I0963797

Jaime Wolf shook his head as though not believing what he'd heard. "I think you mistake the gravity of the situation, Lady Romano. If we don't stop the Clans, who will?"

Romano smiled broadly, then let her gaze sweep the assembly as though to share her enlightenment with all. "You forget, Colonel Wolf, that when the Star League collapsed, General Aleksandr Kerensky led away nearly the whole Star League army beyond the Periphery. They're out there. They have been waiting all this time, waiting for the day mankind would again need their help. They will come and they will save us from the Clans."

Wolf's shoulders sagged. "Lady Romano, have you heard nothing I've said?" He stared around the room in disbelief, once more shaking his head. Though his voice dropped almost to a whisper, no one missed a word in the utter silence that had fallen over the gathering.

"Don't you see?" He leaned forward, grasping the podium so hard his knuckles went white. "Kerensky's people *have* returned. They are the Clans."

BLOOD LEGACY

Other BattleTech Novels:

The Gray Death Legion Saga
    by William H. Keith, Jr.
        Decision at Thunder Rift
        Mercenary's Star
        The Price of Glory

The Sword and the Dagger
    By Ardath Mayhar

The Warrior Saga
    By Michael A. Stackpole
        Warrior: En Garde
        Warrior: Riposte
        Warrior: Coupe

Wolves on the Border
    By Robert Charrette

Heir to the Dragon
    By Robert Charrette

Blood of Kerensky Saga
    By Michael A. Stackpole
        Lethal Heritage

MICHAEL A. STACKPOLE

BLOOD LEGACY

BLOOD OF KERENSKY • VOLUME TWO

FASA
CORPORATION

To Jennifer Roberson and Fred Saberhagen
Thanks for proving overwhelming success does not have to spoil an author by bringing with it an overweening ego. Your example is one to which I pray I can do justice.

The author would like to thank Liz Danforth for tolerating after the battle reports, Donna Ippolito for translating this book from whatever the author uses as a native tongue, Jordan Weisman and Ross Babcock for giving him the opportunity to do the book, and Sam Lewis for designing yet one more 'Mech variant so no rewrite of a battle chapter was necessary. Lasty the author thanks the GEnie Network over which this novel and edits passed through E-mail, from the author's computer, through GEnie, straight to FASA.

Copyright © 1990 FASA Corporation.
ALL RIGHTS RESERVED.
This book may not be reproduced in whole or in part, by any means, without permission in writing from the publisher.
Printed in the United States of America.

BATTLETECH, 'MECH, BATTLEMECH and MECHWARRIOR are Trademarks of FASA Corporation, registered in the U. S Patent and Trademark Office. Copyright © 1990 FASA Corporation. All Rights Reserved. Printed in the United States of America

FASA Corporation
P.O. Box 6930
Chicago, IL 60680

Cover Art: Les Dorscheid
Cover Design: Jim Nelson

Prologue

DropShip Charles Martel
Terra Approach Vector 23917
31 January 3051

The instant he touched the cold stone, Anastasius Focht knew he was seated on the Archon's throne. In the darkness of his dream, the massive doors at the far end of the throne room remained deep in shadow. Yet Focht knew that two mute, enormous *Griffin* BattleMechs stood guard behind him, warding the Lyran Commonwealth rulers and their throne as they had for more than five centuries.

At first, he thought the great, silent room empty but for him, then saw the shadows begin to stir as a form slowly emerged. The silhouette limped toward him, and Focht gradually made out a face he had not seen for twenty years. "This is madness," he said, as though the words could awaken him from this dream fast becoming a nightmare.

The shadowman stopped a dozen meters from the throne and smiled with the smugness of a well-schooled courtier. "Of course, it is, my friend. But when did that ever matter?"

Focht's right fist smashed down on the arm of the throne. "This will end, and end now!" He thrust a finger at the man standing before him. "I know you, Aldo Lestrade, but you have been dead for the past twenty years."

The phantom shrugged as though to say it mattered little. "Physically, yes. I died years ago, poisoned by a whelp I never knew I had sired." He cackled horribly. "But I have lived on within your mind and thrived there. Yes, yes, I know all about the training those Buddhist monks and ComStar Adepts put you through to free your spirit of worldly attachments and concerns. But now you see, Precentor Martial, that I have been there all along, the receptacle for all the ambition you tried to leave behind."

The shade raised its hands to take in the entire room. "And now you have done it. Finally. There you sit on the throne of the Lyran Commonwealth, fulfilling the desire you have long held most dear."

Focht lifted his snow-maned head proudly and stared hard at the shade with his single good eye. "You are wrong, Lestrade. The man I once was desired the throne, but that man is no more." He plucked at the left breast of his long white robe, indicating the golden star insignia embroidered there.

"I now serve ComStar and the Word of Blake. This throne is the rightful place of Archon Melissa Steiner Davion of the Federated Commonwealth, and I recognize her joint rulership with her husband, Prince Hanse Davion of the Federated Commonwealth."

Lestrade laughed softly, but the sound was sinister. "Deny it if you will, old friend, but I am here to prove you wrong. I know the truth of your heart, and it is your desire for power. By giving you this vision of yourself on the throne, I permit you to glimpse the possible future. Use the means in your power and take the throne!"

Banishing his unease, Focht gave a laugh of his own. "It is pure foolishness to believe I either desire the throne or that I would move to take it. It is true that as Precentor Martial of ComStar's forces, I command fifty crack regiments. And yes, that is a force sufficient to depose Melissa if I so desired, but I cannot and I will not."

"Bah!" snarled Lestrade as the healthy glow of his complexion began to fade to a grayish pallor. "You always had to be pushed to see what must be done…"

"Stop!" Focht shot to his feet, towering over the ghost. "You've never been a MechWarrior! You've never understood the code of duty and honor that rules those who pilot these engines of destruction. Placing such an awesome weapon in the hands of an individual implies a similar gesture of trust." Focht's single gray eye flashed with anger. "You betrayed my trust when you were alive. Why would I trust you now?"

Focht turned and waved a hand at the twin *Griffin*s standing behind the throne. "For more than six hundred years, the BattleMech has occupied a central place in the mythology we spin around ourselves like a cocoon then call reality. Since the fall of the Star League, it is BattleMechs that have decided the outcome of our endless wars. It is those very wars that have destroyed most of the means to produce these magnificent war machines. Worse, we have lost so much technology in this long Dark Age that our 'Mechs haven't half the capabilities of those their great-great grandfathers took into battle. In these centuries of Succession Wars, the leaders of the Great Houses lost the vision of a unified humanity. They only saw their greed for another's land or power, and that was how they put the BattleMech to use."

Lestrade opened his mouth to speak, but Focht cut him off. "For centuries, we have told ourselves that the BattleMech is invincible. New models like the *Hatchetman* or *Wolfhound* have shown that improvements are possible, but these designs were still based on technology we understand. They present no *new* threat."

"The same cannot be said of the Clans. Though they, too, fight with 'Mechs, theirs surpass even those our ancestors knew at the pinnacle of man's technological development. Clan 'Mechs move faster, shoot more accurately, and can hit targets at ranges much greater than our machines. What's more, the Clans, as a people, devote their whole existence to firing the engine of war. The defeats they suffered last year were little more than accidents. The Federated Commonwealth attacked them on the poorly garrisoned backwater world of Twycross. And, yes, the Clans forces were crack troops, but Kai Allard-Liao's single-handed destruction of a whole Cluster of frontline Clan 'Mechs can only be attributed to luck."

Lestrade's mechanical left hand worked his jaw around to make it work. "And what of the battle on Wolcott? Theodore Kurita defeated a planetary assault."

"True," Focht conceded with a nod. "He managed to use the Clans' own military conventions against them, but the greater significance of how the Clans function has escaped notice. Some military thinkers of the Inner Sphere believe it only some quirk that makes the Clans bid away troops in order to attack a planet with the minimum number of troops. In fact, it is a sinister omen of things to come. When the Clans stop bidding so boldly, their technological edge will overwhelm our forces. All will be lost."

Lestrade smiled broadly, tearing the desiccated flesh off his lips. "And all the more reason for you to seize control of Tharkad and the throne."

"Have you heard nothing I've just said?" In his anger, Focht grasped the fabric of his nightmare, making the towering *Griffin*s waver, then shift to become the hulking forms of the Clan 'Mech known as the *Madcat*. Mounted on birdlike legs bent backward at the knee, the blocky body thrust the cockpit forward. Above the hip joints rode two boxy long-range missile launchers, and each arm ended in slender, rectangular weapons pods. The slate gray 'Mechs looked like deadly, predators ready to devour any opposition.

"These are the kinds of 'Mech we face now. They have more than double the effectiveness of our machines." This time, Focht took the shadows and formed them into a man-sized suit of armor. The right arm ended in a laser muzzle while the left hand had only three thick fingers. A rocket-launcher rode on the back of the armor suit, and the individual wearing the suit had only a V-shaped black glass slit for a viewport.

"The Clans call these powered suits and the people who pilot them Elementals. This armored infantry can withstand direct hits by 'Mech weaponry. Working in concert, Elementals can take down and destroy a 'Mech." Focht ran the slender fingers of his left hand through his white hair. "The only way mankind can hope to hold back the Clans is by uniting their full resources to defeating the invaders."

Lestrade stared at the armor suit, but seemed unimpressed. "It took no such union to drive the Clans off this time, did it?"

Focht snarled inarticulately, then warped the stuff of dreams again. Against the darkness of the throne room, pinpoints of light began to burn. Above, a system's sun rotated and shot out a massive solar flare. Below, just beyond the whiplash of solar plasma, dozens of waspy JumpShips materialized in the system in two distinct groups. The thick hulls of the smaller group, composed of one massive and four small ships, bristled with weaponry. The larger group, looking skeletal compared to its foes, detached DropShip after DropShip and launched furious flights of fighters in a space-borne assault.

The Precentor Martial gritted his teeth and focused the dream on one fighter. Shaped like a boomerang, the craft made one strafing run from the bow to the stern of the enemy flagship, then turned and came back again. Both the fighter and its wingman were hit in the second run. The wingman's ship drifted away from the battle, but the primary ship boosted forward. Dropping into a long, sweeping dive, it ran its engines higher than they were meant to go. Glowing like a nova, the *Shilone* fighter smashed into the bridge of the Clan JumpShip.

Focht pointed to the gaping hole torn in the JumpShip's hull. "There. That's the reason the Clans have stopped their assaults. That suicide ship killed their ilKhan, the man in charge of the whole invasion of the Inner Sphere. The Clan leaders have withdrawn to elect a new overlord, but the garrison they have left is more than ample to ward the worlds they have taken. Having chosen a new warlord, they will return. This I have from Ulric, Khan of the Wolf Clan, who has never given me reason to doubt him or his words. Once again, it was sheer luck that aided us in our war against the Clans, but to depend on such luck would be suicidal."

The corpse applauded heartily. As his metal hand impacted the other of flesh, the decaying hand lost bits and pieces of skin and fingers. "Spoken like a warrior, Precentor. As such, your analysis of the situation is flawless. You are correct that only the unification of the warring states of the Inner Sphere could defeat the Clans. You speak as a soldier, but I, as a politician, see the impossibility of it all."

"Is that so?" Focht smiled calmly. "Jaime Wolf has gathered the leaders of all the Great Houses to his world of Outreach to discuss the situation. He could forge the ties that will bind everything together."

The sound of Lestrade's teeth rattling loosely in his jaw made an irritating counterpoint to his words. "For that, Wolf would have to be a magician, not a mercenary leader. Hanse Davion and Theodore Kurita can no more get along than light and darkness can abide each other. Twice in the last twenty-five years the Federated Suns has launched an invasion of the Draconis Combine, and twice Theodore Kurita has turned them back. Davion and Kurita are like a snake and a mongoose, each one knowing a single false step could be his death."

Lestrade tried to gesture broadly with his metal arm, but a grinding click in the joint left it hanging useless at his side. "And let us not forget the sisters Liao. The St. Ives Compact ruled by Candace is little more than a protectorate of the Federated Commonwealth. If not for Davion troops stationed there, Romano would have long since have attempted to retake the Compact worlds for the Capellan Confederation. As it is, Romano has made at least a dozen assassination attempts on her sister's life, and she has a bounty out on the heads of Candace's friends and the kin of her husband, Justin Allard. The idea of anyone cooperating with Romano, no matter what the threat to the Successor States, is ludicrous."

The dead Duke's head came up and his lifeless eyes locked on Focht. "As for the Free Worlds League, I'd not expect much from them. Wolf clearly does not trust ComStar, hence the barring of any ComStar personnel from his world and this conference, in particular. As Thomas Marik was a ComStar Acolyte before he took his father's place on the throne, I cannot believe Wolf will be inclined to put much faith in anything Thomas does or says.

"There is also the problem of Thomas' four-year-old son, who has leukemia. It is a cruel blow, but you already know that he has signed the decree legitimizing Isis, his sixteen-year-old daughter by a mistress. Aside from his domestic troubles, Thomas is in a good position to bargain hard for his support because the Clans will have to come through the Lyran Commonwealth before they can hit him. Hanse and Theodore will have to make concessions to Marik for his help. But with the Primus backing him, Thomas still might not give in."

Focht stiffened at the mention of ComStar's leader, and the revenant pounced at this show of anxiety. "Don't try to hide from me, Precentor Martial. Am I not inside your brain and knowing your very thoughts? You style yourself a warrior, and you are good at it, but politics is a minefield. Your Primus, Myndo Waterly, is an excellent player, isn't she? She's convinced that ComStar can work with the Clans until the invaders have bled themselves white in battle, and *then* ComStar can step in, destroy them, and reform all society into Blake's dream of a utopia. Has there ever been a greater foolishness?"

As they spoke, the shade of what had once been Aldo Lestrade slowly disintegrated. His flesh was all but gone and the white of his bones showed through the worm-gnawed rents in his clothing. His death's-head watched Focht with shadow-filled eye sockets, but the bony jaw worked up and down uselessly, no words coming from its throat.

Focht leaned back in the throne. "If you are the container for whatever trace of ambition still claims me, I am pleased to see the state it is in. I am a warrior who commands other warriors. I know better than to dabble in politics." He raised his hand to adjust the patch over his right eye. "I paid a dear price for that realization, but I survived the lesson. You, Aldo Lestrade, did not."

The ghoul laughed one last time. "But what you did not learn, Anastasius Focht, is that you can never escape politics. It is every-where and, someday, it will lay you in the ground, just as it has me…"

Lestrade's skeleton collapsed into a pile of dust, but his laughter continued to echo in Focht's brain until the sound gradually trans-formed into the incessant beeping of the DropShip's visiphone intercom system. Pulling himself up into a sitting position, Focht reached out to punch the glowing button on the console beside his bed.

"Yes?"

The ComStar acolyte on the screen bowed his head. "Forgive me for waking you, Precentor, but you asked to be alerted two hours prior to atmospheric entry. We have just passed that mark and should be on the ground in just under three hours."

Focht nodded. "Call Sandhurst and have them arrange a full staff meeting for ETA plus 30 minutes. No excuses accepted for absence."

The Acolyte paled visibly. "I cannot do that, Precentor."

Focht's voice deepened with a rumble of anger. "Explain."

"The Primus sent us a priority directive while you slept. We are to land at Hilton Head, and you are to brief her immediately on the Clan situation. You will then address the First Circuit."

"Send my message nonetheless. I will leave for Sandhurst as soon as possible."

The Acolyte regained some of his color. "It shall be done as though it were the Will of Blake, Precentor Martial."

Focht broke the connection with the flick of a finger. "Perhaps you were right, Aldo. Perhaps none of us can escape politics, but that does not mean I must succumb to them. One man losing an eye to politics is enough. I cannot allow Mankind to be sacrificed on that same altar. The most elegant speeches may sway the hearts and minds of men, but not one ever stopped a bullet."

"You're *who*?"

Victor Ian Steiner Davion sat stunned in his chair as Romano Liao's shout filled the Dragoons' Grand Council Chamber. In front of him, his father stiffened while his mother reached instinctively for her husband's hand. Romano's voice rang out again. "By all the gods of heaven and earth, I can't believe it."

"I thought, Madam Chancellor, that my statement was clear enough." Jaime Wolf leaned heavily on the raised podium at the front of the chamber. Though the mercenary was not a big man, Victor could see the inner strength that had made Wolf a legendary leader and warrior. His black uniform and short cape only added to the grim expression his face now wore, particularly with the cloak thrown back from the left shoulder to reveal the ruby-eyed wolf's-head epaulet.

"Let me try again." Wolf looked around at the assembled leaders of the Inner Sphere, who gazed back at him with rapt attention. "More than forty-five years ago, Wolf's Dragoons were sent by the Clans to determine the level of military preparedness of your states, those fragments of what had once been the Star League. Since that time, we have worked both for and against every one of the Great Houses of the Inner Sphere."

Prince Haakon Magnusson of the Free Rasalhague Republic angrily raised a clenched fist. "Then I have you to blame for the Clans

1

half-devouring my nation!" Magnusson, a silver-haired man who was neither tall nor particularly strong, put all his strength into the emotion that accented his words. "Was the Rasalhague Republic the choice target for the assault because we are a young nation or was it our reputation for disliking mercenaries?"

Wolf held up his hands to forestall other shouted questions. "Stop! You misinterpret my words." The diminutive mercenary turned to face Magnusson. "The Dragoons had nothing to do with the Clans' choice of targets. They are merely following the same route back into the Inner Sphere by which they left it. The Free Rasalhague Republic just happens to inhabit that slice of known space."

Magnusson returned to his seat at the table set between that assigned to the Draconis Combine representatives and the aisle that split the room in half. Varldherre Tor Miraborg, a sour-looking man with a long, deep scar down the left side of his face, leaned forward in his wheelchair to whisper something to Ragnar, Magnusson's son and the Crown Prince of Rasalhague. It looked to Victor as though Magnusson's heir was listening intently to Miraborg, but it was equally obvious that something in the words had taken him aback.

Hanse Davion rose from his seat with the ease of a much younger man. Though the years had slowed the elder Davion slightly and leeched the auburn from his hair, Victor knew his father took pains to remain physically fit. The Prince of the Federated Suns flashed his son a warm smile as he pushed his chair slightly back and out of the way. As always, the vitality flashing through Hanse's electric blue eyes made Victor confident his father would successfully gauge the problem and find a solution.

"Colonel Wolf, I gather by your answer to Prince Magnusson that you are no longer associated with the Clans?"

Wolf nodded, apparently relieved at an opening to explain. "Our last communication with the Clans occurred just after the Marik civil war in 3014. At that time, our leader believed that a Clan invasion of the Inner Sphere was a distinct, if distant, possibility. Even so, we were ordered to cease communicating information back to the Clans. Since then, we have had no contact with them until their recent broadcast informing us of the death of the ilKhan."

Romano Liao, recovered from her earlier shock, laughed derisively. "And we are to believe this, Colonel Wolf? What proof do you offer?"

Candace Liao, Duchess of the St. Ives Compact, rose from her place at the table to the right of the Federated Commonwealth contingent. Unlike her flame-haired sister, Candace kept a tight rein on her emotions and easily maintained an air of regal dignity. "I would point out, sister mine, that were Colonel Wolf still working for the Clans, we would all have probably died either en route to this meeting, if not before."

"Ha!" Romano waved away her sister's words with contempt. "You have so long clasped a viper to your breast that you cannot see Wolf for what he is."

The Chancellor of the Capellan Confederation would likely have continued to rant, but the savage expression on her face died the moment a slender young man seated behind her rested his hands on her shoulders. The youth threw her a wink when she turned to give his cheek an affectionate pat. As Romano turned back, now composed and in control, Candace slowly seated herself, still glaring at her sister.

Victor's blue-gray eyes narrowed as he studied Romano's son, Sun-Tzu. Clean-limbed and handsome, he did not have the wild look around the eyes that marked both his mother and his sister as seriously disturbed. The tales of paranoid purges and other lunacy from the court in Sian were so rife that Victor took Sun-Tzu's very survival to mean that he was both intelligent and politically astute. From Sun-Tzu's dossier, Victor knew he had undergone only rudimentary MechWarrior training, but the Capellan gave the distinct impression he could fight his own battles.

Victor glanced over to where the St. Ives Compact delegation was seated. Despite Romano's protests, Wolf had accorded the Compact full rights of a sovereign nation. The Dragoon leader had stated that Candace Liao was the ruler of an independent state of the Inner Sphere, even though the Capellans still claimed the realm as "occupied territory."

Behind Candace sat Kai, her eldest son, and her twin daughters, Cassandra and Kuan Yin. In comparison with his cousin Sun-Tzu, Kai fared well. Equally as good-looking and somewhat more athletic, Kai held himself ramrod-straight, as though the whole honor of St. Ives and his family rested on his shoulders. To Victor, the biggest difference between Kai and Sun-Tzu was that Kai's eyes lacked the hungry gleam that flashed from Sun-Tzu's. Perhaps it was because Kai, older than Sun-Tzu as his mother was older than Romano, could press a more convincing claim to the throne Sun-Tzu so coveted.

When Victor looked over his shoulder at his aide, he found the big blond man also staring at the pair, apparently making similar comparisons. "There will be trouble between them," said the Prince.

Hauptmann Galen Cox nodded, a predatory grin stealing across his face. "My money's on Kai. After what he did on Twycross, who'd

3

want to bet against him?"

Hanse Davion, still on his feet, cleared his throat. "I must agree with Duchess Liao's assessment of the situation." Hanse gestured to the man seated beside Candace. "As my Intelligence Secretary can confirm, there has been no overt or covert contact between the Clans and Wolf's Dragoons since they took up residence here on Outreach twenty years ago."

Justin Allard, a slender Eurasian whose left forearm and hand were a black metal prosthesis, nodded in silent agreement with Hanse Davion. Given Romano's legendary hatred for her sister and her sister's husband, she might have risen up again in agitation, but a voice from the Draconis Combine steered the debate into less dangerous waters.

"I would agree that the Dragoons had ample opportunity for treachery in this situation, but I would more have expected some of *us* to try to kill one another than for Colonel Wolf to do the job." Theodore Kurita, Warlord of the Draconis Combine, steepled his fingers as he spoke. "If someone was trying to entrap us, he has succeeded, for here we are, all together, in a most extraordinary gathering. As nothing untoward has yet occurred, perhaps it would be more productive to assume we have not been betrayed."

As Theodore spoke, Victor studied the delegation from the Draconis Combine. Theodore Kurita, the tall, lean Gunji-no-Kanrei of the Combine, sat between his wife and his eldest son, Hohiro. Hohiro had the fierce, noble features of his father, and Victor felt a jolt when their stares met.

The younger Davion could not suppress a grin. *He's just like me. Our fathers have hated each other for as long as they've been alive. Now that legacy falls to us.*

Behind Hohiro, Victor saw a man he recognized as Narimasa Asano, the head of the Genyosha, one of the most feared military units in the Draconis Combine Mustered Soldiery. Then he noticed a beautiful young woman, made up and dressed in ceremonial Japanese fashion, standing between Hohiro and Theodore. A council of war seemed no place for such exquisite and serene loveliness, and it set Victor's mind to all manner of questions about her.

Jaime Wolf looked up from his podium at another contingent of royals from the Inner Sphere. "You are the last to speak, Captain-General. What are your thoughts? Are you in a trap, or can the Dragoons be trusted?"

"I do not think, Colonel, that your questions are necessarily two sides of the same coin." Though Thomas Marik did not rise to speak,

4

he was an imposing figure. Tall and slender, he was severely scarred on the right side of the face and on his right hand, reminders of the burns suffered in the same explosion that assassinated his father. Despite the disfigurement, Marik's strong features and bearing hinted at an inner strength that may have been forged during his internship with ComStar. He wore a purple uniform, but without any rank insignia. Over his graying hair, he wore a short-billed service cap.

Wondering at the addition of the cap, Victor noticed that Sophina, Thomas's wife, also wore one. As did Joshua Simon, all of five years old, who sat holding his mother's hand. The boy's uniform imitated his father's, while the cap hid his baldness. Against the dark-colored uniform, Joshua's skin seemed even more pallid, his eyes sunk deeply in the shadows around them. The boy moved with a languor suggesting utter fatigue, yet was obviously trying to hold himself as tall as possible.

Galen sucked in a sharp breath. "It is true, then. The child is very ill."

"Justin's sources report leukemia." Victor shook his head in pity. "Marik hopes the boy will survive, but the prognosis is not good. Joshua is sensitive to the chemicals they're using to treat him, and they really knock his system out. Look how blue his lips are. It's anemia from the last bout of chemotherapy."

Seated next to the boy, Isis Marik preened herself like a debutante. She, too, wore a paramilitary uniform and had even donned a cap in solidarity with her half-brother. The cap, though, was set at a jaunty angle, flaunting the long, thick braid of abundant chestnut hair that Isis had drawn forward around one shoulder and down onto her breast.

Victor frowned. "It's almost as though she mocks how sick the boy is."

"If he dies, she'll become Captain-General, my Prince." A hint of distaste flashed through Galen's eyes. "You're first in line to the throne, so you may not think much about succession. But being a newly legitimized royal bastard could definitely give someone ideas about power and how to achieve it permanently."

"Well said, Galen. Though she's pretty, I'll do my best to stay away from her." Saying that, Victor stole another glance at the young woman in the Kurita contingent. As a thousand questions about her continued to fill his mind, he shook himself. *This is a council of war, Victor, not some court picnic.*

Thomas leaned forward, resting his hands on the table assigned to the Free Worlds League. "I share the Gunji-no-Kanrei's view that worrying about a trap is immaterial at this point. The Dragoons have brought us here to discuss the Clan invasion and what we should do since they have called a halt to their advance. I think such a discussion would be a most valuable pursuit.

"For my own part, I am not one hundred percent inclined to trust any military force that admits it was once allied with an enemy. Forgive me, Colonel, but the the people of the Free Worlds League well remember the Dragoons for their role in the war between my father and his brother Anton."

"Your caution is understandable, Captain-General," Wolf said. "By the way, we have set up your medical team in our infirmary and have provided them all the equipment you asked be made ready for their use."

Thomas acknowledged Wolf's kindness with a nod. Joshua, meanwhile, sat unaware that he might be the subject of discussion as he dangled his feet idly back and forth above the floor. Victor smiled at the display of innocence, another note as odd as the presence of the beautiful young woman. He knew Jaime Wolf's brother Joshua had been slain in the Free Worlds League Civil War. He wondered if Thomas had chosen the same name for his son by mere coincidence, or if it were a kind of peace offering to Wolf's Dragoons.

Victor looked around the massive room the Dragoons called their Grand Council Chamber. An amphitheater carved out of Outreach's bedrock, it had been paneled with slender strips of oak. Two dozen stepped terraces provided seating for spectators, and a golden oak railing separated the main floor from the spectator galleries. Down on the floor, a semicircle of wooden tables faced the speaker's podium. Victor suspected the Dragoons had removed the connecting pieces that normally bound the tables together so that the Great House leaders would be on equal footing.

Up in the galleries, Victor saw a number of Dragoon uniforms scattered among the small crowd of military advisors and state ministers. The courtiers who had accompanied the various royal parties were hardly necessary for planning a campaign to destroy the Clans, but they were vital to keeping the states of the Inner Sphere functioning. Never before had all these rulers of all the Successor States been gathered in one place at one time, and the stress of maintaining business as usual told on the faces of the civil servants gathered to watch the debate.

Victor noticed Jaime's son MacKenzie Wolf standing toward the back. Tall and slender and with a dark moustache, he cut almost a rakish figure in his black and scarlet uniform, but his bearing suggested he did not find the proceedings amusing.

6

Standing beside MacKenzie were Morgan and Christian Kell of the Kell Hounds mercenary unit. Their scarlet uniforms and waist-cut jackets were distinctive for the way the jacket's double-breast took the form of a black wolf's-head with triangular red eyes. The muzzle fastened at the waist and the two ears fastened at the shoulders. Breaking up the black, campaign ribbons slashed across the left ear of Morgan's jacket, proclaiming the elder mercenary's long career.

The trio's grim expressions reminded Victor of the gravity of the situation. A cold chill ran down his spine as he thought of Morgan's son Phelan—his own cousin—who had been one of the first fatalities in the Clan invasion.

Jaime Wolf sighed heavily. "We are wasting precious time. The Inner Sphere faces the greatest military threat the Successor States have ever encountered, either individually or collectively."

Wolf hit a button on his podium. The room lights dimmed as a holographic map of the Inner Sphere burned to life in the center of the semi-circle. It slowly rotated so everyone could get a good look, then it split into smaller representations of itself, with one hovering before each delegation's table. As Victor leaned forward to study the map, fear writhed like a snake through his belly.

Normally the Successor States and the worlds they claimed formed a rough circle of star systems approximately 370 light years in diameter, with the circle centered on Terra. On this map, however, a huge chunk had been bitten out of the circle, making it a fat crescent with both horns pointing up and away from the chamber floor. Though the ravaged Free Rasalhague Republic lay at the center of the conquered area, bites had also been taken out of both the Lyran sector of the Federated Commonwealth and from the Draconis Combine.

Victor leaned forward toward his father. "I didn't realize the Combine had been hit so hard. They've lost as many worlds as have we."

Hanse pressed his lips together into a thin line. "I daresay, from the expression on Theodore's face, he was not aware that we'd been hard-hit either. Wolf's intelligence network is very good. Things are much worse than any of us dared imagine."

Wolf waved a hand to include all the maps. "As you can see, the situation is most grave. The Free Rasalhague Republic has lost its capital and over half its worlds. The invaders have also made substantial gains in the Lyran Commonwealth and the Draconis Combine. In less than a year, they have managed to take more worlds than changed hands in the Fourth Succession War, and the efforts to stop them have been less than effective.

"My purpose in calling all of you here is to propose that we unite to oppose these invaders. Only a concerted and joint effort can turn back the Clans. Otherwise, we face domination by an implacable foe. Just like the old saying, if the Successor States do not hang together, they will all hang separately."

Romano Liao glanced at her sister as though measuring her neck for a rope, then stood. "I am not certain I share the sense of urgency you seem to advocate, Colonel Wolf. Acting independently, my Lord Kurita and even Hanse Davion have fought off these invaders. And I have no evidence that these Clans are different from any other murdering, butchering, bloody-handed conquerors."

"As you will, Lady Romano," Wolf replied mechanically, but Victor heard the undertone of cold rage in Wolf's voice. "I assure you, however, that the Clans are vastly different than any army that has marched before or will ever march again. Yes, it is true that the Clans stopped advancing after Federated Commonwealth and Combine troops dealt them defeats on two different worlds, but it was not because the Inner Sphere forces had proved themselves superior. The Clans halted their invasion because their war leader was slain at Radstadt, and now they must choose a new one before they can continue to fight. Until then, their line troops will remain in place while the Clan leadership decides on who will spearhead the invasion. When the leaders return again, rest assured that they will come with yet more Clan armies, and if we do not work together, their victory is certain."

Thomas Marik rose and leaned forward with his hands on the table. "I am most impressed by what you have accomplished here on Outreach, Colonel Wolf, and your ability to gather data on the current status of the various states represented here."

The Captain-General pointed to the map glowing in front of him. "This map, for example, is far more complete than the one my intelligence people have been able to assemble, and more complete than any we have stolen from either the Federated Commonwealth or the Draconis Combine." He hesitated briefly as both Hanse Davion and Theodore Kurita nodded a salute to him. "In light of that, and reflecting upon the Dragoons' remarkable career, there is a question I must ask. Do you, Colonel Wolf, believe that it is even *possible* to stop the invaders?"

Victor read no shock on Wolf's face. Rather, the mercenary reacted as though he'd been waiting all along for someone finally to pose the question. "I can only answer on the basis of my experiences within the Clans, and those days were long ago. My men and I were trained in the Clan school of war and it made us very successful when

8

fighting the forces of the Inner Sphere, but we could never claim to be invincible. The Clans fight according to their concept of warfare, but I believe that the tactics of the Ryuken or Federated Commonwealth Regimental Combat Teams could counteract and defeat those tactics."

Wolf looked again at Marik. "To answer your question more specifically, Captain-General, I do believe we can defeat the Clans. The Combine and the Federated Commonwealth paid a high price for their respective victories, but the fact of victory remains. With training and by devoting our full resources to opposing the Clans, I say we can slow and even stop them."

Haakon Magnusson shook his head. "The Clans make our weapons look like toys compared to what they bring to battle."

Wolf's eyes narrowed. "If you surrender to despair now, Prince Magnusson, what chance have you to win back your realm? I have the blueprints and technical diagrams for the new BattleMech technology. Right here on Outreach, the Dragoons have produced, in very limited numbers, BattleMechs based on that technology. It may be dated by Clan standards, but it is still eons ahead of what the Inner Sphere currently has available."

A sudden weariness seemed to settle over Wolf like a lead cloak. "I had hoped for more time to prepare for this invasion, but so be it. My Dragoons have restored Outreach to the training facility it was in the days of the Star League. We have not yet begun mass production of OmniMechs—which is what the Clans call their line 'Mechs—but with the help of Colonel Kell, Dr. Banzai, and Clovis Holstein, we do have working prototypes of many of the new weapons the Clans use. I also have five full regiments of Dragoons ready to take the field against the Clans."

Wolf pushed up the sleeves of his jacket to mid-forearm. "There it is. My cards are on the table. I'll be fighting the Clans, no matter who does or does not join with me. But I say again that if we pull together, we can field an army that will stop the Clans."

Wolf's words sent a shiver down Victor's spine. *He's right. If we don't band together, the Clans will take us apart.*

Romano barked a sharp laugh. "Why should we believe you, Wolf? You've admitted having deceived us before. Why should it be any different now?" She shrugged eloquently, brushing her auburn hair away from the shoulders of her black gown. "I am not worried. The Clans will be stopped."

Wolf watched her carefully, shaking his head as though not believing what he'd heard. "I think you mistake the gravity of the situation, Lady Romano. If we don't stop the Clans, who will?"

9

Romano smiled broadly, then let her gaze sweep the assembly as though to share her enlightenment with all. "You forget, Colonel Wolf, that when the Star League collapsed, General Aleksandr Kerensky led away nearly the whole Star League army beyond the Periphery. They're out there. They have been waiting all this time, waiting for the day mankind would again need their help. They will come and they will save us from the Clans."

Wolf's shoulders sagged. "Lady Romano, have you heard nothing I've said?" He stared around the room in disbelief, once more shaking his head. Though his voice dropped almost to a whisper, no one missed a word in the utter silence that had fallen over the gathering.

"Don't you see?" He leaned forward, grasping the podium so hard his knuckles went white. "Kerensky's people *have* returned. They are the Clans."

DropShip Dire Wolf
Beyond the Periphery
2 February 3051

Sweat-soaked black hair stinging his eyes, Phelan Kell Wolf flew through the air. He twisted into a shoulder roll, bleeding off the energy of the throw that had propelled him across the small room. His left hand slapped the floor mat hard, further breaking his fall and helping to bring his body under control. He knew he could have used the remaining momentum to roll to his feet. Instead, he feigned exhaustion and let himself sprawl out flat on his back.

His opponent, red braid whipping back and forth like a snake, shot after him across the room. Though she stood a third of a meter taller, and outweighed him by seventy kilos, Evantha Fetladral moved quickly and sensuously. A grim smile locked her face into a battle-mask, but wariness burned in her brown eyes. She slowed slightly as she closed, preparing for whatever trap Phelan had laid.

Phelan scythed his left leg through the space occupied by hers. As she leaped above the sweep, Phelan let the momentum of his kick twist him over onto his stomach, then started a second sweep with his right leg. The kick caught Evantha at the ankles and smashed them together as she came down. She landed heavily on the mat, but before Phelan could turn and lunge forward to pin her, she was on her feet again.

She dropped into a crouch and waved him forward. Her sleeve-less gray bodysuit ended at the knees and matched the one Phelan wore. The bands of red at shoulders and thighs were linked by a red

11

flank stripe. Sweat glistened from her nearly bald pate and rippling muscles. "Come on, Phelan. You are good, but you are no Elemental."

The Inner Sphere expatriate wiped his left forearm across his brow. "I didn't think I was supposed to be one. I'm a MechWarrior."

Evantha frowned. "Perhaps that is what you will become, Phelan Wolf, but only if you train well and learn to speak properly."

Phelan winced. *Dammit, I keep forgetting.* Bowing his head slightly, he apologized. "Forgive me. When I get excited, I contract my…"

Evantha's lunge forward made him break off. He spun to the left, just eluding her outstretched right hand, then darted forward. He hooked his right leg behind her right knee, then grabbed her shoulder and threw her down. Fingers stiffened into a spearpoint, he slashed his right hand across her throat.

Evantha slapped the mat three times with her left hand, signaling an end to the fight. "Well done," she said.

Dripping sweat made his eyes burn as Phelan dropped unceremoniously to the mat. "'Bout time. You have been tossing me around the room for the past two hours. Returning the favor was the least I could do."

The giant woman curled up into a sitting position. She used her huge hands to wipe the sweat from her almost completely shaved head, then she dried them on the legs of her bodysuit. "Indeed, it was the least you could do." When Phelan sighed, she smiled. "I am pleased, however, that you let me take no advantage while you were offering your apology. There was once a time when you might have believed that such a formality meant a time-out in training."

"Yeah, time once was…" Phelan crawled toward the edge of the mat and grabbed a white towel from a pile. He tossed it to Evantha, then appropriated another for himself. "Since then, you've been kind enough to beat that misconception out of me."

Evantha played idly with the tail of her long braid. "So much the better. You must remember that you will constantly be watched and tested. Even when an exercise is over, you must be prepared for another challenge. That has always been the way of the Clans, for it is only constant testing and preparedness that has ensured our survival. It has made us what we are. Now that you are one of us, you would do well to understand that."

Phelan nodded acknowledgement, but his thoughts were far away. *I've known that ever since the Clans captured me. Even when I was a bondsman, they were constantly testing me. Khan Ulric pushed me, wanting to see how far I would go in compromising my homeland,*

12

and Vlad tried his best to break my spirit. Now that I have been accepted into the Warrior caste, I am being tested as an equal, not an inferior. If anything, the testing has become more difficult.

Evantha hung her towel around her neck. "Do you want to get a shower?" When Phelan hesitated, Evantha laughed.

"Sorry, Evantha, I still have not gotten used to the familiarity between members of a sibko. Back where I come from, men and women might share duties in the field, but seldom do they share shower facilities."

"You do not seem to mind sharing showers with me."

Phelan turned toward the door and smiled as Ranna slipped into the room. A tall and slender woman who wore her white hair cut very short, she knelt down to give him a kiss. "In fact," she added with a devilish glint in her blue eyes, "I would say you have had vast experience showering with women."

Phelan blushed as both Ranna and Evantha laughed aloud. He reached out to cup Ranna's chin in his left hand, kissed her lightly, then composed his face into a look of innocence. "Actually, my love, I am merely a quick learner under the tutelage of a masterful teacher."

He felt a slight tremor run through Ranna at his use of the word "love," but he was used to that. He knew that the Clanspeople so disassociated love, sex, and reproduction that they no longer saw these things in what Phelan might consider their "normal" relationship. The way he equated love and sexual fidelity was incomprehensible to the Clansfolk, just as their deep fear of interpersonal love was to him.

Evantha heaved herself to her feet. "I remand you to the custody of your most able teacher, Phelan. I expect to see you back here in twenty-two hours for another workout."

Phelan flopped wearily onto his back. "*Ja*, Star Commander. I will be here, right after Carew paces me through antiaircraft tactics."

Evantha threw Ranna a wink. "Be good to him. He did well today."

As Evantha vanished through the door, Phelan reached up to give Ranna's shoulder a squeeze. Touching the gray cotton of her jumpsuit, he felt the large, eight-pointed red star that matched the earring in her left ear. The southernmost point of the star extended down more than twice the length of the other points and turned the insignia into what Phelan had dubbed a "daggerstar." It marked her as a Clan MechWarrior and Phelan envied her that designation.

"So, what shall we do for the rest of the day?"

"We have a problem." Ranna frowned and her fists knotted with frustration. "The whole duty schedule has been shifted around because

13

of the JumpShip that entered the system six hours ago. They sent over a number of DropShips that the *Dire Wolf* has taken aboard, and those ships are carrying many important people. As a result, there has been a mass revision of the duty roster so people can meet with their House leaders."

Phelan pulled himself up into a sitting position and rested both hands on hers until her fists loosened. "How much time until you have to go on duty?"

"About an hour and a half." A sound almost like a low growl rumbled from her throat. "I'd managed to get clearance for us to take one of the 'Mechs out onto the ship's hull so you could get a good look at this triple star system, and then I'd planned for us to have some time together, alone…"

Phelan tipped her head up with his left hand. "Hey, an hour and a half is plenty of time for a shower, *quiaff*? You would not want to go to your duty station dirty, would you?"

She gave him a wry grin. "No, I suppose that would be disorderly of me, *quiaff*?"

"Aff." Phelan stood and pulled Ranna to her feet. "Most disorderly. I think we should do something about that situation."

The figure of an older woman appearing in the doorway stopped them from embracing. Slightly shorter than Ranna and more full-figured, the woman possessed a sensual grace that belied her age. She wore her hair long enough that the red curls hid the shoulders of her jumpsuit. Her blue eyes flashed with amusement as she folded her arms across her chest and leaned against the door jamb.

"Excuse me, children. I do not meant to interrupt."

Phelan turned to face her, slipping one arm around Ranna's waist. "Afternoon, Major…er Colonel Kerensky." When she frowned at that, Phelan quickly corrected his blunder. "I mean Natasha. Forgive me. I still have the habit of addressing you as I did in my time on Outreach."

Natasha Kerensky shrugged eloquently. "No blood, no report. I have two things to tell you. First, after some haggling, Khan Ulric has managed to convince some of the knotheads in the Clan Council that I should be allowed to instruct you in BattleMech tactics." Her eyes became slits. "I don't know if I like him citing my 'advanced age' as the reason I'm suitable for tutor work, but I ain't going to argue with what works."

As Natasha spoke and freely used contractions, he felt Ranna stiffen slightly. Natasha apparently noticed her reaction, too. "Sorry, Ranna, but I spent the better part of five decades in the Inner Sphere.

14

Forgive me if my use of the language offends you."

Ranna smiled coyly. "As you will, *grandmother.*"

Phelan saw Natasha's instant of shock despite her quick recovery. She bowed her head briefly. "*Touché*, Ranna. You are certainly a Kerensky."

"Blood of thy blood. Could I be any less than my forebears?"

Phelan suddenly felt in over his head in a conversation that was traveling well beyond his ken of Clan matters. "Excuse me, but I am catching very little of what you are saying."

Natasha blinked twice, as though waking from a trance. "Right. This is not the place for this talk, nor do we have time for it right now." She turned her attention from Ranna to Phelan. "I am afraid you have to come with me."

Phelan let his disappointment ride openly on his face. "Right now? I have been training for four hours straight, with the last two spent being tossed around by Evantha."

"Builds character." Natasha looked at Ranna. "Cyrilla Ward came over on the *Timber Wolf*. She wants to see Phelan."

Ranna gave Phelan a smile and a nod. "Go. This is important. I will see if I can trade off another duty with someone so I can be free when you are finished."

"I don't understand."

Ranna kissed Phelan quickly. "Just go, and be on your best behavior." She shot a sharp glance at Natasha. "And try to avoid letting her influence cause you to backslide."

Natasha shook her head but did nothing to wipe the proud smile from her face. "Ungrateful child," she muttered as Ranna passed out the door. "Go on, Phelan. Get cleaned up and changed. It's time for you to learn what belonging to the Wolf Clan and the House of Ward truly means."

When he emerged from the shower, Phelan found Natasha sitting on the bench next to his locker. He started at the sight of her, but Natasha just chuckled. "Don't mind me. It's nothing I've not seen before. Don't forget that I was there at your birthing."

Phelan, keeping the towel wrapped around him in kilt fashion, smiled sheepishly. "I've grown up a bit since then."

"True enough, but we're not exactly a sibko and you're not exactly my type." She gave him a more appraising glance. "Well-muscled but lean and ruggedly handsome. You're the type they put on the recruiting posters for the army back in the Lyran Commonwealth."

As she spoke, Natasha swung her body around on the bench to face partially away from him.

Phelan dropped the towel and pulled on clothes from his locker. "I'm afraid the LCAF wouldn't consider me recruiter material. Remember, I'm the one who got punted from the Nagelring."

Natasha laughed heartily. "And no one was prouder than me when I heard the news." She turned to face him again as he stepped into the legs of his gray jumpsuit. "I was ready to clear you a spot as a lance commander in the Black Widow Cluster, but Jaime pulled the plug on that little idea. It's the mark of a good MechWarrior—being able to sort duty from orders and knowing when to act on each."

Phelan zipped up the front of the jumpsuit. "Thanks for the vote of confidence." He closed the locker with a bang, then pounded his right fist against it. "Dammit, Ranna was right. I spend five minutes talking with you, and I start to slip back into my old patterns of speech."

"Try to resist the temptation, boy. It builds character."

"Then why don't *you*?"

Natasha stood up with a sigh. "When you've built as much character as I have, you can let such things slide." She hooked her left hand over Phelan's right shoulder as she led him from the gymnasium and into the Life Services corridor. "Besides, slavish adherence to formal ritual is a sign that one has nothing better to think about."

Phelan nodded. "So, am I allowed to ask questions, or do I have to walk in silence?"

Natasha shrugged as they reached the elevator shaft running the length of the *Dire Wolf*. "Questions about the House of Ward should wait for Cyrilla."

Phelan slapped the elevator call button. "What about you and Ranna?"

Natasha raised an eyebrow, but offered no other reply.

Phelan took that as an invitation to test the waters. "She called you 'grandmother' earlier, and I gathered the use of the term was more than ceremonial. I've not memorized a history of Wolf's Dragoons, but I have never heard of your being pregnant, much less giving birth. *Is* she your granddaughter?"

"Oh, what the scandalvids back in the States would have paid for this story." Natasha waved Phelan into the elevator, then stepped in and punched a button, sending the cage to one of the upper decks. "You are aware, I believe, that both you and your sister were fertilized in vitro. Dragoon doctors pulled ova from your mother, fertilized them with sperm from your father, then reimplanted them in your mother

16

about a year apart."

Phelan nodded. "A wound she took back in 3021 caused some problems."

"Correct." Natasha's face closed slightly. "Suffice it to say, for now, that ova were taken from me before I left the Clans with Wolf's Dragoons."

Before Phelan could ask another question, the elevator came to a halt and the doors opened onto a narrow corridor. Wordlessly, Natasha led him down the hall until they came to a door emblazoned with a wolf's-head device on a shield. Phelan recognized it as the crest of the Wolf Clan and knew it was standard on all the living quarter doors aboard the *Dire Wolf*. What surprised him were the five red daggerstars below the crest. He could see they had been placed there very recently.

Five stars! That's the number of stars that mark Khan Ulric's door. That means whoever this Cyrilla Ward is, she is a very important person within the Clans! And she must be very important within the House of Ward as well.

Before Natasha could knock, the door slid up into the ceiling with a soft whoosh of air. Revealed was a white-haired woman who flung her arms open wide to take Natasha into a hearty embrace. "My God, Tasha, you haven't changed in all these years."

Natasha returned the embrace, lifting Cyrilla Ward off the deck. "Neither have you, Ril."

Cyrilla shook her head, letting her long white hair spread out over her shoulders as she broke the embrace. "It is a good thing you fight better than you lie, or you would have died long ago."

"If only you knew the truth. If not for doctors and reconstructive surgery, I'd long since have ceased fighting and lying all together."

Cyrilla invited both Natasha and Phelan into her temporary suite with a wave of the hand, but Phelan had the feeling she barely noticed him. Wary because of the way Khan Ulric always seemed to be testing him, the young warrior followed Natasha from the antechamber to the main room. Phelan tried to prepare himself for whatever might be waiting, but he grew more anxious with every step. When he saw the trap, he was glad that his caution had allowed him to kill the surprise he might otherwise have revealed.

As they entered the room, another Wolf Clansman rose from his seat and fixed Phelan with an incendiary stare. The man's black hair, combed back to accentuate his widow's peak, gleamed with the oil he used to slick it down. A scar ran from above his left eye to his jawline and was still fresh enough to show the red of wounding.

17

Vlad managed to keep his voice even. "How good to see you again, Natasha." Contempt curled the corners of his mouth as he addressed Phelan. "I trust your leg wound has healed well?"

You mean the place where you slashed me during the adoption ceremony? "Yes, it has." Phelan returned Vlad's stare with his own glower. "I am told there will not even be much of a scar."

Cyrilla placed a bony hand on Vlad's shoulder. "You may go now, Vladimir. I have found our conversation most enlightening." She steered the Clansman toward the door, but he did not break immediately to the pressure of her urging. Making a subtle show of hooking his thumbs in his belt, he framed the buckle with his hands and continued to return Phelan's unrelenting green gaze.

Phelan could not keep his eyes from the buckle. Cast of silver and set with onyx, it showed the hound's-head crest of the Kell Hounds, the well-known mercenary unit of which Phelan was a member before his capture. Tyra Miraborg, the woman who had given it to him, had substituted the green of malachite for the red eyes used in the actual Kell Hound crest, matching them to Phelan's. When he was captured by Vlad and the Clans, Vlad had taken the belt buckle and continued to flaunt it as a reminder of Phelan's inferiority.

Natasha appropriated the low-backed chair Vlad had vacated, but Phelan remained standing. Cyrilla returned to the small sitting room and drew her chair beside the one Natasha had taken. Patting Natasha's left hand, Cyrilla smiled broadly. "After all these years without word, I feared you had been killed."

Natasha turned her hand up to give Cyrilla's a squeeze. "How could I let that happen?" she laughed. "I never forgot our childhood pact that we would finish out our days fighting against the Smoke Jaguars together. Did you think I would renege?"

"No, no, I did not. We will speak more of this later," Cyrilla said gently. She looked up at Phelan, her brown eyes seeming to take measure in ways even more than physical. "So this is Phelan Wolf. Are you worthy of the commotion you have caused?"

"I do not know how to answer that question." Phelan lifted his head and clasped his hands at the small of his back. "I do not know how to judge my worth to the Clan."

Cyrilla watched him like a wolf eyeing a tasty rabbit. "You saved Khan Ulric's life on the bridge of the *Dire Wolf*, *quiaff*?"

Phelan looked down at the floor. "I did what was necessary to help those trapped on the bridge after the ship was rammed. My actions were not heroic. It was simply what had to be done."

"He is modest, *quiaff*, Tasha?"

18

Natasha smiled proudly at Phelan. "I think he'd probably say he is just being honest. He comes from good stock, Ril. He was even entrusted to the Wolves for some of his upbringing. Still, this one can be a bit rash and argumentative at times."

"No doubt because you did some of the raising, Tasha." Cyrilla turned back to Phelan. "Many people want to know more about the bondsman who saved the Khan and claims Ward blood. You are a curiosity that has brought honor to our House, and I thank you."

The former Kell Hound let a grin light his face. "May you and Khan Ulric continue to take pride in my actions."

"Very good, very good, indeed." Cyrilla tilted her head as she studied Phelan for a moment. "But you made a great mistake in pulling Vlad from the wreckage of the bridge of the *Dire Wolf,* young man."

The statement startled Phelan, and he rubbed without thinking at the cut Vlad had given him during his adoption ceremony into the Clan. On one hand, he was praised for saving the Khan, but rebuked for saving another Wolf warrior. "I am confused. Vlad is a warrior of the Wolf Clan. How could I not save him and still serve the Clan?"

Cyrilla considered his reply with a smile. "A valid point. Would you always put duty to the Clan above what might be your best interest?"

"Hypothetical questions are always the ones that get me into trouble when I try to answer them."

"A deft parry. Good." Cyrilla smiled again, folding her hands in her lap. "Do you understand why I think you should have let Vlad die?"

"Not really, but having been with the Clans for a while, I think I can guess."

"Good." Cyrilla leaned back into her chair. "Please explain."

"Bottom line is that the fewer enemies you have, the longer you live." Phelan sighed heavily. "Ever since Vlad captured me in a battle on The Rock a year and a half ago, he has looked for every opportunity to prove that he is superior to me and anyone else from the Successor States. He is not alone in this attitude, but he is perhaps rather more enthusiastic in expressing it.

"Though I beat Vlad in a fist fight on Rasalhague, he could say that I jumped him unexpectedly when he was still exhausted from the recent battle for the world. He lost no face, but Vlad's not one to allow himself so easy an out. Even giving me a severe beating aboard the *Dire Wolf* has not bled off his hatred because I never let him break me."

The elder MechWarrior watching him carefully. "And this leads you to believe..."

Phelan shrugged. "One way or another, Vlad will do anything to get me. He took my adoption into the Clans as a personal affront. He was forced to welcome me into the House of Ward, a duty he seemed particularly loathe to perform."

Cyrilla rested her chin on steepled fingers. "You must have known all this before you found him on the bridge."

The young man nodded. "Yes, but I did not know the body lying there was his until I got to where he was. By then, I really had no choice."

"Even knowing that he hates you with his whole heart and soul, *quiaff*?"

Phelan smiled in spite of himself. "I never said I wouldn't *regret* saving him. I only said I had no choice in the matter." He shrugged. "I am not the sort of MechWarrior who shoots up fleeing 'Mech pilots, and I am not the sort who could abandon someone wounded, be it enemy or friend, if I could do something to save them."

Phelan looked from Cyrilla to Natasha with a rueful smile. "I will say one thing for Vlad. He can carry a grudge further than anyone I have ever met. It's hard to believe he can hate me so much because I shot some armor off his 'Mech. Especially since he blew the hell out of my *Wolfhound* at the same time."

"There *is* more to it than that, Phelan Wolf." Cyrilla pointed to a cream-colored chair near Phelan. "Please be seated. I think, in short order, I can help to clear up that mystery. Do you know what it means to have a Bloodname, *quineg*?"

"Neg."

"Three centuries ago, General Aleksandr Kerensky led ninety percent of the Star League's army from the space you call the Inner Sphere. He detested the civil wars and nationalistic pressures that had wracked the Star League from the time Stefan the Usurper proclaimed himself First Lord. After smashing the Usurper, Kerensky took his people away, hoping to keep them from the path of self-destruction toward which the rest of humanity seemed hell-bent."

She leaned back in her chair, seeming to warm to the task of telling the tale of history. "Kerensky feared that his troops would begin to fight among themselves if they had no common cause to unite them. He reorganized the armies and mothballed seventy-five percent of the BattleMechs and materiel they had brought with them. He told his troops that bringing industry on line to replace parts would take time, so they had to limit the number of machines in use. He set up a system by which pilots were grouped into quartets tested yearly to see which would be the Primary or Secondary pilot for a 'Mech. The other two members of the team would perform support and tactical duties.

"Unfortunately, General Kerensky's death shattered the last bond holding the former Star League troops together. Within a generation, the Star League troops who had left with Kerensky had battered themselves worse than all the damage the Successor States have done to one another since then. Colonies survived by the barest of margins, and cobbled-together BattleMechs stalked the landscape scavenging for spare parts, ammo, and food."

The white-haired woman leaned forward, resting her elbows on her knees. "The only exception was Strana Mechty, the depot world. The name is Russian and means Land of Dreams, so named to encourage people to work together. From there, Nicholas Kerensky and Jennifer Winson led some six hundred Kerensky loyalists on a crusade to destroy the bandits wandering the colony worlds, intending to unite them all under the control of Strana Mechty.

"To these loyalists Nicholas Kerensky gave the highest honor he could imagine within the new society he formed. From that time forward, the surnames of these people would be designated as Bloodnames. Within any Clan, only twenty-five individuals are allowed to claim one of these Bloodnames. And such a claim is acknowledged only after that individual has defeated anyone else who makes a claim on the name."

Cyrilla touched a button on the arm of her chair. A wall panel slid up to reveal a holovid viewing screen. With the touch of another button, the image of a nursery filled with row upon row of babies appeared on the screen. A half-dozen older people wandered among the children, attending to their needs with the gentle care of loving grandparents.

"Nicholas Kerensky launched the Clans on an ambitious plan for rebuilding. Using the most advanced techniques available to our scientists, he began to match warriors and their bloodlines. Children were bred specifically to cultivate those traits that would make them the ultimate in warriors. As you have seen with Evantha, children intended as Elementals are bred for size and strength. Our pilots, like Carew, are bred physically small, but quick of mind and reflex to handle the difficulties of air combat."

"And others, like Vlad and Ranna, are bred to be MechWarriors?"

Cyrilla nodded. "What you see here is a sibko. One hundred children are produced from artificial wombs at the same time and then raised together. Natasha and I were raised in the same sibko, though we do not share any recent ancestors. As the children grow, they are trained and tested to determine if the desired traits have bred true. Yet

21

before the first sibko is five years old, another from similar pairings will be started, and the first sibko will have lost twenty percent of its children to accidents or rejection because of poor test scores."

Phelan frowned, not wanting to accept what he was hearing. "You mean children are allowed to die if their bloodline is not pure? That isn't natural selection. It's monstrous!"

Natasha shook her head. "No, Phelan. You lived for a time as part of a Dragoons sibko on Outreach. From that experience, you know that we do not mistreat children while raising them. Every precaution is taken, but if a child dies, so be it. If a child fails a test, he enters another caste, where he can develop as a useful member of society. Furthermore, only the warrior caste raises its children in the sibko environment. The rest of Clan society functions much as does any in the Inner Sphere."

Cyrilla pointed to the screen, where the scene had shifted to adolescents learning how to fight in light 'Mechs. "Nicholas wanted an army prepared to face any threat, be it from within or without. That was the reason for an enforced breeding program. By the age of twenty, only a quarter of the sibko will be eligible to become warriors. Within ten years, half will have been killed in combat, but the genetic material of any who have proven to be masterful warriors will enter into the Clan breeding program. They will achieve immortality, and for the vast majority, that will be the finest day of their lives. Except for a rare few, the majority will start back down soon after."

Phelan saw anger flash through Natasha's eyes. "Back down?" he asked.

"Yeah, back down." Natasha looked ready to spit fire. "In the Clans, a warrior is ancient by the time he reaches age thirty-five. If he hasn't won his Bloodname, he moves from active duty to training warriors. Ten years more, and he's considered ill-suited for anything more than filling and emptying infants."

"That's absurd!" Phelan looked at Cyrilla for an explanation.

"Not at all. By the time a warrior is thirty, he is facing competition from sibkos that are a generation behind him. By age forty, he fights against children from his own loins. He is at a definite disadvantage."

"But my father was more than forty years old when I was born!"

"And you are clearly superior to him, *quineg*?" Cyrilla looked at Natasha for confirmation, but the Black Widow laughed lightly and shook her head.

Phelan blushed. "Someday, maybe, if I've got a stiff tailwind behind me and he's got one arm tied behind his back. God, this is crazy. At thirty, a warrior starts his slide down!" The young man half-closed his eyes. "I take it, though, that a warrior who has won a Bloodname is on a fast track and stays up longer?"

Cyrilla nodded. "And he is guaranteed a place in the Clan breeding program."

Phelan nodded slowly. "Ah, this puts many things into perspective. It explains Vlad's reaction when he discovered that I claimed a Jal Ward as an ancestor. It also explains why he welcomed me to the House of Ward during the adoption ceremony." He chuckled lightly at the memory of the ceremony. "It must have really burned him to be the one who had to welcome me after my adoption."

Cyrilla smiled broadly. "Jal Ward left with the Star League troops in his father's place during the Exodus. He was one of the loyalists who fought with Nicholas Kerensky. He, his siblings, and all their descendants are eligible to make a claim on the Ward Bloodnames. We trace the bloodline through maternity. Because your grandfather married a cousin who carried the Ward blood means you are a member of the House of Ward."

Phelan frowned. "If this is so, why am I called Phelan Wolf?"

"Two reasons." Natasha ticked each off on her fingers as she explained. "First, anyone who is adopted into a Clan's Warrior caste—an event about as rare as Candace Liao and her sister Romano exchanging a civil word—receives the Clan name as his surname."

Phelan held a hand up. "Then Jaime Wolf and his brother Joshua were adopted into the Wolf Clan's Warrior caste."

At the mention of Joshua Wolf, Phelan saw pain arc through Natasha's eyes. "Yes," she said, composing herself immediately. "Their father 'married' outside the Warrior caste and got two sons on his wife. He petitioned for their adoption into the Warrior caste so his sons could fight beside him if they proved worthy. And so they did.

"However, the second reason you are not addressed with the surname of Ward is because you have not won that right." Natasha gave him a big grin. "Yet. And that is the main reason Vlad hates you so thoroughly. You are his big competition for the next time a Ward Bloodname becomes available."

"What? How could we win Bloodnames? The both of us are too young. There must be thousands of warriors with better claims, and the skills to win the claim."

Cyrilla laughed lightly and shot a glance at the Black Widow. "Natasha won her Bloodname at the age of twenty-two. It was unprecedented at the time, and is a mark still unconquered in the years she has spent in the Successor States. Ulric Kerensky won his Bloodname at the age of thirty, about fifteen years ago. I won my

Bloodname at thirty-six—Tasha always said I was a late bloomer—and have held it for more than forty years."

Natasha patted Cyrilla on the shoulder. "Phelan, you and Vlad are not too young to become involved in the contest the next time a Bloodname becomes open. All the Bloodname houses maintain a list of individuals deemed worthy of competing. The process for selecting and filling positions is arcane and difficult to explain, but consists mainly of nominations by the other Bloodnamed members of the House. They choose their candidates based on performance of duties, scores in testing, and reputation. Though Vlad's performance in the invasion, including your capture, has certainly enhanced his standing, you have attracted enough attention to make it possible to make the list as well. Remember, with the youth bias, burning bright and fast is a big advantage."

"Is making the nomination list the only way to be considered for a Bloodname, *quiaff*?"

Both women exchanged glances. "Neg," Cyrilla answered. "Because politics has a way of excluding the worthy at times, there is a provision that at least one candidate in each Bloodname contest be selected through a series of grueling and often deadly combats. Though many have won their way onto the list in that manner, they often get so torn up during the preliminaries that they cannot perform well in the actual contest."

Phelan chewed his lower lip. "With so many Clansfolk considering me an inferior, my only chance of making the list is probably through the preliminary battling. But giving any consideration to that is folly, *quiaff*? I have not even been accorded full status as a warrior."

Natasha waved away those concerns. "I'll have you up to speed in that department quickly enough. Just remember that Vlad hates and fears you not only because you threaten his chance at a Bloodname, but also because of what you did to him on the Rock. You outsmarted him in combat. Had your 'Mech been the equal of his, your tactics and daring could have killed him. You are the only Ward that Vlad is not certain he can destroy. Be careful he does not find a way to kill you *before* you two ever meet in a Bloodname contest."

Soft ringing tones echoed throughout the ship. Cyrilla smiled as the jump-warning sounds faded away. She stood and quickly punched a button that raised a window in the hull. Returning to her seat, she joined the others digging behind their seat cushions for the restraining straps. Once buckled in, she turned her chair to face the porthole.

A set of five tones sounded, then the *Dire Wolf*'s Kearny-Fuchida drive engaged, warping the space around the JumpShip. At that moment, Phelan felt as though the universe had folded in on itself a thousand times, smashing him down and compacting him into the space of an atom. The light from the stars outside the window expanded until it was as white as a viewport into a blizzard.

Just as suddenly, the universe unfolded again like a huge origami flower. The disk of white filling the viewport fragmented into countless small star dots, and Phelan rubbed his eyes to erase the afterimage. In the space of a heartbeat, the *Dire Wolf* had hurled itself more than thirty light years away from the realm he had once called home.

Cyrilla punched the release button on her restraints and stood framed in the viewport. She smiled, then turned to point toward the blue-green ball striated with white that showed through the window.

"Here we are, Phelan. Welcome to Strana Mechty. Welcome to your new home."

In a headlong sprint, Hanse Davion dashed from behind a boulder to the ruined wall of an out-building, then threw himself forward in a long, rolling dive as yet another target popped up. Twisting into a squat ball, he planted his right foot and tried to turn back toward the mannequin, but the loose gravel gave way and sent him sprawling flat on his face. *Dammit, I'm getting too old for this nonsense*, he cursed inwardly. Spitting out rust-colored dirt, he flopped over onto his back as a series of laser bolts lanced through the air above him.

Hanse jerked the trigger on his laser rifle, returning the mannequin's fire. The ruby darts from his weapon ripped a bar sinister across the target, but not before it adjusted and tracked him. He felt the searing heat of three bolts as they stitched a track down his right flank and leg. Immediately his leg stiffened, locked in a mechanical rictus because of the bulky exoskeleton he wore.

"Justin, I'm hit!"

Without waiting for a reply from his partner in the run through the Dragoons' live-fire range, Hanse dragged himself behind the wall he'd originally sought and levered himself up to his feet. He put all his weight on his left leg and let the rifle dangle from its pistol-grip in his right hand. "I'm mobile, but in name only." He forced a chuckle into his voice. "My kingdom for a horse!"

Hanse marveled at how easily and fluidly Justin Xiang Allard

26

moved from point to point as he crossed to the Prince's position. Still possessed of the litheness and strength of youth though he was close to Hanse's age, the Secretary of the Federated Commonwealth's Ministry of Intelligence molded his body to the available cover and gave the targeting mannequins no opportunity to track him.

Justin glanced at Hanse. "I've got one at two o'clock from your position." He measured the distance between them carefully. "Cover me and I think I can nail it when I'm halfway home."

Hanse nodded and shoved the snout of his rifle around the edge of the wall. With his first bolt, the mannequin oriented toward him and brought its rifle to bear. Hanse clipped off two more shots, both of which passed over the target's head, then he saw Justin's shots burn a triangular grouping just above the robot's midsection.

"Hanse, down!"

Spinning back away from the edge of the wall, Hanse saw another mannequin rise from the ground to his right. Even as he brought his own rifle around and awkwardly pivoted on his locked right leg, he realized he was blocking Justin's line-of-sight to the target. As the mannequin's rifle centered itself on his chest, Davion also knew that he'd never get off a shot in time to prevent getting killed.

When three laser bolts suddenly blasted into the side of the robot's head, the mannequin's laser rifle drooped to the ground without firing a shot. Hanse, heart pounding in his ears, sagged back against the adobe wall and closed his eyes. Rivulets of sweat plowed through the layer of red dust on his face and neck. *That's closer than I ever want to come again.*

"Are you all right, Highness?"

Hanse opened his eyes and saw the concern on Justin Allard's face. "I'll survive. I'm just tired. That was fancy shooting."

Justin jerked his head toward the target as two other men walked around the corner. "Thank them, not me."

One of the approaching men, small and silver-haired, smiled wryly. "My shots missed. You have the Kanrei to thank for saving you."

Taller and more slender, Theodore Kurita barely acknowledged the mention of his title. He surveyed the surrounding area, his tension betrayed only by a vein pulsing in his forehead. It paralleled an old scar that ran from mid-forehead down into his left eyebrow.

I know that look, Hanse thought. *It's the warrior's edge. For him, this is no game.* Letting everyone see that the exoskeleton had locked up to simulate his wound, Davion took two halting steps forward. Shifting his rifle from right hand to left, he offered Theodore his hand.

27

"Thank you. Your skill is most impressive, Kanrei."

The Prince of the Federated Suns half-expected Theodore to snub him, but the Kurita Warlord accepted his hand and shook it firmly. "Perhaps my skill with a rifle is impressive, but my sense of direction is not." He glanced back at his partner. "I fear Prince Magnusson and I are lost. If we had not gotten off our side of the course, I never would have seen your target."

Before anyone could comment, a hiss of static from the communications devices both Justin and Haakon Magnusson wore presaged a message from the Rangemaster. "Range Control here. Time limit's up, gentlemen. Your run is over. Please remove the power packs from your rifles. We'll pick you up a klick out on a heading of oh-four-five degrees."

Justin hit the talk button on his radio. "Roger, one kilometer at oh-four-five degrees. ETA one-half hour. One of us got hit."

"Limp in whenever. We'll wait. Range Control out."

Theodore popped the clip from his rifle and slid it into the open slot on his belt. "I do not believe I have ever found an exercise that so accurately recreates combat conditions."

Magnusson agreed. "Our rifles may have been powered down, as were those of the mannequins, but not by much. I touched a spot where a shot had gone awry and it was still hot."

Hanse slapped a hand against his ribs. "Where I got hit feels like a nasty sunburn. I assume the Dragoons wanted to impress us with the gravity of the current situation."

"A wise approach," Theodore said quietly. "Some among our peers seem not to fully comprehend the danger the Clans present to the Inner Sphere."

Hanse stopped. "Do you refer to Lady Romano, or is your comment directed at me?" He asked the question without recrimination, but Magnusson looked as though Hanse had deliberately insulted Theodore. The Warlord of the Draconis Combine, on the other hand, seemed to weigh his words carefully before speaking.

"May I speak frankly with you, Prince Davion?"

"I would prefer it, Kanrei." Hanse hobbled toward a wind-sculpted rock to lean wearily against it. "What is on your mind?"

Theodore drew in a deep breath. "What concerns me is fighting a two-front war. Both of us know, from our own sources as well as from briefings Jaime Wolf has provided, that the Clans have hit the Draconis Combine as hard as they have hit the Lyran portion of your realm." In deference to Magnusson, Theodore bowed his head in the other man's direction. "Of course, neither of us have lost as much as the Free Rasalhague Republic, but we have been hurt."

"I fought against your surrogate twenty years ago and I tasted my share of defeat as well as savoring a few minor victories." The Kanrei slung his rifle over his shoulder by the strap. "Ten years ago, I battled you directly. In each contest, I have found you more than capable, and if not for a trick or two that you did not anticipate, I might have been left with utter defeats instead of the stand-offs I obtained."

Hanse's blue eyes narrowed. "You underestimate what you have done. After the Fourth Succession War, you rebuilt the Draconis Combine Mustered Soldiery into a force with more flexibility and bite than ever before. In ten short years, you turned it from a military I could have shattered easily into a force I could not destroy. Your drive into my territory in the '39 war forced me to divert my second wave in order to counter your thrusts into the Draconis March. It was a bold strategy that worked."

"It was a gamble." Theodore smiled warily. "A bluff that you could have called. Had you pressed me, you could have cut off my troops from their supply lines and poured straight into the Combine."

"But, Prince Kurita, it was a bluff I could not call." Hanse looked over at Justin. "As my esteemed colleague can confirm, our intelligence reports did not indicate how thinly you had stretched your troops. You had new units with new tactics and new 'Mechs that we did not anticipate. Conquering some worlds in the Combine allowed me to put a victorious public face on the whole enterprise, but we all know how close to a disaster it truly was."

Theodore bowed his head before the compliment in Hanse's words. "That, however, is not the situation now. Your Intelligence Ministry has been most successful in boring new holes into my command structure. You now have the intelligence you need to see what I have where. Deny it if you will, but I cannot afford the luxury of believing you.

"And that, Prince Davion, is what concerns me. When I leaked word that my son was being posted to Turtle Bay, and you responded by posting your son Victor to Trellwan, I had hoped we were silently agreed to let the next war fall to our heirs. I did not imagine a threat like the Clans appearing, but it does make our squabbling over a throne vacant for three hundred years look quite foolish."

Hanse nodded in agreement. "I did post my son to Trellwan in reply to your gesture. I also agree that the Clans are the greatest threat our states have ever faced, individually or collectively." Hanse heaved himself away from the rock and began walking toward the rendezvous point. "United we stand, or divided we fall."

Theodore fell into step with Hanse, and the other two men flanked them as they marched down the dusty trail. It wound slowly down out of the broad canyon that housed the live-fire range and skirted the edge of a dry riverbed. The air was clear as far as the eye could see, and the bright sunlight deepened the red of the rocky landscape.

"I had assumed you would be of that opinion, Prince Davion, but I am advised against acting upon that assumption. On one hand, you stripped troops away from the Dieron district and sent them to the front with the Clans at the same time as I did. This I took as our agreement that the Clans must be stopped, but it also provided you with an opening you could have exploited hideously. My advisors caution me that when you struck at us in 3039 it was because you assumed us to be weak. They believe you are an unscrupulous man who waits to take advantage of us."

Hanse brought his head up. "Do you want my word that I will not send troops into the Combine while the Clans exist as a threat? And would you trust me if I did?"

For a long moment, Theodore said nothing. The only sounds were the whispering desert breeze and the crunch of gravel underfoot. "Would I be wise to trust a man who is also known as the Fox?" Theodore asked rhetorically, then shook his head. "What I can trust, however, is that the Fox is not so foolish as to weaken himself by launching an offensive against a lesser enemy while the Clans threaten the very survival of the Inner Sphere. If nothing else, I have to believe that you will allow the Clans to grind my troops down to give you less to fight when you come for us."

Theodore opened both of his hands. "And that is the thing of it, Hanse. I have no choice but to devote all my resources, if need be, to defend my father's realm from the Clans. Were I speaking with Morgan Hasek-Davion and he and I were to strike a non-aggression pact, I could trust him to uphold his part of the bargain. With you, I must trust that you are too smart to repudiate it."

You know me well, Theodore. Perhaps too well. "I may be an old dog, Theodore, but I am capable of learning new tricks. I admit that my soul has at times ached for a chance to destroy the Combine. Your father and I are old foes, and our rivalry colors the relationship between our two Houses…"

Theodore stopped in his tracks, bringing the other three to a halt around him. "Understand this, Hanse Davion, my father is still the Coordinator of the Draconis Combine. From him, from Luthien, will come opposition to anything you do. They will call you a treacherous

30

dog, and castigate me for entering into a pact with the devil. That, however, is rhetoric. My father will never willfully interfere with defending the Combine from the Clans. So I ask you not to listen to the sound of the Dragon's voice. Rather, you must watch his claws."

Hanse smiled slightly. "I understand," he said, offering Theodore his hand. "I pledge to a non-aggression pact between our realms for the duration of the Clan threat, provided you agree to the same and will not assist your Kapteyn partners in aggression against me. I'll not have you descending on me if I decide Romano Liao needs to be punished for her foolishness."

Theodore met Hanse's grip firmly. "Well-spoken. Had you not included that caveat, I could never have agreed to the deal, for I would surely have believed you mad. I pledge that your state is safe from my armies as long as the Clans remain a threat to the Inner Sphere."

The Dragoons' helicopter raised a cloud of dust some 500 meters down the trail as it went to ground in a cleared landing zone. The Rangemaster dismounted from the craft, but did not head out to meet the quartet as they came in. "Must be that this hike is the last part of our training," Magnusson offered jokingly.

Without warning, another target mannequin snapped upright in the riverbed. Hanse stabbed his rifle at the target and tightened his finger on the trigger. Nothing happened. *Damn! No power pack!*

From his right, a green spear of coherent light flashed across the reddish landscape. It slammed into the center of the mannequin's chest, burning a black hole in the laser-sensitive coating. Sparks shot from the hole like a volcano spitting magma, then the robot exploded. Shrapnel and burning bits of cloth decorated the desert in a circle around the blackened, smoldering skeleton.

Hanse and the others stared at Justin Allard. He held his left forearm parallel to the ground, his mechanical hand snapped back as far as it would go. From his wrist, surrounded by the smoking remnant of his jumpsuit cuff, the muzzle of a laser gun pointed at the target. With a jerk, Justin flexed his metal hand down into a normal position and the laser muzzle dropped back into its hiding place.

Hanse shivered. "I'd forgotten you had that laser built into your arm."

Justin smiled as he tore away the burned cuff. "This refit has the same modified design as the one Aldo Lestrade had built into his artificial arm. It's certainly more efficient than the old one." He sighed. "It's nice to know I've not slowed down that much."

Magnusson stared at Justin in wide-eyed amazement, but Theodore showed no surprise. "The refit, it was done by the dwarf, Clovis

31

Holstein? Is it true he is Lestrade's illegitimate son?"

Justin shrugged. "He did the redesign, but we refitted the arm at the New Avalon Institute of Science. As for the other, I don't know. I've never asked him directly about Lestrade, and my agents in the Lyran Sector seem to have no file on him. But I do believe this device is similar to the one Lestrade used."

The Kanrei smiled. "Then I hope you have better luck with it. The laser didn't prevent an assassin from getting Lestrade."

Justin laughed lightly. "I'll practice until I get faster."

The Rangemaster, ruddy-faced and nearly breathless from his run, drew to a halt. "Are you all right?"

The Prince answered for everyone. "No problem. But I never expected to become a target outside the range."

The Rangemaster pulled off his cap, wiped his forehead on his sleeve, then smoothed the cap back down over his blond hair. "No, I don't suppose you would." He shot a glance at Justin. "Must have been a malfunction that triggered the dummy. We only use it in special cases..."

Hanse exchanged a glance with Theodore and knew instantly that their thoughts ran parallel. *The Dragoons came from the Clans. Perhaps this is the lesson they want us to take away from this exercise: Expect only the unexpected. Maybe they want us to realize that it's our only chance to survive.*

Wolf's Dragoons General Headquarters, Outreach
Sarna March, Federated Commonwealth
5 February 3051

Victor Davion accepted the cup of water from Kai Allard-Liao with a mute nod of thanks. Glancing around the large, rectangular conference room, he saw the others looking almost as bored as he felt. Padded, ladder-backed wooden chairs lined the briefing room walls and surrounded the conference table at its heart. Hohiro Kurita and Shin Yodama, his aide, had seated themselves in chairs at the far corner of the windowless chamber. With his back to the wall, Sun-Tzu Liao sat opposite Victor and the others in the Davion contingent, leaving Ragnar Magnusson the only person who had opted to sit at the massive oaken table that dominated the cathedral-ceilinged chamber. Despite the bright yellow of the walls and the warm gold of the carpet, the room's atmosphere remained cold and full of suspicion.

Galen Cox, at Victor's left hand, leaned his chair back against the wall. "What do you make of my counterpart in the Kurita camp?"

Victor shrugged. "I don't know." He let a smile creep onto his face. "I mean, he can't be as good as you are, Galen, but he must be of some use. Theodore doesn't tolerate sycophants, so I don't imagine his son does either."

"He's more than useful, Highness." Kai subtly pointed at the man as he raised his cup to his lips. "He's wearing his Dragoon-issue jumpsuit half unzipped, just like us, which means he's probably a MechWarrior. And if you look quickly when he turns this way, you can

33

see that he's got tattoos."

Victor took a second, harder look at Hohiro's dark-haired aide. As the Kurita officer adjusted his chair slightly more toward Hohiro, Victor did see a flash of black and gold from the left side of the man's chest. "That's more than just an 'I-love-Mom' tattoo there, isn't it?"

Cassandra leaned forward. "I think my brother means that Yodama appears to be a member of the yakuza."

"Can't be." Galen held out his left hand, then curled his little finger in toward his palm. "He's got all the joints on his fingers."

Kai smiled warily. "That just means he's good."

Just then, the room's double doors opened to admit MacKenzie Wolf and Christian Kell. Like their young charges, the two men wore black jumpsuits with red trim. Though both were MechWarriors, they did not concede to current fashion by wearing the garment half-unzipped. Chris, clasping his hands at the small of his back, took up a position to the left of the doors while MacKenzie Wolf stood at the head of the table.

"If the rest of you would care to join Prince Magnusson and me, we can begin," Mac said. He nodded at Ragnar, who smiled in spite of himself, then opened his hands to indicate all the vacant chairs around the table.

As Victor shot a covert glance at Hohiro, he found the heir to the Draconis Combine returning his look. At the same moment, Sun-Tzu Liao stood and took the seat that placed him at Wolf's right hand. Realizing that both he and Hohiro had been bested in this initial exchange, Victor stood and offered Cassandra his hand as she rose from her seat. "*Aprés vous.*"

Though she stood taller than the Prince, Cassandra accepted his hand, giving Victor a look that said she understood the game and her part in it. She also let him know, with gentle pressure on his hand, that he owed her. "*Merci*, my Prince."

Victor pulled her chair out from the table and seated her, then moved down to the empty chair between Galen and Kai. This put him opposite Ragnar—who, after Victor, was the shortest person in the room. It also put Victor in a position of power that Hohiro tried to trump by seating himself at the far end of the table. Unfortunately, because he placed himself so far from Wolf and the others, he appeared to be snubbing them.

Wolf looked over his shoulder and exchanged an amused glance with Chris Kell. Turning back, Mac shook his head slightly, then addressed them. "As you know, I am MacKenzie Wolf. The man standing behind me is Christian Kell. Chris is one of the finest

34

MechWarriors in the Inner Sphere, and I should know." Wolf's smile broadened. "I taught him everything he knows."

Placing his palms flat on the desk, Wolf leaned forward. "Now the two of us will become your instructors. Some of you have already seen battle, but even with that, the total sum of experience of those seated at this table would not equal what the average Clan warrior goes through in his training. Furthermore, he has superior equipment and knows how to use it. We must attempt to narrow the gulf between you and the average Clansman."

His smile drained away. "Whether or not we can close it is another matter entirely."

Wolf's words took Victor back to the battles with the Clans on Trellwan and Twycross. *It is true that those Clan warriors fight like the devil himself. Even if their machinery wasn't better than ours, we'd still have a hell of a fight on our hands. We outnumbered the Clans on Twycross, and still took far more damage in beating them than we have suffered in similar battles within the Inner Sphere.*

"Preparing you to fight against the Clans will not be easy," Wolf went on. "I suspect you know this, but some lessons have to be learned because they can't simply be taught. Forget everything you already know about war or even life. From this point on, you are not who you were. Now you are ours to shape and mold as we see fit. And be assured, this is not a game like picking power spots at a conference table. This is real, and if you fail, you probably will die. If not here, then out there somewhere."

Wolf straightened up. "Your training will commence immediately. Chris and I have to attend to a couple of details, but we'll be back. Until then, get to know one another, because you'll be working together for a long time."

MacKenzie and Chris withdrew through the doors, which shut silently behind them. With a big smile on his face, the blond, blue-eyed heir to the throne of the Free Rasalhague Republic leaned forward and extended his hand toward Victor. "Hello, I am Ragnar Magnusson. I have seen your picture before…"

Victor, surprised by the open-faced innocence of Ragnar's gesture, hesitated long enough to leave the boy's hand hanging in mid-air for a moment before he responded. In those milliseconds, he saw something like pain or fear flash through Ragnar's bright eyes, but pride came back as Victor accepted Ragnar's hand. "I am Victor Davion. *Angenämt*, Ragnar."

The youngest of the royals smiled radiantly. "You speak Swedish?"

35

Before Ragnar could launch into his native tongue, Victor held up a hand. "I'm afraid that 'I'm very pleased to meet you' just about exhausted my knowledge of your native tongue."

"Oh." Ragnar looked a bit crestfallen, but reinforced his smile quickly enough. "I understand."

Hohiro came around the table and offered Ragnar his hand. *"Roligt att lära känna Er. Mitt namm är Kurita Hohiro."* The Prince of the Draconis Combine turned and indicated Shin with his left hand. *"Får jag presentera Chu-sa Yodama Shin."*

Ragnar bowed to Shin. *"Konnichi-wa, Chu-sa Yodama."*

Having seized upon the language gambit to recover the face he'd lost by being shocked at Ragnar's friendliness, Victor now saw Hohiro using it to leave him in the dust. Before he could think of a way to recover the initiative and the ground he'd lost to Hohiro, Kai rose from his chair.

"Forgive me, please, for interrupting, but I fear neither my Swedish nor my Japanese is sufficient to offer proper introductions." Kai placed his right hand on the back of his sister's chair. "May I introduce Cassandra Allard-Liao, my sister. I am Kai."

As Cassandra stood, Galen also rose from his chair. A moment later, Victor realized what was happening and also leaped to his feet. As Hohiro broke his polite grip on Cassandra's hand, Victor thrust his own hand forward. "Victor Davion."

Hohiro straightened up to full height and swallowed Victor's hand in his own. "I am Hohiro. I look forward to our training together."

If you're as good a MechWarrior as you are a liar, you won't need much training. "And I as well, Hohiro."

With the seven of them exchanging greetings, Sun-Tzu's stony silence stood out in relief. As all eyes turned toward him, and Ragnar took a step to welcome him into the group, Sun-Tzu stood. He regarded them with hooded eyes, then folded his hands into the sleeves of his jumpsuit. "I am Sun-Tzu Liao, the heir to the Celestial Throne of the Capellan Confederation and all its worlds."

Victor saw Kai stiffen and watched Cassandra's hands curl into fists. Hohiro lowered his eyes and Shin's features became an inscrutable mask. Even Ragnar's eagerness faded at the vehemence in Sun-Tzu's voice.

Galen cleared his throat and brushed a lock of blond hair from his forehead. "With all due respect to all of you inheritors of power, I'd really appreciate it if we could avoid titles." He glanced over at Shin and received a mute nod of agreement. "First off, we've got at least five people who will answer to the title 'Prince.' And second, if I have to announce full titles every time I go to talk with one of you, how will I have time to warn you to get your head down in a firefight?"

"I believe Victor and I will agree that titles are superfluous in this context." Hohiro rested a hand on Ragnar's shoulder. "If the Princes of Rasalhague, the Capellan Confederation, and the St. Ives Compact concur, we will dispense with titles."

"Certainly," chirped Ragnar, followed a half-second later by Kai's "Agreed," which tossed the ball firmly into Sun-Tzu's lap. Venom in his eyes, Sun-Tzu stared at both his cousins, then stiffly nodded his assent. Victor suspected that had Hohiro placed the St. Ives Compact before the Capellan Confederation in his request, Sun-Tzu would sooner have died than agree to it.

Ragnar looked over at Cassandra and started to blush. "By the way, not meaning to be forward, but the perfume you are wearing is very pleasing."

Cassandra frowned. "But I'm not wearing any..."

Victor sniffed the air and immediately caught the flowery scent. He looked at Kai. "That's C-34, isn't it?"

In an instant, Kai swept his chair back against the wall and dropped to the floor. Flipping over onto his back, he eased himself in under the table, where he found the gray packet of material stuck to the underside. "It looks like three kilos of the stuff to me. The digital timer shows ten minutes until detonation."

Crawling down beside him, Victor nodded. "Someone from the Clans has gotten here and planted this bomb." The Prince sat upright, his hair just barely brushing the underside of the table as he grabbed the edge and pulled himself upright. "We've got a bomb. We'd best clear out and call a Dragoon detail to get rid of it. Zandra"—Victor pointed to the door—"go. Everyone, let's get out of here."

Cassandra headed for the door, but before she could point out that it was locked, Sun-Tzu's mocking laughter rang out. "Don't bother trying to leave. We are not meant to." His voice dropped to an icy whisper. "Alive, that is."

"What are you talking about?" Victor watched Sun-Tzu warily. *Was I wrong about you, or are you as mad as your mother?* "There's a bomb here."

Sun-Tzu's eyes became jade slits. "I am not a Davion puppet to be ordered about, Victor!"

"Answer his question, Liao!" Hohiro demanded.

"Nor am I a vassal of yours, my Lord Kurita!" Sun-Tzu's right hand came free of his sleeve and with a wave he took in everyone in the room. "Are you all fools? Can you not see that Wolf's Dragoons

37

are playing with you? Jaime Wolf's admitting that his orders came from the Khan of the Clans was to test us. This is most certainly another test. Perhaps it is one that will end in the destruction of the new generation of leaders of the Successor States."

Like his father before him, Sun-Tzu wore the nails on the last three fingers of each hand fashionably long. Reinforced with carbon fibers, they were painted with intricate designs in black lacquer and gold leaf. Light flashed from the gold and shone dully from the razored edge worked onto each nail. "The door is locked and there is no other egress from this room. Even the air conditioning vent is too small for Ragnar," Sun-Tzu sneered. "Or even you, Little Prince Victor. And if the estimate of three kilograms of C-34 is half-right, this whole level of Dragoon Headquarters will be destroyed."

Victor choked down his rage at Sun-Tzu's comment on his height. "So, give us the conclusion you draw from your observation, Celestial Wisdom, if you please."

Sun-Tzu sat down and folded his arms across his chest. "It is obvious. If we have no escape, we are not meant to escape. We should do nothing."

A mild thump from beneath the table made everyone jump, then Kai appeared from below, rubbing his forehead. "Sorry." He glanced over at his cousin, then turned back to the others. "Look, all I can tell you is that the C-34 looks real to me. We've got all of nine minutes to do something."

Hohiro smiled confidently. "Look, this table is built in three sections and is fairly stout. Let's take the two end sections and use them as blast shields." He casually waved the others away from the center part of the table. "Braced diagonally in the corners of the room, each little alcove should provide shelter for three of you. Shin and I will work on disarming the bomb."

Sun-Tzu chuckled mildly. "Brilliant. Cower in the corners. I love it."

"Wait. It's a good idea." Galen pointed to himself and Shin. "The trick is that you royals ought to be the ones taking cover. Shin and I can monkey around with the C-34 until the deadline is up."

Kai raised an eyebrow. "Galen, are you demolitions qualified?"

Galen hedged on his answer. "I took the course offered at the War College on Tamar."

"Not good enough for this thing, I'm afraid. I qualified for underwater demolitions only two years ago and C-34 is what we used." He looked up at Shin. "Do you know anything about explosives?"

38

The yakuza MechWarrior smiled easily. "When I was seven, the *Kuroi Kiri* had me planting packets of C-34 wherever I could to harass Commonwealth troops on Marfik."

"Nothing like on-the-job training." Kai dropped below the table's edge once again.

Victor squatted down on his haunches as Shin joined Kai under the table. "Kai, is there anything you can do to move the bomb?"

"I don't know. I don't think it has a mercury switch imbedded in the plastique because someone pounding a fist into the table could make a connection and set it off. Still, moving the table or the bomb might trigger it."

Shin pointed out that the timer had been stuck into one end of the square packet of explosive. "It might be possible to trim away some explosive to lessen the force of the blast."

Kai nodded and patted down the pockets of his jumpsuit. "We'd need a probe or a knifeblade—non-conductive only—to do the job. Highness, see if anyone has something."

Victor stood. Ragnar and Galen had whisked the south end of the table away and turned it onto its side. They'd wedged it in a corner and set chairs in front of it. Cassandra stood at the head of the table waiting for Hohiro or Sun-Tzu to help her drag it off. "We need something sharp, but it can't be metal." Victor checked his own pockets. "I didn't bring anything with me. Anyone?"

Hohiro checked, but came up a blank. A look of frustration knotted his features, then he turned and pointed to Sun-Tzu. "Your nails."

Sun-Tzu stood quickly, sending his chair flying. Hohiro lunged at him, but Sun-Tzu sidestepped the attack. With a flash of gold, he raked the nails of his left hand through the flank of Hohiro's jumpsuit. Hohiro hissed with the pain, but before Sun-Tzu could slash him again, Cassandra took her cousin down with a kick to the back of his left knee. She grabbed his outstretched right hand and twisted the arm around in an arm-bar that forced Sun-Tzu's forehead to the carpet.

"If you want a nail, I can just break one off."

"No!" Ragnar shouted in a horrified voice.

"What?" Victor looked from Ragnar to where Hohiro pressed his right hand to the cuts over his left flank. "He may think we don't have to do anything about this bomb, but that's a minority opinion. We need one of his nails."

"No we don't. The gold leaf would be conductive." Ragnar grabbed the zipper tab on his jumpsuit and ripped it free of the seams. When he had freed thirty centimeters, he bit through the cloth backing

39

and pulled it entirely away from the garment. Picking at the zipper with his fingernails, he obtained a clear piece of the zipper teeth and started to unravel it.

"The zipper is nylon. Kai can use the nylon line the same way a potter uses a piece of string to slice a pot from the wheel." Ragnar dropped to his knees and handed the nylon strand to Kai. Standing again, he grabbed a corner of the north side of the conference table. "Well? Are you going to help?"

Both Hohiro and Victor exchanged glances. *It's so easy for you, Ragnar, because you're still just a kid,* Victor thought. *You don't realize all that's going on behind the scenes here. You've been included in this group to accord the Free Rasalhague Republic equal status with the other states represented. This sort of cooperation might work fine here, but this is not the real world.*

Hohiro went to the other side of the table and Victor took up a position near its head. Cassandra released Sun-Tzu as the table swept over him, and she took up part of the burden on Hohiro's side. The four of them wrestled it into place, with Cassandra and Hohiro neatly vaulting it to get back into the center of the room.

Sun-Tzu uncoiled slowly and rubbed his right shoulder with his left hand. "If you ever touch me again, witch, it will be the last time."

Cassandra gave him a cold stare. "Don't make any promises you can't keep, *cousin!*"

Ragnar stepped in between Cassandra and Sun-Tzu. "Stop it. You shouldn't be fighting."

Sun-Tzu pushed Ragnar aside, slashing open the right sleeve of his jumpsuit. "I don't need you to defend me, Pauper-prince. You're here in some ridiculous show of putting your father's dwindling realm on equal footing with the Great Houses of the Inner Sphere. Your presence is only barely more palatable than that of this amazon and her brother. Bandits born of a bandit realm, they have less standing than you."

Hohiro wiped his bloody hand on the breast of his jumpsuit. "Sharp words from a bastard."

"Oh, you wound me, sir," Sun-Tzu mocked. "Which is worse in your tradition, Lord Kurita: to be born of unwed parents, or to be born of a union for which a mythical bloodline was created and one that so shames the participants that they dare not announce it to the world until their eldest child is five years old?"

Hohiro started to take a step forward, but Victor's hand on his arm restrained him. "Don't. He's got claws."

Hohiro pulled his arm free and spun on the Prince of the

Federated Commonwealth. He grabbed the front of Victor's jumpsuit with his right hand and pulled him up on his tiptoes. "Keep your hands off me!" He thrust his left index finger at Sun-Tzu. "That one has insulted my parents. No man may so speak and still live."

Victor's left arm came up and around in blow that broke Hohiro's grip. His right fist shot forward and hit home over Hohiro's slashed ribs. Hohiro's left hand shot back in an open-handed cuff that snapped Victor's head around.

Stars exploding before his eyes, Victor reeled back against the upturned table. He regained his balance for only a second before Hohiro tackled him and they both crashed back over the table. Victor felt Hohiro's hands tighten around his throat and blood pounding in his temples, but he refused to signal any sort of surrender. Again and again, he drove his right fist into Hohiro's ribs and occasionally snaked a left hand up into the side of Hohiro's head.

"Enough!" Victor dimly heard the shout above the sound of his own heartbeat echoing in his ears.

"*Hohiro, fusagu!*" The Japanese command brought instant cessation of the pressure on Victor's throat. He sucked in a noisy breath, then coughed loudly as Hohiro straightened up over him. Victor took pleasure in seeing Hohiro hug his left arm to his ribs, and determined to show no weakness by rubbing his own throat. Forcing a grin onto his face, Victor scrambled to his feet.

His grin died immediately.

Standing side by side, Hanse Davion and Theodore Kurita regarded their sons as though both were utterly mad. In the center of the room, Galen Cox and Shin Yodama stood frozen in the position of holding one another back from interfering with the battle between their charges. Ragnar looked positively stricken, Cassandra decidedly angry, and Sun-Tzu smug beyond all reason.

MacKenzie Wolf and Christian Kell flanked Jaime Wolf as he moved into the room. Jaime looked to where Kai lay working on the bomb, then turned on the others with an icy stare. "So this is it? This is the future leadership of the Inner Sphere?" The anger in his voice unabated, he flicked a glance at Hanse and Theodore. "I wish you both long life and more heirs to ward your realms."

"I am especially surprised at the two of you." Wolf crossed the room and stood before Hohiro and Victor. Victor tried to meet his harsh stare head on, but embarrassment forced him to break eye contact and look down at the floor. "Both of you have already faced Clan troops and both of you know that it took everything you had to win out. You had to coordinate your actions, plan your strategies, and

41

possess the vision and flexibility to adapt as the situation changed. But here you let petty jealousies reduce you to behaving like children bickering in a sandlot."

Wolf turned slowly. "Understand this, all of you. The Clans are not going to roll over and play dead just because you command them to do so." He pointed at Kai. "It will take more than one soldier thinking about the objective to defeat them. I had hoped to use you, the scions of the Inner Sphere's ruling Houses, as an example for how we might all cooperate to combat this threat. I had hoped that the seeds of the rivalries that have sundered the Inner Sphere for three centuries had not yet sprouted or taken sufficient root in you.

"If I was wrong, I apologize to you, MacKenzie, and to you, Christian, for assigning you the task of bringing this rabble together into a unit." He looked at Victor and Hohiro. "And make no mistake of it, you will become the unit I need you to be, or you will be discarded. This is no longer a fight of House against House. It is us against the Clans. If I have to manufacture leaders for that war, I will do it."

Wolf stalked from the room. Hanse looked at his son, shaking his head sadly. Turning to Theodore, he rested a hand on the Kanrei's shoulder. "I apologize for my son's behavior. I don't know what possessed him."

Theodore waved off the apology casually. "It is not his fault. He is yet young. My son should have known better."

Together, Hanse and Theodore walked from the room. As the doors closed behind them, MacKenzie Wolf clapped his hands together and smiled coldly. "This bomb test is the least of the challenges you will face in your time here. If you want to fight, we'll give you plenty to do, but unless you start working together, you'll die fighting each other."

He jerked a thumb at the door. "Outside! Move it! You've got a full day of drills ahead of you. Let's try not to screw them up as badly as you did this one."

Despite a nervousness that made him nauseous, Phelan Kell kept his face impassive as he strode down the long stairway from the visitors' gallery. He stepped onto the floor of the huge, circular chamber and crossed it quickly. He managed to step up onto the slowly revolving central platform only a meter or two from the witness box to which he had been called. That act of timing, as Cyrilla had pointed out to him earlier, was no mean feat and would please many of the Clansmen gathered in the chamber.

A stern-faced clerk held out a plaque emblazoned with the old Star League crest. Above it, Phelan recognized the insignia of the Wolf Clan. At the clerk's instruction, Phelan placed his right hand over his heart and his left hand on the cool surface of the plaque. "Do you swear on the honor of the Wolf Clan to tell the entire Truth and not to rest until Justice is done in this matter?"

"I do."

The Clan Loremaster glanced over at Phelan. "Please be seated."

Slipping into the witness chair, Phelan looked out at the assembled Clan Council. Composed of those Clan members who had earned Bloodnames, the Council formed the ruling body for the Wolf Clan. It elected two Khans, who subsequently represented it on the Grand Council, though the election was more a pro-forma acknowledgement of who among the Wolves were the greatest warriors.

43

The Council debated and passed regulations, though the true management of the Clans fell to the Khans. In the main, the Council existed to sit in judgement over matters of honor concerning the Clan and the bloodlines it controlled.

The benches allotted to the Council members filled the first ten tiers of the room, with the remaining dozen devoted to the visitors' gallery. Built along the lines of a theatre in the round, its central dais slowly rotated so everyone could look upon the Loremaster, the Khans, and anyone else involved in the matter at hand. A ring of lights and cameras that moved with the platform provided images to the array of screens hanging from the ceiling, giving each member a view of the faces of the participants.

Each of the Clan Council members had !voting machinery and a communications terminal. Each vote would light up a red, black, or white lucite block, at the same time being tallied as an Aye, Nay, or abstention at the Loremaster's bench. The communications terminal came equipped with a keyboard that allowed typed messages to be sent to other Council members. It also included a headset that permitted public address or private verbal exchanges with other members or with the Loremaster during a debate.

"Phelan Wolf, you have sworn to give full and complete testimony in the matter we are discussing." The Loremaster, whose thinning brown hair matched his eyes, gave Phelan a look meant to be encouraging. "As you are new to the Clan, and the matter we are discussing is your adoption into the Clan, please feel free to ask for any clarification you need to answer the questions."

"Yes, sir." Glancing up, Phelan saw Khan Ulric Kerensky and Garth Radick, the other Wolf Clan Khan, seated above and behind the Loremaster. At first glance, Ulric's white hair, moustache, and goatee made him look older than his fellow Khan, but his leanness and the hungry look in his eyes gave him an aura of youth and vitality. Radick's mousy brown hair and thicker build suggested a man more suited to a sedentary lifestyle, but Phelan knew that could not be true of one who had won a Bloodname. Seeing how Radick's restless brown eyes scanned the crowd, Phelan decided that much went on behind the pleasant mask Radick wore.

A younger member of the Clan came around from a table on the far side of the Loremaster's tall bench. Dressed in a gray jumpsuit, she proudly wore a cluster of three 8-pointed silver stars on her epaulets. Phelan recognized them as the insignia of the Supply and Support division of the Clan's military and assumed this woman to be from the Clan's equivalent of the Adjutant General's office. As she tucked a strand of red hair behind her right ear, Phelan noticed she wore a communications receiver.

She smiled at him openly. "I am Carol Leroux and I will serve as the Inquisitor in this investigation. Were you a full-fledged warrior, you would have an Advocate, but that is not permitted in this type of proceeding. You understand that it is necessary for me to take a devil's advocate position. In addition to asking my own questions—" she touched the electronic device nestled in her right ear—"I will relay questions from members of the Council. Please take as much time as you need to answer them."

"Thank you, Star Colonel," Phelan said, drawing a smile from the Inquisitor when he used the correct form of address. Though he decided to take that as a good sign, his roiling stomach remained unconvinced.

"Very well, Phelan Wolf, please state the name under which you were known in the Successor States."

"I was Phelan Patrick Kell. When captured and made a bondsman, I was frequently addressed as Phelan Ward Kell, with my mother's maiden name substituted for my middle name."

Leroux nodded. "Good. It is best to be complete in your answers." She pressed her hand against the earphone and a strange, predatory look passed over her face as she looked up at Phelan. "As a bondsman, what sort of duties did you perform for Khan Ulric?"

Is that some sort of trick question? Phelan frowned. "As I understood my lot within the Wolf Clan, as a bondsman, every duty I performed was for the Khan."

"Please, be more specific." A hint of irritation crept into her command. "What tasks did you perform at his request?"

Phelan started to pick up Leroux's hostility and his stomach did its best to turn inside-out. Cyrilla had warned him that matters of honor often devolved into heated discussions, but he hadn't gotten the impression that the issue of his adoption would take that turn. *Great. Someone obviously sold my landing zone data to the enemy. This is not going to be fun.*

"I was asked by Khan Ulric to research and provide data concerning the state of preparedness of the Free Rasalhague Republic. Most specifically, I worked up that information for use in the assaults on Rasalhague, the capital world of the Republic."

Leroux's dark eyes widened. "You depict yourself as a researcher, but were you not really an advisor? Did not Ulric Kerensky consult with you exclusively before the Rasalhague assault, *quiaff*?"

"Perhaps I might have been considered an advisor, but I did not

45

see myself in that role." Phelan did his best to keep his discomfort from his expression. "As for who else Khan Ulric consulted or my exclusivity, of this I am ignorant. He never chose to confide any of his plans to me."

"Is it not true that the Khan struck a bargain with you concerning the conquest of Rasalhague, *quiaff*?"

"Aff." Phelan's stomach flip-flopped again. "It was bargained well and done."

His use of the Clan expression to seal a bargaining session took Leroux aback, while Phelan saw several Council members nod approval at his words. He tried to take heart in that, but Leroux recovered in an instant and was at him again. "Did you not, upon his orders, administer a beating to a member of the Warrior caste, *quiaff*?"

Phelan shook his head. "It wasn't like that…"

"Answer the question," she snarled. "Did you or did you not beat a member of the Warrior caste in full view of the Khan and his party on the surface of Rasalhague, *quiaff*?"

"Aff." Phelan immediately looked to the Loremaster and began to speak before Leroux could utter another question. "If I could be allowed to explain my answer."

The Loremaster nodded. "Star Colonel, if you please, let him explain."

Phelan cleared his throat. "My concern in the invasion of Rasalhague was for the people of the world. By that point in time, I had learned that the Clans do not wage war against civilian populations, under normal circumstances anyway. I feared, however, that because the world was the Republic's capital, the defenders might retreat into the cities. All I asked of the Khan was that the assault be as bloodless as possible in terms of civilian casualties.

"He said I might accompany him to the world after it had been pacified. He made good this promise, but during our inspection, a newly unhomed individual approached the Khan to ask for help for his family. He was an old man, but a MechWarrior from the Khan's own party began to beat him mercilessly."

Phelan rubbed his left hand across the knuckles of his right fist. "I asked the Khan to stop the beating. He replied that if it concerned me, I should stop it. The method I chose was to engage the warrior in a fight." The young warrior let a slight smile crack his otherwise serious expression. "I stopped him."

"Then you admit, as a bondsman, that you assaulted a member of the Warrior caste, *quiaff*?"

"If you choose to classify a fist fight as an assault, then my answer is yes." Phelan's green eyes narrowed slyly. "But as I understand my oath, I would be remiss in not admitting that I did assault two Warriors on that occasion."

That admission brought the Inquisitor's head up, and elicited other surprised reactions from some Council members. It was clear that a number of members were feeding Leroux the same request through her earphone, and equally clear that she spoke under duress. "Explain."

"During my fight with the first Warrior, an Elemental outside her armor sought to restrain me. In the heat of battle, I did not realize what was happening and managed to stun her with a lucky series of punches. This happened just before I broke the other warrior's nose with a punch and knocked him unconscious." Phelan cringed inwardly, knowing that Evantha Fetladral had to be present in the Council Chamber, for she had earned her Bloodname well before the invasion of the Inner Sphere. *I don't want to embarrass her, but it's the only way I can see to break this Inquisitor's rhythm. What's going on here? Why am I on trial?*

"Excuse me, Loremaster." Garth Radick's soft voice seemed barely to carry from his throat to Phelan's ears. "I think it is obvious that these questions have little bearing on Phelan Wolf's worthiness as a member of the Wolf Clan. When we adopt someone into the Warrior caste, we require that he has proved himself, heart, mind, and soul, to be a Warrior. I would suggest that Khan Ulric's use of Phelan Wolf as a resource in the Rasalhague conquest proves he has the mind of a Warrior. His choice of personal combat to settle the problem with another Warrior on Rasalhague certainly suggests he has a Warrior's heart."

Garth looked down at Phelan. "Tell us what you did on the bridge of the *Dire Wolf* in the Radstadt system."

"Do you mean when I found Khan Ulric and helped him from the room?"

"No." Garth shook his head, letting a smile grow on his face. "That is a story I believe we have all heard time and again since it happened. I fear any retelling at this point, were you to adhere to your oath of truth, would merely diminish the tale we have all heard."

A mild ripple of laughter ran through the chamber. Garth let it die before he began to speak again. "What I wish to know is what you did on the bridge after that. The technicians had told you that the seal on the hole in the hull was overstressed, *quiaff*?"

"Aff. They had started to evacuate the few rescue teams we had in the room." Phelan shrugged. "I was headed back out, but when I saw

47

a pair of legs move, I went over and freed that Warrior…" He stopped abruptly as the Khan motioned to him.

"Please, you have eliminated an important detail here." Garth looked out at the Council. "This Warrior you found lying there. He was the Warrior who captured you, *quiaff*?"

"Aff."

"He participated in your interrogation, and the first time you met face to face, he assaulted you, *quiaff*? And then, aside from finding the most demeaning labors for you to perform on a regular basis, he also gave you a beating with a neural lash that left your back bloody and raw, *quiaff*?"

Transient tendrils of pain writhed through Phelan's back at the memory. "Aff."

Garth smiled. "And yet, when you saw your tormentor lying there with the seal about to blow on the bridge, you freed him from the debris trapping him and then hauled him out of the bridge. Why?"

"I guess, ultimately, because it was not finished between us." Phelan's head came up and he met Garth's stare evenly. "My tormentor had beaten me in a fist fight, and I returned the favor. In our first encounter, he beat me in a 'Mech duel. If I had let him get sucked out into space, I would never be able to prove who was truly better. I'd never know if he beat me because he is a superior MechWarrior or because his 'Mech was so much better than mine."

From somewhere deep inside him, Phelan's anger and outrage at the abuse he had endured at the hands of Vlad crystallized. "I saved him because if Vlad is going to die, it will be at my hands."

Garth waited as gasps of outrage and a smattering of applause echoed through the chamber. He stood and pointed a hand toward Phelan. "Can there be any doubt, my fellow Wolves, that this man possesses the soul of a Warrior? Can anyone deny him entry into the Warrior caste of the Wolf Clan?"

The Loremaster stood as Garth took his seat again. "I call for the vote on whether or not Phelan Wolf should be accorded the rights and duties of a Warrior of the Wolf Clan. As he has already been formally adopted into the Warrior caste, it would require two-thirds of the Clan Council to reject him." The Loremaster smiled coolly. "May all be advised that the Loremaster of the Smoke Jaguars and the Loremaster of the Steel Vipers have expressed an interest in this pup if we reject him."

He punched a button on his control console. "Register your votes now."

Phelan smiled broadly as Cyrilla and Natasha, stemming the tide of Wolves leaving the chamber, met him at the central dais. "Well, I made it, I think." Seeing the worried expression on their faces, but not comprehending the reason, he asked, "What did the Loremaster mean when he said I had until the end of June to prepare myself for my final acceptance as a Warrior?"

Natasha distractedly waved off his question. "Your birthday is June twenty-seventh. On that day, you will be twenty years old. That is the customary age for a Warrior to test out of his sibko. Depending on how well you do in your testing, you will be assigned duties for the Clan. Don't worry about that. I'll have you in perfect shape. You'll find your test easier than getting kicked out of the Nagelring." Though she tried to make light of the testing process, Phelan sensed apprehension in her tone.

He frowned, but decided not to press her for an elaboration at that point. "If that is not a problem, why do you both look so discouraged?"

Cyrilla pointed to the screen overhead. Phelan looked up and saw the vote still displayed for all to see: 460 Aye. 353 Nay. 187 abstention. "I don't understand. I was accepted."

"True, Phelan, and that is no small accomplishment." Cyrilla laid a reassuring hand on his arm. "The problem is that your margin of victory was decidedly less than what I had hoped. The questions asked of you before Garth stepped in were not intended to prevent your acceptance. As Garth pointed out, those questions affirmed you as a worthy Warrior. Calling for this vote was a smoke screen."

"I'm still missing something."

Natasha's blue eyes flashed angrily. "It's simple, Phelan. Very simple. Those who oppose Ulric are going to mount an attack on him and attempt to depose him. The abstentions are enough of a swing vote to put him out of office, and the number shows that questioning Ulric's judgement the way they did was effective."

"They?"

"The Crusaders, the ones who wanted this damned invasion. If Ulric's foes do oust him, if they succeed in convincing a majority of the Council to support their candidate to replace him, we'll be looking at a major shift in the political balance within the Clans."

The dread in her voice sent a shiver down Phelan's spine and got his stomach going again. "And if that happens?"

Natasha focused her eyes somewhere far away. "Well, Phelan," she said, "you will be home for Christmas, but don't count on recognizing Arc-Royal or any world between here and there."

Wolf's Dragoons General Headquarters, Outreach
Sarna March, Federated Suns
5 February 3051

As Victor Davion watched Hohiro Kurita across the night-darkened terrace, it irritated him less that Hohiro had beaten him in all the physical exercises that day than that his rival seemed not the least stiff from the day's exertions. Victor leaned back against the cold stone balustrade and let it massage away some of the tightness in his lower back. *Obstacle courses, basic weapons instructions, and a cross-country march! If that's training to beat the Clans, the Dragoons have, indeed, sold us out.*

Kai Allard, dressed like Victor and Galen in the olive fatigues of the Tenth Lyran Guards, settled himself against the railing. "Well, Highness, I thought you and Hohiro hit it off well this morning."

Victor turned and gave Kai a withering stare, then cracked a slight smile at the pun. "Blood will out, I guess. It rather surprised me, after that talk about unity, that MacKenzie split us into two teams, pitting the Federated Commonwealth and St. Ives Compact against the Draconis Combine et al."

Kai rubbed his chin ruefully. "I apologize for not having made a better showing of things today."

"Don't worry about it." Victor punched Kai lightly on the shoulder. "None of us were in top form. As I saw it, as long as you beat Sun-Tzu at anything, we were ahead of the game. Zandra smoked Ragnar across the board and Galen kept trading off with Shin. Damned

Hohiro beat the hell out of me. That's why we came in second-best."

Both young men fell silent as others of their class and generation moved out into the garden. Back in the reception hall, the military attaches and actual wielders of power mixed and chatted in a civilized parody of warfare. Galen Cox and Shin Yodama, both of whom had been military men before duty brought royalty into their care, stood at the center of knots of young officers clamoring to know what it was like to do battle with the Clans.

Part of Victor longed to be in that room and to move through those crowds with the same ease his aide enjoyed. He knew he could learn much from what others might have to say, but his title would get in the way. Whether they agreed with him or not, officers would accept his judgement and defer to him just because he was heir to the throne of the Federated Commonwealth. Looking across the terrace at Hohiro, he assumed the Dragon's heir must have felt much the same way.

Victor motioned back toward the ballroom. "Kai, you ought to be in there. I bet every officer in the place wants to know what it's like to be face off with a company of OmniMechs." Though he spoke lightly, Victor realized almost instantly that he'd hit a nerve with Kai. *He still feels responsible for that squad of men who got killed after he ordered them back into combat on Twycross.*

Kai shook his head. "No, I don't think so." He let a slight smile onto his lips and tightened the corners of his gray, almond-shaped eyes. "And it's not for the reason you think, either. Romano is cruising that crowd like a hungry shark, and I don't want to be anywhere near her." His smile broadened suddenly. "Out here, we're safe because she's got no audience."

Victor smiled at Kai's joke, but said nothing as four more people strolled out onto the terrace. Cassandra Allard-Liao and Ragnar laughed about something together, and the two women following them smiled politely. One of the two Victor recognized immediately. Except for her waist-length black hair, she was a physical copy of Cassandra. Victor knew Kuan Yin to be the quieter of the twins and saw in her natural grace the inner strength Kai so often mentioned when speaking of her.

Yet as strong and pretty as she was, Kuan Yin paled in Victor's eyes compared to the other Oriental woman walking silently alongside. It was the same one he had noticed previously among the Kurita delegation, though tonight she was not dressed in Japanese ceremonial robes. She gave Hohiro a smile, but continued her conversation with Kuan Yin.

"Kai, who is that speaking with your sister?"

51

"I don't know." Frowning slightly, he studied the young woman. "I think she's with the Kurita group. Perhaps she's Hohiro's wife. They tend to arrange marriages early in the Combine."

Victor scowled. *Just my luck.* Before he could comment, two more people stepped onto the terrace, deflecting his thoughts. "Trouble at nine o'clock."

Sun-Tzu and his sister Kali strode out onto the terrace as though they owned it, yet Victor saw Sun-Tzu hold back just enough to give the impression that it was his sister who made the big play for attention. Of Kali Liao, the only good thing Victor could think was that her diminutiveness made him no longer the shortest of the royals. In the backlight from the windows arching onto the terrace, her auburn hair took on a halo of gold, but the expression on her face and the look in her green eyes reminded Victor of her mother's wild unpredictability.

The back of Kali's sleeveless black jumpsuit plunged well below the length of her long hair. Its neckline plunged, too, making a long, tapered vee to the wide belt around her waist, accentuating her small breasts. Though no blemish was visible in the half-light, Victor recalled a file that mentioned a faint scar between her breasts. She claimed it was a result of her initiation into a Thugee cult, during which she had cut out her own heart, then put it back again—proving she was loved by her namesake, the Hindu death goddess.

Kali looked around the garden, then stopped when she spotted Cassandra and Kuan Yin.

"I think I'll go over and inquire into the identity of your mystery woman," said Kai. "If you will excuse me."

"Excellent idea."

As Kai headed out toward the quartet that included his sisters, Isis Marik suddenly emerged from the ballroom and slipped her right arm through the crook of Kai's left elbow. Clad in yet another paramilitary blue outfit—this time without the cap—she and Kai looked like a proper military couple until she spoke. Her voice carrying across the terrace and possibly even back into the ballroom, Isis Marik exclaimed, "Finally! I have been looking all over for the heir to the Capellan Confederation."

Sun-Tzu stiffened sharply. "I am afraid, *Gospodjica* Marik, that you are mistaken." He moved to block their line of march and folded his arms across the breast of his golden tunic. "If you seek the heir to the Universal Throne, I am he."

With a look of bewilderment, Isis let her arm slip free of Kai's and stepped between the two cousins. She cocked her head quizzically at Kai. "Is not the eldest child of Maximilian Liao's eldest daughter the rightful heir to the throne?"

Sun-Tzu's eyes became like jade slivers as contempt contorted his features. "The only throne to which Kai Allard has a claim is that of the Federated Commonwealth. But that is only as a lapdog to a Davion, as the Allards have ever been."

Sun-Tzu's remark stung Victor, but he held his ground as Kai forced himself to laugh. "Service to the House of Davion is an honor. Service to the Capellan throne is dancing on the edge of a sword blade."

"Ah, but cousin, to paraphrase Milton, 'tis better to reign in Hell than to serve the court of the butcher of the Successor States. How does it feel, Kai, to know you have ordered men to die to preserve the realm of the greatest aggressor the Inner Sphere has ever known? Hanse Davion murdered 100 million people and left another half-billion casualties in the Fourth Succession War alone! And if that were not enough for him, ten years later he went to war again."

Sun-Tzu saw that his barb about Kai ordering the deaths of his men had hit home. He thrust a finger at the Diamond Sunburst ribbon on Kai's chest. "You go to war and drive men to their deaths, but you reap medals and rewards! Were you the heir to the Universal Throne, what could my people look forward to except the butchery of their young men and women as you concocted some new military crusade to sate your thirst for blood? The Capellan Confederation has not been the aggressor. We were not in 3028, when the Federated Suns launched their attack against us, and we were not in 3030, when Andurien violated our borders."

Sun-Tzu's voice lashed Kai with its ridicule. "And the most perverse of all is that you earned that medal by treachery. You lured honorable Clan warriors into a deathtrap with the promise of single combat. No matter how expedient it might have been, the deed reveals the moral rot in your soul."

Victor saw the mask descend over Kai's face and knew his friend would not reply. *That bastard's aim is true. Give Kai half a chance and he'll always doubt himself.* Victor started forward to rescue his friend, but the situation changed before he could intervene.

Kali had started to drift over like a vulture to pick further at Kai, but Kuan Yin reached out and lightly touched Kali on the arm. Victor would have sworn that Kuan Yin's fingertips merely brushed Kali's flesh, but Romano's daughter jumped back as though she'd been lashed with a neural whip. Kali's eyes flashed and her hands knotted into fists, but Kuan Yin's unwavering hazel-eyed stare cowed her cousin and held her at bay.

53

At that moment, the lovely young Kurita woman stepped forward. "Forgive me for interrupting, gentlemen." The softness of her voice was soothing. "Perhaps it is not my place, but the intensity of this discussion has become so painful that I would ask, please, that you postpone it until another time."

"*Sumimasen. Shitsurei shimash' ta.*" Kai gave her a respectful bow. "I have been most rude. Please forgive me." He straightened up, then turned and walked into the ballroom, leaving the field of battle to Sun-Tzu. The heir to the Capellan Confederation gave the young woman a polite nod, then let Isis Marik steer him out into the shadows of the garden surrounding the terrace.

Victor suddenly found himself face to face with the Kurita woman. The blue of her eyes was a startling contrast to the black hair that shimmered down her back. The delicate beauty of her features put Victor in mind of ancient Japanese woodcuts showing women as perfect as they were serene. Though she stood almost twelve centimeters taller, the smile on her face did not mock his size.

"Thank you for stepping in to stop that fight." Victor shot a glance back to where he had been standing. "I was going to do something myself, but you beat me to it. And, " he added with a sheepish grin, "you certainly did it more gracefully than I could have managed."

"I saw that you intended to help your friend." She hesitated, as though seeking for more precision in her English. "My fear was that you would accept the role as aggressor in the fight. My solution was to make both of them the aggressor. That way, they had to stop or else be branded my torturer. Your friend Kai has courage and strength in him, as well as manners. Sun-Tzu has cunning and strength. I do not think the resumption of this conflict will be pretty."

"Your assessment of Kai is quite accurate. I fear that your reading of his cousin is equally so. If they fight again, I will try to remember your solution to the situation." Victor smiled and gave her a half-bow. "By the way, I am…"

She laughed lightly. "I know quite well who you are, Victor Ian Steiner-Davion, Crown Prince of the Federated Commonwealth, Duke of the Sarna March, Kommandant of the Tenth Lyran Guards."

Victor decided immediately he liked the sound of her laughter. "I am afraid you have me at a disadvantage."

"I am simply Omi."

Omi. The name is familiar. I should know it from somewhere. Victor took her hand and kissed it lightly. "I am most pleased to make your acquaintance, Omi. I would try that in Japanese, but I am afraid languages were never my forte."

"*Do itashimash'ta*. The Nagelring's reputation for languages is not such that you are dishonored by not having mastered a difficult tongue."

Victor allowed himself a frown. "You seem to know a great deal about me, yet I know nothing about you. If you wish, we could remedy that in a pleasant walk through the garden."

Victor saw her about to accept the arm he proffered, but the sharp sound of clicking heels on the terrace tiles stopped her. They both glanced back to find Hohiro standing there, his expression stern.

"Please excuse me, Prince Victor," Omi said quietly, "but I must go. Perhaps we will have another opportunity for that walk."

She turned away and like a curtain descending on a play, Hohiro cut off Victor's view of her. Victor looked up at the Kuritan, but ignored the cold expression on his face. "Who is she, Hohiro? Why did she have to leave?"

The muscles of Hohiro's jaw bunched tightly as he visibly struggled for inner mastery. "She is my sister, Victor Davion, and you will never speak with her again."

Clan Council Chamber, Hall of the Wolves
Strana Mechty, Beyond the Periphery
28 February 3051

"I, Natasha Kerensky, swear on my honor as a member of the Wolf clan to tell the entire Truth and not to rest until Justice is done in this matter."

Seated behind Cyrilla, Phelan smiled at Natasha's defiant tone. It was news to none that she resented being called up for "interrogation by her *peers*." The way she said it left no doubt how few of the Council she considered her equal. The day's session promised to be full of fireworks.

The Loremaster looked down at Natasha as she settled uncomfortably into the witness chair. "Your cooperation in this investigation is most appreciated, Colonel Kerensky. The matter of whether or not Wolf Dragoons are guilty of treason against the Clans is a matter for the Grand Council. We are here to decide if there is sufficient evidence to warrant recommending the Grand Council's jurisdiction."

Natasha looked around the Council with a hard stare not muted by its expansion onto the screens above the central dais. "I believe, Loremaster, that I understand quite well what is going on here." In her black jumpsuit unzipped enough to reveal a red t-shirt with a black widow design, Natasha looked, to Phelan, much more the warrior than the other Council members.

Carol Leroux started to position herself as Interrogator, but Natasha waved away the other flame-haired woman. "Go away, child.

56

I don't want these jackals hiding behind you. If they have questions, let them ask me directly. It's time we deal with the puppeteers, not the puppets."

Leroux appealed mutely to the Loremaster, but before he could respond, one Council member stood up near the front row. "Loremaster, I request you instruct *Colonel* Kerensky that in this place we conduct our business in a civilized manner. She should comport herself with more dignity."

The Loremaster stared the Council member back into his seat, then glanced at Natasha. "Colonel Kerensky, Carol Leroux has been appointed your Advocate in this matter. Burke Carson will be your Inquisitor."

A slender man moved down to the floor of the Council Chamber and adjusted the listening device in his right ear. Even though his head had been shaved to promote good contact with a neurohelmet, the man's build and ease of movement would have told Phelan he was a MechWarrior. And the sneer on his face revealed his contempt for Natasha.

She laughed harshly. "Come then, little boy, and do your worst. Learn why I am called the Black Widow."

Phelan saw a number of Council members nod and chuckle, but many more appeared shocked and offended at her remark. He leaned forward to Cyrilla. "I take it this is a resumption of the political infighting that prompted the review of my adoption?"

"Yes, in some ways it is." She half-closed her eyes. "This is more slashing at the political philosophy that Ulric, Natasha, and I embrace. It is a battle of Crusaders versus Wardens."

Phelan shook his head. "Crusaders? Wardens?"

"It is a complex division in our people, but let me try to simplify it for you. The Wardens believe that the Clans should stay out of the affairs of the Inner Sphere, acting only if an outside force threatens the Successor States. The Crusaders believe that the old Star League was a paradise that they are destined to reestablish. Even if it means destroying the Successor States in the process."

Cyrilla's eyes narrowed. "The problem is that the means they wish to employ cut away at the very heart of what it means to be a Clan Warrior."

The young man shook his head. "I don't understand."

The Ward matriarch's face hardened. "The Crusaders, in pressing a charge of treason against Wolf's Dragoons, seek to block the Dragoons' DNA from ever being used in a breeding program!"

The look that Burke Carson was giving Natasha at that moment

57

reminded Phelan of the look the Honor Board headman had given him the day they kicked him out of the Nagelring. "Perhaps, Natasha, you could inform us of the duties to which the Khan assigned the Wolf Dragoons when he first sent you on the mission to the Inner Sphere."

"Gladly. One of the two Wolf Khans at that time was Nadia Winson. She directed us to seek employment as mercenaries with one of the Great Houses, and she acted at the behest of the Grand Council. Our entry vector into the Successor States, chosen to hide the location of the Clan worlds, brought us first into contact with House Davion on 11 April 3005. We negotiated a contract with Prince Ian Davion and fought against the Capellan Confederation. Over the next five years, we were able to gauge the strengths and weaknesses of the Capellan troops, as well as learn how well the Federated Suns forces worked.

"In 3009, we returned to make our report at the rendezvous point preselected by the Khan. She told us to continue to seek employment with each House in succession so that we might continue to gather information. This we did, moving on to a new employer every five years or so. In 3010, we took employ with House Liao, in 3015 with House Marik, in 3020 with House Steiner, and in 3022 with House Kurita. In 3028, we again entered the service of House Davion, who gave us the world of Outreach as our own in the year 3030."

The slender man folded his arms across his chest. "If your mission was to report on the preparedness of the Inner Sphere, why are there no records of the information you communicated to the Khan?"

Natasha's blue eyes glittered coldly. "Are you saying there is no record or that you are not privy to those records?"

The Loremaster shook his head. "No, Natasha, that answer is not acceptable. Remember, this is the Clan Council. You may not like our reason for asking these questions, but we have the right to do so. Please answer."

The Black Widow nodded reluctantly. "As you say, Loremaster. In 3015, we sent a small party back to the rendezvous and transmitted the data we had gathered on House Liao and House Marik. We also reported the death of Joshua Marik"—her hands gathered into fists— "and of his assassin."

She hesitated, then continued in a slightly subdued voice. "We received no more orders at that time. Our last run for supplies came in 3019. At that time, we were met by Khan Kerlin Ward of this Clan, who issued us a new set of orders."

Carol Leroux, sensing a chance for Natasha to defend herself, pressed for details. "And what were those orders?"

Natasha kept her voice even. "I may not be free to reveal them."

Phelan saw Cyrilla stiffen at that answer, and a number of Council members turned to one another, apparently commenting on the Widow's refusal to answer. The Loremaster's eyes narrowed angrily. "Natasha, you cannot refuse to answer."

Cyrilla stood and settled her earphone and microphone in place. "Loremaster, if I might be permitted. I was a Khan of the Wolf Clan at that time, elected to rule alongside my uncle. I believe that Natasha and the other Wolves in the Dragoons were under strict orders not to discuss their new mission with anyone from the Clans."

From the screen above, the huge image of the Loremaster's face looked down at Cyrilla. "It would seem, then, that we are at an impasse."

"Perhaps not," Cyrilla countered. "Though I was not present at the meeting, I was later privy to the orders given, with no promise of secrecy exacted from me. In fact, Kerlin did that precisely in the event a situation such as this might arise. He was proud of what the Dragoons had done. Were he here now, I am sure Kerlin would free Natasha from her vow of secrecy. He would want to use any and all means to defend the Dragoons' right to participate in breeding programs. Natasha is far more eloquent than I. Perhaps she would give voice to those orders."

Cyrilla bowed her head. "If she does not, I will be forced to report what I know."

Natasha nodded, and a wolfish grin began to spread across her features. "Khan Kerlin Ward charged us with four duties. The first was to continue our survey of the military strengths of the Successor States. He asked us to accelerate our pace, which we did. The second was to examine the problem of training Successor State units to our level of proficiency in 'Mech warfare."

"Third," she said, raising her voice above the din of whispers filling the chamber, "was to locate and secure a world where we could begin to manufacture OmniMechs. The Khan provided us with full technical data on the OmniMechs at that time as well as parts and prototypes for some of the more advanced items your Weapon Masters had created."

The shocked roar threatened to drown her out, but Natasha stood and spoke all the more forcefully. Even the hammering of the Loremaster's gavel did not stop her. "And his last order was to refuse to obey any Khan but himself. He wanted us to prepare the Inner Sphere for the invasion he felt was inevitable and he wanted no outside interference with his plan."

"How dare you suggest Kerlin Ward ordered your treason!" Burke Carson thumped his own chest. "Have you any proof those orders were given?"

Natasha shook her head.

He turned to Cyrilla. "And you, Cyrilla, have you any proof of what you reported?"

"No, Burke, I do not."

Burke turned his attention to Natasha. "So, we have nothing but your word, and the word of your friend, that a Khan ordered you to abandon your original reconnaissance mission and turn it into a crusade to create suitable opposition for the Clans. Such lies are unconscionable in this hallowed body!"

Carol Leroux grabbed Carson's arm. "That is more than enough, Star Commander! You are out of line!"

Furious, Natasha shot from her chair. "How dare you accuse me of lying! I have sworn to tell the truth in this body and I am doing so. I was awarded my Bloodname before your parents left their sibko! I may have been long absent from this Council, but I do recall that we have ways of settling questions of honor. I will meet you on the Field of Combat, Burke Carson."

Carson held his head up high. "A duel of honor is limited to MechWarriors, Natasha Kerensky. Were you one, I would oblige you. As things are now, I have no reason to accept the challenge of an antique."

"What!" Natasha's fist slammed into the railing of the witness box. "How can you even hint I am not a MechWarrior? I have been fighting for the last forty-five years in the Successor States. I brought with me years' worth of holovids and holotapes showing the Dragoons in action." She pointed at a short, bearded man sitting next to her Council seat. "This archivist has chronicled the affairs of the Inner Sphere for the past twenty years and he can cite you, chapter and verse, engagements and results for the whole of the Dragoons career. I have every right to claim the title of MechWarrior, no matter what my age!"

"I am not interested in what fictions your personal apologist might have concocted, Natasha." Carson pointed to the Loremaster. "Ask him. He has the rolls of the Wolf Clan Warriors there. The last time you were tested was in 3003. Though it confirmed your qualification for a Galaxy command, your Galaxy never saw combat. That you commanded a Triple or even a Cluster during your time in the Inner Sphere has no bearing here because it was never officially sanctioned by your superiors. You have no standing as a MechWarrior, Natasha Kerensky, and you were permitted to tutor this Phelan Wolf because we did not know what else to do with you. Had you the good grace and sanity of any other fossil, you would have wandered

60

off to die ages ago."

Amid the growing maelstrom of Council members arguing among themselves and the heated exchange between Carson and Natasha, Khan Ulric rose from his seat. "Enough!" The outrage in his voice cut the din like a laser through smoke. "Both Khan Garth and I have reviewed the material Natasha and her archivist brought from the Inner Sphere. It cannot be denied, in the face of this evidence, that Natasha Kerensky *and* the Wolf Dragoons have been a combat unit of formidable power and influence since they entered the Inner Sphere. Natasha herself has become infamous for her courage and daring. It is inconceivable that you would make such an accusation against her, Burke."

Ulric nodded toward the Loremaster. "Furthermore, we have long had a tradition of granting appropriate status to any Warrior who has been out of action and unable to test for some reason. As I recall, Burke, you were unable to test for six months after your right leg was shattered in a battle with the Jade Falcons. Would you not accord Natasha Kerensky the same courtesy?"

Phelan saw Carson's inner conflict raging on his face. The man hated being forced to agree with Ulric, but had little choice. "That is our custom, as you point out, my Khan, but for MechWarriors of a more recent vintage. If not for Natasha's advanced age, I would not oppose denying her the temporary honor, but what is the purpose? She cannot conceivably win out or even survive testing against Warriors four generations younger. I would also point out that I am not required to accept the challenge of a Warrior whose status is only honorary."

"Acknowledged." Ulric smiled at Natasha. "Are you willing to undergo testing to determine your ranking and status among the MechWarriors of the Wolf Clan?"

The flame-haired MechWarrior nodded solemnly. "I will be prepared to be tested in just under the six months Carson was given for his broken leg. And," she added, shooting him a hooded glance, "I would even be willing to permit Carson as one of my opponents during the testing."

That offer clearly took Carson by surprise. "We shall see if the opportunity presents itself."

"Good." Ulric nodded. "And now back to the original question before us: shall we allow the breeding of the DNA of the Wolf Dragoons?" Ulric looked around the assembly. "It strikes me that Natasha's sworn testimony that the Wolf Dragoons were merely following the Khan's orders resolves the question of treason in a satisfactory manner. How can one commit treason if treason is defined as working against the will of the Clans but the Khan is the embodiment of that will?"

Burke Carson pressed his hand against his earphone and repeated the question coming through to him from a Council member. "Your question is valid, my Khan, and can only be answered in the consciences of the members present. My question, however, is of a different nature. Colonel Kerensky, if you were under orders not to obey the orders of anyone but Khan Kerlin Ward, why did you return to the Clans at this time?"

"I returned to the Clans because, for the first time since our mission began, we received a broadcast demanding all members of the Clan Council return in preparation for the election of an ilKhan. As I was the only member of the expedition who had attained a Bloodname before we left, I was the only one bound by my duty to the Wolf Clan. I did not see my attendance here as contradictory to my orders." She smiled evenly. "In fact, I saw my return as a way to keep faith with those orders."

Carol Leroux smiled slightly. "What do you mean?"

Natasha leaned forward. "The Khan charged us with the duty of preparing the Successor States to oppose an invasion. As a member of the Clan Council, it is my duty to advise the Clan and its Khans on the wisdom of continuing the assault on the Inner Sphere."

Sarcasm dripping from his voice, Carson turned on Natasha again. "And, pray tell, what would you advise us?"

"I would advise that your successes so far came because you took the Inner Sphere by surprise. The time it will take to elect a new ilKhan and resume the assault will negate that advantage. Your superiority of weapons and materiel will be slowly reduced as the Successor States are able to bring newer model 'Mechs on line. Already, as was seen in the Combine and the Lyran sector of the Federated Commonwealth, the Inner Sphere's troops learn quickly and can counter your attacks." Natasha leaned back. "I would advise, ultimately, that the Clans leave the Inner Sphere and never return."

"And leave our Star League in the hands of its destroyers?"

"The Star League ceased being ours when we abandoned it!"

A sharp rap of the Loremaster's gavel stopped their argument cold. "As Khan Ulric has pointed out, the discussion wanders from the issue of the disposition of Dragoon genetic material. We have heard that the Dragoons apparently obeyed the Khan's orders in both letter and spirit. That we do not agree with or sanction those orders is not grounds for recommending review of this matter to the Council of Khans. An excellent point made earlier was that this question can only be decided in the consciences of the Council members.

"I now call for a vote on the matter. As it is most serious, it will require a two-thirds majority to deny the inclusion of Dragoons' DNA in breeding programs. An Aye vote is for destruction of all sperm and ova taken from the Dragoons when they left on their mission. A Nay will kill the matter here and now, allowing our brave brethren fulfillment of their destiny. You have five minutes to post your vote."

Phelan watched as Cyrilla reached her hand toward the red Aye button on her console. "Wait! What are you doing? How can you deny Jaime Wolf and his people the right to reproduce?"

Cyrilla patted Phelan's knee. "Phelan, the moment Natasha and I reported that Khan Kerlin Ward gave the Dragoons orders to do what they did without reporting back, the issue was closed. There is no way that two-thirds of the Wolves will vote to have the Dragoons' DNA destroyed. The records Natasha brought back with her contain so much information that our scientists have only begun to analyze it. As each Blood House has members within the Dragoons, they will not deny themselves the chance of discovering a genetic diamond in the rough. Therefore, knowing the issue will be defeated, I choose to sow discord among the Crusaders by helping inflate their vote total."

"Wait, wait. How can you be sure the vote will go the way you want it to?"

Cyrilla sighed. "Phelan, those of us who have been around for a long time build up a storehouse of favors owed from members of other Houses. We also exert considerable influence over our own kin. Through exchanging a few favors with other Houses, I was able to gain an accurate picture of how the voting would likely go, and to change some minds so we could manufacture a pleasing picture for our Crusader friends."

Phelan nibbled on his lower lip. "How close will it get?"

Cyrilla shrugged. "Close enough that the Crusaders will believe they can replace one or both of our Khans in the next election."

Ah, I think I see now. "With the vote ending up closer than they expected, they will believe themselves closer to victory and will not work as hard to gather the votes they need."

"And those Wardens who have consistently underestimated the Crusader threat will be alarmed at the situation." Cyrilla smiled knowingly as she punched the button that registered an affirmative vote. "After the final vote is tallied, one of the Crusaders, an Elemental by the name of Karl Nevski, will issue a preemptory challenge of the vote. Evantha Fetladral will accept the challenge."

Confused again, Phelan furrowed his brow. "Even a fair vote can be challenged through combat?"

"Certainly." Cyrilla laid a hand on Phelan's shoulder. "We are the Clans, we are warriors. Our final court of appeal has always been the battlefield. If Nevski's forces can defeat those gathered by Evantha, and do so convincingly in the eyes of the Loremaster, the vote will be overturned."

Phelan shook his head slowly. "The ultimate in might making right."

"It is tradition among our people," Cyrilla said. The elder Ward smiled as her eyes focused far away. "You see, Phelan, within the Clans, fighting does not end when you leave the cockpit of a 'Mech. There is always conflict everywhere. He who is not ready for it will be destroyed by it."

ComStar First Circuit Compound, Hilton Head Island
North America, Terra
5 March 3051

Precentor Martial Focht bowed deeply to Primus Myndo Waterly as he entered the room. Standing in the midst of her personal chamber, he felt uncomfortable and more than a little intimidated. He cleared his throat before speaking. "I came as soon as I received word you wanted to see me." He was about to apologize for the sweat-stained fatigues he wore when the Primus signalled him to be silent.

She turned slowly from the large window overlooking the courtyard below, obviously fighting back the urge to unleash her fury. "I am not pleased that you were 'out of radio contact.' Were I of a suspicious nature, I might think it was an attempt to somehow evade me." She still wore the formal robe of her office, but her mane of long white hair was loose rather than bound.

Anastasius Focht closed his one good eye and shook his head. "Far from it, Primus. I was engaged in an exercise that demanded total radio silence. We have been simulating the effects of long-term operation in Clan-occupied areas. In this way, we can better determine the abilities of our troops in a long campaign against the Clans."

The Primus raised an eyebrow. "That is foolishness. *Our* forces will not be fighting the Clans."

"Apologies, Primus. I meant the term 'our' to refer to troops from the various Houses of the Inner Sphere. I did not mean to imply we would be engaging the Clans in the near future."

The Primus smiled with the condescension of a parent correcting an errant child. "We will never fight the Clans as long as there is a chance of taking them over from within. They are the hammer for reforging mankind, and ComStar is the anvil on which the New Man is being beaten into shape."

"Primus, I acknowledge the truth of what you say. Blessed be the will of Blake. These exercises, however, are necessary so that we can calculate what resistance the Successor States are likely to offer our allies when battle is joined again. The successes of the Davion forces on Twycross and the Kurita forces on Wolcott were a surprise."

Myndo nodded and turned away. She touched a hidden panel beside the round pane, and a shade slowly descended over it. As the light from the window died, the computer equalized the room's illumination by bringing up the interior lights. Their glow burnished the oak-panelled walls and floor with rich highlights.

"I appreciate, Precentor Martial, your desire to maintain our troops as an ace-in-the-hole if the Clans do become unruly, but I think your time is better spent assessing the strengths and weaknesses of potential targets for Clan conquest."

Focht's grim expression pulled his lips into a taut line. "At this point in time, Primus, the Clans have the ability to take any world they choose. Because of the ilKhan's death, most of their front-line troops have withdrawn to a position somewhere beyond the Periphery. This withdrawal comes because many of these elite troops have Bloodnames—a kind of hereditary order among them, as near as I can tell. These Bloodnamed individuals will elect a new ilKhan.

"Though the troops they have left behind to garrison their conquests are not normally seen as offensively capable, they could easily start adding to the Clans' holdings."

Myndo gestured casually toward the desk and data terminal in a corner of the chamber. "This I know, Precentor. I have read your reports and have found them, as always, to be informative and concise. I have noted, however, that you and I disagree on the worlds best suited to Clan conquest."

"I am not certain I follow your meaning, Primus." Focht was beginning to feel uneasy. "Worlds are selected based on their garrison strength, the value of their resources and industry, and the overall size of their populations. We choose those with high resources or industries, but weak defenses and low populations, as the primary targets. They are easier to take and hold."

"Perhaps for the military this is true." The Primus' blue eyes glittered like ice. "ComStar, on the other hand, has other interests.

Because the Clans see fit to let us administer their conquered worlds and to reeducate the populations, your criteria are flawed. By advising the conquest of worlds with larger populations first, we gain a larger audience for the Sacred Word of Blake."

The Precentor Martial forced himself to count silently to ten. With equal deliberation, he clasped his hands behind his back. "Primus, I understand your desire to gain access to as many people as possible within the conquered territories. However, to advocate the conquest of high-density population worlds increases the chance of civilian casualties."

"And you see a problem with that?" Myndo's eyes flared wide. "Bloodshed is just what people need to shake them from their complacency. If civilians die, it only builds resentment against the Clans, making it all the easier for us to play the role of savior when we come as intermediary between the populace and the Clans. The passion of the people becomes our passion, and through it, we can enlighten them."

"Surely, Primus, you would not advocate the commission of atrocities against civilians?"

Myndo vetoed that idea with the wave of a hand. "Never, Precentor Martial, would I issue such orders. But you know as well as I that the people of worlds where civilians have suffered are more quickly transformed into a docile citizenry."

"I see." Focht looked down at the golden ComStar insignia inlaid into the floor of the chamber. "Then I take it the re-education programs are going well?"

"Not as well as I hoped, but the withdrawal of the Clan leadership has lifted some of the pressure from the people. Some of them dare believe the Clans will not continue the invasion, though our agents assure them the Clans intend to fight on. Yet, in just over a year, the people of many a conquered world see ComStar as the only means to getting things done. If we can continue as advocates for the people against their conquerors for another two or three years, we will be able to engineer a mass uprising to overthrow the Clans when the time is right."

Focht's head came back up. "What news of the negotiations on Outreach? Is Wolf going to be able to unite the feuding factions of the Inner Sphere into an army?"

The petulant look that swept the Primus' features was an eloquent answer. "We have little or no news. We have not infiltrated any agents into the cadre of outsiders Wolf allows on his world. Even if we had, it would be impossible for such an agent to report until he was out of the system. As nearly as we can tell, people are going into Outreach, but no one has left. I believe this means that negotiations are not proceeding as smoothly as Wolf had hoped, for no action has been taken in direct response to orders issued from Outreach."

"On the other hand, Primus, it could also mean negotiations are going very well, and the planning precludes the issuance of orders."

The Primus shrugged. "Either way, I do not believe the armies of the Great Houses could ever pose a threat to the Clans, even if united. Was it not you who time and again has underscored the technological advantage the Clans have over any forces in the Inner Sphere? Reading your reports, it has occurred to me that cooperation between the Great Houses would result in the Clans abandoning their silly practice of bidding away strength. Only we can stop them, and we will do it from within."

"I realize, Primus, that you disdain dealing with hypothetical situations, but the current state of affairs does demand some speculation." Focht rubbed the white stubble on his chin with his left hand. "Twenty years ago, a Star League memory core fell into the hands of Hanse Davion. A covert ComStar assault on the New Avalon Institute of Science failed to recover or destroy it. Since that time, a number of technological advancements have emerged in medicine, planetology, astrophysics, and other sciences. These suggest that the computer core provided breakthroughs to the rediscovery of much knowledge lost after the First Succession War."

"Yes, but we have seen no developments in weapons or 'Mech technology."

"True, Primus, but it would not be the first time that the Successor States have withheld information from us. It could be that they are keeping a tight guard on the secret of new advancements. You will recall that twenty years ago House Davion revealed a new myomer fiber that made 'Mechs faster and stronger than ever been before."

Myndo's eyes narrowed. "But that myomer fiber combusted when in contact with a gas Davion scientists had created. That was why Davion did not outfit his 'Mechs with the pseudomuscle, but was more than willing to let House Liao have the secret so he could use it against them. I remember well the raid on Sian, Precentor Martial. I also know that two decades of research by Liao scientists have not succeeded in finding a way to coat or change the muscle so that it is not combustible in the presence of that gas."

"I do not bring this to your attention to upset you, Primus." Focht held his hands open in a gesture of peace. "I do hasten to point out, however, that the triple-strength myomer has not been released for use in industrial 'Mechs where the gas is not usually present. It strikes me as likely that the myomer is the subject of continued classified researches. Even if the Davion scientists have not found a way to make the myomer immune to the gas, they could equip their 'Mechs with the more powerful muscles anyway, just as House Liao has done with recon 'Mechs like the *Locust* and the *Raven*. These 'Mechs could be used on airless worlds or ones constantly lashed by storms to present the Clans with a nasty surprise."

"We shall inform the Clans of the gas and instruct them in its use."

Focht nodded. "I have already done so, Primus. That is not the issue. I explain all this to emphasize that we do not know the state of Davion weapons research on a secret that is twenty years old. How can we be certain Davion or Kurita or even Thomas Marik has not initiated a weapons research program that will close the technological gap with the Clans?"

The Primus recoiled with shock. "Close it? Is that possible in twenty years?"

The Precentor Martial sighed heavily. "Probably not, but they could narrow it. If the core started them on the road to restoring 'Mechs to the level and ability of their Star League precursors, the gap narrows precipitously."

Only the whisper of rustling silk broke the silence as Myndo paced. "I see your point. You must somehow determine the capabilities of such Star League-era weapons in the hands of current Mech-Warriors. We must be able to alert the Clans to potential difficulties."

The Precentor Martial barely succeeded in repressing a smug grin. "By using some of our own Star League-era 'Mechs in the exercise I was running, it was just such data I was attempting to gather."

Displeasure arced through the Primus' eyes. "Do not rebuke me, Anastasius Focht. I know well who and what you truly are. Do you forget I am the one who rescued you from a life of mind-numbing boredom and made you the head of my armies? You have served me well, but you may yet push me too far."

"Apologies, Primus. I did not mean to offend." Focht bowed his head remorsefully, but part of him rejoiced at having stung her. As he brought his head up, he adjusted the patch over his right eye. "Have you yet reached a decision on the matter of the message to Morgan Kell? I promised Phelan Kell that I would communicate to Kell that his son is alive."

"Yes, I have. You are forbidden to communicate news of Phelan Kell to any of his kin." Myndo's face became an implacable mask. "If

Morgan Kell or anyone on Outreach had even a hint of Phelan's survival, it would not only tip them to our involvement with the Clans, but it might also set them to thoughts of negotiating with the Clans. That must never happen."

"As you will it, Primus."

"Do not look so glum, Anastasius. You know there is no other way." Her eyes focused distantly and Focht knew she no longer saw him. "As difficult as this time is for humanity, it is only by passing through the cleansing fire of the Clan invasion that man can become worthy of what we, inheritors of the Word of Blake, will one day offer them."

Nestled in the 'Mech simulator's metal cocoon, Victor Davion cursed. "Dammit! Galen, can you get over here? I have a situation..."

The computer-projected enemy *Centurion*—a humanoid BattleMech whose right arm ended in the muzzle of an autocannon—stepped clear of its hiding place in the narrow canyon. The right arm came up and swung into line with the breast of the Prince's *Victor*. Victor flicked a glance at the armor diagram on his secondary monitor and chose not to duck back to cover. *I can take whatever his autocannon will dish out, and can give back as good as I get.*

As Victor brought his own 'Mech's muzzle-arm up, the *Centurion* cut loose. The simulator cockpit whirled, blurring the vision of the computer-construct landscape. Victor jerked against the command couch's restraining straps as the cockpit stopped abruptly, then experienced a severe jolt as special reaction pads in the chair pounded into his back.

The view screens showed him sky.

"Christ Almighty, what's he packing in that thing?" The armor diagram showed that all the armor had been stripped away from the right side of the *Victor*'s torso. The chain feed for the autocannon ammo in its right shoulder had been blasted to pieces. The sheer impact from the assault had been enough for the computer judging the contest to determine that the *Victor* would have been knocked to the ground,

71

a judgement that put the Prince at a severe disadvantage.

Victor forced the BattleMech into a sitting position and cut loose with twin blasts from the lasers mounted on its left forearm. The scarlet fire ripped straight lines through the canyon, splashing red highlights over the striated rock, but it missed the *Centurion*. Still, the hastily snapped shots forced the *Centurion* pilot to duck back, giving Victor just enough time to regain his feet again. The computer, using Victor's own sense of balance as reported through the bulky neurohelmet he wore, brought the BattleMech upright.

"Galen, where are you?"

"Coming up behind you, boss. What's the score?"

"Him lots, and me nothing. *Centurion*s pack a Luxor D-series Autocannon, right?"

"In the right arm, yeah." Galen hesitated. "That is, all except one I know of. That one's got a Pontiac 100, just like your *Victor* there."

Victor pounded a fist down against the arm of his command couch. "Damn! *Yen-lo-wang* has a Pontiac. That had to be Kai." A shiver ran down his spine. "And if that was Kai, the rest of his lance can't be far behind."

"Roger. I've got visual on you."

The computer projected an image of the entire 360-degree area surrounding Victor in a 160-degree arc in front of him. Twin crosshairs stood in the middle of the display, each under control of the joysticks on the arms of his command couch. At the right edge of the display, beyond the gold bars that showed Victor the limits of his weapon firing arcs, he saw the computer projection of Galen's *Crusader* marching into the canyon behind him.

"You know, Highness, from behind, your 'Mech looks fine."

"Looks are deceiving." Victor punched up a damage report. "The armor on my right side is gone completely. The autocannon is useless because the ammo feed mechanism is shot. I'm lucky Kai didn't get a stray shot into the magazine."

The LRM pods on either of the *Crusader*'s arms flicked open. "Where is he?"

"I don't know. Where's the other half of our lance?"

Hohiro's voice boomed an answer to the question into the Prince's neurohelmet. "I am here, coming up behind Hauptmann Cox. Has your *immortal* assault 'Mech run into some trouble?"

Victor ground his teeth. "You might put it that way, *Sho-sa*. We've found Kai Allard and he's running in a modified *Centurion*."

"If you find a *Centurion* too much to handle, Kommandant Davion, I would accept command of the lance."

"If you and Yodama would be so kind as to keep up with Galen and me, we might be able to trap Kai's people and have it out with them." Back behind Galen's *Crusader*, Victor saw the blocky form of Hohiro's *Grand Dragon* wander into view. The LRM launching rack jutted forward from the 'Mech's chest like the muzzle of a beast. Its right arm had no hand because the forearm housed a PPC, and Victor saw a medium laser underslung from the 'Mech's left forearm. He knew the *Grand Dragon* to be a nasty 'Mech in a fight, and would have preferred battling it out with Hohiro to being on the same side with him.

Galen's voice cut into the commlink. "I think you two should remember that we're fighting against Kai and the others, not among ourselves. Victor, you know well enough that we're going to have to work together to beat Kai. *Sho-sa* Kurita, if you've not learned to be wary of Kai yet, you probably will have by the time this simulator exercise is over."

Shin Yodama, bringing his *Phoenix Hawk* up behind the *Grand Dragon*, overrode the commlink. "Scatter. Incoming!"

Up over the computer horizon came three swarms of long-range missiles. The narrow canyon took some out as they impacted the lip or slammed into outcroppings and exploded in brilliant balls of computerized flame. A series of detonations rocked Victor in his pod as missiles peppered his 'Mech's left leg, blasting digitized armor into fragments. The *Victor* started to topple again, but the Prince jammed the useless autocannon into a canyon wall and kept himself upright.

The missile barrage hammered the two Kurita 'Mechs. The missiles savaged the armor on Hohiro's chest and right leg. A rippling series of explosions crushed armor on Shin's *Phoenix Hawk*, leaving the right side of its chest pockmarked with craters. A second wave of missiles following immediately after the first blasted yet more armor from Hohiro's *Grand Dragon* and chipped away at the armor over the *Phoenix Hawk*'s chest and right arm.

Victor escaped the wrath of the second wave, but Galen did not. A quintet of missiles arced into the *Crusader*'s right knee. Great chunks of half-melted ferroceramic armor shot from the fireball engulfing the joint. The *Crusader* staggered and dropped to one knee as another set of missiles struck it full in the chest. The impact knocked the *Crusader* sideways, but Galen caught it on one hand and kept the 'Mech from going all the way down.

The fire in the 'Mech's chest did not subside with the end of the missile barrage. More explosions wracked the humanoid *Crusader*, making it shake as with a giant case of hiccups. Fire geysered from the hole in its chest and out through its spine, then a massive blast obliterated its chest and sent its arms and legs flying throughout the canyon.

"Galen's out. Move!" Victor started his 'Mech running down the canyon toward where he had seen Kai's *Centurion*. "Missiles must have breached the armor and touched off his short-range missile magazine. Move it, or we'll get pounded by another flight of LRMs." Victor suppressed a shudder as he realized that if Kai's attack had hit his autocannon magazine, his 'Mech could easily have been torn apart from inside. "Kai spotted for the rest of his lance and they brought the missiles right down on top of us."

Victor cut around the corner into another canyon and saw, after a short distance, that it opened to the right into a broader canyon with a flat, level floor. Better yet, a 'Mech stood its ground and waited for him. "Move, guys. I've found them."

His computer identified the BattleMech as a *Cataphract*, but Victor knew it by another name. Because the ungainly beast looked like something cobbled together from various parts of other 'Mechs, most Federated Commonwealth MechWarriors called the Liao 'Mech a "Frankenstein." An autocannon barrel jutted forward like a lance from the center of its chest. Its right arm was identical to a *Marauder*'s, down to the PPC and medium laser in the boxy weapons pod that substituted for a right hand. The left arm was styled after the right arm on most *Shadow Hawk*s, except that the medium laser was mounted on top of the arm instead of below it. That led most weapon experts to conclude that the whole system had just been transplanted with a refit on the elbow and hand. The bulbous body and birdlike legs again drew comparisons with the *Marauder*, but somehow the *Cataphract* did not offer the same menace as its predecessor.

Victor dropped his crosshairs onto the *Cataphract*'s outline and hit the button beneath his left thumb. Twin spears of laser light stabbed out at the awkward 'Mech. The first shot boiled away armor on the *Cataphract*'s left flank, letting gobbets of it drop like rain onto the canyon floor. The second carved a hot scar through the armor on the 'Mech's head, making the pilot flinch. The 'Mech, complying with the motion of the pilot, took a skip-jump to the left, but stayed upright and brought its weapons to bear.

A bolt of blue lightning leaped from the PPC and caressed the *Victor*'s right arm. Molten armor coursed down the limb like blood from an open wound. The two medium lasers bracketed the assault 'Mech, each stabbing into the armor on an arm. The autocannon's stream of slugs slashed a bar sinister across the *Victor*'s chest, but

74

nothing penetrated armor to cause internal damage.

With his autocannon out of commission, Victor sent his 'Mech racing forward to beat on the *Cataphract* with the useless weapon. A quick blow could knock the autocannon out of commission, and being in that close would make the PPC much more difficult to aim. Victor smiled as he raised the 'Mech's right arm. "It's all over now, Sun-Tzu."

Out of the corner of his eye, he caught movement. To the extreme right edge of his display, he saw Kai's *Centurion* step away from its hiding place near the canyon mouth. The autocannon came up, and even as Victor tried to cut to one side, the weapon vomited out a rain of metal.

The depleted-uranium slugs hit the *Victor* in its already damaged left leg. The projectiles blasted away the battered remnants of armor clinging to the leg, then zipped through the myomer muscles corded in the 'Mech's thigh. Sparks flew as shells chipped away at the ferro-titanium femur, snapping the inorganic bone in half.

As the lower half of his 'Mech's left leg dropped away, Victor fought a losing battle to retain his balance. The 'Mech twisted as it fell, smashing its back against the far canyon wall. The command couch's special panels punched into Victor's own back, crunching him between them and the restraining belts. The blow stunned him for a moment, leaving him unable to do anything but watch as Hohiro and Shin entered the canyon.

From his vantage point, Victor saw the other two members of Kai's lance, an *Orion* and a *Catapult*, both 'Mechs with LRMs in their arms. The *Catapult* directed both its fifteen-missile flights at the *Phoenix Hawk*, while the *Orion* concentrated on the *Grand Dragon*. The *Cataphract* brought its weapons to bear on Hohiro, while Kai swung his autocannon around to take the *Phoenix Hawk*.

The missiles covered the mouth of the canyon in a sheet of flame. The explosions stripped all the armor off the *Phoenix Hawk*'s arms, and a subsidiary blast took out the medium laser mounted on the underside of the right forearm. Even more damaging, the missiles hitting the left arm shredded the myomer muscles in the upper arm, leaving it dangling and useless. More explosions sent sheets of armor flying from the 'Mech's left flank and leg, with two scoring hits on the *Phoenix Hawk*'s head.

The *Grand Dragon* fared better, as most of the missiles undershot the target. Even so, they managed to whittle away armor on the 'Mech's chest and left leg, providing the *Cataphract* with viable targets for its attack. Yet even as the fire condensed into black smoke, the *Grand Dragon* had sighted in on the *Cataphract* and the two 'Mechs exchanged volleys.

The azure bolt from the *Grand Dragon*'s PPCs lashed hunks of armor from the *Cataphract*'s left arm, but failed to penetrate it fully. The medium laser mounted in its left breast stabbed out and melted more armor over the left flank that Victor had previously hit, but again failed to do more than damage armor. In return, the *Cataphract*'s autocannon peeled a strip of armor from the *Grand Dragon*'s left flank. The Liao 'Mech's medium lasers missed their target, but the PPC made up for the misses with a vengeance.

The cerulean energy whip flayed the last of the armor from the *Grand Dragon*'s left leg. As it dropped away, the particle beam sliced like a scalpel into the myomer fibers in the thigh, melting them like candles. The *Grand Dragon*, having lost control of its left leg, started to tip, but Hohiro shifted the 'Mech's weight back over onto its right leg and kept the machine upright.

Kai's *Centurion* fired at the *Phoenix Hawk* from point-blank range. The autocannon's salvo hit the *Phoenix Hawk* in the right shoulder, spinning the 'Mech around like a toy. Sparks flew as the large laser shorted, and a string of firecracker pops sounded as the machine gun's ammo cooked off. The *Phoenix Hawk* slammed into the canyon wall face-first, then rebounded and dropped to its back on the rocky floor.

Another concentrated volley of rockets brought Hohiro crashing down. He struggled to rise up again, but Kai blew the *Grand Dragon*'s right arm off at the elbow with a shot that could just as easily have destroyed the cockpit. The computer controlling the exercise asked if Victor wanted to surrender, and he reluctantly replied in the affirmative.

As the screens died and the hatch at the back of the simulator opened, Victor unbuckled himself from the command couch. He set the neurohelmet back on the shelf over his head, then rubbed his eyes with both hands. "What a disaster. I'm never going to hear the end of this." He gave himself a few seconds to dream up some excuse that could explain how he'd managed to lose his whole command of battle-hardened veterans to Kai and some rookies, but nothing even remotely viable occurred to him.

Victor was the last one to reach the lounge area outside the simulator pod room. Kai was already there, flanked by his sister Cassandra on one side and Ragnar Magnusson on the other. Hohiro and Shin stood nearby while Sun-Tzu scowled at the assembly. Galen straightened up from the drinking fountain near the door and just shook his head.

Victor sighed heavily as he crossed to where Kai was standing. He offered him his hand. "Damn, you did good work out there. I haven't ever been nailed that badly."

Hohiro agreed. "Taking down four heavy BattleMechs, with only one of your command taking any damage at all is remarkable."

Ragnar beamed. "Sun-Tzu *wouldn't* have taken any damage if he'd done what Kai told him to."

Sun-Tzu spun Ragnar around with a hand on his right shoulder. "I am not a little weakling to be ordered about by an inferior."

Galen moved between Sun-Tzu and Ragnar, while Hohiro laughed. "You can hardly consider a MechWarrior with three kills to his credit today an inferior, Sun-Tzu. Your 'Mech, as well as the *Catapult* Ragnar piloted and Zandra's *Orion*, are well-suited to long-range combat, while *Yen-lo-wang* is built for infighting."

"Kai ordered all of us to stay back," Romano's son snarled, "so he could steal the glory of the kills for himself."

Victor shook his head. "No, Sun-Tzu. Kai placed himself in extreme jeopardy to act as bait for a very well-sprung trap. I should have known better than to lead my lance straight into it. Kai used his personnel in the best possible way, taking the most dangerous jobs for himself. Had Kai not been there, you would have died at my hands."

Shin bowed his head toward Kai. "I would also note that Kai moves with *Yen-lo-wang* as though the 'Mech were part of him. I knew, from seeing the *Victor* tumble, that the *Centurion* had to be lurking off to the right side of the canyon. Even knowing that, however, I could not follow his movement well enough with my weapons to be able to target him." Grinning at Kai, Shin added, "I am very glad I only have to face you in simulator battles."

Sun-Tzu snorted derisively, turned on his heel, and stalked off. Kai blushed, then shrugged. "Thanks for the kind words, guys, but don't forget, this was a unit exercise. My lance beat you, not me. If Zandra, Ragnar, and Sun-Tzu hadn't softened you up…"

"Or put us down," Galen interjected hastily.

"…I'd have been squashed like a bug." Kai looked at each one of the opposition lance members. "All of you are really good. We just got lucky."

Victor rested his fists on his hips. "Give it up, Kai. Just admit you're damned good, will you?" He looked over at Hohiro, who responded with a begrudging nod. "You smoked us, period. End of sentence."

"No." Kai held his up hands and waved off the praise. "I'm not that good. I've never been that good. In simulator battles at home on Kestrel or St. Ives, I regularly get my head handed to me."

Cassandra laughed aloud. "At home, the only person he can beat is me, and he doesn't think that sufficient for bragging." She gave Kai a playful punch in the ribs and Kai blushed.

Victor shook his head. *In his day, Justin Allard proved himself the best MechWarrior in the Successor States by becoming the champion of the Solaris games. And Candace Liao had a brilliant career as a MechWarrior before she left the army and entered government service. It's not that you aren't good, Kai, it's just that the league you played in at home was so superior that you don't dream of how special you really are.*

Victor threw his arm around Kai's shoulders. "If I may be so bold as to speak for the rest of the Inner Sphere, welcome to the world outside the Allard house league. We're sure glad to have you on our side."

Strana Mechty
Beyond the Periphery
2 April 3051

Having cinched the cooling vest snugly to his chest, Phelan Wolf pulled on his gunbelt and strapped it into place. He let the holster ride down on his right hip and left the ties dangling down toward his boottop. Unable to suppress a smile, he walked from the locker room and met Natasha Kerensky a short way down the hall.

She raised an eyebrow. "You look like a Nagelring cadet who's smuggled beer into his dorm room."

Phelan shrugged. "That is about how I feel. I have been down on Strana Mechty for just about two months and been training like a dog the whole time." He stretched out his arms. "I am in better condition now than ever before, but it is almost two years since I last piloted a 'Mech. It feels like a part of me has been missing."

Natasha shoved her hands into the small pockets of her cooling vest. "I can understand that." She flicked a glance at the gunbelt. "So you're one of those rocket rangers who wears a gun in the cockpit?"

The younger MechWarrior blushed. "Yeah. Knowing that Romano Liao would do anything to take a shot at the Kell Hounds, I always felt better when armed. It may be silly to wear it for a workout in a simulator, but if I wear it in the cockpit, I will wear it in the simpod."

Natasha shook her head. "No simulators."

"Damn." Phelan frowned and irritation seeped into his voice. "I was looking forward to some 'Mech exercise. I thought that was what we were finally going to do."

The flame-haired MechWarrior laughed lightly. "No. You misunderstood me. Simulators are for children, so we don't use them. You'll be mounting up in a real 'Mech, an OmniMech. This will be like no other ride you've ever had." She planted her hand in the small of his back and gave him a slight push. "Move it. Let's get you saddled up."

Natasha ushered Phelan into the 'Mech bay, but all the pushing at his back could not budge him once he had stepped into the cavernous room. Towering above him, alien and fearsome, BattleMechs filled the room. Standing ten meters high and massing as much as one hundred tons, the awesome war machines were lined up, rank upon rank, as far as Phelan could see. The gray color scheme favored by the Wolf Clan predominated, but Phelan also saw 'Mechs painted in various camouflage patterns suitable for jungle, arctic, and urban combat.

Phelan smiled at Natasha. "I'd forgotten how impressive a sight this can be."

The older MechWarrior gave him a slap on the back. "It's the guys whose breath isn't taken away by this sight who worry me."

Phelan studied the 'Mechs more closely. "I don't think I've ever seen any like these before. I don't recognize the designs."

"That's because these are OmniMechs. The designs change according to the mission." She pointed toward one of the smaller, non-humanoid 'Mechs with a cylindrical body and legs canted back like a bird's. Its skinny arms ended in twin muzzles. "That *Kit Fox* is yours for this first run. Get set up inside and set the radio to channel seventeen. I'll brief you as we head out to the range."

Phelan ran up the steps of the gantry two at a time and dropped through the hatch topside of the *Kit Fox*. Standing in the cockpit, he secured the hatch, then looked around for the reactor switch. Wrapping both hands around the red bar, he flipped it down into the "On" position and locked it in place. Beneath him, in the heart of the 'Mech, he felt the thrum of the engine. The lights came on in the cockpit and the computers began their check routines just as they always did, but Phelan sensed something beyond the ordinary in this 'Mech.

He dropped into the command couch and flipped a button on the console to his right, opening a radio channel to Natasha. "Something's screwy here, Natasha. This 'Mech looks like it masses maybe thirty tons, but the vibrations are those of some monster engine."

He heard a light laugh crackle back through the speakers. "You're sitting on top of a Starfire XL engine. It's about half the weight of a conventional, but puts out the same amount of power. You've also got an endo-steel skeleton and ferro-fibrous armor, both stronger than normal, if a bit bulkier."

"In other words, this box I am in is tougher, tighter, and lighter than anything I have ever piloted."

"In a nutshell. Wait until you bring the weapons on line."

Before he could do that, though, Phelan knew he must confirm his identity with the computer. That would be the last in a sequence of steps he took to prepare himself to take the BattleMech onto the field. He settled back into the command couch, telling himself to take the procedure one step at a time, lest he forget something because of the long layoff. Drawing in a deep breath, he recalled the litany of things he must do, then started at the top of the list and worked his way down.

Phelan found the medical monitor patches and cables in a compartment built into the right arm of the command couch. He peeled the backing off each and stuck the patches onto his thighs and shoulders. Taking the cables, he clipped the rounded end to the bead on top of the monitor patch, then snaked the cable through the loops on his cooling vest. He let the connector jacks dangle at his throat.

Next he removed the cooling vest's cable from the small pouch on the vest's right side. Snapping it into the jack to the side of the command couch, he felt the icy caress of coolant fluid begin to circulate through the vest. Trapped between a layer of goretex on the inside and ballistic cloth on the outside, the coolant would pull heat away from his body during the exercise. That was important because the fusion engine and the various weapons produced enough heat to overwhelm pilots who did not have help in dissipating it.

Phelan again keyed the radio. "Natasha, I think this cooling vest may be defective. The circulation seems to work fine, but it does not feel as cold as it should. It is probably just old coolant."

"Negative, Phelan. Your vest is fine. The Clans perfected heat exchangers for their 'Mechs that have roughly double the capability of those you're used to. As a result, the heat output is less. What's more, the coolant in your vest works better and is not poisonous if some of it gets splashed into a wound."

Phelan let out a low whistle. With machines that ran cooler and could pump out more power, it was little wonder the Clans had fared so well in their invasion of the Inner Sphere. The decreased weight of body, engine, and armor meant these OmniMechs could support more weaponry. *With all this special structure, I can't wait to see what I have online for weapons.*

From a shelf above and behind the head of the command couch,

Phelan drew down his neurohelmet. It was as bulky and heavy as any he remembered, and he settled it down over the padded collar of his cooling vest. He fidgeted with it until the neuroreceptors were pressed to the right spots on his head, then used the velcro fasteners to secure the helmet to the vest. Finally, he snapped the medical monitor jacks into the plate at his throat and fastened the chinstrap into place.

Phelan reached out and punched a button on the right side of the command console to start the identification sequence. A computer-generated voice sounded through the neurohelmet's speakers. "Kit Fox 349287XL3341 online. Proceed with voice identification."

"I am Phelan Wolf."

"Voiceprint pattern match obtained. Working…"

Panic tightened Phelan's throat. The computer would ask him to complete the initiation sequence by reciting a password of some sort. Because a 'Mech was loaded with specific data about the pilot that owned and used it exclusively, the password was usually personal and nearly impossible to guess. In training cadres, the passwords were general so that anyone could use a training 'Mech. Because no one had given Phelan the codeword for the *Kit Fox*, he supposed it must be one of those all-purpose ones.

Worse yet, he could not use the radio during the initiation sequence to ask Natasha for the correct code. *If they handle things the way we did in the Kell Hounds, the 'Mech will freeze up and I'll be trapped in here until someone overrides the anti-intruder programming. With my luck, it'll be Vlad who shows up to let me out of this 'Mech.* He rested his right hand on his pistol. *Well, I can always use this to avoid the embarrassment, though shooting Vlad would be a bit drastic.*

The computer came back with its flat voice, but the cadence and wording of the statement was one hundred percent Natasha. "Complete the initiation sequence, kid, and you only get one shot at this: What was the nastiest 'Mech company in the whole Inner Sphere?"

"The Black Widow Company."

"Affirmative. Welcome aboard, Phelan Wolf. Time for you to earn your pay as a MechWarrior."

Phelan laughed aloud and gave a clap of the hands. The computer shunted power to the weapon systems. The primary and auxiliary monitors filled with data as the computer checked and double-checked all systems. Phelan studied it for a moment, then opened a radio link to Natasha. "What does it mean when the weapons' initialization program says 'Verifying configuration'? That's hardwired into the system, *quiaff*?"

"Neg. These are Omnis, Phelan. The weapon pods on these creatures are modular. The *Kit Fox* usually carries lasers, an autocannon, and a short-range missile launcher, but the one you're riding has been dolled up. For one thing, I had arms installed on your *Kit Fox* this morning because you were used to running around in a *Wolfhound*. I figured you'd be more at home with this array than any other."

Phelan glanced over at the auxiliary monitor. Each arm ended in a large laser side by side with a medium laser, or so it appeared to Phelan. "Large beamers with mediums riding sidecar, right?"

"More or less."

Phelan realized she'd not told him everything, and that Natasha was loving every minute of his wonderment at what the OmniMech had to offer. He grabbed the joysticks on the ends of the command couch arms and used the foot pedals to start the *Kit Fox* walking forward. "I am ready to go. After you." By concentrating, Phelan managed to move the left arm in a fluid wave toward the far end of the 'Mech bay.

"Not bad. Are you one hundred percent operational?"

"Almost." Phelan punched a button on the left side of the command console. Instantly, a targeting display materialized about halfway between him and the rectangular viewport to the outside. Totally computer-generated, it provided a 360-degree view of his surroundings in a 160-degree arc. Gold lines broke the display into a triptych whose center portion displayed his firing arc. Two gold crosshairs floated within the display, responding to Phelan's movement of the joysticks.

Natasha's 'Mech led the way out of the BattleMech hangar and then south toward a targeting range. Her 'Mech looked akin to his *Kit Fox*, but the chassis was much larger and appeared to be heavier. Its arms ended in the weapon pods commonly found on a *Marauder*, lending the BattleMech that general look. In fact, Phelan would have classified it as a *Marauder* variant, except for the LRM launcher pods mounted on each shoulder. That made it look more like a *Catapult*.

Something clicked in the back of Phelan's mind. "Natasha, that looks very much like the 'Mech type Vlad was piloting when he captured me."

"You've got good eyes. It's the very same. After repairs, of course."

Phelan gasped in surprise. "You dispossessed him?"

"Rank hath its privileges." Natasha's warm, throaty laughter filled his neurohelmet. "Vlad only had this *Timber Wolf* for the expeditionary force anyway. In the real fighting, he used another Omni that fit better with his Star's make-up."

She brought her 'Mech to a stop at the targeting range's firing line. Bringing the *Kit Fox* alongside her, Phelan studied the range. He immediately punched up double magnification on his vislight scan. "I mark targets out at 300 meters. I know these weapons can do it because I saw Vlad take out some targets at this range and beyond."

"I've reviewed his battlerom, so I know what he did. I want you to shoot the nearest target. Use the medium lasers. You've still not seen everything an Omni has to offer."

Phelan dropped both crosshairs onto the ragged ferrocrete dolmen the computer marked at 305 meters. When the computer had a target lock, a gold dot pulsed in the center of the crosshairs. Flicking a glance at his control panel, Phelan saw the medium lasers were controlled by the joystick's trigger. He tightened his fingers down on them.

Used as he was to lasers that produced one sustained beam of coherent light, the Omni's weapons surprised him. Each medium laser spat out a series of micropulsed bolts that peppered the target with laser fire. Whereas normal lasers often slashed a trench through a target's armor as the target moved, this weapon chewed away at one spot, with the computer making small corrections in targeting to keep the bolts following one after the other.

"Sonovabitch! What the hell is this?"

Natasha laughed heartily. "Your medium lasers are Kolibri Pulse lasers. The problem with straight-beam lasers is that the material they vaporize helps diffuse the beam, lessening their damage. The pulses allow for vaporized material to disperse, increasing the ability to hit. The rapid cycling makes the weapon run hotter, but the higher damage potential is worth it."

"I'll say." Phelan smiled proudly. "Damn, it feels good to be back in a 'Mech. I wish Ranna could see me in this thing."

"She can."

Natasha's remark coincided with another *Kit Fox* moving from behind a low hill approximately 450 meters to Phelan's right. It appeared just beyond the bar that marked the edge of his firing arc, and brought up an arm that ended in the muzzle of an autocannon. Phelan saw a flash, then felt his 'Mech rock with the impact of a volley. He fought to control it and kept the machine upright. Still, before he could bring his machine around, the other *Kit Fox* vanished.

"My God, she's using live ordnance! Is she crazy?"

All levity dropped from Natasha's voice. "No, she's just doing her job. I told you before. Simulators are for kids. Her shells are underpowered, just as are your lasers. That goes for the other two *Foxes* hunting you out there."

Phelan swallowed hard as the computer assessed the damage to his armor. "That stuff may be down-powered, but it still ripped up some armor. This is just a training exercise."

"You'll have to watch your step because you can get killed out here. That's the problem with simulator combat. Even if you screw up, you get another chance. But a real battle never offers that sort of mercy."

"But Natasha, that's crazy. Think about how many perfectly good MechWarriors you must lose in these live-fire exercises."

The tone of her reply was cold, but Phelan sensed that the anger was not directed against him. "Good, perhaps, but not perfect. And that's what we aim for. Son, sibkos start out with a hundred or more children, but by the time the majority reach your age, they're down to thirty or less. Some die and some just leave the sibko. I don't know if it's right, but that's the way it's done."

She continued on, a trace of anxiety seeming to edge her words. "The breeding programs keep producing better and better warriors, but sometimes I wonder if it makes that much difference. By the time you're ready to test out, I guess we'll both learn the answer to that question."

Phelan shook his head. "The only answer we can accept is that, no, it cannot make that much difference."

"Maybe that's it, Phelan. What we'd have to prove is that someone who's been trained in a different system can match the Clans' best, and that one of the best from long ago is still damned good."

"I'll take one half of the assignment if you'll take the other."

"Bargained well and done." The fire returned to Natasha's voice. "And watch your contractions. You youngsters should really speak well, you know."

"I hear and obey." Phelan turned his 'Mech from the firing line. "You fighting in this exercise, or just along for the ride?"

"Today I am an observer."

"Then out of my way." Phelan wiped his perspiring hands on his cooling vest, then took hold of the joysticks again. "The odds are not quite to my liking, but I have never backed down from a fight. Let us see if your people are really as hot as they think."

Natasha watched the mechanical figures move across the quartet of screens without actually seeing anything. *My God, they all move so*

85

flawlessly. Have the sibkos really come this far in the time I've been away? A slight chill ran over her and suddenly she began to feel her true age. The long decades of battles, death, and destruction descended upon her with all the weight of a DropShip.

"Natasha?"

Ulric's voice snapped her out of her dark thoughts. "My Khan." She blinked her eyes, then reached out and touched a button on the console, freezing the four images. Using another dial, she slowly brought the room's lights up, but not too bright. "I have been reviewing the battleroms for Phelan's first training run."

The Khan stroked his goatee. "And?"

"And I think the sibkos have done superior work turning out well-trained and disciplined MechWarriors."

"Indeed." Ulric gave her a small smile, as if to say he'd anticipated her answer. "How would you say Phelan Wolf stacks up against them?"

Natasha allowed herself a wry grin of her own. "He's rough around the edges, though I imagine that's more from inactivity than lack of skill or training. Our MechWarriors can outshoot him now, but that advantage won't last long once he gets used to the new weaponry. If Phelan had been in a 'Mech the equal of Vlad's, he'd never have been captured on The Rock. We both know that."

Ulric dismissed her statement with a quick wave of the hand. "Hypothetical. Will he be able to test out in four months, *quiaff*?"

"I believe so."

"And will you?"

Ulric's question squeezed Natasha's heart. "Excuse me?"

"You needed to study those battleroms only once to come up with your assessment of Phelan's performance, *quiaff*? I saw his talent right away, as did Cyrilla. I must therefore assume that your continued review was an attempt to assess the skill level of those against whom Phelan fought. I also assume that you were measuring them against yourself."

"I appreciate your concern, Ulric, but how can the fate of one MechWarrior be so important to you?"

"You would be surprised, Natasha, at the importance I attach to you and Phelan." He folded his arms across his chest. "In your case, my political opponents are opposed even to allowing you to test out as a warrior at your age. Of course, if you fail, I will simply tell them that courtesy demanded I permit you to try."

"How convenient."

"Your victory would help to demonstrate their pitiful shortsightedness. If you do, indeed, test out, I will need to know in advance in order to make the most of the opportunity."

Ulric's voice became less confrontational as he explained himself, but still Natasha felt as though he had her under an electron microscope. "You wear a Khan's mask well, Ulric. You do the House of Kerensky proud."

"Coming from you that is most welcome praise." He turned to face the bank of monitors. "So, is the Black Widow still as deadly as ever?"

Natasha's blue eyes narrowed into a killing glare, but Ulric did not notice. "As you know," she said, "Black Widows only kill their mates, not their offspring." She stabbed a finger at the monitor that contained Ranna's battle ROM image. "Ranna is very good. The others are adequate, which is to say better than the standards set forth by the Successor States."

"You avoid my question," Ulric said sternly.

Always probing, always searching. You are, indeed, a Khan. Natasha shook her head. "Not avoiding, my Khan, merely considering my answer. Watching their performance in a training exercise, I can judge them only as a spectator. I cannot say how they would perform in battle against me, and that is what you are asking me. Would I control the battle and force them into foolish moves? If so, all the training in the world would mean nothing. I would own them."

"So you need more input before you can answer, *quiaff*?"

"Aff." Natasha felt her stomach twist into a knot. *Being a MechWarrior is not all reflexes and youth. Experience counts for more than the Clans have ever admitted. This I know to be true.*

She looked up and saw Ulric staring at her. She had to force a thin smile. " Have no fear, my Khan. I will test out."

Or I will die in the attempt.

Kai Allard-Liao smiled as his mother smoothed the shoulder of his uniform jacket with a loving caress. "Don't worry, mother. Nothing can go wrong."

Candace dropped her hand from his arm as a fleeting sadness showed briefly in her gray eyes. "You say that so easily, but your aunt is more than capable of causing trouble. It is she who has demanded that you testify before this council of leaders. I can't help but believe she has something nasty up her sleeve."

Justin reached out with his good right hand to give his wife's shoulder a squeeze. "Beloved, try not to ascribe to maliciousness what can better be explained by stupidity."

The ripple of laughter from all three Allards filled the room. Kai felt especially good to see his parents together and somewhat relaxed. Within the pressure cooker that Outreach had become, his little free time seldom seemed to coincide with theirs.

Kai took his mother's hands in his own. "Don't worry. I am ready for anything Romano will throw at me." *And I won't embarrass you.* "I trust Colonel Wolf to keep things in line."

Glancing at his father, he added, "Besides, Father could always just shoot her!"

Justin snorted a laugh, then shook his head. "Now you know why I sit on your mother's left in these councils. She can't get her hands on my left arm."

"This is not as funny as it seems to be to you." Candace's expression tightened, but her eyes blazed fire. "From a military view point, Romano may be virtually impotent, but she is hardly powerless. Indeed, I consider her one of the most dangerous women alive."

Her gray gaze flicked to Justin's black-steel hand. "And as for using that on Romano, I would not. Not here, not now. But if she ever strikes at one of you or the twins or Quint, even death itself will not keep me from avenging you."

Kai felt an abrupt shift in his father's mood. "As in everything else, my love, I gladly share with you this vow." He gave Candace a hug, then steered her toward the door of their chamber. "We'll see you in the Council, Kai. Just be yourself and nothing will go wrong. We love you, and I doubt there are any prouder parents anywhere in the Successor States."

Kai tugged at the waist of his dress gray jacket as he seated himself to one side of Jaime Wolf's podium. He glanced over to his left and flashed his mother and father a nervous grin. Beyond them and seated all around the semi-circle, he saw the royalty of the Federated Commonwealth, the Free Worlds League, the Free Rasalhague Republic, the Draconis Combine, and the Capellan Confederation gathered to hear him speak, but he noted that none of the other young royals had chosen to attend. He hardly blamed them for wanting to spend their free time elsewhere.

Jaime Wolf nodded in Kai's direction. "I regret taking up your free morning this way, Leftenant Allard-Liao. We have all read the report you wrote after the incident on Twycross. For myself, I found it an insightful, concise, clearly written document. This judgement is not shared by all those gathered here, however, which is the reason we are asking you to answer questions that may further enlighten some of us."

Wolf made no attempt to hide his displeasure at having to devote time to this meeting, when so many other matters were pressing. From what his parents had said, Kai knew that Romano had instigated the whole circus. Glancing over at his aunt, Kai felt ice creep into his bowels. The nasty look in her eyes told him she would show him no mercy.

"Thank you, Colonel Wolf." Kai bowed his head politely. "I wish to be of service."

"Good." Wolf looked out over the ruling families. "Well, then,

Leftenant, perhaps you will begin with what happened on the planet Twycross on 10 September of last year."

Kai nodded, as his thoughts wound back in time. At first, the words came slowly. "The Tenth Lyran Guard was involved in an operation intended to liberate Twycross. We believed that the Clans—in this case, the Jade Falcons—had moved all their line units from the planet. We thought that by striking at a world behind their lines, we would face only garrison troops. If we succeeded in taking the world, we could slow their advance because it would mean they had to pull line troops to hunt us down.

"On Twycross, we set up our position in a place that offered us maximum cover and reduced the battle to the closer ranges that favor us over the Clans. The weak point in this position was a mountain pass known as the Great Gash. Our troops placed explosives at the highest point in the pass, and we had a company of 'Mechs down at the westernmost end. We believed the enemy had no troops to send through the Gash, but we were taking no chances. Because of a storm in the area, however, radio contact was poor, so we did not have a full grasp of what was happening at the far end of the Gash when our troops met the Clans on our chosen battlefield."

"So, Leftenant, at some point early on, Victor Davion dispatched your lance to check on the Gash?" Wolf's encouraging smile eased some of the tightness in Kai's chest.

"Yes, sir. He instructed me to go to sector 0227. We had a landline there at the field hospital. Victor told me to use it to communicate to him what was happening. I…"

Kai faltered. Through the far doors, a trooper in Dragoons uniform was leading a visitor to a seat in the observers' gallery. The visitor wore a uniform similar to Kai's, but her clothing bore no rank insignia. He recognized her short black hair and though he could not see the color of her eyes from here, he knew her gaze was polar blue. *What is she doing here?*

Kai recovered himself after only a moment's silence. "…I discovered sector 0227 under attack by Toads—ah, the Clans Armored Infantry, what you have called Elementals. I defeated the half-dozen operating in the canyon and ordered an evacuation of the hospital and all the personnel."

"Excuse me," Romano purred, "but did you not also order some men back into the Gash area to detonate the explosives?"

Kai struggled to keep his voice from trembling. "Yes, I did."

"Knowing, as you did, the capabilities of the Toads, you must have sent only men armed with weapons able to defend them against assault by the Toads." Romano's statement stabbed at his heart like a dagger. "I mean, to do otherwise would have been ordering those men to their deaths. Such an action would be very irresponsible, wouldn't it, Leftenant?"

Kai swallowed hard. "Yes, Madam Chancellor, it would be irresponsible." He raised his head and tried to return her stony gaze with calm. "I accept that their blood is on my hands. I made a mistake, which I cannot undo. I can only vow never to repeat such a mistake."

Romano's lids lowered like a tigress lying patiently, waiting for the right moment to strike. "You made a mistake? Is that how you classify sending men to their death? A mistake? What kind of twisted philosophy pervades the Federated Commonwealth military to permit you to make such a statement?"

"Madam Chancellor," Wolf interrupted sharply, "your questions are far from the subject of our inquiry here."

"I do not…"

"Enough!" Wolf snapped. The irritation drained from the Colonel's face as he returned his gaze to Kai. "After the evacuation had begun, you engaged more Toads. In the course of your battle with them, what happened?"

"I fought with the Toads—at least two dozen of them—and forced them back through the Gash to the highest point of the pass. Once there, I saw a reinforced battalion of Clan 'Mechs. These were front-line units—what you said were called OmniMechs—that we thought had left the planet. Because radio communication was impossible, I knew that the only way to stop them from pouring through the Gash and falling on our troops was to seal the pass."

Kai's gaze flicked up toward the woman in the visitors' gallery. "I challenged the Clansmen to single combat, then instructed Dr. Deirdre Lear—my unwilling passenger—to pull the circuits that controlled the magnetic containment shielding for my fusion engine. As the first 'Mech engaged me, I ejected. The fusion engine explosion triggered the pentaglycerine we'd used to mine the Gash."

Kai hesitated as he relived that moment of boulders smashing down and burying enemy 'Mechs. "The *Hatchetman*'s ejection pod carried the doctor and myself to safety, while those Clan 'Mechs were destroyed." Kai's hands tightened into fists, then opened again. "I had no choice."

Romano stood abruptly. "You had no choice? You make it sound as though you were dispatching a rabid dog, not facing fellow MechWarriors. They deserved the honor of the combat you offered them. You could have met them and defeated them honestly, but you resorted to treachery instead. Have you no honor?"

Hanse Davion's fist slammed into his table. "Colonel Wolf, once again I see my *esteemed colleague* from the Capellan Confederation conducting a personal vendetta against her sister in our councils. This time, however, she directs her attacks against a surrogate who does not deserve it. I would request you to admonish her again to keep her remarks to the subject at hand. Criticizing a man for a decision—one I believe was correct—made in the thick of battle is not our purpose here."

Romano's green eyes blazed. "I would maintain that Kai Allard's conduct is very much the subject at hand. Colonel Wolf has asked us to unite our forces to face this mutual threat, has he not? Yet Allard's conduct shows a gross disregard for the lives in his command, and he apparently has no sense of position or honor. Am I to trust my troops to actions where they will have to work under AFFC commanders? How convenient it would be for those commanders to consider my troops expendable, and order them into a similar slaughterhouse situation so that the F-C need not lose any of its own men."

She smiled cruelly. "Given Hanse Davion's lust for my realm, he could entice me to send my troops against this supposed Clan threat as a prelude to another of his invasions. How can I trust my Confederation's security to men like Allard?" Romano turned to Kai. "You cannot justify your actions, Leftenant."

Kai trembled with anger, but his self-doubt stopped him from shouting out a hot denial. *She's right. You know she's right,* a voice whispered inside his mind. *You're less a warrior than you are a butcher.*

He forced his fists to unknot, then looked Romano straight in the eye again. "You are correct, Madam Chancellor. I cannot justify my actions with any motive other than personal greed. I could not allow myself the luxury of honorable conduct when I stood to lose friends and comrades in a battle, comrades I valued above all. And I cannot assure you that should I be part of an operation that included your troops, or in which your son served, that I would not have to order the troops to fill a hole in a line, and that the order might not mean everyone would die…"

"Ha!" she crowed triumphantly.

Kai's even voice overrode her shout of victory. "…but I guarantee that in any such situation, I would be at their head, leading the way."

Kai closed his eyes and inclined his head forward. "I live with the nightmares of what happened on Twycross. And the only thing that allows me to do so is the resolve never to order others into danger I would not be willing to face. If I have to consign men to death, I will be there with them. That, ultimately, is the burden of being a leader. And a burden I am willing to shoulder. It may not be what you call honor, but it is honor enough for me."

Kai let the door to the Council Chamber swing shut behind him, then slumped against the wall. Even as he was leaving the witness stand, Wolf had called Deirdre Lear to come forward. Kai knew that the whole situation on Twycross would be picked apart to the minutest detail, and that most of it would consist of Romano trying to make points in her forever war with Candace. *Thank God I don't squabble like that with my sisters or brother.*

"You, Allard." Hohiro Kurita filled the narrow corridor with fists on his hips.

Kai straightened up. "Yes, *Sho-sa*?"

The angry expression on Hohiro's face matched the grim tone of his words. "I'm looking for Victor Davion. Where is he?"

"I don't know." Kai shrugged wearily. "What difference does it make?"

Hohiro's rage cooled in the face of Kai's apathy. The Kurita Prince hesitated for a second, then forced a stern note into his voice. "It makes a difference to me. I believe he is with my sister."

Kai smothered a smile. "Well, my question still stands. What difference does it make?"

"What difference?" Hohiro reacted as though Kai's words were an autocannon hit between the eyes. "He is with my sister, and I do not know where they are. This is not done in the Draconis Combine."

"We aren't in the Draconis Combine."

"Our traditions govern the conduct of my family and our people no matter where we are. It is a dishonor for an unmarried woman to be in the company of a man who is not blood kin."

Kai's chin came up. "If you are suggesting that Victor Davion would comport himself in any way not becoming of a gentleman, I would say you that you are foolish." The young officer's gray eyes narrowed. "But this isn't really about your sister's honor, is it, Hohiro? You told Victor he was not to see your sister again, and you're angry that he may have violated your demand. This is between you and him, whereas it should really be between him and your sister Omi."

Hohiro stiffened. "It is a matter of family honor."

"Ha!" Kai snorted and gave Hohiro a reproving glance. "It is a matter of your ego and your struggle with Victor for dominance of our little community on Outreach. You're missing everything Jaime and MacKenzie Wolf are trying to do here. If I didn't know better, I might think you've being staying up late having long talks with my aunt."

"Perhaps, Leftenant Allard, you do not understand…"

"Oh, I understand, all right. Maybe better than you do." Kai's anger at Romano boiled up suddenly, and for once, he could not keep from venting it. "You and Victor see yourselves as heirs to a warrior tradition so honorable as to be sacred to you. You've both ignored the fact that your fathers are committed to a truce that could see us through this Clan crisis. The two of you use our training exercises here as a way to compete with one another, and you're clubbing yourselves to death to do it.

"You are both fine MechWarriors. You understand how to fight as individuals, and you've got a stunning grasp of strategy and tactics. And you both possess knowledge of the Clans that could only be improved through mutual cooperation. The trust your fathers place in you is more than justified, except when the two of you insist on behaving like feuding children."

Hohiro tried to hide behind his impassive mask, but Kai would not stop. He could see in Hohiro's dark eyes that many of his shots hit home. "And now this nonsense about prohibiting Omi and Victor from meeting. Face it, just like you and me, Victor and Omi are nobles. They have probably not the slightest chance of knowing happiness or love in any conventional sense. They have no equals in the world with whom they can relax and be themselves. Their marriages will be arranged, their mates chosen for them, and even extra-marital lovers will have to be politically correct, lest there be some scandal that could harm the empire.

"Now, you and I both know how slim are the chances of your sister and Victor falling in love. And the chances of them consummating *any* sort of relationship are slimmer yet. That leaves the chances of marriage virtually non-existent. But that does not preclude them from being friends, and through their friendship, gaining a greater understanding of one another's nation. Your sister will likely replace Constance as Keeper of the House Honor. In that capacity, she will be a brake on you when it is time for you to take power. As a friend of Victor, she could easily serve in that capacity for him as well."

Kai shook his head and waved Hohiro away. "But I don't imagine you'll listen to me because your samurai blood is thundering through your head and drowning out any sense. Pity. You and Victor would be much more effective as friends than enemies."

As Kai tried to walk past him, Hohiro reached out and caught

Kai's shoulder. Kai spun about quickly, but fought the instinct to raise his hands for Hohiro was not poised to strike. "*Sumimasen*, Allard-*san*." Hohiro bowed his head. "I am indeed foolish, and you are right to rebuke me. All is not exactly as you have described, but enough so that you have given me much to consider."

The Kurita Prince gave Kai a half-smile. "I am concerned for my sister, but your points are well taken. Perhaps you could communicate to Victor my apprehensions. In the Combine, perception becomes reality with surprising swiftness, and I wish only to protect my sister from damage to her honor."

Kai nodded. "I can do that."

"And I, in turn, can and will take a new look at Victor Davion. Perhaps Outreach is a place where the old tradition of rivalry gives way to a more practical one."

Kai smiled and even chuckled lightly. "I hope so." *And if you two succeed in patching it up, maybe, just maybe, I can get you to talk to Romano.*

Clan Council Chamber, Hall of the Wolves
Strana Mechty, Beyond the Periphery
25 April 3051

Phelan Wolf looked questioningly at Cyrilla, who was laughing. "It is getting nasty. How can you laugh?"

She shrugged easily. "I dearly love watching Conal make a fool of himself."

Off to their right, a Clanswoman stood in place, haranguing her fellow Wolves. "We face the most important Clan election since before we left the Inner Sphere. Soon we must choose a new ilKhan, and the Khans we elect today will affect the outcome of the other election. One of them might even be chosen as the next ilKhan. This, if for no other reason, is why we must replace Ulric Kerensky."

The young MechWarrior frowned. "I do not know, Cyrilla. The speakers have been hammering Ulric pretty hard. All were obviously Crusaders whose main objection is that he is a Warden. It looks grim to me."

"So it might appear." A spark of amusement lit Cyrilla's brown eyes, but her voice took the tone Phelan had come to associate with lessons for him. "If you know a storm is likely to do damage, you button up as tightly as possible, then you wait for the storm to blow itself out before trying to pick up the pieces and rebuild. The arguments we have heard seemed to build one upon another and to pick up momentum. But their foundation is quicksand."

"It is?" Phelan narrowed his green eyes. "The speakers say that

Ulric abrogated his responsibilities by not honoring the compromise made when the invasion was planned. They have accused him of everything from stupidity to outright treason."

Phelan jerked his head in the direction of a handsome, dark-haired man seated just below their place. "And they push Conal Ward as a logical replacement for Ulric. If only half of what the speakers say is true, Conal could be a good leader."

Cyrilla folded her arms across her chest. "He may, indeed, be a good leader, but I think he has overstepped his bounds here. Conal backed Nevski's challenge to the Dragoon's DNA vote, and yet that effort failed badly, thanks to Evantha's own persuasive skills.

"You know enough of our ways to realize that we place efficiency and superiority in military arts above all else. A Khan is one who has strong support within the Clan. The Clan members know he will bring them victory at the lowest cost possible. Right now, Conal shows himself a master of politics and rhetoric, but all this talk has not won a single battle in the Inner Sphere. Ulric, who is no novice when it comes to politics *or* war, will be re-elected."

The younger man eyed Cyrilla suspiciously. "More of your behind-the-scenes bargaining?"

"I would not be a House Ward Leader if I did not mind the affairs of all Wards, would I?" Her brown eyes flashed impishly. "I warned Conal not to push himself as competition for Ulric. I told him I would publicly endorse Ulric if Conal became a contender for Ulric's seat. This would point up Conal as a divisive influence within House Ward—something that would make most Clanfolk uneasy."

She smiled at Phelan. "We Clanfolk like people who know how to take and follow orders."

Phelan shook his head. "That explains why they view me with apprehension."

"Oh, not so much as you think." Cyrilla sat back in her chair. "If the reports of your 'Mech exercises are accurate, it is true that you operate in an unorthodox manner. But you get results. As a people, we also appreciate and respect that. Our society does not particularly encourage individuality, but we are capable of recognizing and understanding its value."

Phelan looked down at where Ranna sat beside Natasha. "I wish my unorthodox methods would work better against Ranna. She is my bane."

"And as she is also your lover, she knows you better than the others with whom you must fight." Cyrilla tapped her left index finger against her lips as she reflected for a moment. "When faced with three-to-one odds, a MechWarrior would usually take up a defensive position and try to inflict as much damage as possible on anyone who came after him. He knows the other side will send their least experienced warrior first, then the next level of experience, and finally the best of their number. Your willingness to play hunter instead of hunted is a shock, as is your willingness to shoot at more than one opponent at one time."

The younger MechWarrior shrugged. "That is how we do things back home. Aside from some strange battles with Draconis Combine warriors, most combat is a semi-organized free-for-all. Up 'til now, the Clans have not seen much of our fighting style because your 'Mechs are so much better than ours. Now that I fight in a 'Mech on a par with yours, the Clan rules of battle do not function as effectively."

He let a smile brighten his face. "And I do not know if Ranna is effective against me in a battle just because she is my lover. Not only is she a good MechWarrior, but she has patience. That seems to be a quality many of your people lack. With generations of children being born in lab facilities every five years and a Warrior's slide to oblivion starting at forty-five years of age, a long-term view is not very common here."

"Ah, yes, the famed Kerensky vision." Cyrilla nodded. "Ulric has it, as do Ranna and all the Kerenskys since Aleksandr himself. It is something in the Kerensky bloodline. Freebirth! I have tried to get the Keepers of our Bloodline to arrange for its blending into the Ward line, but the Kerenskys seem reluctant to give us the genetic material we desire."

Cyrilla laughed lightly. "Actually, Natasha is without the Kerensky vision. She has ever been one for action now rather than later." Cyrilla pointed down toward where Natasha sat. "She is the only Kerensky with an unblooded aide. For a Kerensky to bring one to a Clan Council is almost as serious a breach of House honor as Natasha's conduct and language here."

From Cyrilla's smile, Phelan guessed that she did not find Natasha's conduct particularly shocking or heinous. "What is it with unblooded aides? Vlad is over there with Conal, and I see other young people I assume to be unblooded who are with individuals you point out as part of House Ward. I know enough of the Clans to understand that this is significant, but I have yet to puzzle out the true meaning."

"You do recall my saying that candidates for a Bloodname are selected by nomination from within the House, *quiaff*?"

"Aff. Or by combat."

"Well, bringing an unblooded aide to the Clan Council, especially one convened to elect the Khans and the Loremaster, is an endorsement of sorts. It lets others see who an individual favors. Conal favors Vlad and I favor you."

Phelan bowed his head. "I am honored."

"And when the opportunity arises, you will honor me by winning a Bloodname."

"I hope to prove myself worthy of your support." Phelan chewed on his lower lip. "Why would it be a breach of honor for a Kerensky to bring an unblooded aide to a Clan Council meeting if everyone else does it?"

Cyrilla shrugged. "The Kerenskys are supposed to hold themselves above this political infighting. It is a tradition that began with Nicholas, but apparently, ends with Natasha. Those years in the Successor States have changed her, honed her to an edge that I think will cut away at the heart of the Clans."

"When she tests out as a Warrior, it will certainly start some tongues wagging, *quiaff?*"

"Aff, in a very big way. If Natasha can regain status as a warrior, we will have to question the idea of retiring warriors at an age when they may not yet have reached their peak. And if you test out, we will have to question the superiority of our ways over those that shaped you."

"I will do my best to make you proud."

Cyrilla nodded. "I anticipate no problems. I have more confidence in your ability to win than I do in my ability to figure out what Conal is up to. I am beginning to think he has some plan in mind here."

Phelan frowned. "It seems obvious to me. He wants to defeat Ulric and become a Khan. His desire must have outweighed your warning to him."

"Perhaps that is what we are supposed to believe. I do not like the fact that all the speakers attacking Ulric and backing him are fringe members of the Crusader cadre of our Clan. Those I would have assumed to be Conal's strongest supporters have been the least vocal during this debate."

"Maybe Conal is saving his big guns for later. Perhaps this is his way of bidding away supporters so the fight will not escalate into something he cannot win."

"An interesting analysis." The old woman's eyes narrowed. "While we do bid away troops when staging a battle, our political fights have never operated in that way before. He has to be up to something."

Cyrilla fell silent as her eyes focused beyond Phelan. He spun around and saw Conal Ward rising to speak.

"Loremaster, my Khans, and colleagues. I have heard many people castigate Khan Ulric for his conduct during the first stage of the invasion of the Inner Sphere. They note that by conquering more worlds than did any of the other Clans, he has violated an agreement under which the invasion was begun. They suggest that by pushing further than any other Clan into the Successor States, he has disgraced and dishonored us. They say that by prematurely launching waves, he has goaded other Clans into disastrous acts of daring that resulted in serious defeats for the Jade Falcons and Smoke Jaguars."

Conal's voice was strong, and he knew how to shift the tone and speed of his delivery to catch his audience in his rhythm. An engaging speaker, he had a warrior's dignified bearing to emphasize that his substance was equal to his style.

"I have also heard these same speakers extol my virtues and set me up as the man to replace Khan Ulric. They cite my experience in leading our Heavy Cavalry Galaxy and my past successes in campaigns against the Snow Raven and Ghost Bear clans. They remind you that I won my Bloodname at the age of twenty-seven and that four Clans have offered to trade for my genetic material. They point out that my offspring, though only ten and fifteen years old, already dominate their sibkos.

"I have heard these words and I must plead guilty to the vanity that makes me take pride in them. I will not, however, let anyone suggest that my actions make me worthy to replace Khan Ulric. There are others here—Cyrilla Ward, Natasha Kerensky, and Anton Fetladral, for example—who are far more suited than I to the position of Khan. Indeed, both Cyrilla and Anton have served in that role before and should be considered for service again."

Phelan heard Cyrilla chuckle. "Oh, he is good, is he not, Phelan?"

"I guess so…" Phelan gave her a hard look. "Do you know what he is doing?"

She shook her head. "No, but at this rate, I imagine he will succeed."

Conal rested his hands on the hips of his gray jumpsuit. "Of course, saying they are suitable to replace Khan Ulric sounds as though I endorse Ulric's removal as Khan. I do not!"

That statement brought shocked cries from some Council members and battered others into betrayed silence. Phelan saw more than one member who had spoken of Conal in glowing terms blush deep crimson, though several others turned purple with rage. Through it all, Conal smiled, as did Vlad, and waited for the furor to die down beneath the pounding of the Loremaster's gavel.

"I do not support the removal of Khan Ulric because the arguments against him are foolish. How can we reject a man who has brought our Clan closer to fulfilling the goal of this invasion than any other? Can we fault him for taking an unfair advantage when the Wolf spearhead was directed at a heavily populated and heavily defended portion of the Successor States? Can we listen to the cries of foul by other Clans when their plan to hobble us failed, *quineg*?"

Conal looked around the room, his dark eyes flashing with enthusiasm. "You seek to rebuke him, but I say we should exalt him. He *is* a man of vision, and he looks beyond the goal of the invasion to the time beyond. He sees into the future, and it is one in which the Wolves occupy their rightful place within the history of both the Clans and of mankind. To oppose him, to vote against him, should be considered high treason against the Clan.

"Politics is a necessity, yet must it blind us? Ulric and I have had our differences in the past, yet I acknowledge him as an excellent leader. This is a time for the Wolves to come together, lest the other Clans destroy us on the eve of our victory. Let us not deliver ourselves to our enemies. Let us present such a united front that they would not dare think to attack us."

Thunderous applause greeted Conal's speech, and some of his closest supporters rose to give him a standing ovation. When Phelan turned to see Cyrilla's reaction, he found the white-haired woman shaking her head.

"He is amazing, *quiaff*, Phelan?"

The young man nodded. "If he had not taken himself out of the running for Khan, that speech would have won him the spot instantly. Even some of those he embarrassed have recovered and are applauding him wildly. If he is only planning for the short term and wanted to reap adulation, he got his wish."

"Yes, but is that all he wanted?"

As the applause gradually died down, Carol Leroux stood. "Loremaster, though the request may seem ill-mannered, I have no choice. After hearing that speech, Conal Ward has shown us all that he is, indeed, worthy of our trust. As he declines nomination as Khan, I ask that his name be placed in nomination for Loremaster of the Wolf Clan."

A hundred voices seconded that nomination, and Cyrilla punctuated it by hammering her fist into the bench top. "Oh, crafty dog. Conal, I underestimated you."

Phelan felt confused. "I am missing something. Does not this

101

mean an end to the threat to Ulric?"

Cyrilla shook her head resolutely. "Far from it. It just means the battleground has shifted from the Wolf Clan Council to the Grand Council. There they can vote to censure Ulric for his conduct, and within their confines, strip him of his power. He would still be a Khan of the Wolf Clan, but the Loremaster would fulfill all duties, including voting."

"Then you must stop him."

"I cannot." Cyrilla nodded a salute to Conal. "Because he circumvented my threat this time, to react would be a poor move. Besides, after that speech, he will win no matter what I do."

Phelan ground his teeth. "But that means the Crusaders have won. From what you and Natasha have said, that also means the Successor States stand no chance."

Cyrilla rested her left hand on Phelan's shoulder. "Do not lose heart yet, Phelan. There is a battle to be waged in the Grand Council. As well you know, as long as there is life in Ulric's body, he is more than able to handle both himself and his enemies."

Shin Yodama slid open the door and entered the small receiving alcove. The room's austerity seemed familiar rather than harsh because the quarters were so similar to his own on far-distant Luthien. In fact, the stark simplicity of the furnishings made him feel very much at home, as the arrangement made perfect zen sense. When he remembered that *gaijin* lived here, it was something of a shock.

Beside the door was a small rectangle of carpet upon which stood a pair of boots and a pair of slippers. Without thinking, Shin pulled off his own boots and donned the slippers. Placing his boots next to those of his host, he walked forward across the polished wooden floor and bowed.

"*Konnichi-wa*, Major Kell. I thank you for the invitation to visit." Shin looked around the room and smiled. "I envy you your surroundings."

The black-haired mercenary returned the bow. "Thank you, Yodama-*san*." He waved the Combine MechWarrior to a pile of pillows on the floor. Shin noted that, like himself, Christian Kell wore a short kimono and a regular pair of trousers. The difference was that Chris' kimono bore no Kurita crests. Shin, proud to display the crest on the breast, back, and sleeves of his kimono, started to fit the lack of crests into the rumors about Chris circulating through the Kurita community on Outreach.

"Please excuse my rudeness, but I wish to speak directly about the reasons I asked you to meet with me." A bell rang in the small kitchenette. "I have some *saké* warming," Kell said. "Please make yourself at home."

As Chris returned to the kitchenette, Shin turned to examine a rice-paper painting on the wall. Done in brush and black ink, it depicted a hastily painted 'Mech shielding a woman from a coiled serpent. The simplicity of the work contrasted sharply with the bold strength of the brush strokes. Down the side of the drawing, Shin saw a number of commentaries in Japanese that said much the same thing.

"You are a talented artist."

"Thank you." Chris set the tray with a *saké* flask and two small cups on the floor before seating himself on a pillow. "What little skill I have is in my blood."

Shin seated himself and smiled. "If you inherited but half that much skill from your father, I applaud the alliance Wolf seeks to forge. I have no desire to face Patrick Kell's son in combat."

Chris stopped for a moment and Shin felt as though the man's jade stare were slicing through to his soul. Then Chris bowed his head and smiled slightly. "You are good, Yodama-*san*. You probe without asking questions. Had the ISF arranged this meeting earlier, much could have been resolved before now."

Shin frowned. "Your meaning escapes me. I am no gossip, but stories about you abound. In our training, I have found you an excellent leader and teacher. Would I be human if I did not take an interest in what shaped my *sensei*?"

"No, no, your point is well taken." Chris poured the rice wine into the small cups, then raised his. "To success in our endeavors."

Shin matched the gesture, then the two men sipped the raw liquor. Shin felt it burn its way down to his stomach, but relished the sensation. "I commend you, Major. It is the perfect temperature."

"No inborn skill there, just years of learning how many seconds the microwave requires for the result."

Both men laughed and drank again. "I have two reasons for asking you here this evening. The first concerns the training group. I have noticed, over the last five weeks, that the tensions between Victor Davion and Hohiro Kurita have begun to lessen. Both have shown a marked improvement in their development as a result."

"*Hai*. I believe Kai Allard spoke with Hohiro and that Omi-*sama* has also encouraged cooperation with Victor."

"I know." Chris smiled and Shin felt himself warming to the man. "I have spoken with Galen Cox about encouraging Victor to work with

Hohiro. I would like you to do the same thing. Nothing overt or direct, but subtle and thereby more effective."

"*Wakarimas,* Chris-*san.*"

"*Domo.* Their ability to work together is vital to our effort. If they can get along, line troopers will try to do the same. Each can lead by example, and such example will prevent our coalition from collapsing because of infighting."

"I agree. I believe the extended field operation you have scheduled for the end of this month will teach them once and for all the need for cooperation. If you permit, I will speak with Galen Cox personally so we can better coordinate our efforts."

"Excellent." Chris refilled their cups. "The other reason I wished to speak with you is because of the inquiries that your Internal Security Force agents have been making about me."

Shin shook his head. "The ISF has never been discreet."

"No, and I fear some of my comrades within the Dragoons have been spinning great stories out of nothing to feed to your boys. I think I should clear things up."

Shin stiffened. "Major, I can see from your quarters and your manner that you have a great understanding of the Combine way of life. You should know that we respect your privacy and do not require you to make a confession as in some tawdry holodrama. I am honored that you have chosen to speak with me, but I fear I am most inappropriate as a relay to the ISF."

Chris' eyes glittered mischievously. "I do not think so, Shin Yodama of the *Kuroi Kiri.* I believe I can trust you to counter rumors that are wrong."

As he spoke, Chris unknotted the sash on his kimono and pulled his left arm back through the sleeve. He bared the left side of his torso, revealing a brilliantly colored tattoo that ran from collarbone to navel and down to mid-forearm. Highly stylized, but still recognizable and beautiful, it depicted a black and red wolfhound locked in mortal combat with a blue and green dragon. Each beast had its teeth sunk into the throat of its enemy in a yin/yang design that suggested the equality and necessity of opposites. From their wounds, blood dripped down to fill the outline of a man. Stars surrounded him, and in his hands, he clutched a sword and a pistol.

"I am Christian Kell of the *Ryu-no-inu-gumi* of Murchison. I believe, as one yakuza to another, we can trust each other."

Yakuza? A Kell? Shin caught himself staring at his host and looked down immediately. "*Sumimasen,* Keiru-*san.* Forgive my staring. I had no idea, having never seen you in a cooling vest."

105

"No offense, taken, Yodama-*san*. I know it must be something of a shock." Chris smiled broadly. "You looked only slightly less surprised than my uncle Morgan when he first saw the tattoo almost ten years ago."

Shin shook his head to clear it. "So the rumors that you were raised in the Combine are true?"

Chris shrugged and sipped *saké*. "More or less. My father was Patrick Kell and I was born on Murchison about six months before his death. As nearly as I can determine, he never knew I existed. I believe my mother meant to tell him in their last visit together, but she feared he would want to retire and settle down if he knew there was a child. She believed that would have killed him slowly, and would have trapped her, so she never spoke.

"My mother made her living as an artist, but had connections within the yakuza community in Akumashima. When she traveled offworld, I was left in the care of a yakuza family. As I grew older, I accompanied her on her travels, though we did not go far after the 3039 War."

Shin's brown eyes narrowed. "Murchison was taken by the Federated Commonwealth in the war."

"Yes, and the occupation forces shut down all the routes my mother had used to leave and return at will. I have no doubt that the loss of freedom was what ultimately killed her. In fact, it was not long after the occupation began that she became ill. Yet if not for the occupation, I would never have left Murchison.

"You see, mother never told me my father's true identity. She believed that if Patrick had known about me, he would have retired and not have been killed on Styx. When Murchison became part of the Commonwealth, the indoctrination of its people included exposure to countless documentary and holodrama broadcasts glorifying the Steiner-Davion heritage. That and the fact that I came to look more and more like my father as I matured compelled her to send me away. Then she died."

Shin looked down at the floor. "I am saddened by your loss."

"*Domo arigato*." Chris chewed on his lower lip for a moment. "As much as her death hurt me, I do not hold it against her for making me go. As I cleared out her things, I found her diaries, which was how I came to know my father at long last. I did not have to look very hard. After his death, she addressed every entry as though it were a letter to him.

"I decided to seek out Morgan Kell. The *Ryu-no-inu-gumi* managed to smuggle me off-planet. I found my uncle on Arboris, right here in the Sarna March. Among my mother's things was a message concerning my lineage that she had verigraphed to Morgan Kell. Morgan accepted me immediately, took a leave of absence from the Hounds, and brought me here to Outreach for training. That was in 3042."

"Your training must have gone well." Shin returned Chris' smile. "The first I heard of you was after the Ambergrist Crisis in '45. Rumor had it that you were a clone of Patrick Kell whom Hanse Davion had produced in some biomedical lab at the New Avalon Institute of Science. That you handily tied up a Liao battalion with only a company did not go unnoticed."

"And is remembered still, if Lady Romano's cold reaction to me is any indication." Chris refilled their cups. "I think that should supply you with enough information to make your ISF happy and to stop them from further annoying the Dragoons with their questions."

Shin nodded in agreement. "That will leave them the mystery of Kali Liao's supposed death and resurrection during a Thugee cult ceremony."

Chris laughed. "No mystery there. Psychotropic drugs work wonders, especially when the subject has only a nodding acquaintance with reality anyway. A light cut on her flesh and keeping her juiced until it heals into a scar produces a miracle. No, if your ISF boys want a mystery, have them puzzle out a ComStar mystery for us."

"ComStar?"

"Yes. The Precentor Martial recently sent my uncle Morgan a message. It consisted of only one line, and that line was the famous old quote from Mark Twain—'Reports of my death have been greatly exaggerated.'"

Montayana Foothills, Outreach
Sarna March, Federated Commonwealth
1 June 3051

As the last trace of red sun sank behind the saw-toothed horizon, Kai Allard shrugged off his pack. He leaned back against one of the boulders that surrounded the circular clearing Victor had designated as a good spot for their camp that night. By his compass and the map, they were only a half hour's march from their target. With the overhanging cliff above and the broken terrain surrounding, the campsite provided cover from spotting aircraft and patrolling 'Mechs.

Off to his left, Victor and Galen also dropped their packs and slumped to the ground. Opposite them, Hohiro and Shin likewise dumped their gear. Cassandra and Ragnar put their things down next to Kai's while Sun-Tzu paced the clearing like a trapped animal.

Kai looked at his chronometer. "We've made it here a couple hours ahead of schedule. Let's get some food in us, then get some sleep."

Sun-Tzu glanced contemptuously at Ragnar. "You, fetch firewood."

Kai countermanded that order. "No."

Sun-Tzu's face hardened. "Then send someone to do it. Cox or the yakuza."

"I said no."

Ragnar stood up, determined to keep the peace between Kai and his cousin. "Don't worry, Kai. I'll get it. I don't mind."

Kai laid his right hand on Ragnar's left shoulder. "I said no because we're not going to have a fire." He pointed off in the direction of their target. "Victor chose this place because it offers us maximum cover. Lighting a fire would immediately reveal our presence. Surprise is our only advantage in this operation, and I don't want to give that away."

Victor chuckled as he rummaged around in his rucksack. "Besides, you don't want these rations warmed up. Cold, you can scrape the congealed fat right off the top. This stuff must be left over from the Second Succession War."

Sun-Tzu scowled. "Leave it to the aggressor to be so over-prepared for war."

Victor snorted derisively. "Hey, if you Capellans had put up even token resistance twenty years ago, we'd have been through this stuff and would have had to make more."

Sun-Tzu took a half-step toward Victor, but Galen stood up quickly, his readiness a warning. Disgusted, Sun-Tzu threw down his pack. He dropped to the ground and sat with his elbows on his knees and his hands covering his pouting face.

Kai looked at him and shook his head. *He's no more a Mech-Warrior than Ragnar, but at least the kid tries.* Kai realized that as tensions between the Davion and Kurita factions within the group eased, Sun-Tzu successfully focused the divisiveness on himself. He shrugged, feeling helpless to change things, and dug into his pack for a can of rations.

He held up his discovery for all to see. "I've got a can of alleged beef stew here that I am willing to trade for almost anything. It even has a biscuit."

Galen shook his head. "Nope. No rock bread and gristle chunks for me."

Ragnar offered a can to him. "Chicken in naranji sauce and noodles."

Kai failed to keep the surprise from his voice. "You want to swap that, straight up? That's the only stuff any of us have found edible on this outing."

Shin held up two cans. "Ragnar, I'll give you two pork and beans for it."

Victor dug quickly to the bottom of his pack. "I'll see your two beans and toss in half a chocolate bar."

"Too rich for my blood." Kai smiled at Ragnar. "Looks like you've got a firm offer from the Prince of the Federated Commonwealth. Play hard to get and you might get more. Maybe even a planet."

"But be careful," cautioned Cassandra. "The last time a Davion started giving up worlds, he gave away half the Capellan Confederation."

Everyone, save Sun-Tzu, enjoyed a laugh over that joke. Yet, weary as they all were, Sun-Tzu's resentment sobered them enough that thê laughter died prematurely.

Ragnar shrugged. "I'm not offering it to Victor. If you want it, Kai, it's yours. If not, I'll eat it." To the group at large, he added, "I may be the youngest here, but that doesn't mean I was born yesterday or born ignorant. This is worth at least three cans of beans, a whole chocolate bar, and someone taking my watch for me."

"Keep it, Ragnar. You might as well enjoy the meal because tomorrow is going to be nasty." Kai popped open his stew and shuddered as the odor reached his nose. Losing his appetite, he set the can on the rock. "Yeah, one more thing. About the watches. They're going to be two hours instead of the normal one. Sun-Tzu will take the first, followed by Ragnar, Cassandra, and me in that order. I'll get everyone moving well before dawn so we can hit the enemy before they're out of their sleeping bags."

Sun-Tzu looked up. "No. I'm tired. I don't want the first watch."

Kai sighed heavily. "I set the watches based on who seems to be most tired. Not only do I feel you have more stamina than Ragnar or my sister, but you're very difficult to awaken when it's your turn for the watch. I'd prefer not to have to worry about it. You have the first watch."

Sun-Tzu looked at Victor and Hohiro. "And they do not have watches? I know why you make an exception for the Davion, but why for Kurita? Have you, like your father, turned traitor?"

Cassandra scrambled to her feet, fists balled, but Kai stepped forward and stopped her without a word. He acknowledged the fury in her brown eyes and blessed it with a nod, but signalled her back to Ragnar's side with a look. She acquiesced, but only reluctantly, and Kai knew her anger still simmered only a degree or two below a rolling boil.

"Let me explain this to everyone, just so we're all clear here. Victor, Galen, Shin, and Hohiro are our primary strike force. Their job is to get to the enemy 'Mechs and to secure a lance. For this, I want them well-rested and sharp. I do not think interrupting their sleep will help in that, so I have exempted them from watches for this evening."

Kai indicated the rest of them by opening his hands. "We are the diversionary force. Our job is to create as much mayhem and confusion as possible to cover the others on their way to the 'Mechs. Because

110

we do not face the complicated task of trying to strip out the code modules for a 'Mech in mid-raid, I think we can get by with a bit less sleep. As it is, by taking the first watch, your sleep will be uninterrupted. Is that clear?"

"I see what is clear." Sun-Tzu picked at his trimmed fingernails, then stood abruptly. "I see everything clearly. This is a conspiracy."

Ragnar set his food down. "Look, I'll take the first two watches. I can do four hours. I've never needed much sleep."

Sun-Tzu gave him a sour look. "Away, puppy. I don't need you to defend me. It is obvious that all of this is a plot to embarrass and degrade the Capellan Confederation. Why else would they have put you in charge and have your Amazon sister here? To elevate you to the position of commander of this exercise is an insult to legitimate nations, and for Davion and Kurita to condone it proves their complicity."

Kai kept his voice even. "Sit down, Sun-Tzu."

Sun-Tzu's voice dripped scorn. "I take no commands from you. Treason runs in your veins, and that House Davion depends upon the Allards makes them worthy only of contempt."

He turned and focused fully on Ragnar. "You, on the other hand, are fit only for ridicule. The Free Rasalhague Republic never was anything more than a joke that the Draconis Combine played on your people. Your freedom is based purely on the promise of those who were once your masters. If the Combine decided to revoke your independence, do you think anything could stop them? And now you have lost your capital and over half your worlds."

Ragnar shot to his feet. "Then you should realize how much alike we are, Sun-Tzu. Each of us has lost half our realm to outsiders. We should be brothers, you and I, in resolving not to lose the rest of our worlds."

Though Ragnar meant his plea to be calming, it had the opposite effect. Sun-Tzu's voice rose in pitch as he screamed at the Prince from Rasalhague. "Never presume equality with me, boy. It is well you toady up to Kai and Cassandra. You all come from bandit nations that have no right to exist."

He whirled. "And how appropriate it is that a yakuza attends a Kurita and that a Lyran sucks up to a Davion. You're all whores playing into the hands of whatever plot Hanse Davion and Jaime Wolf have hatched. You know the Dragoons are part and parcel of the Clans. Wolf said so himself. And here we are, going through a sham to delay any real planning while the Clans regroup."

Ragnar reached out and touched Sun-Tzu's arm. The Capellan

spun, his right hand a blur as it came around to smash Ragnar down. But before the blow could land, Kai shot forward and caught his cousin's wrist in his right hand.

Shrieking like a wild beast, Sun-Tzu ripped his hand free from Kai's grip. For half a second, Kai looked into his cousin's green eyes and saw the vicious emotions that drove him so. Then brilliant stars exploded, eclipsing the view of his cousin, as Sun-Tzu's right foot swept up in a roundhouse kick that blasted Kai to the ground.

Shimmering balls of rainbow light danced before his eyes and dirt ground beneath his teeth. The left side of his head felt as though he'd been hit with a mallet, but the ringing in his ears failed to block out Sun-Tzu's angry words of triumph.

"Do not touch me, quisling whelp! There now, you've a taste of what will happen if you ever attempt to complete what your mother and father started. The Capellan Confederation is not yours. It is mine. You will never get your hands on it—this I vow—no matter how hard you try to embarrass me."

Kai's own anger erupted. His hands reached out and gathered Sun-Tzu's ankles together. As his cousin fell, Kai pounced on his chest and pinned his arms to the ground by grinding his knees into Sun-Tzu's biceps. He grabbed the front of Sun-Tzu's jumpsuit in his left fist, then slapped him twice in quick succession.

Kai's voice dropped to a menacing growl. "I hope this gets through to you now because, until now, it hasn't. I do not want it now, nor have I ever wanted, the Capellan Confederation. The Celestial Throne is yours, and you are welcome to it. If Victor asked me to lead an invasion into the Confederation, I would counsel against it. If I never see or hear of fighting between our realms again, I will die a happy man."

Without letting go of his cousin's jumpsuit, Kai stood and dragged Sun-Tzu to his feet. "The first watch is yours."

Sun-Tzu staggered back but said nothing when Kai released him. Blood still pounding in his ears, Kai turned away and stalked off beyond the circle of stones that marked their campsite. He wandered off and down around a small hill that hid the camp from view. Seating himself on a stone, he closed his eyes and hugged his arms around himself.

How could I have been so stupid? He knew that hitting Sun-Tzu was no solution to the problem. It probably wouldn't be more than twenty-four hours before the council of leaders would call him up again to explain his conduct. Kai's cheeks began to burn as he imagined his parents' disapproval.

112

Behind him, he heard the sound of gravel crunch beneath booted feet. He knew instantly that it was not Sun-Tzu because the noise was not loud enough. "It's all right, Zandra. I'm fine."

"Forgive me, Leftenant Allard," said Hohiro. "I did not mean to intrude on your thoughts."

Kai turned slowly. Despite a half-full moon and a dozen smaller satellites of various colors orbiting above them, Kai could not see more than Hohiro's outline. "It is no intrusion, Hohiro. I should apologize to everyone for my conduct, and I might as well start with you. I am sorry you had to witness that, that…"

"That loss of control?" Hohiro shook his head. "No apology is necessary, Kai. In fact, I come here to tell you I admired your command of self. In your place, I would have beaten him senseless."

"That's the problem. Sun-Tzu is already senseless. Beating him would only reinforce everything he's known his entire life. And as much as you thought I controlled myself, there had to be another way."

The Kurita Prince leaned back against a dark dolmen. "There are times when the only solution is violence."

"Hohiro, you and I are both warriors. We condone the use of violence to solve problems, and I have to admit that sometimes it seems the only way." The image of Clan 'Mechs being crushed under tons of stone flashed before his inner eye. "But killing Sun-Tzu is not an option, and beating him only deepens his fear."

"His fear?" Hohiro scratched at the stubble on his chin. "I've never seen anything in him but hatred."

Kai clasped his hands at the nape of his neck and hugged his forearms to his head. "It's there, believe me. I saw it in his eyes before he nailed me. Think about it. He's grown up in a nightmare. He learned to hate and fear me the way Romano hates and fears my mother. He was barely five years old when our grandfather supposedly committed suicide, so he grew up with the rumors that his own mother ordered his death. As much as he loves Romano, somehow he has to reconcile the loving face she shows him and the demonic mask she displays to the people. With the same spontaneity that could make her suddenly give him a present, she could order the death of thousands. She institutionalized torture as a test of loyalty and no matter how much he wanted to deny it, he had to be afraid she would one day ask him to prove his loyalty in that way."

Kai swallowed hard. "Somehow he survived in that madhouse. He has worked long and hard to appease his mother and to deflect her from murderous rages. He has fought to hold together a realm that his mother could so easily tear apart, but for what? He looks at the St. Ives

113

Compact and the Federated Commonwealth and he knows we could sweep the Capellans away at any time. He knows his troops wouldn't even slow us down. The only way he could make us pay would be to whip his people into a suicidal frenzy that would destroy all he has sought to preserve."

"But you have told him you have no interest in the Capellan throne."

Kai shrugged in exasperation. "But each denial seems only to convince him that I am trying to lull him into a false sense of security so I can crush him."

Hohiro's head came up. "Perhaps that is because he hears beyond your words to the truth."

"What?"

"You yourself said it earlier. We are both warriors. We know that some problems can only be solved by violence, and we have accepted the responsibility of the power given to us. You deny wanting to rule the Capellan Confederation, and that may be so, but you and I know it is not the whole truth. If Sun-Tzu turned out to be as mad as his mother or your grandfather, if people were being slaughtered wholesale for his amusement, if minorities were being killed in some genocidal drive for a pure race, I believe you'd go after him. And you would do anything to destroy him."

"No."

"Yes." Hohiro folded his arms across his chest. "I've watched you, Kai, and I also read carefully the reports the ISF has prepared on you. Our analysts have labeled you a coward. They claim you are afraid of war and only became a MechWarrior so that you would not disgrace your parents by not doing so. They interpret your tendency to overwork plans as excessive timidity. They insist that your victory on Twycross was sheer accident, that your escape pod's rocket blasted the shielding from your fusion engine in a malfunction."

"Is that what you think?"

Hohiro shook his head. "What I think is that our ISF agents are fools. You're not afraid of war. You're afraid of what would happen if you ever let yourself go. You're terrified that you would not stop, that you would not know how to draw the line. At Twycross, you ordered a half-dozen men to return to their post and to blow the Gash. You had to issue that order—it was the right one at the right time—because you had no way of knowing you would make it into the Gash. If their 'Mechs had been a half-minute faster, you would have arrived too late. What you fear is that you are capable of ordering men to their deaths without a second thought.

114

"I come from a tradition where life is not held so dear. Instead of ordering men into battle against foes, I can 'invite them onward.' A pretty euphemism for ordering someone to die, isn't it? I have that sort of power of life and death over anyone in my realm. Because of it, I also share your fear."

Hohiro hesitated a moment, then plunged on. "I know what it is to look in the mirror and wonder what kind of a monster I could become. That is natural, and what's more, it is vital. My father has taught me that if we did not question ourselves about the uses of power, we would never notice the boundary between just use and despotism until we'd overshot it by light years. If we did not question ourselves, we might not have a clue that we had gone too far until we started to drown in the blood of our victims."

Kai winced as Hohiro's words seemed to touch the core of his being. "No, no, you're wrong."

"He's right, Kai." Victor joined them, with a nod toward Hohiro. "I heard what Hohiro had to say and I concur fully. Morgan Kell first brought the same point to my attention, back when we all arrived on Outreach in January. He said you were one of those rare warriors who keeps a tight rein on himself because you fear what would happen otherwise. 'Just be thankful he's on your side,' Morgan said. 'If he ever cuts loose, there's not much in the Inner Sphere that could stop him.'"

Hohiro bowed his head in a salute to Victor. "Colonel Kell is a shrewd judge of character, and a warrior of long and distinguished career. It does not surprise me that he saw this so clearly."

The Kurita Prince stepped forward and rested his hands on Kai's shoulders. "Kai, the power we possess is given only to a few because of the immense responsibility that comes with it. We are the arbiters who must sometimes decide whether to risk a small group to prevent suffering by a greater number of people. Even at the best of times, in the most clear-cut of cases, this is not an easy decision. You just have to trust yourself and your innate sense. You have resolved to do the right thing, and you will."

Kai turned away. "I've wrestled with this demon since Twycross, and even before that. I thought my initial solution was right, but Twycross proved me wrong."

He turned around again and let his arms fall to his side. "I've decided the potential for wielding such power in error is too high. In the future, if ever I am forced to issue orders that are suicidal, I will give them. But I will also lead those troops personally."

A slightly lopsided grin spread across his face. "Perhaps your ISF people were right, Hohiro. Perhaps I am a coward. I believe it is much harder to live with the knowledge that I had to push people into a situation that caused their death than to die with them in that effort. I refuse to treat life so cheaply, no matter what the cause or how great the justification. If that proves to be my epitaph, I will rest well through eternity."

Kerensky Sports Centre
Strana Mechty, Beyond the Periphery
1 June 3051

"So, when you dropped your 'Mech down on its haunches and cranked the torso back to give your arms more range, I had to break off. It was a good move."

"Thank you, Carew." Phelan Wolf nodded solemnly as his companion finished his explanation of the exercise they had just completed. Carew was a small, slender man of the type common among Clan pilots. His unruly shock of blond hair made his head seem yet bigger, and his large green eyes gave him a look of childlike innocence. Still, in all the time Phelan had spent training in antiaircraft maneuvers with him, the MechWarrior knew his friend to be anything but childlike or innocent.

Carew shrugged. "With Natasha, Ranna, Evantha, and me training you, the only question when you test out is whether you should do it as a MechWarrior, a pilot, or an Elemental."

Wearing shorts and T-shirts in place of their cooling vests, the two men marched up a grassy slope to a massive plateau. The flat expanse had been sectioned off into a score of playing fields, each carefully delineated by a chalk line. Each field was split in half across the middle and each end had a circle surrounding a goal approximately two meters square and located four meters from the end line.

The players out on the field wore helmets with a mesh cage to protect their faces, padded gloves, arm guards, and padded torso protectors with a red or blue circle in the center. They carried sticks whose length varied, depending on the player's position on the field, but all had triangular nets on one end. Phelan noted that defensive players carried sticks as tall as they were. As most of them were Elementals, that meant they were long, indeed. Offensive players, mostly pilots like Carew, had short sticks that could be whipped around very quickly. Midfielders carried sticks about a meter and a half in length, as did the goalie, but the net on his stick was four times the size of the others.

Phelan smiled. "Hey, lacrosse. We used to play this on Outreach and I played for the Academy during my time at the Nagelring."

Carew nodded. "I think you'll find this game a bit different than what you played on Outreach." He held up his hand to forestall Phelan's question. "I've been talking to Natasha's archivist about the differences between how we play here and they play there. But if you go on this field thinking the game is the same, you'll get yourself killed."

Phelan looked out at the field and watched the players chase the ball around for a while. The red team caught and tossed the small white ball back and forth, working it in toward the blue goal. One of the midfielders cut across the middle, caught a pass from a forward, and sent the ball whistling in at the goal. The goalie scooped it up and started it heading back down the field.

"I hear what you say, Carew, but aside from a lot of butt-ending by players, it does not look that different."

"Butt-ending?"

"Smacking another player with the aft end of the stick. You know, a *foul*?"

"Foul?"

Out on the field, one blue player jabbed his stick into the ribs of a red player, crumpling the victim. "Yeah, like that, spearing. That's a foul. It's illegal. Against the rules."

"Phelan, we have no fouls. You get points for that sort of thing."

"Oh." Phelan watched the game for a moment, winced as another player got hit hard, then shrugged. "Well, that's almost the way we played at the Nagelring. It's not *that* different."

The small man smiled. "Ah, but that's the difference that makes all the difference. If you have the ball, you are considered 'live.' That means anyone who hits you with the butt end of his stick in the circle takes a point from your team. You can poke back, but while you're carrying the ball, that's not usually a good move. Each goal is worth fifty points to your team. The game goes for an hour, or until a team is forced into negative points. The teams start with one hundred points, but forcing a team to retire early is less difficult than you might think."

"Hmmm. Interesting variation." Phelan took another look at the game. "Unlike everything else around here, the game is not coed."

Carew shivered. "Play against women? No thank you. They are vicious. The only thing worse than playing against a woman in sport is fighting against one for a Bloodname, or so I understand."

"I see." Phelan pointed to the nearest game. "Do you think they could use a couple of new players?"

"Could be, but only you could play in that game. The red team is House Ward and the blues are House Demos. The players are all unbloods, so they *should* let you play."

"Should?"

"The guy who took that last shot on goal was Vlad. As I recall, the only thing you two agree on is that one of you will be killed by the other."

"True." Phelan frowned slightly. "Which is your House?"

Carew shrugged. "I was born into House Nygren."

Phelan heard annoyance and resignation in his friend's voice. "You say that as though it were a curse."

"It is, after a manner of speaking. Nygren has never had a strong fighter pilot contingent. Twenty-five years ago, the Wolves beat the Jade Falcons in a battle, and Nygren got genetic material from House Malthus that was thought to contain the DNA that gives Malthus pilots their edge in combat. I am a product of that line."

"So why so glum? You should have a leg up on other folks when it comes to a Bloodname contest. You've got an edge."

Carew shook his head. "Just after the second generation was produced from the spoils of our victory, we learned that the genetic material came from a cadet branch of the family. Though Wolf scientists claimed the genes were the same as those we were seeking, the subterfuge embarrassed some of the Nygren elders. This has left a taint on those of us born of that victory, making our chances of being nominated for a Bloodname slim or simply nil."

"And to work through the open battling would be relatively worthless." Phelan reached out and gave Carew's shoulder a squeeze. "Sorry about that, my friend. Perhaps when we return to the Inner Sphere, you will achieve something that will force them to nominate you."

"Perhaps." Carew pointed over at the game. "Half-time break. This is your chance to get into the game."

Phelan grinned. "You don't mind watching?"

"Go on. Natasha's archivist had some information about you that he passed along. House Demos has a bad gene. They all gamble too much." He smiled broadly. "If you live up to the rumors, I can earn some favors at this."

Chuckling, Phelan turned from his friend and crossed to the knot of sweaty players on the sidelines. He approached a balding, brown-haired man he recognized as the one who had been speared. When the man looked up, Phelan placed him as someone he had fought in a 'Mech training session. "You are Emilio, *quiaff?*"

The man drained his cup of water and drew another from the cooler. "Aff, and you are Phelan."

"Right. Need another player?"

Emilio shrugged. "Vlad, do you want another warm body out there? My breathing is getting ragged. I think Carter popped one of my ribs with that last point-touch."

"Phelan?" Vlad's voice mixed disbelief with scorn. "Has Cyrilla decided to let you play rough with the rest of us?"

Phelan turned slowly and saw Vlad surrounded by the other players of the team. Half of them shared Vlad's disdainful look, but the others—mostly Elementals—seemed merely to await Phelan's reply. Phelan smiled easily. "I do not know about playing rough, Vlad, but it strikes me that is not necessarily the object of this game. If I score goals, the number of times I poke someone else is irrelevant, *quiaff?*"

Vlad raised an eyebrow. "You will find that hitting is not as rough as being hit." He gave Phelan a fish-eye, then nodded slowly. "You can play."

Phelan hopped over the sideline bench and started to rummage through a pile of equipment. Vlad slapped his stick against the bench, bringing Phelan around with his hands up to ward off a blow. "Hey, I want equipment."

"And you shall have it." Vlad pointed his stick at Emilio. "Give him yours. You are my right wing, Phelan."

"No! No need to make him give me his stuff. There's plenty here."

Vlad did not even acknowledge Phelan's protest. "Emilio, give Phelan your equipment."

"As you wish, Star Commander."

Emilio peeled off the torso vest and held it up for Phelan to slip into. "Hope it protects you better than it did me."

Phelan's green eyes smoldered. "Why are you doing this? Why do you not stand up to him?"

Emilio shook his head. "Look at me. I am thirty-two years old and

120

I am an unblood. My career will be finished soon. It is a wonder that Vlad and the others allow me to play at all. I know enough to make way for the new generations."

In Emilio's words Phelan heard the resentment that was building as a result of Natasha's insistence at testing out to be a warrior. "But with age comes experience. Does that count for nothing?"

Emilio watched Phelan, then shook his head. "You have so much to learn, Phelan Wolf. Experience is what I give to those I teach. Here, take the vest and the benefit of my experience in this game. Remember that you are live when you have the ball, and you remain live until someone else takes it away. The Demos players will take all the cheap shots they can. The circuitry in the vest will not award points for them, but they hurt anyway."

"Got it." As Emilio unsnapped his arm guards, Phelan snaked the two straps on the torso jacket through his crotch and fastened them at his hips. He adjusted the cup so it felt comfortable, then pulled on the arm guards. Foam over hard plastic, they felt like a light exoskeleton. The gloves were still clammy from Emilio's use, as was the chin strap on the helmet.

Emilio knelt down and opened a green equipment chest. From it, he pulled a U-shaped piece of plastic. He coated it with an aerosol spray and handed it to Phelan. "Here, bite down on this and clench your jaw for ten seconds. It is a mouth guard. The spray temporarily heats the plastic so it can remold to your teeth."

"Fanks," Phelan mumbled gratefully.

"Score some goals. We are down 67 to 75. See the defenseman on the right, *quiaff*? That is Carter, and he is the one who got me."

Phelan nodded and ran out onto the field. *This society is so confused that good warriors get tossed aside at an age when they would just be entering their prime in the Successor States. Does their breeding program really make them that much better?* He sized up his opposition and clamped down on the mouth guard. *Here's where I find the answer to that question.*

Vlad and the Demo's center met at the midpoint and bent down for a face-off. They pressed the backs of their nets together, and a referee placed the ball between the two sticks. At his whistle, both men struggled for possession of the ball. Vlad lunged forward, then spun off to the left. The ball popped loose on that side, and he scooped it up.

Phelan shot forward and arrowed in toward the goal. He threw a little head fake at Carter, then breezed by him. He raised his stick to catch Vlad's attention, and they made eye contact, but Vlad dumped the ball off to the attacker in the corner. As Phelan pulled himself back out to a more proper position, a pass came to the center forward, but the goalie stuffed him and Carter picked up the ball.

"Stupid ape." Phelan watched as Carter carried the ball like an egg in a basket. Most players, by working the head of the stick back and forth in a semi-circular motion known as "cradling" the ball, used centripetal force to keep the ball in the net. Carter made no attempt to stabilize the ball. Rather, he slowed his pace to let the nearest Ward attacker close with him, then he snaked the butt-end of his stick out to spear the man in his red circle.

The attacker went down clutching his chest, and foul or no foul, Phelan saw red. Instead of backing to cover his counterpart on the Demos team, he sprinted toward Carter. Phelan held his stick by the butt-end in his right hand and pulled it straight back in obvious preparation for a slashing stick-on-stick check. Given ample warning, Carter cradled the ball briefly, then pulled it back and away from Phelan.

This better work! Phelan purposely cut wide to the left, as though Carter's infantile move had somehow faked him into the error. Still holding it in one hand, he let his stick rise up over Carter's head, then whipped it down hard. Phelan caught Carter's stick just beneath the head and bounced the ball loose. Dodging back right, Phelan scooped the ball into his net. Two steps further in, he planted his right foot, cut to the left and shifted his hands around for a left-handed shot.

He snapped the stick down and directed the shot at the ground less than a meter in front of the net. The ball hit the grass and skidded about four centimeters before it bounced up. The goalie's sweeping save sliced through the air a hair's-breadth behind the ball. The vulcanized rubber sphere slipped inside the goal just beyond the post.

Phelan raised his stick triumphantly in the air. Other players cheered, but as he turned around, Carter and Vlad seemed to be competing to see who could glare at him the hardest. Feeling buoyant, Phelan trotted over to Vlad. "I could have done that five seconds earlier if you had passed me the ball when I was open."

"Carter had you covered."

"Yeah, on your wish-list and in his dreams."

"You got lucky, Phelan."

"Luck's what others call talent when they have none, Vlad."

Vlad's brown eyes smouldered. "Well, we will just have to see if you are as good as you think. Get back where you belong."

Phelan took up his position for the face-off. *Now if I were Vlad and I hated me as much as he does, what would I do?* Phelan smiled. *Yeah, buddy-pass.*

Blue won the face-off and brought the ball down into the Wards' defensive zone. A couple of quick passes resulted in a shot on goal, but the goalie made the save. He passed off to a defenseman, who worked the ball up to the left wing. As their line swept past midfield, the left wing passed to Vlad. Vlad cradled the ball for a couple of seconds, then looped it over to Phelan.

The high pass came slow, leaving Phelan no choice but to wait for it. He took a quick glance over his shoulder and saw Carter bearing down on him. *Thanks loads, Vlad.* Phelan clamped down on the mouth guard and prepared himself for impact.

He caught the ball with his back to Carter. Phelan knew that nothing short of a brick wall would stop Carter from blasting through him, and he had no time to dodge. Determined to make the best of a very bad situation, the MechWarrior ran his hands up to the head of the stick and tucked the shaft beneath his right arm. As Carter's huge form eclipsed the sun, Phelan shoved back and up as hard as possible.

Carter impaled himself on the butt-end of Phelan's stick. Cartilage cracked in his sternum and his gloves flew from his hands as his arms shot out. He hung suspended in air for a second or two, then dropped directly onto his tailbone. Croaking as he tried to suck in a breath, the big man lay on the ground with his hands clutched to the blue spot on his chest.

The impact knocked Phelan forward. Cradling the ball close to his own chest, he rolled and came up with it still in his net. Vlad streaked toward the middle and Phelan shot the ball at his head. The other MechWarrior deftly plucked it from the air and whipped his stick down and around in an underhand shot. It rocketed up and over the goalie's right shoulder to catch the corner of the goal.

"Hey, Vlad," Phelan called out. "Nice goal. We do good things when we work together."

Vlad spun and poked at Phelan's chest with his stick. "Drop dead."

Phelan parried the blow sharply down. "You know, our fighting makes about as much sense as the citizens of Free Rasalhague hating mercenaries. We don't have to like each other, but we can work together for the common good."

"The common good?" Vlad laughed contemptuously. "That you are here at all is because of your good luck. That you are a warrior is my bad luck, but in no way should you dream you have the right to consider yourself a member of our group. You are here only until the testing process proves what I have known all along: you are the dregs of a degraded society. When you fail your testing, you will be discarded."

"And when I pass?"

"You will not. Six weeks or six hundred weeks from now, you will not pass." Vlad's grin, twisted by the scar on his face, showed no mirth. "I guarantee it because I will be one of the pilots fighting against you. And believe me, I shall end your charade then and there."

Phelan snorted, then pointed at Carter. "Just be sure you get it right the first time around, Vlad. You will never have a better chance. If you blow it, it will be my turn, and I assure you, I will not miss."

Winddancer Plains, Outreach
Sarna March, Federated Commonwealth
2 June 3051

Victor Davion pulled his night-vision goggles a centimeter off his face and let cool air bathe his flesh. Settling the goggles back in place, he glanced at his chronometer for the twentieth time since taking up his position. *Fifteen more seconds. I hope the others are in place.*

Ahead of him, at the camp's northern perimeter, stood four BattleMechs. Each had the cylindrical body and back-bending legs that made it look so much like a *Marauder*, but the underslung arms ended in a configuration that Victor found unique. The 'Mech type also looked to mass less than a *Marauder* because of the overall downscaling of the design. He knew Wolf's Dragoons had begun to produce some of their own 'Mech designs with the facilities on Outreach, but this was his first look at any of them.

Two guards wearily trudged their way through picket duty. It was already toward the end in their watch, and the rosy hint of dawn on the horizon seemed to have sapped the last of their strength and caution. The two seemed more interested in chatting together and stamping their feet to keep warm than in surveying the surrounding brush.

Victor picked up his laser rifle and sighted in on the two guards. Like everyone in the commando team, they wore harnesses and helmets fitted with infrared sensors. If shot by one of the downpowered lasers, a signal would go off, telling the target he had been hit and killed. Victor did not think the gear was as effective as the exoskeletons used for training at the Nagelring, but they were lighter and thus

125

preferable for this long expedition.

Wolf had placed the company command out on the plains, and they knew only to take all necessary precautions against a possible raid. Like most field units, they had split their command into its three lances and placed them at three points around the camp. That made it more difficult for an air strike to destroy the command. They also kept their fusion engines lit so the 'Mech pilots could spring into action with a minimum of delay.

As the last second ticked off on his chronometer, Victor centered his rifle's crosshairs on the southernmost guard and stroked the trigger twice. He saw the monitor lights on the target's harness light up and heard the distant keening before his second shot. He smiled, even knowing that both he and Hohiro would try to claim credit for that kill, then sprinted toward the waiting 'Mechs.

His compatriots likewise shot out of their hiding places and ran to their war machines. Victor's had an *Uller* torso, but twin-barreled arms. Slinging his rifle over his shoulder, Victor vaulted onto one of his 'Mech's flat feet, caught the barrel of the large laser and swung up onto the lower arm actuator. Like an acrobat on a high wire, he walked to the 'Mech's elbow, then scrambled up to the shoulder and onto the torso. He dropped in through the hatch and pulled it secure behind him.

Tossing the laser rifle onto the jumpseat behind him, Victor settled into the command couch. He reached under the console on his left and popped open an access panel. He withdrew a circuit board and lay it face-up in his lap. He popped a chip from the board, then pulled another computer chip from a pouch on his cooling vest and snapped it onto the board. He replaced the circuitry, then strapped himself into the command couch.

After slapping the medical monitor patches onto his limbs, then hitching them into the neurohelmet he'd pulled on, he keyed the vocal link to the computer. "Initiation Sequence Override, engage now."

The computer replied after a moment's hesitation. "Authorization code required."

"Able Tango Xray Foxtrot."

"Verification obtained. Welcome aboard Kit Fox 0038W."

Victor breathed a heavy sigh of relief. The primary and secondary monitors came alive with streams of data about the weapon systems as they came online. The display showed that the large and medium lasers in both arms had been powered down to exercise levels, but Victor knew a concentrated blast would be enough to damage a 'Mech and possibly kill the pilot.

This may only be an exercise, but someone can still get hurt.

Victor hit a switch and adjusted a dial to set the radio to the agreed-upon tactical frequency. "Raider Deuce, I'm up and running."

"Raider Ace ready for the road," Galen called out.

"Raider Three and Four operational."

Galen's 'Mech lurched forward and headed back in toward the main encampment. Victor swung onto a path parallel with his and hit the button that brought up his projection display. Punched on magnification, he picked out the laser flashes of a running firefight in the center of the camp. Switching over to magnetic resonance scanning, he picked out the shapes that bore an X on them. Quickly, he tagged each with a computer ID number and shot the data out to the other raiders.

"I have our ground troops on magscan and have shot you their labels. The tinfoil strips backing their harnesses worked. Commencing antipersonnel fire."

Victor grabbed the joysticks on both arms of the command couch and lowered the crosshairs onto their targets. He toggled a switch to the left on the console, which dropped the laser's power level yet again, then he swept the right Kolibri pulse laser across the line of defenders.

The other 'Mechs laid down a pattern of fire that took out the other enemy ground troops. The X-forms on Victor's magscan started running for the lance of 'Mechs standing to the north. Galen started his 'Mech toward the south and indicated, with a wave of his right arm, that Shin should join up with him.

"Raider Three and Ace will check the third lance. You two make sure our buddies get buttoned up."

"Roger, Ace."

Victor toggled his weapons to anti-'Mech levels and flicked his scanner back to vislight. With the sun just barely beginning to creep up over the horizon, he got enough light to see Kai boosting Ragnar up to the 'Mech's arm. Cassandra and Sun-Tzu had already reached their cockpits. And when he saw Kai sprint to his 'Mech and start the climb up onto it, Victor could not suppress a smile.

Victor's pleasure died quickly as he looked up to see the right arm of Sun Tzu's 'Mech swing into line with Kai's. Though the motion might have been the kind of move any pilot would make as he began to acclimate to an unfamiliar BattleMech, something seemed wrong. Victor couldn't be certain one way or another, but the shiver that had run down his spine was instinct enough.

Lunging forward, he slid his laser muzzles over Sun-Tzu's left shoulder. The scream of weapon on armor was strong enough for Victor to hear it even within his cockpit, and the bump of muzzle against cockpit was none too gentle. Sweat stinging his eyes, he punched up a tightbeam channel to Sun-Tzu on his radio.

"Don't even think it. Not only will I kill you if you shoot, but I promise to reduce Sian to a cinder in your name."

Bleed-over crackled into his neurohelmet. "…willingly erase the Liao-Shang line from the rolls of mankind." Hohiro's voice poured through the static strong and angry. Victor glanced at the edge of his display and saw Raider Four with its lasers also centered on the *Kit Fox*'s cockpit.

Sun-Tzu lowered his 'Mech's arm. "Treachery runs so deep in your hearts that you mistake innocent actions for conscious betrayal. It is you who are perfidious, not I."

Victor dropped his voice to a low growl. "That may be true, little worm, but let it be a warning that you'd best be careful what you do from here on out. An innocent mistake on your part might cause Hohiro or me to have a 'weapons malfunction.' You'll be a lot more likeable in a eulogy than you are now, so I'll gladly deliver it."

Victor broke off the channel and opened another one to Hohiro. "Great minds think alike, do they not?"

Victor actually heard Hohiro laugh. "When small minds abound, they must."

"Thanks for keeping an eye out for Kai."

"I always watch out for my allies."

"As do I." Victor backed his 'Mech around to face Hohiro. "Appears Raiders Ace and Three have formed a team. Need a wingman?"

Leaning against the garden's stone railing, Victor forced a smile as Galen handed him a mug of beer. Ignoring them, Sun-Tzu and his sister, seated on a stone bench in a far corner of the garden, spoke in hushed whispers. Their words did not carry, and besides, Victor did not understand Chinese, but he guessed that if he knew what they were saying, it would probably make him sick.

"Ground control to Victor."

Victor looked up at Galen. "Sorry, my friend, I was just thinking about part of the exercise."

"I get the feeling something happened between you and Sun-Tzu while Shin and I were off disabling the third lance."

"It was nothing."

"Nothing?" Galen's blue eyes glittered. "I come back and find you and Hohiro thick as thieves and you say it was nothing? Hell,

ComStar could award Sun-Tzu a Peace Prize just for getting the two of you to speak together."

"A Peace Prize?" Victor chuckled and drank some of his beer. "No worry about that happening. The little rat did something and Hohiro and I probably overreacted. As for us being thick as thieves, what were we supposed to do? You and Shin became best buddies and Cassandra appointed herself Sun's babysitter. Kai and Ragnar were a natural pairing, so Hohiro and I had to work together."

The older MechWarrior shook his head. "Now I think you're going for a prize in understatement. Shin and I got shot to pieces when that reinforced company of bogies dropped down on us. Sun-Tzu proved about as useful as a *Rifleman's* tissue-paper aft armor and there was only so much Cassandra could do fighting alone. You and Hohiro fought beautifully together. You really tore up the enemy."

Victor raked his blond hair with the fingers of one hand. In Outreach's dry atmosphere, it had all but dried from his recent shower. "We did some damage, but Kai and Ragnar sent them packing."

Just then, Kai, Cassandra, and Ragnar stepped from the ballroom and Victor straightened up. He set his beer down on the railing and fished a gold coin from his pocket. "Kai," he called, then flipped the coin to his friend, who deftly caught it in one hand.

"Fifty Kroner?" Kai frowned. "What's this for?"

"Remember we placed a little bet about the exercise? Ten Kroner a head to the winner?"

Kai started to toss the coin back. "I only got four."

Victor held his hand up. "You can owe me. Hell, you and Ragnar saved my butt out there. I ought to pay you a thousand times that."

Kai smiled self-consciously and blushed. "My duty and my honor." He clapped Ragnar on the back. "If not for a reliable pilot protecting my rear, I never could have done it."

Ragnar blushed, the color deepening when Cassandra added, "I'd like to have a decent wingman sometime. Next exercise, Ragnar's with me."

Sun-Tzu grumbled from his corner, but Victor barely noticed as Hohiro and his sister stepped from the reception inside. Meeting Victor's gaze, she returned his smile of pleasure. Hohiro read the expression on his sister's face, then looked angrily at Victor.

So much for our alliance. Victor turned away and recovered his beer. Only Galen's greeting warned him of their approach.

"Evening, Hohiro. How nice to see you again, Lady Omi."

"Evening, gentlemen." Hohiro smiled politely and Omi gave them a silent nod. "I have just been telling my sister about today's

129

exercise. Once again, Victor, I must thank you for helping me when that lance overran my position."

Victor shrugged. "That's what wingmen are for."

"True, but most wingmen who had warned their partner about the folly of a maneuver would have let him die." Hohiro swallowed audibly. "Especially when their partner expressly forbade them to come help."

Galen shot Victor a wink. "There's your problem, Hohiro. Victor is so contrary that if you toss him into a gravity well, he floats up. I know of only one way to get him to obey orders like that."

Victor rubbed his jaw. "Yeah, quite an effective little persuader you are."

Slipping her right hand from her brother's elbow, Omi pressed her hands together. "I believe Hohiro characterized your action as both bold and heroic."

He said that? Victor blinked. "He probably realizes that in the Armed Forces of the Federated Commonwealth, a bold MechWarrior is one who manages to survive his own stupidity, and a hero is a bold MechWarrior who survives rescuing other bold MechWarriors from even greater stupidity." His gaze flicked over at Kai. "Happily, there are exceptions to that rule."

Omi smiled. "And I think present company proves an exception as well." She stepped away from her brother, placing herself between him and Victor. "In fact, if you are of a mind to, Prince Victor, I would gladly take that walk you suggested months ago."

Victor looked up at Hohiro, knowing Hohiro was aware that he and Omi had taken more than one walk together since that first invitation. "If your brother does not mind."

Hohiro smiled solemnly. "I trusted you with my life today and you safeguarded it better than I did. I believe I can trust you with one whom I hold more dear than life itself."

"*Arigato gozaimas*, Hohiro-*sama*." Victor offered his left arm to Omi, and she slipped her hand through the crook of his elbow. "I accept the weight of your trust and am honored by it."

"That is well, Victor Davion." Hohiro's eyes became dark slivers. "Our lives are too short and our duties too great for us to add yet more fuel to a centuries-old bonfire. Perhaps someday you and I, too, will be able to walk together as friends."

Grand Council Chamber, Hall of Khans
Strana Mechty, Beyond the Periphery
19 June 3051

Flanked by two Elementals in black armor, Phelan Wolf marched to the small dais just to the side of the high bench. Taking his place on the black marble stand added at least another head to his height, but still left him that much shorter than the armored figures to either side. A shiver ran down his spine as he looked out at the Khans gathered in the dimly lit, semi-circular chamber.

Though not nearly as large as the Clan Council Chamber of the Wolf Clan, the dark room seemed much more oppressive. The places for member Khans were carved from granite, with red velvet cushions on the seats and backs. They were arranged in five rows of eight, with the center aisle splitting the rows in half. The black stone used for their desktops was streaked with a pattern of white that reminded Phelan of the luminescent nebula clouds and stars seen from the observation deck of a JumpShip.

The slate wall paneling and recessed lighting increased the gloom and deepened his anxiety. Even the seventeen colorful banners hanging down from the ceiling did not break the graveyard mood of the room. Three obvious breaks in the spacing and six empty seats in the Khans' area suggested to Phelan that three of the original twenty Clans no longer existed. Phelan shuddered to realize that a people able to destroy parts of their own society would surely have no qualms about destroying the states of the Inner Sphere.

Even more unsettling was the style of clothing the Khans wore here in the Grand Council. Except for Phelan, the only other person whose face was not hidden by a mask was Conal Ward. Each Khan wore an exquisite headpiece that transformed him from a human into an anthropomorphic representation of his or her Clan. Phelan had seen the masks worn by the Smoke Jaguars, Jade Falcons, Ghost Bears, and Wolves during his adoption into the Wolf Clan warrior caste, but a baker's dozen new images confronted him in the Chamber. It brought home to him again that it was much more than mere distance separating the Clans from the Successor States.

Phelan glanced over at Conal Ward and gave him a slight nod.

Ward, whom the assembly had chosen to act as Loremaster while they elected an ilKhan, replied with a nod of his own, then turned to face the assembled Khans. "Let the chamber be sealed so that none of this debate may escape. If the accusations prove baseless, the questions we ask will blow away and be forgotten like ashes. Otherwise, the accused will have thirty days to prepare a defense."

In unison, the assembled Khans intoned, "Seyla."

The two Elementals split up and left Phelan alone on the dais. One took up a position by the side door through which the Loremaster and Phelan had entered the room. The other mounted the stepped aisle that split the chamber in two and stood with his back to the chamber's double doors.

The self-importance in Conal's voice did nothing to ease Phelan's mind. "Phelan Wolf, do you know why you have been summoned here before the Khans?"

The look on Conal's face told Phelan the Loremaster had something up his sleeve. Still, Phelan refrained from telling the Khans what Natasha had instructed him to answer. "It is not my ken to know the will of the Khans, Loremaster, but only to do all I may to fulfill their wishes."

Conal's face settled into a mask of superiority. "The Clans are without an ilKhan during this most important time. The ilKhan is the war leader of all the Clans and is chosen by the Council of Khans as the instrument of their combined will. He is charged with the duty of fulfilling their mandate. More important, he rules until his replacement or his death to safeguard the Clans from the folly that has destroyed the Successor States."

"That I understand, Loremaster."

"Good, then your tutors have taught you well." Conal gave him a patronizing nod. "All Khans are eligible for election, but before that election can begin, charges against any Khan must be resolved or set

132

aside for later judgement. In this case, we have called you to answer a most serious charge against Khan Ulric of the Wolves."

Phelan's eyes narrowed. *No surprise. Cyrilla was right. The battleground has shifted.* "I vow not to rest until justice in this matter has been done." Phelan saw Ulric nod as his response anticipated the Loremaster's next question.

Conal recovered after only a heartbeat's hesitation. "Very good, very good, indeed. The charge against Ulric is this: that he knowingly engineered the death of the former ilKhan, Leo Showers of the Smoke Jaguars. To your knowledge, is there any truth in this charge?"

The bald-faced affront of the question shocked Phelan. He instantly shook his head with vehemence. "Not only is the charge baseless, I must call it ludicrous as well." He felt his temper rising, but fought to keep it under control.

A Khan from the Steel Viper Clan stood. "But you do not deny that the ilKhan died when Khan Ulric did not?"

"No, of course I do not deny it." Phelan swallowed hard and forced his hands to remain clasped behind his back. "I was there. I was the first person onto the bridge after the Rasalhague fighter hit it. The hull had a hole in it bigger than this dais, and anything that wasn't hitched down had been sucked into space. Debris had ricocheted like shrapnel through the area. That there were any survivors at all was a miracle."

He took a deep breath and tried to calm his racing heart. "When I found Khan Ulric, he was buried beneath the panels of the holotank. He had blacked out and was unable to leave the bridge without assistance."

A Smoke Jaguar Khan stood up under the banner of his Clan. "Such a state could be feigned."

Phelan's nervousness and disbelief boosted into his anger. "You can't fake cyanosis. His skin and lips were blue from oxygen deprivation and he came around only after I fitted him with an oxygen mask."

Phelan's ire peaked at Conal's expression of contempt. He drew in a deep breath. "But that is less important than the idiocy of what is suggested by these charges. A fighter slammed into the hull of the ship and breached it. Fifteen meters higher and it would have shattered the bridge bulkhead, purging vast chunks of the ship's atmosphere. If Khan Ulric wanted to use such a risky method to kill the ilKhan, it would have been stupid for him to remain on the ship, *quiaff*? Why would he endanger the *Dire Wolf* at all when he could have had a supposed 'sniper' from the Rasalhague resistance troops shoot the ilKhan on the ground?"

The Smoke Jaguar Khan slammed his fist into his marble bench. "I will not be lectured by a *freeborn* whelp!"

"Show respect!" Conal snapped at Phelan.

Phelan's nostrils flared. "You demand a vow of my ceaseless pursuit of justice, then you seek to hobble me. I submit, Khan, that you would not need a lecture from a *freeborn* whelp if you had the brains of the average *surat*!"

The Khan trembled with rage at being compared with a bat-winged monkey native to one of the Clan worlds. He started to sputter, but Phelan gave him no chance to speak. "Face it. This charge is born of the fact that Khan Ulric and his Wolves ripped through one of the most densely populated regions of the Inner Sphere while the rest of you moved at the speed of a stunned snail. And now your spite makes you want to strip the Wolves of their best leadership. Instead, you should be choosing Ulric as your ilKhan. He's the only Khan who accomplished anything in the invasion of the Inner Sphere, and those of you with *stravag* brains between your ears should see that."

Conal's eyes blazed. "This is the Council of Khans! You are a visitor here. Watch your language and your tone!"

Phelan folded his arms across his chest. "I mean no disrespect, but I cannot fulfill the oath I have sworn to serve my Khan and the Clans if I do not protest this idiocy, *quiaff*?" He turned to face the Khans. "As for my language, Natasha Kerensky once told me, 'Slavish adherence to formal ritual is a sign that one has nothing better to think about.' I might suggest that within this, a warrior society, the same applies to those who fight with politics when what is called for are a warrior's skills."

A number of Khans chuckled heartily at that, but their laughter only made Conal angrier. "This conduct would not be tolerated from one who *is* a warrior, much less an untested foundling." With a flick of his hand, he summoned the nearest Elemental. "Remove him."

Phelan spitted the Elemental with a harsh stare. "Ease off, Ace. I've already laid two Elementals out in my career. You don't want to be the third." Holding his head high, he set his face in a grim mask. "I may not have tested out, *yet*, but that does not invalidate what I have said. I am slowly coming to understand your ways, but nothing I have learned leads me to believe injustice is a trait for which you select. If it is, perhaps I should just return to being a bondsman."

He stepped from the dais and swept past the Elemental. Slipping through the side door, he let it swing shut behind him, then slumped against the wall of the corridor. Balling his right fist, he slammed it against his thigh. *You moron! That's exactly the kind of thing that got*

134

you tossed out of the Nagelring. Eventually, Phelan, you have to learn that to get along you have to go along. It's a good thing Cyrilla couldn't see that performance. She'd never consider me for a Bloodname slot if she had.

Levering himself away from the wall, he rushed on past Natasha's archivist waiting in the hallway, far too distracted to notice the man or acknowledge his greeting. Further down the corridor and around a corner, Phelan stopped at a door showing the wolf's-head crest of the Wolf Clan. He knocked twice, then opened the door and entered the small office. Cutting through the door in the back corner, he came into Ulric's private office.

Natasha rose from the chair behind the large desk and applauded. "Thought we'd lost you there for a moment. You did great." Cyrilla, seated across from her, nodded her approval.

Phelan blinked. "What? The proceedings were supposed to be…" He glanced back at the cabinet half-hidden by the open door. A monitor showed a view of the Grand Council Chamber. "You saw?"

Cyrilla nodded and pointed to the remote control at the monitor. The sound started to come up. "All the Khans have access to this closed-circuit system. Watching the charade certainly violates the spirit of the Council regulations, but not more than a handful of the Khans can keep a secret anyway, so no harm is done."

Like Khan Ulric's cabin aboard the *Dire Wolf*, his office contained the bare minimum of furnishings required to serve its purpose. The padded leather chairs seemed the only concession to luxury. The ample surface of the sturdy desk was spread out with campaign maps. The other steel and glass tables and shelves were clear except for a few holovid albums and some small stone carvings.

"I thought Conal was going to pitch a fit when you backed that Elemental off." Natasha shook her head. "That was brilliant."

Phelan shrugged sheepishly. "That's what happens when you think with your adrenal glands."

"If you did all that in your panic mode, I want you in any unit I form up."

Cyrilla held her hand up. "Quiet. They're voting on Ulric."

The picture focused on the Clan banners as the Khans voted. A line along the bottom of the screen kept track of the totals. An obvious pattern arose right from the start, and by the end of the ballot, the vote exonerated Ulric overwhelmingly. Cyrilla clapped and Natasha cursed happily. Phelan just smiled.

"Now down to brass tacks. What's your read, Ril?"

The white-haired woman wrinkled her brow in thought. "The

135

Crusaders have to push for one of their own as ilKhan. I would have bet on Kincaid Furey, but Phelan's ripostes hit home. He does not have the sense of your average *surat*, and everyone knows that."

"Speak of the devil." Phelan pointed at the monitor as the camera focused on the Smoke Jaguar Khan.

Kincaid had regained control of his temper and stood stock-still. "I stand to apologize to Khan Ulric for having suspected him of complicity in the death of Leo Showers. I know my suspicions were fueled by my anger at his success. Perhaps it does take the anonymous delivery of truth to point out one's own limitations. Perhaps the first limit is seeing how easy it is to be mistaken."

Cyrilla's jaw dropped open and she paled visibly. "Oh, *freebirth*! No, they can't do this!"

"What?" Phelan looked from Cyrilla to Natasha's blank stare, then back to the monitor.

"Having been so abruptly acquainted with my stupidity, I now seek to remedy it. I, Kincaid Furey, nominate for the position of ilKhan, Khan Ulric of the Wolves."

Confusion knotted Phelan's brows in a frown. "What's going on? You two are reacting as if the world had ended. Isn't it good to have Ulric as the ilKhan?"

Natasha shook her head. "No, it's not good at all. Recall that Conal told you the ilKhan is to rule in accordance with the dictates of the Grand Council? That means Ulric will have to push the Crusader agenda if it is reconfirmed. From what Ril has told me, there are enough votes in the Council to endorse a resumption of the invasion."

Cyrilla nodded in agreement. Phelan saw that the color had returned to her face, and her brown eyes had angry sparks in them. "It gets worse. Not only do they hamstring Ulric, but he has to appoint his Wolf Khan replacement from within the Wolf Clan Council."

Phelan felt a sinking feeling in the pit of his stomach. "Let me guess. The Loremaster has traditionally been the person elevated to the position of Khan in such cases, *quiaff*?"

"Bargained well and done." Natasha gathered her long red hair back with her hands, then tipped her head back to stare at the ceiling. "They boxed us good on this one, eh, Ril?"

"They eliminate Ulric as a force and get a Crusader as a Wolf Khan."

As Cyrilla nodded with resignation and they heard no other candidate nominated as ilKhan, Phelan suddenly felt inexplicably giddy. "I think you may be selling Ulric short."

Cyrilla raised an eyebrow. "You see a way out of this trap?"

Phelan shrugged. "I do not, but that does not mean Ulric cannot find one. I saw him work through many tricky situations during the invasion. He managed to make ComStar dance to his tune and pay the piper. The Crusaders may be good, but I think Ulric might be better."

Along the bottom of the screen, the vote tallies appeared quickly. Without opposition, Ulric was elected easily. A number of Khans chose to abstain from the voting, and Phelan guessed those were Warden Khans protesting the railroading of their most successful comrade.

From the monitor came the sound of the Khans thumping their fists against their desktops to show approval. Conal Ward made a great show of vacating the ilKhan's chair. He offered Ulric his hand, then wandered up into the Council seating. All smiles, he plopped down into Ulric's old seat.

The camera shifted back to Ulric at the ilKhan's high bench. The ilKhan slowly removed his mask and set it on the bench. He smiled, stroked his goatee thoughtfully, then motioned to one of the Elementals. "Please escort Loremaster Ward from the chamber."

Kincaid Furey rose in mild protest. "Is that necessary, ilKhan? Your first act as ilKhan is to appoint your replacement as Wolf Khan. You can allow him to stay."

Ulric blinked innocently. "Why would I do that?"

"Well, because…" Kincaid started to answer, then abruptly fell silent.

The Elemental took Conal Ward by the elbow and started him up the center aisle. Before Conal had cleared the chamber, however, Ulric made an announcement. "As my replacement, I choose Natasha Kerensky."

Conal tore his arm from the Elemental's grasp. "What! You can't do that!"

"Please, Conal, your language. Consider where you are."

Phelan turned to Natasha. The famed Black Widow paled and stared at the screen. "Tell me he didn't say that, Ril."

Cyrilla started to laugh. "You heard it, Tasha. You are it."

"I'd sooner be Romano Liao's sister."

Conal posted his fists on his hips. "You know the tradition. The Loremaster is always selected to replace a Khan who has been elevated or otherwise rendered unable to serve."

Ulric steepled his fingers. "Not always, Conal. It has never happened when the Loremaster has declined the job."

"But I have not declined."

Ulric grinned cruelly. "Oh no? Did you not, during the Wolf Clan elections, say that you were unworthy to replace me? In fact, I seem to recall that you suggested Natasha Kerensky as a possible candidate for Khan. How can you complain when I merely acknowledge the wisdom of your recommendations?"

"Zap!" Phelan laughed. "Cut by your own knife, Conal!" He smiled at Natasha. "So much for that protest."

Natasha's eyes narrowed. "Never make it stick, Ulric." Her grin grew. "I've not tested out as a MechWarrior yet, so they'll never let you elevate me to that position."

Kincaid looked positively forlorn as the Elemental drove Conal from the room. His face tightened. "IlKhan, you cannot choose Natasha Kerensky. She has not yet tested out as a MechWarrior. Because she does not have active-duty status, she cannot become a Khan."

"I believe you are wrong, Khan Kincaid." Ulric nodded at the Elemental near the side door. "If you will bring in the witness."

The Elemental opened the door and conducted Natasha's archivist to the stone platform Phelan had earlier occupied. The small man looked a bit nervous, but a devilish light played through his eyes. He smoothed his dark beard nervously with one hand, then he smiled and nodded to the ilKhan.

"For those who do not know, this is Gustavus Michaels. He accompanied Natasha Kerensky from the Inner Sphere and provided us with a detailed history of the Wolf Dragoons detachment since they left the Clans. He is quite conversant with Natasha's career and will assure you that she is very much a MechWarrior."

Kincaid folded his arms across his chest. "He has no standing here. His word about her exploits in the Inner Sphere means nothing."

With a wave of his hand, Ulric gave Michaels leave to speak. "If you will permit me, Khan Kincaid," the small man began, "the ilKhan did not ask me here to report any of the original data I have gathered. Instead, he asked me to research the background of all those who have been appointed Khans by the election of an ilKhan or a tragedy that forced replacement. What I found were four instances of a Bloodnamed individual chosen to serve as Khan despite his active-duty status being under revocation or scrutiny. In two of those cases, the newly appointed Khan was in a coma."

Michaels smiled broadly. "And I can assure you that Natasha Kerensky is definitely not in a coma."

That remark brought a grin to Natasha's face and softened her sour expression. "He had this all planned out. When I get my hands on him, I'll kill him."

"Which one, Tasha, Ulric or Gus?"

"Yes."

The camera focused back on Ulric. "That should answer any questions you have, Khan Kincaid. Though I appreciate your concern that matters be conducted properly, let me remind you that I am the ilKhan. I need not justify my decisions to you. You may unseat me, if you wish, if you are *able*. You chose the landing zone, now you fight from it."

"Natasha Kerensky is the new Khan of the Wolves. What say you?"

"Seyla." Though a few voices were subdued, a confidence rang through the affirmation of Ulric's choice.

Ulric stood and leaned forward on his fists. "We have already wasted too much time, my Khans. We have elected a new ilKhan and have many important matters at hand. First and foremost is the invasion. The sooner we settle our differences, the sooner we can complete our conquest of the Inner Sphere."

Hanse Davion shot from his chair, outrage etched clearly on his face. "I don't give a damn what Kai Allard or my son did to Sun-Tzu yesterday, much less a month ago. Your irrelevancies and tantrums are a constant obstruction to what we have to do here. You son's inability to work with others is not a central issue in this debate."

"I believe you mistaken, Hanse Davion." Romano glared at him like a tiger. "As I have suggested before, and will maintain forever, the microcosm of the training unit involving my son is a reflection of the universe at large. Let us not even mention the gross breaches of protocol and the ridicule to which he has been subjected. Let us only consider the physical abuse he has suffered at the hands of a pretender to my throne, and the death threats from your son."

As Hanse sat down, Justin Allard stood up slowly. "With all due respect, Madam Chancellor…"

"Sit down, Allard. Though I don't see Davion's lips moving, I hear his words coming from your mouth. You have no standing here, no legitimacy."

Hanse saw Candace Liao lay her left hand on her husband's right forearm, then rise to stand beside him. "You will not dismiss me so easily, sister dear. What Prince Davion has been trying to explain, in words you can understand, is that the problem is not with our sons, it is with *your* son. Just as the problems between our troops and your

140

troops are problems with you. We face ravening hordes from beyond known space. It is a threat to us all. We need to band together to face this danger."

Romano threw back her head and laughed hysterically. "Ha! Band together! You would know all about that, wouldn't you, dear Candace? Twenty years ago, you joined forces with our enemies. Is that how you want us to face this threat now? You would have me do as you have done? Am I to give my troops over to Hanse Davion so he can destroy them as he will your forces? How stupid do you think I am?"

Candace's gray eyes blazed. "I have long since ceased any attempt to plumb the depths of your stupidity, Romano."

"Ladies, if you please!" Thomas Marik stood at his bench to Hanse's left. "Let us not have personal enmities divide us when we face more fundamental problems in our effort to oppose these Clans."

To Hanse, Thomas Marik looked haggard. Hanse knew that young Joshua Marik was not responding to medical treatment here on Outreach and that the Dragoon physicians were doubtful of the boy's survival. *Still, they say the boy's a fighter. Perhaps he will outlive us all.*

Thomas looked around the room with the calm authority he'd developed as a ComStar Adept. "Lady Romano's objection to sending her troops so far from home is well-founded. Her nation, among all of ours, has suffered the most from predation by its neighbors." He inclined his head toward Prince Magnusson of Free Rasalhague. "Your holding excepted in the current crisis."

Resuming his thread, Thomas went on. "Because of history and her desire not to repeat it, she is wise to be cautious."

"Bah." Hanse waved that objection away. "I give her my word that none of my troops will set foot in her realm until twenty years after the Clans have been defeated."

Thomas smiled less than sympathetically. "I am sure you offer that assurance in the spirit of cooperation, but I think Lady Romano is not so easily calmed. Recall that the most recent battles she has fought were against my Free Worlds League."

Hanse grinned wolfishly. "Then you offer her a pledge of non-aggression and let's get on with this."

"*Touché*, Prince Davion." The Captain-General brought his hands together in a prayerful position. "I think, though, given my nation's reputation for instability and your willingness to launch an assault on the very day of your wedding may leave any guarantees we offer still suspect. Even the wording of your statement suggests that

141

your troops *would* end up in her holding whenever the truce ended."

Hanse pointed at Theodore Kurita. "The Kanrei and I have concluded a non-aggression pact. If the two of us can trust one another, why cannot Lady Romano trust you and me?" *Because she's mad, that's why.* The second the thought hit him, Hanse saw it reflected in Thomas Marik's eyes.

"That is a question only she can answer." Marik bowed his head briefly, then brought it back up. "I did not rise to answer for her, nor to adjudicate your dispute. I am more concerned with my doubts about committing troops to this effort. From my border to the front is a distance of somewhere between 260 and 320 light years. This means nine to eleven jumps in a JumpShip. Simply stated, I do not have the resources needed to deliver troops in the numbers needed to be of any help."

"Nonsense," Hanse snarled angrily. "The rest of us are willing to do whatever it takes."

"To commit the necessary numbers of ships would gut my economy. Unlike the rest of you, I am not a dictator who rules by divine fiat." The fire-scars on the right side of Marik's face made him look yet fiercer. "If I drive the economy into the ground to help stave off an enemy threat, the Parliament will vote me out. And I'm not sure they wouldn't be right to do so."

Magnusson smashed his fist against the top of his desk. "How can you consider politics when this threat affects us all? We are not whistling in the dark while strolling through a graveyard. The danger is real. If the Clans return by fall, their rate of progress would put them on Atreus in two years. They would reach Sian even quicker if they split the Federated Commonwealth. If you don't do something, you will end up in the same grave as half my people."

Thomas shook his head. "With all due respect, Prince Magnusson..."

"No, Captain-General, there is no need to wrap your excuses in platitudes to hide your contempt for my nation. In your eyes, I am due no respect. You are only marginally more acceptable to me than Lady Romano because you are more silent, but neither of you understand the true horror of the Clan invasion."

The white-haired Prince pointed to where Morgan Kell sat behind Melissa Steiner. "Ask Colonel Kell how it feels to lose a son to the Clans." He turned and pointed behind him to a military officer in a wheelchair. "Ask Tor Miraborg how it feels to lose his daughter to the Clans. Ask me how it feels to watch someone like Tyra Miraborg take her fighter into the hull of a Clan JumpShip in a suicidal attempt

142

to save my life. Ask any of my people what it is like to be driven from their homes, from their worlds! And if that does not tell you anything, only think back to the wars of ten years ago to recall that hollow feeling in your soul when the enemy threatens everything you hold dear.

"If you do not act now, you will know that feeling yet again."

Melissa Steiner rose to her feet. "I know that feeling only too well, as do others in this room. Colonel Wolf and Colonel Kell have both pledged their mercenary units to the fight. Hanse and I have agreed that we shall devote our forces to opposing the Clans. Candace Liao has promised her crack units, and we know Prince Magnusson and the Kanrei will contribute everything they have to defeating the enemy. I do not enjoy war, but I acknowledge that there are times it must be fought."

She turned and held out a hand in Romano's direction. "Madam Chancellor, *I* promise no Federated Commonwealth troops will disturb your sovereignty. *I* promise your troops will not be used as cannon fodder against the Clans. I make the same promises to you, Thomas Marik. Join us."

As Melissa sat back down, she slipped her left hand into Hanse's right. He felt her trembling and gave her hand a squeeze. When she looked up at him, he nodded reassuringly. "Yes, Melissa. If this is what we must do, if these are the promises we must make, I abide by your words," he whispered gently.

Romano stood with a languid motion that suggested great weariness. She stifled a yawn with the back of her right hand, then discarded her act with a look of disgust. "Keep your promises, Archon Steiner. As Hanse Davion's brood mare, you are amusing, but I have no doubt he would disregard your assurances as quickly as any he himself made. I will not sacrifice my people on an altar of hollow promises built solely on your vanity."

The Chancellor from the Capellan Confederation turned her cold eyes on Prince Magnusson. "As for you, my dear Prince, your nation and your son are of the same age. Given what I hear of his prowess in a 'Mech, I would guess they have the same life expectancy. Your nation is nothing more than a Combine prefecture given the illusion of freedom. If by now you do not realize the joke that has been played on you, more's the pity."

She raised her hand in a salute to him. "How curious it is, Prince Magnusson, that your people's hatred for mercenaries now turns to adoration for them. The citizens of Rasalhague may choose to forget events of the past because of present problems, but I do not have that luxury. Each morning I see from my window the overgrown remains

143

of a 'Mech company that Hanse Davion destroyed in my capital. I will not be duped by him, nor talked into being duped by the rest of you. I remain unconvinced that the Fox has changed, and I *know* his old ways breed true in his children."

The scar over Magnusson's right eye stood out in stark white contrast to his florid features. "I pray, Lady Romano, that you are staring at those mouldering 'Mechs when the Clans take your capital away from you. Then you can lament not believing the Fox when he was telling the truth. There is no way out unless you choose to trust us, Romano. Otherwise you will be caught in a trap of your own making. Remember that when the trap snaps shut."

Thomas Marik rose again to speak, but Hanse barely listened. *Our only chance to defeat the Clans is to band together.* "Hang together or hang separately, as they used to say." He glared at Romano. *All of us with our heads in the noose, and she's playing with the gallows lever. I hope to God the Clans are as divided as we are. If not, the days of the Inner Sphere are numbered, and those numbers have damned few digits.*

Phelan Wolf twisted his gunbelt around and tied the holster down to his right leg. Turning to present himself to Natasha, he tried to force a smile of confidence. "Ready as I'll ever be."

She returned the smile, but shook her head. "God above, your language has deteriorated."

"It's the company I keep."

Natasha slung her arm around his neck and guided him toward the 'Mech bay. "Look, kid, you'll do fine. I've got your 'Mech configured in a way that will do maximum damage. It's unique, like my 'Mech. I tagged your Omni with the name *Lone Wolf.*"

Despite the big grin on Natasha's face, the younger MechWarrior felt something was wrong. He nodded grimly. "I hope that name's not an omen. I know it's not traditional, but are we working together out there?"

Natasha slapped the flat of his belly with the back of one hand. "You better believe it. The second I launch on one of your targets, it becomes a free-for-all." Her voice lost some of its jocularity and settled into a colder tone. "I need it like that because I'm going to have to ace my trio and kill one of yours to make these idiots sit up and take notice. Hope you won't mind me stealing one of your targets."

"Take them all. They're small."

Her laugh was half-hearted. "Can't do that. You'll have to take

one to be put on active duty. That's the only way to get you in my unit."
Serious again, she exhaled slowly. "On the other hand, only by taking four 'Mechs will I get a Cluster command. But if that's what it takes to get through the age bias, then I'll do it."

"I have no doubt that you will succeed, Colonel," Phelan said, though Natasha sounded as though she were still trying to convince herself of that fact.

"Are you so certain?"

The young man nodded confidently. "I recall your once saying that old age and treachery will beat youth and beauty every time. Sure, we'll be facing warriors younger and faster than you, but none of them will take either one of us seriously."

"Except Vlad."

"Yeah," Phelan said as his mouth soured, "except Vlad. This isn't going to be easy, but if anyone can do it, you can."

Natasha gave Phelan a sly smile. "Yes, I definitely want you in my unit."

Halfway down the row of BattleMechs in the hangar, Natasha gave Phelan a gentle shove toward his machine. "Here you go, kid. Warm it up and check all the weapons. I'll be online on Tac 29. We won't be able to communicate once the test starts, but until they give the word, we can exchange data."

"Roger."

"Phelan, remember that we have some advantages. They don't know about the configurations of our 'Mechs, but we're running assault 'Mechs that'll outmass any one of them. They're running non-standard heavies, so we can't be sure what we're up against. The most important thing for you to remember, however, is that this is live. The testers are volunteers who are willing to risk death. That doesn't mean you go out to smoke them, but if it happens, it happens."

"I know that. With Vlad out there, though, I think they're going to be going directly after me."

Natasha shrugged. "He'll let the others soften you up first, then he'll take you. Play smart and you'll be ready for him."

"Thanks. Good luck."

"Save the luck for the other guys. Old age and treachery will do fine for me." She threw him a wink and headed off to her own 'Mech.

Phelan paused and look up at his BattleMech as it stood there waiting for him. Six times his height, the war machine was painted black except in two spots. On the right hip, he saw the red wolf's-head crest of the Kell Hounds, the mercenary unit owned by his family. On the head was painted a mouth with sharp white fangs, war paint reminiscent of the markings on the 'Mech he'd lost when captured by the Clans almost two years ago.

Phelan made a couple of guesses from the exterior about the weaponry arrayed in the machine. The blocky shoulders were dotted with missile launch ports. The right arm ended in a blocky weapon pod with three laser muzzles poking from it like stubby fingers. The left arm ended in a muzzle, but it bore none of the telltale circuitry he would have expected on a PPC or laser, and it looked nothing like the autocannon muzzle hanging from the weapon pod underslung on the torso.

A box with six launch tubes was attached above the cockpit, just aft of the hatch. As he mounted the 'Mech, Phelan took a close look at it and decided it was a "fire and forget" packet of missiles. *One shot and it's gone.* The coding on the side of the launcher indicated that these were short-range missiles. *If I have to use them, it will mean that things have gotten a bit dicey. Still, just like wearing this pistol, it's nice to have something for emergencies.*

Phelan dropped into the cockpit, sealed and pressurized it, then brought the 'Mech online. As he satisfied the computer that he was the pilot assigned to the machine, it gave him a full readout of the 'Mech's offensive capabilities. He saw a number of things that confused him, so he switched the radio to Tac 29.

"Natasha, I have a couple of questions for you."

"Ask away."

"The LRM launcher in the left shoulder is loaded with Swarm missiles in its first twelve racks?"

"Swarms are LRMs that will saturate an area with submunitions. Our foes will be grouped together like Siamese triplets at the start of this operation. Standard procedure is for them to engage us one at a time. You've shown how to really screw them up when you just start nailing anything and everything. The Swarms will ladle out damage generously."

"But won't that get all of them attacking us at once?"

Natasha's laugh survived computer modulation intact. "Of course. Would you prefer that they use a strategy that makes them comfortable or uncomfortable?"

"Point taken. This LBX autocannon has Cluster loads."

"Shotgun shells. It'll sand all the armor off a foe. Once you've softened him up, your lasers ought to cut him to ribbons."

Phelan nodded to himself and studied the auxiliary monitor. "Gauss rifle in my left arm?"

"Great weapon. It uses magnetic currents to launch a ball of ferrous metal about the diameter of a melon. Generates next to no heat and packs one hell of a wallop. The only problem is that its power requirements are fairly heavy. If you try to shoot it and the lasers at the same time, the computer will have to cycle and allocate power, so it will take a bit longer to get your salvo off."

Phelan looked up and through his cockpit canopy and saw Natasha's BattleMech stride into view. It had the same bird legs as his 'Mech and a cylindrical body built up at the shoulder to accommodate missile launchers. On the 'Mech's right side, Phelan saw the stubby muzzle of an autocannon and a triangular configuration of laser muzzles in the chest. Both arms ended in slender sets of two weapon barrels in an over-and-under arrangement. Natasha's 'Mech was painted black, and the red hourglass marking of a Black Widow spider emblazoned the 'Mech's abdomen.

Phelan smiled as he read the computer's name for her 'Mech. "Widowmaker? That's appropriate. Looks like you're loaded for bear, Colonel Kerensky."

"For Wolves, Phelan. I know that isn't precisely the Kell Hounds color scheme on your 'Mech, but you're no longer a hound. You're a Wolf now—we both are."

Phelan started his BattleMech forward. "Let's go prove it to the others, shall we?"

Two sets of three BattleMechs stood waiting to test the warriors. Their paint schemes allowed the outlines of the 'Mechs to blend with the red rocks and sandy terrain, but the visual trickery did not fool Phelan's weaponry. "I've got my three targets over on the left. I wonder which one is Vlad?"

"It doesn't matter, does it?" Natasha's 'Mech moved slightly forward of Phelan's position. "Tell you what. I'll mark the 'Mech of yours closest to my set." She sounded tentative, then seemed to recognize it and uttered a soft curse. "Dammit, these young pups won't get to me."

Phelan said nothing.

"Sorry, Phelan. I don't like this, but there is no other way to make a difference. When we get the go-ahead, let him have it with your long-range weaponry. I'll toss a barrage of missiles at the *Mad Dog*, but I'm going to take one of my own targets with my beams."

"Confirmed."

Ulric's voice boomed through the speakers in Phelan's neurohelmet. "Natasha Kerensky and Phelan of the Wolves, this is your testing time. Every aspect of your performance will be examined and evaluated. The rating generated by this process will determine your duties until the next testing period. Defeat no enemies and you will lose your status as a Warrior. Defeat one and you will be given a 'Mech assignment. Defeat two and you will earn the right to be a Star Commander. Three kills will earn you the rank of Star Captain. Do you understand this, *quiaff*?"

"Aff."

"Very well. Natasha, your targets are designated by red triangles on your tactical scanner. Phelan, your targets are blue squares. Your foes already know that defeat here will not reflect negatively on them in any official way. Natasha, Burke Carson is one of your opponents, and Vladimir of the Wolves is set against Phelan. As both of you know, this is very important. Neatness does not count. You have won as long as you are operational and your enemy is not. Even if you have to drag yourself off the battlefield with your arms, you will be victorious."

Ulric's voice lost power as he opened lines to all the 'Mechs on the battlefield. "Let the testing begin!"

Phelan dropped the crosshairs on his battle array down to cover the torso of the 'Mech sandwiched between his and Natasha's group. He hit both buttons on top of the targeting joysticks and tightened down on the trigger under his left index finger. He felt a rush of heat as the 'Mech rocked back with the recoil.

Natasha's flight of LRMs reached the *Mad Dog* first, so Phelan's missiles screamed into the roiling fireball already consuming the 'Mech. LRMs sprayed the whole torso and peppered its head, blasting armor into ferro-ceramic splinters. Phelan saw the 'Mech stagger slightly, then the Gauss rifle's silvery ball projectile slammed into its left shoulder. The impact crushed armor and spun the massive war engine to the ground. It rolled back toward one of its teammates, but that pilot deftly danced his machine out of danger.

Phelan pulled his BattleMech back, taking cover behind a low hill. A glance at his secondary monitor gave him a status report on the downed 'Mech, making him shudder. "Computer shows his cockpit was hit. He's dead or wounded, just for a *test*."

Phelan worked around to the left, splitting off from Natasha to engage his own testers. Clearing the low hill, he saw one of his targets standing over the damaged 'Mech while the other headed straight toward Phelan's low hill. The computer identified that OmniMech as a *Warhawk*.

Stepping up onto the hilltop, Phelan spitted the 'Mech on his crosshairs and fired a second barrage. The twin missile flights bracketed the incoming Clan 'Mech. Missiles exploded armor on the *Warhawk*'s arms and legs, with minor damage to its right flank resulting from two errant warheads. The Gauss rifle's sphere hit the barrel of the PPC mounted in the left arm and skipped along it to slam into the *Warhawk*'s elbow, but it failed to damage the gun before it discharged its particle beam.

Both of the *Warhawk*'s two arms ended in weapon pods that housed particle projection cannons mated with pulse lasers. The PPC's azure beams sizzled out and stabbed into Phelan's *Lone Wolf*. One lashed the 'Mech's right arm, flaying armor from shoulder to elbow. The other beam burned a jagged scar down the Omni's right leg, dropping steaming sheets of armor onto the hilltop.

Phelan's body jerked hard to the right as he fought the controls to keep his 'Mech upright. He moved the crosshairs back on target as the *Lone Wolf* recoiled from the damage the *Warhawk* had done. He let it move in forty meters and dipped his 'Mech's right arm as though it had taken more than just damage to the armor. *Just how contemptuous of me are you?*

The *Warhawk*'s pilot kept coming and brought its weapon pods up to fire. One PPC beam shot over the *Lone Wolf*'s head, but the other whipped across it like a blue scourge, vaporizing armor and the canopy on Phelan's 'Mech. A stinging mist scorched his exposed arms and legs, but the cabin's depressurization blew most of the molten glass back out. Sparks shot from two or three panels and a secondary monitor died in a puff of smoke.

The computer calmly informed him that his life support systems had been destroyed, but Phelan knew that was of little concern on a hospitable world like Strana Mechty. The pulse laser fire to the *Lone Wolf*'s left arm had done nothing but melt armor. *I have to end this now, or I'm in a serious world of hurt.* He forced the pain of his arms and legs away, then let the *Warhawk* have everything at point-blank range.

One flight of missiles missed its target, but the second blasted armor from both arms, baring the myomer fibers and workings of the PPC and pulse laser of the *Warhawk*'s left arm. One of the trio of pulse lasers mounted in the *Lone Wolf*'s right arm shot wide of the *Warhawk*'s body. The other two ruby beams carved armor from the center of the 'Mech's body and its right flank, leaving parallel smoking scars.

Muzzle flashes from the autocannon strobed into the *Lone Wolf*'s cockpit, and the pungent odor of high explosives filled it. The cloud of metal chewed into the *Warhawk* on its right side and blasted a huge chunk of armor from the Omni's right arm. The Gauss rifle's ball whistled from the muzzle, catching the *Warhawk* in the right arm. The limb shivered under the impact and the armor shattered like glass.

Phelan's left ring finger tightened on the SRM launcher button. The six missiles shot from their box and raced at the crippled *Warhawk* like sharks heading for bloody water. Three missed the Omni, but the trio that hit did serious damage. One augured into the left arm and exploded, scattering bits and pieces of 'Mech skeleton. Subsidiary detonations sent chunks of PPC and pulse laser whirling away. The missile striking the right arm hit higher up. Though it nibbled away at the 'Mech's ferro-titanium bones, it did no damage to its weaponry.

The last missile aimed for the *Warhawk* dead-center, but it detonated prematurely. A boiling cloud of liquid fire washed over the 'Mech and clung to it like a fiery blanket. The pilot tried to pull away from the flames, but the *Warhawk* had been hammered so badly in a such a short time that it was grossly off-balance. The 'Mech clawed at the earth to remain upright, but succeeded only in raising a cloud of dust. With the screech of stressed metal and the staccato popping of armor plates breaking, the *Warhawk* crashed to the ground and broke off its own left arm.

Phelan now looked for the 'Mech his computer had named "Executioner." He couldn't find it on his screen nor could he see it through his viewport. He immediately knew Vlad was its pilot. *Dammit! I'm naked here and I don't know where he is.*

The young MechWarrior started his *Lone Wolf* forward. He stepped down hard on the *Warhawk*'s right knee, snapping the joint. He pumped one round from the Gauss rifle through the 'Mech's right shoulder, sending the *Warhawk*'s arm pinwheeling off in a shower of sparks. "That means you're going nowhere."

Realizing he had yet to face his deadliest enemy, Phelan's guts started to flipflop. As Natasha had predicted, Vlad had let the others batter the *Lone Wolf* before he chose to engage it. Convinced that mobility and a continued, long-range duel gave him an edge, Phelan headed down the hill and back toward the *Mad Dog*'s wreckage.

Adrenaline jolted through his system as he saw movement on his battle display. The *Executioner* appeared in his aft arc. Phelan cursed the loss of his secondary monitor and shunted a data feed to his auxiliary monitor. Immediately, the computer filled it with an information scan of the OmniMech. He saw that each arm mounted a Gauss rifle and each side of the torso was arrayed with one large laser and two medium lasers.

Unable to fire any weapons, Phelan cut hard to the right, making the *Lone Wolf* do a hop-jump that bounced him forward against the command couch's restraining straps. A silver ball skittered through the space he had just vacated. It skipped across the rocky landscape, bouncing off outcroppings of sedimentary rock, striking sparks wherever it actually hit. A second or two later, another Gauss rifle projectile whizzed over the *Lone Wolf*'s head.

"Shit!" Phelan shot forward, pushing his 'Mech for all the speed it could muster. He broke to the left, then back to the right. He knew that would make him a difficult target to hit, but did not find much comfort in that. *I used this same tactic when I fought Vlad for the very first time. It infuriated him because I refused to stand and battle it out like a "civilized" warrior.*

Knowing how much Vlad hated him, Phelan had to admire the man's control. When Vlad fired his first shot, the *Lone Wolf* had been well within the optimum range for all his weapons. Instead of letting loose with everything, the Clansman had carefully triggered one Gauss rifle and then the other. *He's taken the name of his 'Mech to heart. This is not to be a slaughter. He intends it to be an execution.*

Phelan hunkered the *Lone Wolf* down behind a small mesa and readied all his weapons systems. With all his missiles and the ammo for the autocannon, he could be in big trouble if Vlad managed to get damage through his armor. Touching off a rack of missiles or starting the autocannon ammo exploding would destroy the *Lone Wolf* from the inside out. Packing only energy weapons and Gauss rifles, Vlad didn't have to worry about explosive ammo getting hit.

A fragment of something he'd heard suddenly hurtled forward into Phelan's consciousness, and it was as though a blindfold had been torn from his eyes. "Vlad isn't in control. Natasha warned me about the power requirements for a Gauss rifle. Vlad hit the triggers for everything in his first shot. He's got the Gauss rifles set up as his primary weapons, so they get first crack at the power from his fusion engines!"

Phelan popped the *Lone Wolf* up to its full height and spotted the *Executioner* at half a klick and moving quickly. As Vlad brought the Omni around, Phelan cut loose with twin missile flights. With golden explosions, five missiles cratered the armor on the *Executioner*'s right leg. Over half the other flight ground into the 'Mech's left arm and blew out armor chaff.

The impact knocked that Gauss rifle off target, its round shell sailing high and wide of the *Lone Wolf*. A second later, however, the *Executioner*'s right-arm weapon launched its projectile in an electric flash. The *Lone Wolf* lurched to the left as the ball pounded the 'Mech's left hip. Armor shards flew through the air and the 'Mech slewed half about.

Phelan twisted his body back onto the command couch and dropped the *Lone Wolf* into a crouch. "Jesus, Mary, and Joseph!" His primary monitor showed him that the upper portion of his left leg armor had been utterly destroyed. "One more shot like that, and I lose the leg!"

He knew Vlad would be a tough nut to crack, but confirmation of his power problem gave Phelan some hope.

Phelan backed the *Lone Wolf* from the mesa, then worked to the left. He picked a spot between two jutting stone formations and stood there. His computer marked the *Executioner* at 300 meters, and Phelan hung both crosshairs on him. The second the dot in the middle of them flashed, Phelan sent two missile flights and a Gauss rifle shot at Vlad, then immediately ducked down. Through the open canopy, he heard the missile explosions.

Suddenly the earth shuddered beneath the *Lone Wolf*'s feet. Dust and pebbles rattled into the cockpit as a silver ball gouged a divot from the embankment that hid Phelan. A scarlet energy beam sliced through the air right behind it, but neither attack did any damage to the *Lone Wolf*.

"He's figuring out what I've learned about his 'Mech. He may be a son of a bitch, but he's not stupid." For a half second, Phelan wondered idly why he hadn't stayed a bondsman. Anger at himself chased the thought from his mind. *You're a warrior, that's why. Now be smart, hit hard, and run.*

Twice more Phelan managed to use the terrain and his superior mobility to snipe at the *Executioner*. By circling, he managed to keep the right side of Vlad's 'Mech in his sights. The missiles scoured armor from the 'Mech's right leg, torso, and arm, leaving them covered with the tattered remnants of ferro-fibrous plating. But the Gauss rifle did the most critical damage. It punched through the weakened armor on the *Executioner*'s right breast, destroying the laser. The large laser dropped down to crush one of the pulse lasers.

As dark smoke poured from the hole in the *Executioner*'s chest, Phelan leaped his 'Mech up onto the ridge line he'd been using for cover to bring his autocannon into play. Vlad turned his 'Mech to meet Phelan head-on. Without a second's hesitation, all weapons oriented on their targets. At 200 meters, the two warriors let everything fly.

Phelan's paired flights of missiles shot from the *Lone Wolf*'s shoulders, drawing gray contrail lines in the air. Missiles chipped away at the armor over the *Executioner*'s heart and blasted armor from its right leg. More missiles poured through the hole in its right side and yet others chopped into the armor at the 'Mech's left shoulder.

Bracketed by the missile tracks, the trio of pulse lasers found their target easily. One drilled a hole through the *Executioner*'s right arm, evaporating its last armor. The second sent a stream of molten ceramic coursing down the 'Mech's left leg. The last blasted a staggered line of holes down the 'Mech's face in a crude parody of Vlad's own scar.

Phelan's autocannon tracked poorly and ripped away all but the last bit of armor on the *Executioner*'s right leg. The Gauss rifle's argent sphere pulverized the armor on the 'Mech's left arm, sending jagged sheets of it to the sand. Though the fire laid much of the arm bare, it did not destroy the *Executioner*'s own Gauss rifle.

Vlad's return fire rattled and shook the *Lone Wolf*, leaving Phelan feeling like a rock being shaken in a tin can. The first Gauss rifle slug blasted into the *Lone Wolf*'s left arm, snapping the limb off at the elbow and spinning the 'Mech to the left. Phelan's Gauss rifle careened off to explode down in the trench he'd previously used for cover.

With his altered priorities in place, the *Executioner*'s battle computer cycled through his lasers before it got to his remaining Gauss rifle. The pulse laser in the shattered right breast stitched a half-dozen steaming holes in the *Lone Wolf*'s right leg. The other two pulse lasers both melted a deep hole in Phelan's right flank. The *Executioner*'s large laser lanced its red beam through the left side of the *Lone Wolf*'s chest as Phelan brought his machine back under control and turned it to face Vlad.

The *Executioner*'s right-arm Gauss rifle spat out a hunk of metal about thirty centimeters in diameter. Nothing more than a silver blur, it shot straight into the middle of the *Lone Wolf*'s chest. Phelan's teeth smashed together as the whole torso pitched up, jamming him down into the command couch. Vlad disappeared from view as the empty canopy filled with a vision of the cloudless blue sky. Phelan clawed at the arms of his command couch and tried to step back to steady the 'Mech, but the ridge offered him no footing.

For a time that felt like forever, he knew the horror of freefall in a BattleMech.

The *Lone Wolf* hit the ground with all the grace and gentleness of a huge rock. The abrupt landing smashed Phelan down into the command couch and whipped his head back against a cockpit rein-forcement. His neurohelmet prevented his brains from being spattered all over, but he still saw stars. His left arm jammed its elbow against the edge of a console, numbing it to the wrist. He bit his tongue, tasting blood from that and from where the neurohelmet mashed his lips against his teeth.

Sparks flew through the cockpit as monitors and control panels shorted out. Warning klaxons blared, then were choked off by a pop and a puff of smoke. Pouring in through the skeletal remains of the cockpit canopy structure, dirt and stones ricocheted off broken equipment and Phelan's battered body. One large piece cracked the viewport on his helmet as it bounced off to the back of the cockpit.

Then he heard nothing except the rattle of debris and the steady whispered rumble of the fusion engine. His left arm felt on fire as feeling returned to it, but a visual inspection showed only a small cut on the forearm. He brushed away the dirt that had pooled at his throat and started to unbuckle himself from the ruined 'Mech.

What stopped him was a bizarre and terrifying sound from outside. Thud, scrape, thud, scrape, it reverberated powerfully through the ground and into his 'Mech. To Phelan, it was the noise made by the deranged, one-legged maniac that haunted scary stories he'd heard as a child. As quickly as he clubbed that childhood fear down, another more insistent horror rose in his heart. *That's Vlad. He's coming for me.*

Phelan moved instantly to action. Working the right joystick around and pushing the 'Mech's foot pedals, he found power still going to his 'Mech's limbs. The total absence of monitors meant he had no idea whether any of his weapons were still operational. Without his battle array, he could only guess if a weapon was on target, but he knew that a 'Mech at point-blank range would be very hard to miss.

That's a point Vlad won't overlook.

Using his 'Mech's right arm, he pushed off against the ground. The *Lone Wolf* started to move toward the right, but caught only after a shift of a few degrees. Phelan pushed harder, but heard armor panels buckling, so he stopped. As he relieved the pressure on his right arm, the *Lone Wolf* sank back to its original position.

Despair clutched at his heart. *I'm wedged in tight. I've got no weapons. There's nothing I can do. I'm going to die!*

From somewhere deep inside, he heard a voice that could only be his own. *If you're going to die, Phelan Kell, you'll die a man.*

He clenched his jaw and swallowed hard. Working his left arm around to ease its numbness, he waited.

Thud, scrape, thud, scrape. His pulse matched itself to the thunderous cadence of Vlad's approach. A thousand different plans for escape flashed through Phelan's mind and were rejected. He knew he couldn't run because Vlad would gladly hunt him down and kill him whether he were in a 'Mech or not. Calling out to Natasha would do no good. As nearly as he could tell, his radio was out, and during the test, it would be jammed anyway.

Vlad did not keep him waiting long. The *Executioner* pulled itself up onto the ridge and stared down at the *Lone Wolf*. From shoulder to foot, the entire right side of the 'Mech's body had been stripped of armor. Impact craters and laser burns dotted the rest of the 'Mech's hide like disease sores. Smoke drifted from the ruined half of of its chest and hung over the body like a wispy cloak.

Vlad's laughter echoed from the *Executioner*'s external speakers. "So this is how it ends? I would have expected more of a fight from a *warrior* as great as you."

Phelan flicked open his helmet's face plate. "If you were any sort of opponent, I might have really put my best effort into it."

"A mistake, Phelan. I regret that I cannot offer you the luxury of learning from it. I would have let you live to wallow in your dismal failure, but I have not been given that choice." The *Executioner*'s left arm swung its Gauss rifle muzzle in line with Phelan's cockpit. "You embarrassed Conal in the Grand Council and he has demanded your death."

Phelan snorted contemptuously. "If you had the balls God gave a sand flea, you'd come down here and slit my throat."

"Fortunately, Phelan, I have the brains God gave a man and I remember you wear a gun in the cockpit. Nice try."

"A warrior's got to try."

"A fitting epitaph. Too bad it's too long to inscribe on the thimble they'll use for your remains. Farewell, Phelan."

Phelan swept his 'Mech's right arm up and dropped the boxy weapon pod down to cover his open cockpit. At the same time, he stabbed both command couch foot pedals to the floor.

The *Lone Wolf*'s right arm slammed back into the cockpit like a hammer. The canopy skeleton shattered and raked jagged pieces of metal through the cockpit. One sliced through the surface of Phelan's cooling vest, instantly filling the air with the acrid scent of 'Mech coolant. Fist-sized hunks of armor rained down from the weapon, their jagged edges nicking and cutting Phelan's arms and legs.

Once armor fragments stopped clattering around in the cockpit, the only sound in the eerie quiet was the bass undertone of the fusion engine. Vlad did not curse him or taunt him. He heard no sound of Vlad's 'Mech limping to another position. *Could my kicking out with my feet have shaken the ground enough to knock him down?*

Phelan peeled the *Lone Wolf*'s arm away from its face. Pressing the limb to the ground, he pushed off again and the OmniMech seemed to move much more freely. He rolled it over to the left, then gathered his feet under him. Slowly and cautiously, he raised the 'Mech to its full height and looked out over the edge of the trench.

The *Executioner* lay on its face. Still-glowing stumps and the bubbling burning ends of myomer muscles were all that remained of its right arm and right leg. The hole in the right side of the 'Mech's torso had expanded all the way to the midline and beyond. From it, Phelan saw a thick cloud of gray smoke, and the scent told him the *Executioner's* gyro had been reduced to scrap.

Static crackled through the speakers in his neurohelmet, followed quickly by Natasha's nervously giddy laughter. "It's official, Phelan. The exam is over. Thanks for opening up Vlad for me and keeping him busy so I could line up that long shot."

Phelan shuddered. "Yeah, well, entertaining Vlad seems to be a specialty of mine." He felt blood trickle down from a scratch on his right arm. I'm just glad you came along when you did."

"Why, Phelan Wolf, I think you're the first person outside the Dragoons ever to say that to me."

"And no one ever meant it more, I can assure you." Phelan's *Lone Wolf* slowly scaled the side of the trench. "I'm happy you got your quartet of 'Mechs, but I hope you'll understand if I never want to do this again."

Tetsuhara Proving Grounds, Outreach
Sarna March, Federated Commonwealth
22 July 3051

Kai Allard wiped his sweaty palms against his cooling vest. "I copy, Victor. I appreciate your advice. Heaven knows I can't hope to do as well out there as you did."

Victor's voice made it through the speakers full of confidence. "Kai, Hohiro smoked my mark, so I know you can do better. I'm counting on it. The honor of the Federated Commonwealth rests on your shoulders."

Kai shivered. "You had it easy. Shin was your wingman. I've got Sun-Tzu out here, which means I've got four people hunting me."

"He'll have his hands full with the crew they've arrayed against him. As long as you don't shoot any of his targets, his folks will leave you alone and yours will leave him alone. Remember, you've got an Omni and they're just running normal 'Mechs. You'll dust them in no time."

"Don't waste your money betting on me."

"Can't," Victor laughed. "No one will give me good odds."

Another voice, one Kai instantly recognized as that of Jaime Wolf, cut into the channel. "Sun-Tzu Liao and Kai Allard-Liao, this is your time of testing. Though all energy weapons are powered down and projectiles are phantom rounds, damage will be assessed at full value by the computers monitoring the exercise. Still, caution is important because the 'Mechs are subject to damage. Fall off a mesa and land on your cockpit and you'll be as dead as you would be from a head shot in a battle. Do you understand?"

"Roger, Colonel." Kai heard the echoes of Sun-Tzu's reply a moment later.

"Your mission is to defeat the foes arrayed against you. You may cooperate, but radio communication will be jammed for both sides of the battle. You may shoot at enemies not assigned to you, but that frees your foes to pursue your ally and vice versa. These exercises are usually complicated enough that such additional confusion is not necessary. You will be ranked according to the number of foes you destroy and the amount of damage you do. Good luck. The exercise will commence in thirty seconds."

Kai took one last glance at his primary monitor. It reported all weapon systems operational, and Kai smiled at the array he had been given. The LRMs, the extended range large laser, and the Gauss rifle would all hit at longer ranges, letting him pick apart enemies working in closer. At closer range, his heavy autocannon and battery of pulse lasers would do some serious damage. This *Daishi*, whose name meant Great Death, looked like it would live up to its name.

Across the battlefield, he saw a frightening group of enemy 'Mechs. Allotted to him were an *Archer*, a *Blackjack*, and a *Battle-Master*. He evaluated the 'Mechs in terms of threat and formulated his plan of action. The *Blackjack*, he knew, had the lightest armor. A concentrated assault in the form of missiles, large laser, and Gauss rifle could take it out of battle almost instantly. The *Archer*, with two batteries of LRMs, was built for long-range combat, which meant he'd have to close with it or duke it out at a distance.

The *BattleMaster*, Kai decided, should be his second target. An assault 'Mech, it was heavily armored yet somewhat under-gunned, especially for a long-range duel. Hitting it early would mean that Kai had a better chance of having all his weapons available to attack it. If he ended up closing with the *Archer* last, he could use his close-in weapons to deal with it.

He glanced over at the other *Daishi* standing 250 meters to his left. Like his 'Mech, the blocky war machine stood on back-canted legs. Its stubby, cylindrical arms ended in weapon muzzles, a Gauss rifle left and large laser right. The autocannon rode high on the left shoulder, and opposite it, the hulking LRM launch mechanism rose like a hump on its right shoulder. The trio of pulse lasers were mounted just below the *Daishi*'s chin on the right side of its chest.

Kai snorted grimly as he noted Sun-Tzu had his weapons pointed at the enemies they faced. The second he learned of his pairing in the exercise, Kai vowed to stay away from Sun-Tzu. Even if one of Sun's foes presented Kai a clean backshot, he had decided not to take it. *I don't care what it could do for my score. If I do anything to interfere with his performance, I'll never hear the end of it.*

The digital display flashed down to 00:00, and Kai's combat display came up. Instantly, he dropped the crosshairs for his weapons onto the outline of the *Blackjack*. His right thumb punched the button on top of the right joystick, launching a full flight of twenty missiles at the 'Mech. His left hand hit the thumb button and firing button under his index finger, bringing the Gauss rifle and large laser into play.

Missiles dotted the *Blackjack*'s head, chest, and left flank with computer-animated fireballs. The large laser swept across the top of the 'Mech's left thigh like a surgeon's scalpel, leaving a deep, nasty scar in the computer's image. The Gauss rifle's phantom projectile streaked across the landscape and smashed the *Blackjack* squarely in the knee. The impact shivered most of the armor from that leg and dumped the *Blackjack* to the ground.

Kai darted his *Daishi* forward twenty meters and off to the right, anticipating his foes' plan for him to retreat. The twin flights of missiles from the *Archer* overshot him by that margin. The particle beam from the *BattleMaster*'s pistollike particle projection cannon burned wide, bringing a smile to Kai's face. *If I can keep you guys guessing...*

Suddenly, missile detonations wreathed the *BattleMaster*'s arms in fire. "You idiot, Sun-Tzu, you hit the wrong target!" Kai glanced at the secondary monitor updating the *BattleMaster*'s damage, but took no satisfaction at the report. "Stupid accident and now whatever gets past him comes after me. Why did I have to be paired with him?"

Though the battle had been going on for only a few seconds, everything suddenly stopped as a ring of fire blossomed around Sun-Tzu's canopy. The duraplast viewport blew out and away as the explosive bolts detonated. An intense light flashed to life from within the dark cockpit, then Sun-Tzu's command couch rode a rocket into the sky. Without even slowing, the couch shot over the line of hills beyond the enemy 'Mechs and disappeared from view.

It took several seconds before Kai counsciously registered what Sun-Tzu had done. The Capellan had not accidentally targeted the *BattleMaster*. He had selected it most carefully and deliberately. In shooting it, he had guaranteed that all the enemy 'Mechs—a full half-dozen of them—could attack either or both the young MechWarriors. Having ensured that the battle would become a chaotic fray, he then punched out to leave his hated cousin alone.

Part of Kai wanted to cry out that the test was no longer fair, then thought how the men he had sent against Elementals on Twycross must have cursed him the same way he wanted to curse Sun-Tzu. *They had no choice. Neither do you.*

That cold truth settled around him like a burdensome cloak, but he took his hopelessness and hatred and wove them into fury. Instead of that hollow feeling at his core, he felt a furnace of emotions. With his mind clear, Kai took up the gauntlet Sun-Tzu had hurled at him.

He again targeted the stricken *Blackjack*. With help from the *BattleMaster*, it had begun to regain its feet, but five missiles and the brilliant scarlet beam of Kai's large laser chopped off its right leg at the knee. Meanwhile, the Gauss rifle's silver slug pounded its way through the armor on the 'Mech's left flank and crushed the left side of its torso. The 'Mech twisted in the *BattleMaster*'s grip, then flopped to the ground.

Kai kicked the *Daishi* into high gear, cutting back to the left. He turned sharply, presenting his back to the *Archer*. It cut loose with two score LRMs and delivered over half of them on target, blasting armor from the *Daishi*'s head, back, right flank, and right arm. The computer, simulating the damage, threw the gyro out of phase for several seconds, but Kai fought the controls and managed to keep the loping *Daishi* upright.

Before the *Archer* could fire again, Kai put a hill between him and the enemy task force. A quick review of the damage to his armor revealed about half the rear armor blown off, but he dismissed that problem almost immediately. *If I let anyone into my aft arc, I deserve to die. Damn you, Sun-Tzu. There's got to be something I can do.*

Communications. He knew the Dragoons jammed radio broadcasts during the tests, but he wondered if they would lift the jamming now that Kai was alone. He switched his radio over to the tactical frequency the other trainees had used to communicate before the battle. A bone-twisting squeal ripped through the neurohelmet's speakers at first, then died abruptly.

He smiled as he brought the *Daishi* to the end of a small valley and cut back north toward his enemies. Kai quickly punched up a frequency command for the computer and sent out a standard code. *If they're not jamming everything, maybe this will work.* He hit the Enter key, then crossed his fingers for luck.

The secondary monitor flashed twice, blanking the outline of the *Blackjack*, and replacing it with geological survey satellite feed of data from seismic sensors in the area. Kai magnified the image several times until he got an area roughly two kilometers in diameter, centered on himself. He ordered the computer to sort for and pinpoint areas of seismic activity, then set the threshold at .01 on the Richter scale. He laughed out loud when the computer painted six squares on the screen and appended their Richter ratings to them.

He continued to work his way north. As nearly as he could work out from Richter ratings, the *BattleMaster* and one of Sun's opponents had headed directly out after him. The remaining two of Sun's foes had come in slowly, but they appeared more interested in using Sun's 'Mech as cover against any southwestern approach by Kai than in hunting him. The *BattleMaster* and its wingman headed west once they passed through the low hills, obviously seeking to drive him north.

The *Archer* appeared to be moving very little. As a result, its icon kept vanishing from the screen. Kai knew, both from the parting shot that had hit him and the way that warrior waited, that the pilot in that machine was cagey. That worried him because he knew the only way he would survive was by his enemies getting so cocky that they came at him using no strategy at all.

I wish I knew the access codes to some of Wolf's spy satellites. Rather have the feed from those than from this rockhound bird. Kai narrowed his eyes and took one last look at the weather report. "It's now or never," he told himself. "Last stand, part one."

Cutting east, he brought the *Daishi* up over a ridge line a little more than 250 meters from the *Archer* and almost twice that from Sun-Tzu's abandoned 'Mech. Standing on either side of it were 'Mechs Kai identified as a *Marauder II*—the bigger, nastier brother of one of the deadliest BattleMechs ever made—and a *Thunderbolt*. The *Marauder* shared the *Daishi*'s hunched frame, and clawlike weapon pods capped its skinny arms. The flight stabilizers marked it as jump-capable, but made it look no more graceful than its companion.

A desperate scheme popped into Kai's brain, and after a nanosecond's study of the primary monitor and its readout on his 'Mech, he decided to take the gamble. Even as the *Archer* twisted left and launched two missile flights, Kai brought his weapons to bear on the empty husk of Sun-Tzu's *Daishi*. "You're supposed to be a big killer, well, do it!"

The *Archer*'s missiles hammered the *Daishi* mercilessly. Red highlights dotted the right flank of his computer outline like spots on a leopard's pelt. The computer informed him of 40 percent reduced armor on his right arm, and a bloody circle showed where missiles had also destroyed armor on the 'Mech's foot. It again threw the gyro out of phase, but Kai wrestled the *Daishi* upright after a stumble and kept

162

his weapons on their mark.

The missiles from Kai's LRM launcher chipped armor from each flank. The large laser in his right arm melted more of the same on the 'Mech's right side. Having bracketed his true target, Kai corrected his aim by a millimeter for the left crosshairs, got a target lock pulse, then punched the thumb button and uttered a short prayer.

The computer tracked the Gauss rifle's ball straight to and through the blackened hole that used to be the *Daishi*'s cockpit. For a half-second, nothing happened, then the computer calculated the probable result of such a shot. The *Daishi*'s torso plumped as if pregnant, then exploded.

On the computer array, its left arm swung around and hit the *Thunderbolt* with the Gauss rifle. The rail gun's capacitors detonated, then a subsidiary blast from within the *Daishi* sprayed the *Thunderbolt* with shrapnel and Gauss rifle slugs. The *Daishi*'s body, reacting to the force of the explosion on its left side, teetered to the right, colliding with the *Marauder*.

Kai realized the computers must have cut power to the *Marauder*'s gyros and legs because it went down beneath the *Daishi*'s outline as though if it had been tackled. The *Thunderbolt* also fell and the computer quickly updated the 'Mech's status, reporting that the armor had been stripped from its right side. Looking closer, Kai saw that the 'Mech's head had been destroyed as far as the computer was concerned.

Acting on pure instinct, he sent the *Daishi* flying forward in fits and starts. The erratic pattern made the *Archer* miss with two volleys, yet kept his weapons dead on the tangled wreck of 'Mechs ahead of him. As he closed to less than 100 meters, Kai let the *Marauder* have a blast from the autocannon, and the computer showed the 'Mech's right leg amputated as a result of the attack.

Glancing at the earthquake display, Kai realized that neither the *BattleMaster* nor the other 'Mech had any way of knowing what had just happened. The *BattleMaster*'s companion had gotten 200 meters ahead of the larger 'Mech and was racing west, almost parallel with Kai's current position. Cutting south, Kai put a hill between him and the *Archer*, then raced into battle with the *BattleMaster*'s point man.

A *Hoplite*! Kai laughed cruelly as he intercepted the barrel-chested 'Mech at point-blank range. Built for scouting and support missions, the *Hoplite* was neither armored nor armed for an extended battle with an Omni like the *Daishi*. The pilot brought his autocannon to bear. The hail of metal it spat out shredded the armor on Kai's right leg, but failed to even slow him..

In reply, Kai let the *Hoplite* have everything but a barrage of missiles. The autocannon stripped the armor from its right flank, and the computer reported further internal damage. The Gauss rifle tore armor from the 'Mech's left leg, while the lasers worked on the right leg and left arm, shaving armor from both.

Sliding across Kai's approach path in a cloud of red dust, the *Hoplite* hit the ground and sprawled forward. Off to his left, Kai saw the *BattleMaster* enter the canyon the *Hoplite* had just traversed. Without a moment's hesitation, Kai dropped the left crosshair onto the *BattleMaster*'s gigantic silhouette and swung his right arm over to drop the laser's crosshairs onto the prone *Hoplite*.

The large laser's ruby beam lanced into the *Hoplite*'s right breast. On the computer projection, it melted away the *Hoplite*'s skeleton. As one of the trio of pulse lasers added stream after stream of staggered bolts to the area, the computer indicated damage to the *Hoplite*'s engine and gyro. The other two completed the destruction of armor on the *Hoplite*'s right leg.

Kai waited for the *BattleMaster* to bring its PPC up before he triggered the Gauss rifle. The blue bolt of artificial lightning arced through the canyon and slashed a jagged gash across the *Daishi*'s left thigh armor. The Gauss rifle, in return, smashed into the *BattleMaster*'s left fist, shattering armor and snapping off a finger.

Kai swung his *Daishi* around to bring all his weapons into line with the *BattleMaster*, and its pilot suddenly realized that his 'Mech was not well-suited to battle waged at a distance. Kai waited to see if the warrior would quickly reverse course or would resign himself to his fate and carry out a charge.

He charged.

The PPC hit the *Daishi* again. The blue beam melted a diagonal scar over the barrel of the Gauss rifle, but did no damage to its mechanism. Setting his 'Mech, Kai let the *BattleMaster* have it with his long-range weaponry.

A grouping of five missiles drilled into the *BattleMaster*'s chest, dropping shards of computer-drawn armor to the ground. The Gauss rifle's ball cored the missiles' fireball. The computer stripped layer after layer of armor from over the *BattleMaster*'s heart, but it showed plenty of armor still protecting the 'Mech's chest.

Missiles and the large laser were more effective on the 'Mech's left arm. The computer showed Kai's assaults had denuded the arm of shielding as the large laser's beam sawed through it. The computer's projection of myomer muscles snapped apart. The arm fell slack, nothing more than dead weight on the *BattleMaster*'s left side.

The assault 'Mech closed to within 100 meters and brought other weapons to bear in addition to its PPC. Kai watched his computer update the outline of the *Daishi* with new damage and grimly acknowledged the pilot of the *BattleMaster* as very good. The PPC slashed more armor from the Gauss rifle, but still failed to breach its protection. The four medium lasers, two each mounted in the left and right flanks of the *BattleMaster*, seared armor from the *Daishi*'s chest and right flank. One scarlet beam cut back across the *Daishi*'s left leg, combining with a PPC scar to mark the limb with an X.

Kai's eyes slitted as he centered his crosshairs on the *BattleMaster*. *I have got to end this now.* The gold dot in the center of the crosshairs flashed in fast syncopation with his heartbeat as he triggered all his weapons. The rush of heat vented into the cockpit threatened to overwhelm him, but he held the weapons on target.

Missiles chipped armor from the enemy 'Mech's left flank, left arm, and right leg, while only two of Kai's trio of pulse lasers hit their target. The first left a trail of six smoking holes in the armor over the *BattleMaster*'s midline. The second vaporized the ferro-titanium bones in its left arm, and the computer erased that limb from the 'Mech's outline.

The large laser's bloody beam swept out from the *Daishi*'s right arm muzzle, spearing straight into the *BattleMaster*'s blocky chest. The computer painted a heat glow over the damage to the 'Mech's chest, and Kai smiled. *That's damage to the engine. That monster's going to be running hot now.*

The autocannon in the left side of the *Daishi*'s chest sent out a stream of depleted-uranium phantom slugs and obliterated what little armor remained on the right arm. The computer showed the PPC disintegrating as the slugs punched through its housing. Myomer muscles parted easily and hung like frayed pieces of rope from the 'Mech's skeleton.

The lights in the cockpit dimmed as the Gauss rifle cut loose. Its sphere hit the *BattleMaster* in the shoulder socket and ricocheted into its left breast. Medium lasers exploded and their muzzles tipped toward the ground. The computer painted the 'Mech's outline with a series of subsidiary short-range missile explosions that shattered what little of the skeletal structure remained on that flank. In a burst of fire, the computer's image of the boxy SRM launcher on the *BattleMaster*'s shoulder vaulted into the air. The 'Mech's whole left side collapsed, and behind the computer projection, the actual machine crashed to the ground.

"Yes!" Kai slammed his right fist down on the command chair's arm. "Five down and one to go."

An inner voice reminded him, with chilling truth, that cockiness would kill him. He tried to ignore it, to let his emotions override it, but the more he tried to push the thought away, the stronger it became. *It's a game now, Kai, but what about when it's real?*

Kai snarled and looked at his secondary monitor. The *BattleMaster*'s fall had created enough of a seismic disturbance that the satellite failed to paint the *Archer*'s position until it took the last step into the canyon beyond the *BattleMaster*. Looking up, Kai spotted its squat form immediately. At just over 200 meters, it stood at its optimum range and flicked open the armored covers over the LRM launch tubes mounted on each shoulder.

Kai flicked a glance at the edge of his combat array, then at his primary monitor. *I've taken too much damage to engage it straightaway. If I run...No, I can't. But if I charge...*As he searched for a solution, the *Archer*'s first two flights scattered missiles all over the *Daishi*. They blasted its cylindrical chest and right flank, gouging deeper holes into the already pitted armor. A flight of five missiles completed the armor destruction job begun by the *BattleMaster* on the Gauss rifle, while five others tore sheets of armor flying from the *Daishi*'s left shin.

The computer snapped the gyro out of line for half a second, bringing Kai out of his deliberations. He kept the 'Mech upright, then started it hurling down the canyon at the *Archer*. Despite the bumpy ride and the leap over the fallen *BattleMaster*, Kai dropped his crosshairs onto the *Archer* and triggered only two weapons to keep the heat down.

The LRMs exploded like a string of firecrackers on the *Archer*'s chest, leaving an uneven line of craters on the computer image. More missiles tore at the armor on the 'Mech's left shoulder, but did little more than dent it. The Gauss rifle's projectile slammed into the *Archer*'s right arm, shivering off most of the armor from the computer projection. Yet it failed to do any serious damage.

Kai knew that much damage should have made the computer dephase the gyro, but if it had, the enemy pilot's sure hand on the controls had recovered without noticeable effect. *Why did I save the best pilot for last?*

The inner voice answered him. *Because you knew he would kill you.*

Kai ground his teeth. "I'm not dead yet!"

You are. You've just not acknowledged it.

The *Archer*'s missile barrage hammered him. More armor flew

166

from his chest, leaving his right flank open. Missiles blasted into the Gauss rifle, and Kai winced as he saw the weapon disappear. Even worse, he saw the left arm evaporate and damage appear on the outline of the 'Mech's skeleton.

Fighting the gyro decycle, Kai kept the *Daishi* rushing in at the *Archer*. Desperate, he dragged the crosshairs down onto the *Archer* and fired even before he had a confirmed weapons lock. The autocannon tore chunks of armor from the *Archer*'s leg, but failed to knock the 'Mech down. The trio of pulse lasers hit, with one melting away armor on the *Archer*'s right flank. The other two completed the destruction of the 'Mech's right arm that the Gauss rifle had begun. Myomers parted like smoke as the lasers pulsed into them, leaving the limb hanging like a wet rag and the medium laser a useless collection of lenses.

Kai smiled. "Got him!"

You know that's not nearly enough to stop him.

At closer range, the *Archer* only became that much more deadly. His missiles tore into the *Daishi* like piranha. They chewed away the last bits of armor on the Omni's right arm and took revenge for the loss of the *Archer*'s medium laser by destroying the *Daishi*'s main weapon. More important, the missiles devoured the right leg of Kai's 'Mech, weakening its muscles and skeleton enough that the next bone-jarring footfall snapped the limb like a rotten stick.

Kai's stomach rose to his throat as the computer cut the gyro. He struggled vainly against the controls, trying somehow to manhandle the Omni upright against the forces of gravity. His momentum kept the *Daishi* moving forward, so that it hit on its chin, bounced once, then slid along the canyon floor.

Sparks flew in the cockpit and Kai's chest ached from being thrown against the command chair's restraining straps. The computer's warning lights told him he could not eject, but that was no cause for panic. *If I never get out of here, it'll be too soon. How could I have been so stupid? Charging an* Archer. *I should have waited. I should have ambushed him somehow.*

You failed, Kai. You failed because you stopped to think and because you exulted in your victory. It was the moment you counted yourself a winner that you doomed yourself to defeat.

The voice was right. "When I act, somehow I manage to do the right thing. When I hesitate, when I wait and I over-think a problem, I screw up. This is it. This is the last time."

Kai nodded to himself in the fastness of his cockpit. *I've embarrassed myself and my family horribly in this defeat. Never again! I'll die before I let it happen again.*

Phelan Wolf set his face into a mask as unrevealing as those worn by the people assembled in the small reception room. He wore the snug-fitting gray leather pants and sleeveless jerkin they had given him, with the long cloak thrown back at each shoulder, bunching the wolf-fur that topped his shoulders and the back of the cloak. The silver knife he had received upon acceptance into the Warrior caste was thrust into his boot scabbard.

Gathered in the dim room were two score people, each wearing the formal leathers appropriate for a Clan Conclave. Each also wore an exquisitely worked wolf's-head mask that hid his or her features beneath its snarling expression. At one time, Phelan realized, he would have viewed this assembly as a fiercely hostile audience. *Now I am one of them.*

Looking around, he could not be certain of the identity of anyone there, though he assumed Evantha was among the Elementals gathered at the back of the hall. He was almost positive that two female Wolf MechWarriors standing together were Cyrilla and Ranna, and he guessed the stiff-backed man in front of them to be Vlad. He looked for Carew, but could not place him among the aerospace pilots crowded toward the front.

When one of the Wolves stepped forward, an overhead light flashed on to spotlight a crystalline podium on the dais at the far end of the room. Only when the Wolf who mounted the dais removed his mask did Phelan pierce the secret of his identity.

Ulric gripped the edges of the podium and began to speak. "I, Khan Ulric Kerensky, am the Oathmaster! All will be bound by this Conclave until they are dust and memories, and even beyond that until the end of all that is."

From the forty people gathered inside the room, Phelan heard one response, "Seyla."

"This night, it is our joy and honor to accept into the ranks of active MechWarriors one who has proven to be a fulfillment of Nicholas Kerensky's dream and one who was a foundling, but a foundling with a strong heart and vital spirit. We accepted him into the Wolf Clan as a bondsman, then welcomed him as a Warrior. Now he is to stand among us as a MechWarrior."

Ulric raised his right hand. "Phelan Wolf, the Conclave bids you forward."

Phelan held his head up as he marched down the aisle. The leathers clung to him like a second skin and he flushed slightly. Though he felt eyes boring into him, he did not turn his head to meet the gaze of those gathered around him. He knew they watched him to take his measure, for he was now a brother on whom they would come to depend.

Ulric gave him the barest of nods as Phelan stopped to the right of the podium. "Phelan Wolf, have you undergone the training and passed the testing required of those who wish to achieve MechWarrior status within the Wolf Clan?"

"As I have been instructed, I have, my Khan."

"Do you understand the rights and responsibilities of a Mech-Warrior within the Wolf Clan?"

"With my heart and soul, my Khan."

Ulric looked up. "Are these affirmations acceptable to the Conclave?"

"Seyla," whispered the Wolves.

"Very well." Ulric nodded to someone standing behind Phelan. "From this day forward, Phelan Wolf, you have all the rights and responsibilities, honors and duties attending to your status. Because you killed two 'Mechs during your test, you are eligible to join a combat unit at the rank of Star Commander. In fact, the commander of a line unit has already given you a place. Congratulations."

"It is my honor and my duty to serve to the best of my abilities."

A Wolf bearing a silver tray appeared at Phelan's left shoulder. From that tray, Ulric took a small lapel pin stamped with a symbol that the new MechWarrior instantly recognized . The design was the eight-pointed star with an elongated southern point, the one Phelan called a daggerstar. It marked him as a MechWarrior.

Ulric pinned it to the right breast of Phelan's tunic. "Let this symbol show the world what we have found in your heart and mind and soul."

The ilKhan then lifted the second item from the tray, and the aide withdrew. Cast in metal and decorated with enamels, the mask seemed possessed of a savage lupine spirit. Its white teeth stood out sharply against the glassy gray flesh of the muzzle, and the upthrust ears gave it a look of attentiveness. For a single moment, Phelan felt as though he were looking into a mirror, then Ulric settled the mask over his head.

Ulric turned him to face the assembly. "I give you Phelan of the Wolves and demand you recognize him as a MechWarrior."

"Seyla."

From within the mask's protective anonymity, Phelan felt fully one with the Clan. Some part of him remembered who he had once been, yet it no longer mattered. Phelan Kell had died during his transformation from bondsman to Warrior, and Phelan Wolf had taken his place. Still, until this time and this place, Phelan Wolf had been a creature of two worlds. With his acceptance by the Warriors, Phelan's integration of past and present began.

"Seyla," he said softly.

Ulric's aide pulled at Phelan's elbow and backed him to the dim edge of the circle of light. Without thinking, Phelan reached up his left hand to touch the pin. The cool metal felt good to his fingers, as though all his time and training were now distilled into this one symbol. *I am again a MechWarrior, and no one will take that away from me ever*.

Ulric leaned forward on the podium once more. "The Conclave bids forward a Warrior whose exploits are legend both within the Clans and in the Successor States. She left us almost fifty years ago, yet returns even more skilled than before her departure. In her testing, she accomplished what no other Warrior has ever done: she destroyed four opponents, killing Burke Carson. If anyone doubted the stories of her career in the Inner Sphere, that performance confirms their truth. Natasha Kerensky, come forward."

Phelan marveled at the woman striding down the aisle toward the podium. He knew, from the history of the Clans and Wolf's Dragoons, that she had to be at least seventy years old, but her leather-sheathed body didn't look a day over a young forty. Even more youthful than her form was Natasha's lightness of movement and confidence of bearing. Her spirit burned so brightly that it had kept her young, Phelan decided. *Young and so very dangerous.*

Natasha's leathers were black with red trim, a holdover from her days as a member of Wolf's Dragoons. On her right breast, she wore the red daggerstar she had earned even before Phelan's father had entered the Nagelring. At the waist of her tunic was emblazoned a red hourglass shape. *The Black Widow's mark.* He smiled slightly. *Natasha will never change.*

The ilKhan took the wolf mask that his aide handed him. It differed only from Phelan's in being black instead of gray. Ulric settled the mask on Natasha's shoulders, then presented her to the audience. "I give you Natasha Kerensky and demand you recognize her once again as a MechWarrior."

Phelan joined in as the others chorused, "Seyla."

As Natasha retreated to Phelan's side, Ulric addressed the crowd. "It is my duty to inform this Conclave that Natasha Kerensky's performance in the testing has forced reevaluation of some criteria we use in assigning duties. A person of her age is usually charged with raising a sibko and imparting her wisdom to the young. That is how it has been since the Clans were born, and we hold dear the tradition.

"Still, it is a practice that not all have found easy to accept. Warriors have pointed out that within the Scientist caste and other lower orders in our society, an individual's useful lifetime is measured in terms that make a Warrior's career appear like that of a mayfly. Some argue that those other pursuits are not as demanding of total mind-body integration as are our duties. However, until Natasha's recent testing, no assault had ever been mounted against it.

"Because of her exceptional scoring, the ilKhan has granted her an exceptional request. He agrees with her assessment that she has been a MechWarrior too long to easily accept 'herding crawler commandos.' She has been granted command of a Cluster that she will form from her own choice of Wolf Warriors. She has received the rank of Star Colonel and will remain in command until such time as she or the ilKhan decides that the Cluster is non-functional."

Ulric pulled himself up to his full height. "All are to abide by the rede given here. Thus it shall stand until we all shall fall."

"Thus it shall stand until we all shall fall," echoed the assembled Wolves. Their applause at the end of the ceremony made Phelan blush, but the sound trailed off quickly enough as the people filed out of the room. Cyrilla and Ranna, having removed their masks, fought through the crowd toward Phelan, while Ulric was shaking hands with the newly welcomed warriors.

"Congratulations, Natasha, Phelan." The ilKhan smiled warmly. "You both performed excellently in the testing yesterday. You, Natasha, turned many a head with those four kills to your credit. And Phelan, your stature grew for allowing Natasha that fourth kill."

Phelan pulled off his mask and shrugged. "Allow? I really did not have any choice. If she had not finished Vlad, he would have killed me."

Natasha, tucking her mask under her right arm, turned to him. "No, Phelan, Ulric does not mean 'allow,' as in present me the opening, but 'allow,' as in agreeing that I could take one of your kills. Had you not agreed to work together, I would not have shot at Vlad. Even though it might have been the cause of your death, I would not have dishonored you by robbing you of that kill. That, not the lack of skill, is the reason no one else has killed four 'Mechs in a test."

Cyrilla shook her head. "You underestimate your performance, Tasha. Many, many others have tried to bag a quartet. Two pilots agree to allow one another to shoot at their targets so that each has a chance of killing a fourth. The problem is that they end up trying to track more than just their enemies and they lose sight of their objective. They get shot out or even killed well shy of their allotted three, much less four."

"Perhaps," Natasha said, then looked over at Ulric. "I wish to thank you for giving me a Cluster. I know you told me it was my 'ransom,' but it is far more generous than I deserve."

Phelan frowned. "Ransom?"

Ulric smiled. "It is the custom among our people to grant a Warrior a gift upon achieving full status as an active Warrior. We refer to this as a 'ransom' because of the ancient tradition of a captor ransoming a Warrior after his capture." He glanced at Natasha. "Despite Natasha's protestations that my gift is too generous, the ilKhan is possessed of great wealth and may disburse it as he sees fit. Giving her a 'Mech Cluster should keep her so busy she will stay out of his hair."

The older man turned slightly to address Phelan. "I have a 'ransom' for you as well, Phelan. It reflects my great pride at seeing you qualify as a MechWarrior. It is also an inadequate token of my appreciation for all you have done for me. I cannot fully repay the debt I owe you for saving my life, but I trust this gift will make a dent in it. Ranna?"

Ranna slipped her left arm through Phelan's right and led him out of the room. As he started to ask where they were bound, she pressed a finger to his lips. "This is supposed to be a surprise, lover, so I'm not going to answer any questions."

She took him down the stairs and toward the south end of the building. As they neared the 'Mech bay, she took firm hold of his elbow. "Close your eyes."

"If I do that, I can't see."

"I'll tell you when to open them again."

He shut his eyes and felt her kiss each one of his eyelids. Yielding to the pressure on his arm, he let her guide him through the corridors. He knew they'd entered the 'Mech bay when the clicks of their heels echoed away to nothingness. The sharp scent of 'Mech coolant and the cloying odor of autocannon high explosives also clued him to their location, but he could not accurately gauge how far they had gone or where they were standing when they stopped.

Ranna squeezed his elbow once, then let go. "Open your eyes, Phelan."

It took a second or two for his eyes to focus within the dimly lit cavern of a room, then what he saw took his breath away and freed a thousand memories. His mouth dropped open and he fell to his knees.

The BattleMech standing in the berth before him rose to five times his height. From toes to throat, its slender, humanoid form suggested speed and agility. Its left arm ended in a fully articulated hand, but the right arm showed a laser muzzle where a hand would have been. The black 'Mech mounted three laser ports on its broad breast, two at the shoulders, and one dead-center.

The 'Mech's head looked like no other in the 'Mech bay. Its jutting muzzle, tall, pointed ears, and dark viewport eye-slits formed a perfect wolf's-head image, just like Phelan's ceremonial mask. Together they transformed the 'Mech from an oversized toy soldier into a mechanistic avatar of an ancient wargod.

Bright tints broke the 'Mech's somber color scheme in only three places. Phelan saw the hound's-head crest of the Kell Hounds painted in black on a circular red field on the 'Mech's right shoulder. The eyes of the hound had been painted green to match Phelan's. Opposite it, on the left shoulder, Phelan saw a red hourglass and realized immediately that it meant Natasha had chosen him to serve in her new unit.

Phelan smiled when he looked at the 'Mech's muzzle, which had been painted with long white fangs in a snarling face. It matched perfectly the design he'd used to decorate his last 'Mech. *That was over three years ago, back when I got myself expelled from the Nagelring and joined the Kell Hounds.*

Choking down the huge lump in his throat, he turned to Ranna. "This is *Grinner*. This is my *Wolfhound*. How is it possible? Vlad blew it to hell and back on Sisyphus's Lament when he captured me."

173

Ranna came to stand behind him, hands resting on his shoulders. "The head assembly formed your escape module. It contained the computer files we needed to reproduce the general design. Of course, we've modified it a bit."

Phelan frowned. "Modified it? That's one of the most modern designs in the Successor States."

Ranna patted his right shoulder. "True enough, but the technology used to put it together was old when the Star League fell apart. We replaced the skeleton with one made of an endo-steel alloy. It's a bit bulkier to stabilize in sheering-strength situations, but it's much lighter than the original internal structure. The power plant is brand new, and it provides the same power and speed at half the weight. The heat sinks built into it work at roughly double the efficiency of those you had before."

She hunkered down behind him and pointed over his shoulder. "The armor is made of a ferro-fibrous compound that is layered together and tempered to give it increased strength at a lighter weight. As a result, *Grinner* is carrying roughly 50 percent more armor than before. Your forward medium lasers have been replaced with the latest in pulse lasers. Both the large laser in the right arm and the medium in the back are now the extended-range variety so you can hit your foes further out. And your targeting system has been been adjusted accordingly."

She directed him to look at the 'Mech's head and ears. "The edging on the ears is part of an electronic countermeasures system that will make the 'Mech harder to spot and also able to jam many of the advanced targeting systems used nowadays. We wanted to mount an anti-missile system in there as well, but the engineers felt it would violate the original design objectives for a 'Mech that did not need to be supplied with ammo. If they get a laser-based system working, however, they're just aching to slap it on your machine."

Phelan stared at the machine as though it were a ghost from the past. "You don't know what seeing this does to me, Ranna. It reminds me of how much I've changed and how much I've lost. That 'Mech was part of Phelan Kell. To see it standing there leaves me in awe that the ilKhan did this for me. It also makes me wonder if I have not betrayed my people by abandoning them."

Ranna slipped her arms around his chest and gave him a squeeze. "Phelan, you should understand two things about the ilKhan. First of all, he began this reconstruction project even before you started training for your test. He was that confident in you and took great pride in your vindication of his judgement.

174

"More important than that, though, is that he asked me to say that he knew *Grinner* would rekindle memories of what you left behind in the Inner Sphere. He is glad of that because he does not *want* you to forget what you were. The Phelan Kell we captured is the basis for Phelan Wolf, a MechWarrior of the Clans. Because you have known life in the Inner Sphere and have been tempered by it, Ulric says you are stronger than Warriors who have known only the Clans."

Phelan nodded. "Perhaps he's right. Remembering who and what I was will make me stronger." He clasped her arms. "And it's strong warriors he'll need. Ulric the Warden becomes Ulric the Crusader and launches us back at the Successor States."

"That is true, Phelan, but do not mistake methods for ends." She settled her chin on his shoulder. "The only way Ulric can defeat the Crusaders is to beat them at their own game. As long as he is in the lead in our quest for the goal, he can dictate terms and rules. He'll need you and Natasha and the rest of us to keep that lead. It is up to us to make sure that our drive to win does not crush those whose only crime is inhabiting the worlds on our path."

Phelan straightened up, turned, and lifted Ranna to her feet. "Thank you for bringing me here. This is incredible. I must go and thank the ilKhan."

He started to walk off, but she grabbed his left hand and stopped him. "You can do that tomorrow."

"Tomorrow?"

"Yes, tomorrow," she said firmly. Ranna slipped one of his arms around her and kissed him on the cheek. "Tonight, my love, I want to give you another ransom." She nibbled at his earlobe. "It is a present I think you will enjoy unwrapping, and I do not think you want to delay getting it in any way."

Kai Allard cringed as his mother rose and cut her sister off in mid-tirade. "No more lies, Romano. I've seen you indulged and shielded your entire life. Even here, people have bent over backward to please you. For the sake of your pitiful forces, we've mollycoddled you and elevated you to a rank you could only deserve in your demented dreams. I will not sit here and listen to you slander my son."

Romano's green eyes sparked fire. "The she-bear rises to defend her cub! Cannot your son fight his own battles?"

Candace shook with rage. "He fights his own battles, and those of your son, as I recall. Your tale is absurd. Sun-Tzu punched out accidently after targeting one of my son's targets? Romano, even you were not that incompetent in a BattleMech. If your son is not an outright coward, he's a schemer who tried to engineer an embarrassing defeat for my son. Had Kai not proven himself worthy of the challenge, you'd be denouncing him as a failure. Because he won despite your son's trickery, you argue that he will lead your troops into untenable situations because he believes in his own invincibility."

Candace turned to face Jaime Wolf. "You were there, Colonel. Your *Archer* destroyed Kai's *Daishi*. Did you find him invincible?"

Romano's harsh laugh usurped Wolf's answer. "Dare you imagine, Candace, that your son could stand against the greatest warrior in the Inner Sphere? Even cheating as he did, he is not that good and you cannot be that arrogant!"

"Lady Romano, I am more than able to answer questions on my own," Wolf snapped irritably. "Kai Allard-Liao's actions speak for themselves. His use of the geological survey satellite feed was not cheating—it was incredibly resourceful. The first 'Mech he downed was piloted by his father, once the undisputed champion of Solaris VII. The *BattleMaster* he destroyed had Hanse Davion as its pilot. My son MacKenzie and Christian Kell were at the controls of the *Marauder* and *Thunderbolt* he took down. Sven Ngov, one of my better Dragoons, piloted the *Hoplite*. Acting alone, Kai Allard-Liao used his head and took down five of the best MechWarriors the Successor States have ever seen."

Wolf looked over at Kai. "And it was by no means assured that I would not be his sixth victim. One more exchange and I might have turned the Dragoons over to his lead."

Feeling all eyes on him, Kai looked around self-consciously. His father and Hanse Davion were smiling proudly. Theodore Kurita and Hohiro acknowledged his warrior skill with simple nods. Victor, Cassandra, and Ragnar wore big grins and Prince Magnusson seemed to be wishing he could clone a hundred of him. Thomas Marik, on the other hand, seemed to watch him warily, and Romano's savage stare threatened to burn holes through him.

Sun-Tzu was the only one who refused to look at Kai.

Romano pulled herself erect. "So this is it, then? You all unite against me! Very well. I shall deal with the Clans when they set foot in my realm, and not before." With that, she turned on her heel and stalked from the room. Stunned, the rest of her entourage followed slowly. Kai noticed Isis Marik watching Sun-Tzu intently, and he saw his cousin nod to her as he walked past.

Wolf waited for Romano to fully exit the council chamber, then addressed Thomas Marik. "Well, Captain-General? I would not characterize you as Romano Liao's ally in all this, but you have been closer to her than any others. Will you leave us, too?"

Thomas Marik rose slowly, revealing his sickly little boy seated behind him. The dark circles under the boy's eyes mirrored his father's haggard expression. "Colonel, I do not dispute or question the bravery of Kai Allard. Though I do not have Lady Romano's objections to the suggested plan, I do have my own reservations. I cannot fail to recognize our common threat, but I am uneasy about putting your new 'Mech weaponry into production within the Free Worlds League. You want me to export ninety percent of what we produce to the Federated Commonwealth and Draconis Combine."

Wolf frowned. "That is now a problem? I thought we had

177

agreed…"

"In principle, yes." Marik sighed wearily. "However, my advisors have pointed out that payment for these parts is to be made on a long-term schedule, the last not due until 3110. How can I ask my people to approve that agreement when neither the Draconis Combine nor the Federated Commonwealth might survive that long?"

Theodore Kurita gave Marik a withering stare. "Captain-General, if we do not get the field modification kits, it is you who carve our epitaphs. If we do have them, we can throw the Clans back."

Thomas raised his hands. "Kanrei, I understand the trap of circular logic, but I cannot be certain my enemies will see it the same way. My nation is a democracy, not a dictatorship. I cannot…"

"Bah!" barked Hanse Davion. "You could impose those production quotas using the powers of the Emergency Action Laws enacted after your father's assassination. Do not use the excuse of politics to justify your refusal. You mean to gouge more out of us, more worlds and more technology."

The Captain-General struck an air of noble innocence. "Far be it from me to use this crisis as a means of ransoming your freedom. However, some immediate and material gains for the Free Worlds League would make it easier to justify this agreement to my people."

Hanse shot to his feet. "Cut to the chase, Thomas. You will make our equipment as long as we give you something, right?"

"If you choose to see it that way."

"I do." Though Hanse had his back to Kai, the young MechWarrior could easily imagine the Prince's expression as he hunched forward. "Very well, Captain-General, I will give you something no one else can. I will give you your son's life."

All color drained from Marik's face. "What?"

"You heard me. The New Avalon Institute of Science knows no equal in the Inner Sphere for its medical research. Candace Liao, for example, successfully battled breast cancer at the NAIS a half-dozen years ago. Since then, our oncology researches have proved very promising in cases of leukemia, even in advanced cases such as your son's. Give me—give us—our weapons and I will give you your son."

The Captain-General of the Free Worlds League leaned heavily on his table, then looked back at his son. The boy gave his father a brave grin, but even that effort seemed to fatigue him. Thomas reached back to rub his hand affectionately over the boy's bald head.

He turned back to Hanse Davion and Kai saw tears streaking his face. "You would use the life of a sick child against me? If I don't agree, you will consign my son to death?"

Hanse nodded solemnly. "Yes! As readily as you would consign our sons to death without those 'Mechs. I'm not out to win a Peace Prize and I don't care how history remembers me. All I care about now is ensuring that there *will* be people who can remember. This effort may be futile, but it would be criminal cowardice not to make it."

Hanse's voice softened slightly. "If bargaining for your son's health is the only way to communicate to you the urgency and gravity of this situation, then so be it. I regret it comes to this."

Shaken, Thomas Marik sagged down into his chair. "How soon can the treatments begin?"

"I have a command circuit of JumpShips linking me with New Avalon. It will take three days to get Joshua up to the ships, and then less than a week to get him to New Avalon. Your wife can accompany him, as may your doctors. They will be provided housing, security, and complete anonymity."

"Then you shall have your machinery." Thomas fixed Hanse with an unforgiving stare. "I entrust my son to you because I cannot deny him a chance at life. I give you your war toys because it is true that your son deserves the chance you are giving to mine. Do not imagine, though, that this makes us friends or allies. I will not forget— I cannot let myself forget—that you are the devil incarnate."

Hanse made no reply as he sat down, but Kai read a look of grim satisfaction on the Prince's face. Melissa reached out for her husband's hand. "Can they save Joshua?" she whispered.

The Prince of the Federated Commonwealth shrugged slightly. "They will do what they can, everything they can, just as I have done." His blue eyes darkened. "It will have to be enough."

Hanse's words set Kai to deep reflection. *Could I ever find it in myself to be that confident?* he wondered. *Then again, if I have to sacrifice so much of my humanity, would I want such confidence?*

Jaime Wolf spoke slowly, his voice low, in keeping with the somber mood that had fallen over the chamber. "It is good that we have reached an agreement concerning the OmniMechs because the exercise evaluators have completed the review of the training cadre's performance. As all but one of its members are here, I will take this opportunity to announce their scores. A perfect score on this exercise was 300 and could be obtained by 100 percent destruction of three foes, with no damage to the 'Mech of the pilot being tested."

Wolf smiled cryptically. "It should come as no surprise that Kai Allard-Liao scored highest in the exercise. He ended up with a score of 445 points, based on 520 points for the damage he did, less the 75 percent destruction of his 'Mech. To my knowledge, this high a score has never been achieved anywhere, within the Clans or here on Outreach. That he achieved it fighting against such tough opponents only makes it the more impressive.

"Hohiro Kurita earned a score of 255, to come in second. Victor Davion scored 235. Galen Cox and Shin Yodama scored 195 and 193, respectively. Cassandra Allard-Liao scored 189 and Ragnar Magnusson scored 157."

Wolf raised one eyebrow. "And because you will ask, Sun-Tzu Liao ended up with a score of minus 62 points.

"Because of their scores, Kai and Hohiro will be given *Daishi* chassis OmniMechs to configure in whatever manner they choose. We all agreed that it was important for the sons and daughters of the Inner Sphere's royal houses to present a united front, and these scores and performances seem to auger well for the chances of an alliance that can defeat the Clans."

Kai felt his mouth go dry as he stood up. "Excuse me, Colonel Wolf."

"Yes?"

He swallowed hard. "I am honored to be given an OmniMech, but I must refuse it."

Victor shook his head. "No, Kai, don't do this for me. You won it fair and square, and Hohiro blew past the mark I set."

Kai forced himself to smile. "Victor, though we are friends, I would not sacrifice a *Daishi* to soothe your feelings. It's too fine a machine to let go so easily." Kai looked back to Wolf. "Colonel, I already have a 'Mech that I wish to pilot in battle. It was my father's, the same one that took him to the pinnacle on the Game World and that saw him through desperate battles in the last war. In that 'Mech, he carried my mother from the Capellan homeworld."

He looked down, avoiding Wolf's probing stare. "For this reason, I ask you to let another pilot have the OmniMech you so kindly wish to award me. *Yen-lo-wang* safeguarded my father and mother in most dangerous times. It will do the same for me."

Jaime Wolf nodded slowly. "As you wish, Leftenant Allard. Your *Daishi* will be assigned to Victor Davion. Whatever I might think of your decision, no warrior could deny your request."

Wolf shifted his gaze to Hanse's son. "Victor Davion, you have here a friend more valuable than all the worlds in the Inner Sphere. By stepping down, he allows you and Hohiro Kurita to remain on equal standing with one another. Let this selflessness be a reminder of the kind of deeds that may yet be necessary if this alliance is to endure and be victorious."

ComStar First Circuit Compound, Hilton Head Island
North America, Terra
17 September 3051

Primus Myndo Waterly smiled as Precentor Tharkad grew angrier. "Calm yourself, Ulthan. This is not the First Circuit. I do not need your histrionics, nor am I obliged to tolerate them here in my quarters." She pointed beyond him to the Precentor from the Draconis Combine. "Why can't you maintain your composure, as does Sharilar?"

The purplish hue of Ulthan Everson's beefy face did not look terribly healthy, but the color began to return to normal as he looked first at Myndo, then back at Sharilar Mori. "Why can't I be more like her? Because I was not raised in the repressive samurai society that produced her *or* you, Primus. Precentor Dieron might be able to hide her emotions, but how could she not feel the same outrage?"

Thick white eyebrows bunched like clouds over his blue eyes. "Just how long have you known the Clans were planning to resume their invasion of the Inner Sphere?"

Myndo shrugged, then tugged the golden pleats of her silk robe back into their proper position. "I have always known they would resume the war, Ulthan. We all have. As for knowledge that they were actually returning, I suppose I learned in early July that they had elected a new ilKhan. It seemed obvious that they would start their return shortly after that."

Ulthan Everson blinked his eyes in amazement. "You've known

for two months, but this is the first you've thought to tell us of it?"

Myndo's dark eyes glittered like black pearls. "Until the actual return, I did not believe it was necessary to bother you with such things. You have enough on your hands administering the areas the Clans have already conquered. Even now, the Precentor Martial is on his way to meet them, and he will report to me as needed.

"By the way, Ulthan, I was most pleased with the upswing in the popularity of our Blessed Order in the occupied worlds of the Federated Commonwealth. You have done well."

Sharilar pressed her delicate hands together. "Primus, I believe Precentor Tharkad wished to learn of the return as early as possible to make certain the Clans will find no fault with our policies. I share this concern because a new ilKhan could easily decide not to continue the liaison with us, robbing us of the chance to spread the Word of Blake among the masses."

Bright girl, so like me at her age. Myndo smiled indulgently at the woman who had assumed the Precentorship she had held before her accession to Primus. "This was a dilemma I foresaw long ago. However, the new ilKhan is Ulric of the Wolves. In the past, he was quite eager to use our people to pacify and administer the worlds he took, so I assume he realizes the benefits of alliance with us."

The Primus smiled coldly as she watched Precentor Tharkad pace impatiently before her. "I think, Sharilar, that Ulthan has another objection to my tardiness in informing him of the Clans' return. You still do not like my policy of working with the Clans, do you, Ulthan?"

The Precentor from Tharkad stopped short and shook his head. "Not one bit. We know virtually nothing about these Clans. They are supposed to be the remnants of General Kerensky's Star League army, but we have no actual proof that is true."

"But neither do we have reason to doubt their pedigree."

"Don't we, Primus? Kerensky left the Inner Sphere to avoid war. If they were his heirs in philosophy as well as blood, why are they returning in such an aggressive manner? They seem more the heirs to a thousand Periphery raiders than to one so noble as Kerensky."

"An interesting point, Ulthan, but it is utterly immaterial." Myndo lowered herself into the backless U-shaped chair by the semi-circular window and spread her skirts out into a golden fan. "The Clans are returning. We are letting them shatter this fledgling renaissance so we may bring the true order Jerome Blake directed us toward three hundred years ago. When the Clan invaders have exhausted themselves, we will lead a revolution that liberates those they have captured. It is a simple plan, but it will work."

Ulthan's head came up. "But you will not allow us to warn the people of the Inner Sphere that their year of peace is at an end?"

Myndo waved that away as though it were an annoying fly. "Why should I? Their own agents on the captured worlds can get the word out in some manner."

"But Primus," Sharilar put in, "if ComStar is not providing transmission of those messages, the only way the leaders will hear of the return is when more worlds fall."

"True, Precentor Dieron. Quite true." Myndo took in a deep breath. "Pity they weren't watching their borders instead of chattering away on Outreach, isn't it? By late next month, they should know of the return. I can't wait to see what their response will be."

"Neither can I." Ulthan clasped his hands behind his back and stared out the window. "Of their reaction, this I do know: it will be the best and most cunning thing you or I can imagine. There is an outside chance, Primus, that you have decided to back the wrong horse in this race. If so, you can expect from Hanse Davion and Theodore Kurita all the help you have shown them."

Myndo threw back her head and laughed aloud. "That, Precentor Tharkad, is something I shall remember when I am dancing on both their graves."

Kai felt a shiver run down his spine as his father led him wordlessly through the dark corridors leading to the Dragoons' 'Mech bay. "Is something wrong, father?"

Justin stopped and rested both his hands on his son's shoulders. "Wrong? No, Kai, nothing is wrong. If I am quiet, it is my preoccupation with all that is happening. I'm afraid my mind is off wondering about the Kurita ship that just showed up in the system and the message they beamed to Outreach. We intercepted it, of course, but our crypto section is having no luck cracking the code."

Kai felt the heavy weight of his father's mechanical left hand on his right shoulder. "I was afraid I had done something to upset you."

Justin laughed and dragged his son forward into a hug. "I don't know what made you think that, but nothing is further from the truth. You have done nothing but make your mother and me proud. Perhaps I don't say it enough, but I love you very much, and any father who says he is more proud of his son is a liar."

Kai wanted to say a million things in response, but the lump in this throat effectively blocked the words. He embraced his father tightly, desperately relishing the little-boy sense of security it gave him. He swallowed hard and fought to keep a waver out of his voice. "You know I would never do anything to bring shame on you or Mother, don't you?"

Justin held Kai out at arm's length. "If I were keeping a balance sheet, even one entry in the negative column would go unnoticed. Kai, you are everything your mother and I wanted to be when we became MechWarriors. You are a thoughtful leader and a damned fine warrior. When I'm your grandfather's age, I'll be telling all my friends that yes, once, a long time ago, I could beat you in simulator battles."

Kai saw the mirth in his father's eyes and the laughter in his voice, but still could not fully believe it. "Then you are not angry that I shot you out first in the test?"

Hanse Davion's Secretary of Intelligence threw his head back and laughed heartily. "Angry? God no. I knew I was your logical first target, and I told both Hanse and Jaime that I'd be down first." He threw his son a wink. "Hanse said I had more important work to do off the testing field, so he didn't let me hide behind his *BattleMaster*."

"And you weren't angry about my declining an OmniMech?"

"No." Justin paused, brushing a hand over his eyes. "In fact, your choice of *Yen-lo-wang* honored me more than you will ever know. That 'Mech was my lifeline on Solaris, on Bethel, and on Sian. There is no other pilot in the Inner Sphere that I would prefer—that I would allow—to take *Yen-lo-wang* into battle."

He pointed toward the 'Mech bay with his artificial hand. "That is even more true now than ever."

Kai frowned. "What do you mean?"

Justin said nothing and led his son into the 'Mech bay. This portion of the huge hangar was cordoned off with thick curtains hanging down from the girders overhead. Kai knew this was the section of the 'Mech bay where repair and refit work was done on BattleMechs, but he had no idea why *Yen-lo-wang* might be here. Last he knew, the modified *Centurion* was insystem, but no one had used it, much less damaged it.

As he stepped through some scaffolding, Kai saw Hanse Davion speaking with another man. That man stood only waist-high to the Prince and wore his graying hair down to his shoulders. His small, stubby-fingered hands were fitted with waldo-devices to extend his reach and strengthen his grip. As Kai entered the clear space at the *Centurion*'s feet, the little man appraised him with a quick glance, then smiled roguishly.

"So you're the one who's forced me into this hurry-up job, eh?" His brown eyes twinkled impishly. "Are you worth it?"

Hanse Davion answered for Kai. "He is, Clovis. Worth it and more."

The Prince looked over at Kai. "Leftenant Kai Allard-Liao, this

185

is Clovis Holstein. Clovis, this is the finest MechWarrior of his generation. Excepting perhaps present company, he could be the finest MechWarrior since Aleksandr Kerensky left the Inner Sphere."

The dwarf raised an eyebrow and whistled long and low. "Quite a billing, but it fits with everything else I've heard."

Kai blushed deep red. "The Prince is too kind."

"Hope not. I've put a lot of work into refitting your tin beastie here, and I want to be sure it'll be in good hands."

Kai looked up at the towering war machine. Humanoid in configuration, its right arm had a gun muzzle at the wrist, but Kai knew it now housed a weapon other than its former heavy autocannon. The left arm ended in a hand, but Kai saw two laser muzzles mounted on the underside of the forearm, where no weapons had been before. A glance at the Mech's smoothly armored chest told him that one of the lasers had been moved from its mount in the center torso. The head remained unchanged, with the Romanesque helmet sensor array that gave the 'Mech its name intact.

Clovis grinned. "All right, kid, you've spotted the two lasers on the left arm. Those are Spitfire pulse lasers. We moved the one in the center of the *Centurion* to the arm, added another, and packed three heat sinks into that assembly to bleed off their added heat."

"Do I still have the laser that covers my back?"

"Still there, though it's also been upgraded to a Spitfire." Clovis pointed at the *Centurion*'s right arm. "We swapped out the Pontiac 100 autocannon and replaced it with a Von Ryan Rail Gun. The ammo is stored in the right side of the 'Mech's chest and the feed mechanism is all magnetic. If you lose power to the feed system and you want to lean heavily to the side, you can probably use gravity feed to pump a round into the chamber, but that's not one hundred percent."

Kai chewed on his lower lip. "Can I muzzle-load it?"

Clovis looked surprised. "Yeah, if ammo's spilling out of your side, you could muzzle-load it. It'll shoot anything that magnets can jet along, though your average girder has lousy ballistic qualities and is likely to damage the bore. Again, using non-reg ammo is only for desperate situations."

"Got it."

The dwarf clapped his hands together in a clash of metal. "The real prize is inside. We stripped the old engine out and put in an extra-light Miata 200. It'll kick out the same amount of energy you're used to, but it's lighter. We needed that weight savings because your 'Mech's been fitted with experimental myomer fibers. They are much stronger than normal—roughly triple-strength—but have some unusual properties."

Kai glanced at his father. "Are these the same ones you tricked House Liao into using? Do they still burn in the presence of a particular chemical agent?"

"No." Justin folded his arms across his chest. "That formula has been heavily modified in the past twenty years. We now have a 3X fiber that won't burn, though it has only a narrow range of operation."

Clovis continued the explanation. "What you have are muscles that only pick up their extra strength when heated. Their operational range just begins as they edge into the yellow range on your heat monitors. Below that, they're normal. In the yellow, they increase your speed and strength."

Kai frowned. "But running that warm will affect my ability to target enemies."

"It does cook the targeting circuits a bit." Clovis pointed again at the laser assembly on the left arm. "You'll find a switch in the cockpit that pulls those three heat sinks offline. That will help boost your temp almost immediately. You can shut down more to do it faster, and I'll help you rig a switch to do so if you want, but the increase in strength will be a great help if the fighting gets close and nasty."

Kai looked from Clovis to his father and Hanse Davion. All three men grinned when they saw how overwhelmed he was. "I don't know what to say. You made these modifications just for me?"

Justin shrugged. "More or less. Clovis wanted to show off the triple myomers, and because of *Yen-lo-wang*'s days on Solaris, it had all the diagnostic circuitry already built. When you passed up an Omni in favor of *Yen-lo-wang*, the Prince ordered the other modifications."

Hanse nodded. "Because you deserve the best 'Mech possible when out there and because you're in my son's command. Victor gets reckless, and even though Hauptmann Cox does an excellent job keeping an eye on him, I want someone else out there I can trust with his life."

"Kai Allard-Liao is a wise choice for that job, Prince Davion."

Kai spun at the sound of another man's voice behind them, his hands reflexively coming up into a position to fend off an attack and deliver a counterstrike. He forced them down and bowed. "*Konnichiwa*, Gunji-no-Kanrei."

Theodore Kurita solemnly returned the bow. "And to you, Leftenant. My agents have reported the nature of your new 'Mech and I envy you."

Hanse's blue eyes narrowed. "Is there something I can do for you, Theodore?"

The Kanrei reached into a pocket of his robe and withdrew a sheet of paper. "I thought, Hanse, that you would be interested in the news that the Clans have begun their return." He handed the sheet to Justin. "This is a condensed version of the message my ship sent this morning. It's not literal enough to let you crack our code, but it contains all the necessary data. The Clans have elected a new ilKhan. He is apparently the leader of the Wolves. As they have been the most militarily successful Clan thus far, I suspect this means the war will now resume."

Hanse looked at Justin. "Confirm or deny?"

"I can do neither, Highness. Our agents on the border worlds report no attacks. And agents we may or may not have on the occupied worlds have not been able to report to us. I do not know if they are still alive, or if ComStar is merely holding up their communications. Neither have our ships probing the territories had time to report back in any great detail."

Hanse's lips formed a grim line. "This is sooner than I would have hoped. It will take another year for Thomas Marik to bring his factories online with total production."

Theodore nodded. "I have taken the step of ordering a number of factories to turn out field modification packages. As we repair and refit, we can use new components to rebuild our 'Mechs."

"Agreed." Hanse gave Theodore a grin that reminded Kai of Hanse's longtime nickname of "the Fox." "My compliments to your spy for getting you the information so soon."

The Kanrei returned the grin. "I will communicate your praise to our network. We believe the assaults will begin again by October's end. That gives us six weeks to prepare our defenses."

"I don't suppose this new ilKhan would favor giving us more time." Hanse rested his hands on his hips. "Again, thank you for letting me know about this."

"There is another matter we should discuss," Theodore said quietly. "It concerns Victor and Omi." Hanse looked at Clovis and Kai, but Theodore indicated with a wave of the hand that they might remain. "According to ISF files, Clovis Holstein can be trusted with a secret, and Kai is already aware of the situation. In fact, the reason I come to speak to you is because of something he said to my son."

Clovis cracked a grin. "The easiest way to keep a secret is to not know it. Gotta go anyway. Promised my wife I'd meet her fifteen minutes ago."

Hanse dismissed Clovis with a nod, then shook his head in mild disbelief. "Your daughter and my son becoming friends. Who would have believed it?"

"Shakespeare?" Justin offered casually.

Everyone laughed briefly, then sobered as their initial embarrassment wore off. "I have spoken with Omi about her friendship with your son. Apparently, they are only friends, not yet lovers. She has obediently offered to break off all communication with Victor and to atone for any dishonor her actions may have brought to House Kurita."

Theodore's blue eyes flicked at Kai. "That is exactly what I would have required if Hohiro had not told me of his conversation with Kai. Kai believes that my daughter and your son offer one another an otherwise nonexistent opportunity of spending time with a peer. It is true that they cannot simply be themselves with most people they encounter. I managed it, but only because my father all but disowned me. That freed me to meet a woman with whom I fell deeply in love."

Hanse's eyes focused distantly and a smile tugged at his lips, then he returned just as swiftly to the here and now. "Though I gained my bride in different circumstances, I have found with her a deep union beyond title or bloodline. There were thousands of women more than willing to bear Davion heirs, but only one I wanted."

"Yes." Theodore looked a bit uncomfortable. "And if your wife is the least bit like mine, she will make you pay dearly if we interfere in this budding relationship."

Hanse sighed heavily. "I'd rather spend a day with Romano Liao than a minute with Melissa if she were to get wind that I'd done something to cause a break between Victor and Omi. If Victor is happy, so is she."

"But we both agree that it would be a disaster if they fell in love. We could never allow their union to be consummated or legitimized."

"Absolutely not!" Hanse massaged his forehead with his left hand. "The Draconis March would figure it was Victor's brideprice gift to you, and the religious nightmares of such a wedding would be the death of me."

"There is a silver lining to the idea," Kai offered. Hanse and Theodore looked at him with surprise. "Considering what happened at the last big state wedding, at least you know Romano Liao wouldn't show up."

Hanse and Theodore looked at one another, then broke out laughing. Justin chuckled, too, but shook his head reprovingly at his son. Kai waited for the laughter to die. "I am not trying to speak for Victor," he said, "but I know him pretty well. I can assure you, Kanrei, that he has nothing but the utmost respect for Omi. Given half a chance, I know he could fall for her, but it isn't a very realistic possibility. The two of them getting together would certainly strengthen the united front we want to present the Clans, but I would agree that such a union would prove internally divisive. The point is, they're not going to have any more time together after we all leave this planet. They'll probably exchange holodisks and personal confidences if you'll allow it, but I think both are more than aware of the futility of their situation."

Hanse weighed Kai's words carefully. "You're saying that they have chosen not to let the hopelessness of their situation spoil their friendship here?"

"That's what I think. When are they ever likely to meet one another again face to face?"

Theodore shook his head. "In all likelihood, never." He looked at Hanse. "I am not adverse to allowing our children to continue their acquaintance. Shall we allow them to correspond?"

"Knowing how it feels to get any mail at all at the front, I would be most pleased if Omi wished to communicate with my son. I see no difficulty with that." Hanse paused, again seeming to gaze into some other time, either distant past or future. "Ah, Theodore," he said finally, "can you imagine, a Davion-Kurita wedding?"

"It would be a Kurita-Davion wedding, Prince Davion," Theodore laughed. "Your Draconis March would secede and my father would have me assassinated." His smile turned rueful. "But who knows, if the Clans do us enough damage, we might just have to let fate play its part and let our children pick up the pieces."

Wolf's Dragoons General Headquarters, Outreach
Sarna March, Federated Commonwealth
23 September 3051

Victor Davion smiled broadly to see her slipping into the night-shrouded garden. "*Komban-wa*, Omiko-*san*."

"*Arigato gozaimas*, Victor-*san*." She lowered her eyes and bowed to him. "Your Japanese has so improved."

"I've had an excellent teacher and more than enough motivation to study hard." She started to blush and look away, but he reached out and gently took her chin in his right hand. "I say that not to flatter you, but because it is true."

She took his hand in hers and kissed the palm. "I have had a most willing student." Omi looked up abruptly as a distant roar intruded on the stillness of the garden, overpowering the whirring of crickets. Then the night sky lit up as a bulbous metal form rose slowly on a brilliant torch. The DropShip's flame burnished golden highlights onto Omi's smooth skin and hair.

"The only way I could come to the garden unescorted was because my ISF chaperone believes you are aboard that ship. Until I got your note, I thought we would have no chance to say goodbye." She looked at Victor warily. "From your father, you have inherited the cunning of the Fox, and from your cousin Morgan, you inherit the courage of the Lion. Won't there be trouble when they find you are not onboard the ship?"

Victor shook his head. "No. Kai convinced the pilot that he and

I had to attend a last-minute briefing. He's off saying goodbye to his family and I am here with you. We'll take a shuttle up and reach the ship in a half a day."

"How fortunate to have such a resourceful friend."

"He's not the only friend I'm lucky to have." Victor sighed heavily. "I suppose your father spoke to you about us, as my father did with me?"

She nodded solemnly, and Victor was glad she had let her black hair hang down over the shoulders of her green silken kimono. "My father tried to be most reasonable. He told me we might communicate with one another, but I suspect he gave in on that point because he knew he could not stop us. He seems terrified that you and I would fall in love."

Victor grinned unabashedly. "That's roughly the same read I got from my father. Kai says they joked about a romance and possible marriage between us. But he also said that despite their dread of the political problems, it seemed that either one would cut off his own arm before causing his child unhappiness."

Omi's eyes half-shut. "So, Victor Davion, are we falling in love?"

Victor started to speak, then clamped his mouth shut. Omi intrigued him more than any woman ever had and he also found her immeasurably desirable. *But is this love, or am I infatuated because I can never have her?* He looked down. "Omi-*san*," he teased, "perhaps I'll be the last to know."

He brought his eyes up to meet hers. "I do care for you, very deeply. Part of me wants to say I love you, but I don't know if I have the strength to shoulder all that would imply. I'm also afraid that if I said yes, and we were to become lovers, I would lose you as a friend."

Omi smiled tenderly at that. "Your confusion mirrors mine. I know that part of your allure is a fascination with the forbidden. But you also have great heart and a quick mind. You are not afraid to say what you think and you do not suffer fools who seek you out because of your title. These qualities I rarely see beyond my family in the Draconis Combine, and that is why I think I could be very happy with you as either friend or lover.

"But, as you say, to fall in love would also present us with a whole host of problems."

"Your grandfather would refuse to come to the wedding and mine would be spinning in his grave! Ryan Steiner would accuse me of selling Skye to the Combine and the Draconis March would try to join with Free Rasalhague so I'd not cede half of it to your father."

192

Her laughter buoyed Victor's spirits. It was so easy to be with her and talk to her in a way that would shock others who would take these matters oh-so-seriously. In public, he could start a war by saying that he thought Sun-Tzu Liao was an ass, but with Omi he risked no such interstellar incident. And if not for her, he'd never have come even close to beginning to understand Hohiro.

Omi coiled a lock of dark hair around her finger. "Any pregnancy would have to produce twins and we would have to say they were both born at the same time or risk a war over which child was heir to which throne. It would be a nightmare."

"Not a path to be taken lightly."

Before she could reply, another voice pierced the night. "Omi?"

Recognizing it instantly as Hohiro's, Victor sank back into the shadows. The lights from the building silhouetted Omi's brother as she turned to face him. "*Hai*, Hohiro-*san*?"

"Oh, you are alone." Hohiro looked around, but gave no sign he saw anything amiss. "I came looking for you because I saw Kai Allard down near the shuttle bay. He had been forbidden to leave the shuttle area so he asked me to seek out a friend of his. Kai said they had been 'busted' and faced serious disciplinary action if they did not report to their ship immediately."

Victor knew Hohiro addressed his sister in English for his benefit. Omi obviously understood this, too, because she replied, "I think, if he were here, Kai's friend would thank you very much. If I see Kai's friend, I will pass the message on to him."

"Good, I would not like to see him in trouble. You might add that I, Hohiro Kurita, am betting him ten ounces of gold per enemy 'Mech that I claim more enemy kills than he."

Victor almost stepped from the shadows to accept that wager, but Omi raised her hand to stop her brother's words. "And I tell you, Hohiro, that I would be most saddened if either one of you died because of such a bet. You wager far more than gold in this war against the Clans. It is the future of the Inner Sphere that is at stake. Work together as you have here, and we all shall win."

Hohiro gave his sister a short bow of respect, then retreated from the garden. Omi waited for the sound of his footsteps to fade away, then turned back to Victor. "You heard?"

Victor abandoned his shadowy sanctuary. "Yes. I have to go."

"Wait." From around her neck, Omi pulled an oval-shaped piece of bronze on a leather thong. She held it out to Victor. In the half-light, he saw Japanese symbols and realized it was a dragon biting its own tail. The center of the bronze had a square hole in it, through which the thong had been looped to let the medallion hang lengthwise, but Omi slipped it off the leather before placing it in Victor's hands.

"This is a swordguard, isn't it?"

"*Hai*." Omi nodded. "It and a swordsman's skill are all that saves him from an enemy. You have the skills of a warrior, but I want you to have this, too."

"*Domo arigato*." Victor smiled and slipped it into his pocket. "I will keep it with me." He shrugged helplessly. "I regret that I have nothing to give you."

She reached out and caressed his right cheek. "Give me your promise that you will be safe."

"That is the one thing I *cannot* promise you," he said.

Her voice returned stronger. "Give me your promise and it will be so."

Victor stepped closer and slipped his arms around her slender waist. "Yes, Omi, I promise."

His mouth found hers, and though their kiss was brief, the warmth of it stayed with Victor long after he had left the garden and Outreach and Omi behind.

26

DropShip Dire Wolf, Nadir Jump Point
Engadin, Wolf Clan Occupation Zone
15 October 3051

Phelan Wolf heard a hiss as the ComStar shuttlecraft cracked its hatch. The boxy yellow ship had touched down lightly in a shuttle bay manned by Elementals in their armor. Once the *Dire Wolf*'s hatch was secured, the Techs provided the bay with a breathable atmosphere and Phelan entered through an access port on the deck level.

The shuttle's hatch twisted sideways, then slid into the interior of the ship. A short ramp telescoped out and down, but even before it had touched the deck, the Precentor Martial appeared in the hatchway. Tall enough that he had to dip his white-maned head to get through it, the ComStar envoy steadied himself with a strong grip on either side of the opening. His long white robe was loosely belted at the waist with a piece of white rope. The only other color on him was the black of the patch covering his empty right eye socket.

The Precentor Martial smiled at the sight of Phelan, and the MechWarrior returned the smile heartily. He met the older man at the base of the gangway and offered him his right hand. The Precentor Martial accepted it in both hands and shook it firmly.

"It appears, Phelan Kell, that you have fared well since we said our goodbyes on this very deck."

"That I have, Precentor Martial." Phelan directed two bondsmen to haul Focht's baggage to his room. "I was adopted into the Wolf Clan Warrior caste just after you left. I am now known as Phelan Wolf."

Focht bowed his head. "Please excuse my ignorance and accept my congratulations. If I remember the symbolism correctly, the red star patch on your shoulder means you are a MechWarrior as well?"

The younger man nodded. "For about three months now. This black and red jumpsuit is the uniform of my regiment. Officially, we are the Thirteenth Wolf Guards, otherwise known as the Wolf Spiders."

"And led by Natasha Kerensky herself."

Phelan chuckled lightly. "You don't miss a trick, do you?"

"ComStar knows all." Focht smiled enough for Phelan to know he was making a joke, but the young MechWarrior suspected the statement was not far from the mark. "Natasha's passage from Outreach was noted by some of our waystations, so we assumed she had made contact with the Clans. We took that as confirmation that the Dragoons were once part of the Clans, though that alliance no longer appears to be in force."

"I believe the history is correct, but I do not know the Dragoons' current status." Phelan waved the Precentor Martial toward the exit port. "As much as I enjoying talking with you and look forward to another such opportunity, the ilKhan has asked me to escort you to him immediately upon your arrival. If you don't mind."

"Not at all." Focht adjusted the patch over his right eye. "I am most pleased to see you have been made a MechWarrior." His voice dropped to a discreet whisper. "It should make it much easier to gather information, as we discussed a year ago."

Phelan chewed his lower lip. "I know I agreed to spy for you, but that was before. Much has happened since then. I am afraid I cannot betray the Clans."

Focht looked surprised. "Cannot? Phelan, these people are still attacking your home."

The MechWarrior shook his head. "These people are now *my* people, and this is my home."

"I see." Focht looked hard at Phelan, who felt as though he were being x-rayed. "I should have expected this. Converts are always more zealous than someone born to a cause."

"As well you would know, Precentor." Phelan's face closed up. "Before I was thrown out of the Nagelring, I do not recall seeing any ComStar initiates studying there. That means you had a life before ComStar, which makes you, too, a convert."

They continued down the corridor in silence until they reached an elevator tube. Focht broke the silence. "Even as a convert to ComStar, I have been willing to bend the rules, for a *friend.* "

Phelan's head snapped around. "You sent my parents a message about me?" He felt his pulse begin to pound as images of his family and friends began to float before his inner eye. Then and there he realized no matter how fully he accepted the Clans as his new family and friends, he could never let go of the people he had known before. *This concern for both sides is what the ilKhan wants from me. Natasha and I both have loyalties to the Clans and to the Inner Sphere. Are we here to temper the Clans in their fight?*

Focht waited until they had entered the elevator and Phelan had it moving toward the bridge. "The Primus forbade me to tell your family anything about you, so I tried to get around it by sending a kind of coded message to your father. I used a famous quote by the ancient writer Mark Twain about the exaggerated reports of his death, hoping he'd be able to puzzle it out eventually. But that was the best I could do."

"Thank you." Phelan picked distractedly at a fingernail, "but I know nothing of importance to tell you, Precentor. Natasha is a Khan of the Wolves and Ulric's election as ilKhan was not without surprises. His enemies agreed to elect him ilKhan, believing they could manipulate him, but he quickly set them straight. As for his invasion plans, he has confided nothing to me."

"Ulric is a very wise man. I have no doubt that whatever he has planned for the Inner Sphere will be most challenging."

The elevator stopped and the door opened onto a darkened corridor. Phelan led the way toward the bridge, remembering this same scene nearly a year before when the ship had been damaged in a battle. He looked at the Precentor Martial over his shoulder. "You know, running to the bridge after the Rasalhague ship hit us, I never believed we would find anyone alive."

Focht half-closed his good eye. "If not for your quick thinking and that tool you had created to open the lock, no one would have survived."

"Funny how things work out, isn't it?"

"The irony of the universe has not escaped me."

The two Elementals standing on either side of the hatch to the bridge gave no clue that they saw or cared about Phelan conducting the Precentor Martial in to see the ilKhan. Manning the various stations on the bridge were some two score crew members. Despite their brand new equipment and the routine way they seemed to go about their tasks, Phelan felt a shiver down his spine. His eyes flew up to where a catastrophic hole had been ripped in the hull, but nothing remained to show it had ever been there.

He guided Focht forward to a central area enclosed by a circular palisade of black panels. Slipping into the holotank through one of the four openings, they came immediately into the midst of a holographic space map. Star pinpoints large and small burned brightly, and the names of many were identified by floating labels.

At the heart of the galaxy, Ulric stood talking with Natasha Kerensky. He looked up and smiled at Focht, but waited until Natasha had finished speaking before he moved to welcome his guest. The look of pleasure on Ulric's face was in stark antithesis to Natasha's dark expression.

The ilKhan offered the Precentor Martial his right hand. "I am most pleased your Primus has sent you to us again."

Focht shook Ulric's hand heartily. "And I am happy to return. The Primus asks me to advise you that ComStar offers all the support at its disposal."

"Excellent." Ulric half-turned and waved Natasha forward. "This is Natasha Kerensky, formerly of the Wolf Dragoons."

"And now in command of the Thirteenth Wolf Guards." Focht took her right hand and kissed it. "You are even more beautiful than I remember, Colonel Kerensky."

Natasha's expression turned arctic with suspicion. "We've met before?"

The Precentor Martial shrugged. "It was a lifetime ago. You'd not remember me, for I was but one of many warriors who dreaded fighting against your Black Widows but dreamed of fighting with them."

Natasha withdrew her hand from his. "And I thought ComStar's Precentor Martial would be nothing more than a eunuch in a seraglio. You have charm and wit, yet are modest. A most dangerous combination, indeed."

Focht raised his hands in protest. "I am not here as an enemy, Colonel. I am here to help."

"That is a very good thing, Precentor," said Ulric, taking control of the conversation, "because our strategy has shifted." The ilKhan reached out to touch the glowing dot at the end of one star's name tag. Instantly, the label expanded to become a scrolling window of data. From where Phelan stood, he only saw the letters in reverse through the body of the translucent computer projection. That hardly mattered, for he'd studied enough world reports to know it was providing as timely information as the Clans had about the military forces on that planet.

"I will need you to provide very accurate and up-to-date information on the worlds we choose to hit. Instead of continuing to roll forward like a blanket, we are going to cherry-pick worlds. We will target the most heavily defended worlds in a sector, bypassing and cutting off lesser worlds. We hope that when the key worlds fall, the disruptive elements of the bypassed worlds will flee, allowing us to scoop up those planets with little or no struggle."

Focht nodded thoughtfully. "Getting the data should present no problem at all, provided you can give me a list of worlds you want to hit within two weeks of your attack. I do not need that much time to gather the information, you understand, but it gives my people the lead time to prepare for the aftermath of your invasion and the period of pacification."

"Fine." Ulric positioned his hand at the bottom of the window and pushed up. The computer sucked the data window back up into the label. "We want to force the Inner Sphere militaries to concentrate their forces, which should stop their attacks on worlds behind the lines. It will also be more of a challenge for our forces. With the addition of three more Clans to bolster those that have not fared as well as the Wolves, we must provide opportunities for glory in battle."

"Then the suggestion I had in mind might not be welcome."

"Speak freely. Nothing is forged of titanium as of yet."

The Precentor Martial pointed to a relatively minor world. "I thought it might be possible to use the offices of ComStar to negotiate the surrender of worlds you do not attack. This places us as a buffer between you and the populace, making implementation of pacification policies all the easier. If the negotiations fall through, you can still hit the world with whatever force you choose."

"A kind of 'carrot and PPC' approach to world conquest, eh, Precentor?"

"A most interesting turn of phrase, Colonel Kerensky." Focht clasped his hands behind his back. "I offer this idea merely with the thought of speeding your ability to secure your rear area. Politicians are not warriors. They often gladly give away what an army could not take in a millennia."

Ulric laughed politely. "Point well-taken, Precentor, and one spoken like a warrior. To call a politician untrustworthy is redundant, and to call one honest is a contradiction in terms. However, anyone who is aware of how the politics of a situation might affect him can sail through the obstacles."

"Good charts, strong ship, and a sextant have made it possible to weather more than one storm," Focht said amiably. "If you do not mind, I would welcome a chance to rest a bit before we continue."

"A splendid idea. Natasha and I have some things to discuss before we can decide on potential targets." Ulric escorted the Precentor Martial to the edge of the holotank. "Phelan will take you to your cabin. We can meet later for dinner. In say, four hours. We should be prepared to give you the names of some worlds for study by then."

Focht bowed his head. "I am your humble servant, ilKhan Ulric. The Peace of Blake be with you."

27

Unity Palace, Imperial City, Luthien
Kagoshima Prefecture, Draconis Combine
30 October 3051

Shin Yodama concentrated so hard on the holographic display of the battle data that he did not hear her enter the room. The first clue that he was no longer alone was a flash of white he saw out the corner of his eye. Thinking it another messenger, he turned, his expression became a scowl of irritation, then quickly bowed his head.

"*Sumimasen*, Kurita Omi-*san*. Forgive me. I had not expected to see you here."

Omi smiled forgiveness. "It is I who must apologize for disturbing you, Yodama-*san*."

Shin glanced over to the desk where Hohiro normally worked. "Your brother is not here right now. The doctors wanted to check his leg to make certain the osteomylitis has been contained after the injury on Turtle Bay. They say it's routine."

"I know." She pulled the chair from her brother's desk and slid it over beside Shin. "But it is you I have come to see. No one else can answer my questions. My father is far too busy and Hohiro refuses to acknowledge my interest in military matters. It is presumptuous of me, but I am sure neither my father nor my brother would object to my discussing my question with you."

Shin began to feel uneasy. "Though I cannot imagine refusing any request you would make of me, Lady Omi, I am reluctant to place myself in any path opposed to your father's or brother's wrath."

"I assure you, Yodama-*san*, that they have not forbidden my interest. Rather, they have neither the time nor inclination to indulge it." The holographic display covered the right side of her face with glowing green and red neon lines and symbols. "I merely require some general information so I may do my part to help control rumors."

Shin straightened himself up at his desk. "What is it you wish to know?"

Omi went straight to the point. "Have the Clans resumed their attacks?"

Shin's fingers flicked across the keyboard and summoned up a projection map of the Draconis Combine. Roughly triangular in shape, a sizable chunk had been sliced out of its left side. The conquered worlds occupied a green zone on the map, while the rest of the Combine appeared in red. Where the two colors met, one world burned with a golden light.

"That is Marshdale. So far, this is the only world the Clans have attacked in renewing the invasion. That is odd because Marshdale is the most heavily defended world in that section of the Combine. Hyner, Byersville, and LaBrea are virtually naked in terms of military forces."

Omi frowned. "Could it be that they have decided to be more cautious because of the defeat on Wolcott?"

Shin conceded her point with a nod. "Possibly, but something about it strikes me the wrong way. On Turtle Bay, the Clans did nothing I would class as cautious. What's more, we now face the Clan known as the Smoke Jaguars as well as another one calling itself the Nova Cats. With reinforcements, I would have expected an increase in hostilities, not a reduction."

"Are the Smoke Jaguars and Nova Cats working together, or do they work independently, as did the Smoke Jaguars and the Ghost Bears in the initial invasion?"

"I am not certain." Shin typed a request into the computer and it exchanged the stellar map for a projection map of Marshdale. The planet first appeared as a sphere, then the ball split and flattened out. A number of red dots glowed on the six continents to mark battles, most of them occurring next to the gold dots pinpointing cities.

"The Smoke Jaguars have landed on three of the continents, and the Nova Cats have landed on the other three. Though our sources report radio intercepts of information exchanges between the two commands, they've seen nothing even close to combined operations. In fact, the Nova Cats have allowed two regiments to escape to Smoke Jaguar continents, and as nearly as we can make out, have made no attempts to follow. All our information is almost three days old."

"ComStar is not permitting our forces to send out messages?"

"No."

Omi pulled her kimono tightly closed at her throat. "So the only information we have comes through these mysterious Black Boxes that Hanse Davion does not realize we have?"

Shin was not quick enough to veil the look of surprise on his face. "I am afraid you have me at a disadvantage, Lady Omi."

"Forgive me, Yodama-*san*." Her eyes closed halfway in a look of innocence that Shin knew to be utterly synthetic. "I assumed you knew we had captured one toward the end of the Fourth Succession War. We used the information it gave us to great advantage in the '39 war and were able to monitor much of the Federated Commonwealth's action against the Clans because of the copies we had made. I was unaware, however, that my father had actually authorized distribution of the machines."

Shin swallowed hard. "I can only tell you that I know our information is traveling much slower than ComStar would send it. You seem far more knowledgeable about this matter than I." Shin surrendered with a shrug of his shoulders. "It may be as you suggest, but I do not know."

Omi smiled briefly, then folded her hands in her lap. "At least our Black Boxes have been directionally shielded so that our information is not broadcast for all to see." She pointed to the display. "Can you call up data intercepted from the Federated Commonwealth's transmissions?"

Shin nodded. "It is possible." He typed a simple command into the computer. "I have summoned up the information we have on one particular unit, just to see how the others from Outreach were being positioned. Here it is, the data on the Tenth Lyran Guards."

Shin saw Omi's intense interest flash for the briefest instant across her face, but he hid his notice of it. "That is the unit to which Hanse Davion's heir has been assigned, is it not?"

"Yes, Omi-*san*. Victor is a Kommandant, Galen Cox is a Hauptmann, and Kai Allard a Leftenant. From what we can determine, their Regimental Combat Team is being placed on Alyina. That may have changed by now, as the reporting time for such data is quite long. It is possible the Guards will be shifted to counterattack a world the Clans target."

Omi watched Shin like a hawk. "Tell me what you thought of Victor Davion, Yodama-*san*."

Her directness startled Shin. Not only was it highly irregular that she be concerned with his opinion, but her tone suggested she placed a certain amount of weight on his judgement. "I can only do that from a warrior's point of view, Lady Omi."

"That, and from a yakuza point of view, yes?"

"*Hai*." Shin tugged his left sleeve down at the wrist to hide a piece of the black and gold tattoo. "I think Victor is most capable as a warrior. He is good in single combat and can also work with other warriors in a coordinated fashion. He and Galen Cox almost seem to share one brain at times. Victor is also gifted in tactical and strategic skills. If not for his physical size, he might be considered a model warrior."

She smiled at that. "And his faults?"

"I would not call them faults so much as passions. He is fiercely loyal to his friends, and at times, he acts impulsively to aid them. Still, in the training on Outreach, he learned from his mistakes and became less likely to place himself in jeopardy as time went on."

Shin smiled, remembering something else about Victor. "He does not suffer courtiers gladly. I think Prince Davion would rather slog through mud with friends who value him sincerely than be among those who do him homage because of his bloodline. That could make his life more difficult, but it also adds a disarming directness to his interactions and will keep truly valuable men by his side."

"And your judgement of him from a yakuza viewpoint?"

"If he were an *oyabun*, we would own the world. As a police magistrate, he would be death itself."

Omi stood slowly and wheeled the chair back to her brother's desk. "Thank you, Yodama-*san*, for giving me so much of your time. One more question and I will leave."

"If you feel you must leave…"

"I must let you get back to your work." Her expression betrayed a trace of fear, but her voice remained calm and even. "You say Victor is loyal to his friends. But what of this alliance my father has made? Will the Davions wait to stab us once we turn our backs?"

Shin exhaled slowly as he considered her question. "Were it up to Victor, no, we would have nothing to fear. That is not to say that I do not trust your father's judgement implicitly. Yet we have all grown up hearing stories of the craftiness of the Fox. I would certainly not want to see the Combine lulled to sleep by any promise of Hanse Davion's for fear we might never waken again."

DropShip Barbarossa, *Inbound*
Alyina, Federated Commonwealth
16 November 3051

Kai Allard stopped halfway through the hatch and turned around. "You needed something, Highness?" Other officers leaving the small briefing room slipped past Kai one by one to eventually leave him alone with Victor.

"Close the hatch."

Kai heard the tension in Victor's voice, but knew him well enough to intuit that it was something more personal than business on Victor's mind. "What's the matter?"

Victor looked up at him and blinked his gray eyes. "Sorry, Kai. I must sound like the heat death of the universe is imminent or something." He cracked a smile. "Nothing so terrible, I assure you. I just wanted to speak to you alone in order to pass on some personal information that came with our orders. No one else is getting any personal communications because of our cutting ComStar off…"

"Got it." Kai sat down on the edge of the conference table. "What's happening?"

Victor dropped into a well-padded chair and put his feet up on the table. "Our parents made it back to New Avalon without incident. My brother Peter went AWOL from his NAIS company during exercises so he could be there when they arrived. He wants to ship out here immediately."

Kai chuckled lightly. "Peter always was a bit headstrong. He's the only cadet who's ever given Firsties more trouble during hazing than they gave him. What made him think he wanted to be out here?"

"I'm not sure." Victor shrugged. "I think he heard that Ragnar Magnusson is younger than he is and I gather his grades have been less than stunning."

"My father said Quint was a bit irked about having to stay at the Sakhara Academy while we were training on Wolf's world." Kai rotated his fist to loosen up his forearm. "I guess Cassandra and Kuan Yin convinced him to stay at the Academy."

"There's more," Victor said gravely. "Intelligence from Sian reports that Romano has put your mother and father under an edict of death. I'm sorry."

"Again?" Kai forced himself to take the threat lightly. "This is at least the tenth report we've had of another assassination plot. All the others that have leaked were dismal failures. The ones we didn't foresee came close, except that the agents always managed to bungle them. The assassins all got picked up coming in-system at St. Ives or Loris."

"Even so, we're tightening security here, just in case Romano's insane enough to go after *you*."

Kai nodded. "I appreciate the warning, but we'll have to tell the Liao assassin to take a number. After the Clans are through with me, he can do his worst."

"I suppose."

Kai sensed a sudden shift in Victor's mood. "There's something else. Are you still upset at our assignment to Alyina even though the Clans bypassed it in favor of Devin and Pasig?"

"No. I'm certainly not happy about it, but it could be worse. Alyina has some good defensive positions." Victor glanced down at his hands, then back up at Kai. "My father said that various folks in the Draconis March have been reminding him of their loyalty and that they wouldn't ever want to be faced with a choice between staying with the Federated Commonwealth or allying with another state."

"What?" Kai couldn't believe what he heard. "That's treason, isn't it?"

"I suppose. From what I can make out, Liao agents in the Sarna March have been spreading stories of a torrid romance between Omi Kurita and me. Of course, it eventually got to folks in the Draconis March and they reacted unfavorably, to put it mildly. There has been no incident, mind you, but I don't appreciate their interest in my life."

"Ah." Kai narrowed his eyes. "But you and Omi Kurita didn't seem to be carrying on a big romance. Has something changed that I don't know about?"

"Not unless you want to call a goodbye kiss a big romance." Victor pounded his fist on the table. "I barely know her and now I've got people protesting about a phantom relationship. How dare they?"

Kai got up and began to pace the room. "Victor, don't you realize how many people's future rides on you? You turned twenty-one back in April, and if it hadn't been for our training, you would certainly have been officially invested as the heir to both thrones of the Federated Commonwealth. Hell, your father might even have abdicated in your favor, which some were predicting at that time—war or no war."

"What has that got to do with anything?" Victor demanded angrily.

"It has to do with how others react to your behavior. The people in the Draconis March only feel safe as long as they believe you hate the Dracos as much as they do. They know you and your father keep the Draconis March strong to prevent the Kuritans from trying to take it away. They like that. It reassures them, makes them think you're following in your father's footsteps.

"Now they hear you're romancing Theodore Kurita's daughter." Kai shook his head. "They figure she's bewitched you and that you'll begin to start making excuses for the Dracos. Then poof! They're suddenly Theodore's vassals."

"That's ridiculous."

"To you and me, but not to them." Kai stopped his pacing and leaned his hands down on the conference table. "Look, I trust you to make the right decision, no matter what. If you want to romance anyone—save Kali Liao—I'll back your play. But you've got to start looking at things the way others might interpret them."

Victor sighed and hung his head. "I've been thinking just these kinds of things, too, of late. Even if I don't like the situation, you're right and I must be careful. But, Kai, only you can help me."

"Whatever you need."

"Rumor and damage control mostly. Try to get it out that this 'romance' is merely idle gossip. With you and Galen and my cousin Morgan to back me, who will doubt that I've got my head on straight? Which I do, by the way."

Kai laughed. "I'll agree with that. After all, didn't you find the most interesting woman on Outreach?"

"Our mothers excepted."

"Of course." Kai opened the hatch. "Don't worry, Victor. Before long, we'll all have way too much on our minds to worry about who is romancing whom." He threw his friend a friendly salute. "Later."

Kai glanced at his chronometer, thinking that if he moved quickly, he still had a chance to reach the sick bay before the change of shift. Using an access ladder to descend two levels, he then cut through a maze of narrow corridors and bulkheads. Passing through the hatch, he tugged the sleeves of his shirt down into place and gave the orderly at the reception desk a smile.

"Is Doctor Lear in?"

The orderly glanced at the clock on his desk. "She still has a few minutes on her shift. Name?"

Kai jerked his thumb toward the interior office. "I'll announce myself."

The orderly nodded and Kai passed through the examination room to the small office for the medical watch officer. He knocked on the bulkhead and braced himself for her response.

He almost thought she was glad to see him, then the look on her face changed immediately to the dark mask of anger and hatred she reserved for him, though he'd never learned why.

"Afternoon, Leftenant Allard. Something I can do for you?"

Kai did his best to ignore her icy tone. "I have seen the assignments for the landing on Alyina. Your field hospital will be located in sector 2750."

She nodded, her blue eyes full of suspicion. "We've been assigned to take over a veterinary hospital attached to the agrocomplex at Tassa."

"I know. My company is assigned to cover that area." Kai looked down at his feet. "Tassa is close enough to what could be a front that things might get nasty. I'll do my best to keep you informed so you'll have plenty of time to ready patients for evacuation, if necessary."

"You are most kind, Leftenant." Deirdre closed the chart on her computer desktop and prepared to open another. "If there is nothing else, I have work to do."

"Actually, there is something. I want to say thank you."

"For fixing your legs on Twycross?" She waved away his thanks as trivial. "I was just doing my job, Leftenant, as were you when you kidnapped me and killed those soldiers." Anger rippled through her words, but Kai thought her usual cutting tone had lost some of its edge.

He shook his head. "No, I mean...of course, I appreciate you for that, but it was what you did on Outreach, in the Council of Lords, that I wanted to thank." He gave her a weak smile. "Romano certainly subjected you to some badgering."

208

White fury flashed through Deirdre's eyes. "What makes her so hateful? She did everything to force me to say I considered you to be the worst officer imaginable."

"But you didn't."

"No mean feat. The worst officer ever to live was present in the room, and he's a Davion. Compared to him, you are a paragon of virtue." She searched Kai's face with what seemed a mixture of pity and wonderment. "As much as we have our differences, I am not blind to how much more caring you seem than most officers in this army. I've had enough of hatred in my life. I don't intend to give Romano any more fuel for her anger."

"My parents asked me to convey their gratitude, too. They wanted to meet you, but you headed off planet too quickly."

Kai noticed she stiffened slightly at the mention of his parents, then visibly fought down the reaction. If possible, her tone became even more formal and her manner more distant, but not so much as in the past. "I had to do some things before taking assignment aboard the *Barbarossa*," she explained. "It was obvious how proud they are of you, and happy that someone else vindicated their belief. I require no thanks from them, however."

As Deirdre Lear turned back to her computer files, Kai understood that the interview was over. "Well, thank you again for the support," he said lamely.

As he turned to leave, her voice made him look back. "Kai...Leftenant...thank you for offering to keep me informed on Alyina. And for organizing the evacuation of my field hospital on Twycross. We lost some men, but many more would have died if the Clans had broken through."

Kai gave her a nod, then slipped into the corridor. Out there, he leaned his head against a cold bulkhead and closed his eyes. *The Clans came closer to a breakthrough on Twycross than I have come with you, Deirdre Lear*.

Kai smiled and flexed his fingers. "Since sector 2750 is in my company's area of control," he said aloud, "I should familiarize myself with the background of all personnel being assigned to it. Let us see, Dr. Lear, what clues your files may offer in solving this little mystery. And I won't rest until I know why you hate my family, and what can I do about it."

JumpShip Dire Wolf, *Assault Orbit*
Memmingen, Free Rasalhague Republic
20 November 3051

Phelan Wolf watched Natasha Kerensky shake hands with Star Colonel Marcos within the confines of the bridge holotank. As she turned away, he saw the predatory grin on her face. Head held high and stride springy with pride, Natasha returned to her bidding station.

Phelan relinquished his place at the bid computer keyboard and moved over to a general access terminal. "How do you think the bidding will go?" he asked.

She threw him a wink, which prompted both Phelan and Ranna to smile. "You two pups watch this. Marcos won't know what hit him. Give me first bid because of my age, will he!"

Phelan shook his head. Having seen Cluster commanders bid away men and materials in preparation for a planetary assault a dozen times on at least a dozen previous occasions, he still could not get used to it. He knew the ground rules. A commander went in to attack with whatever he had bid, but could bring down reinforcements equal to his rival's last bid, without penalty. Ultimately, he could bring down as much as the opening bid in the contest for that planet, but his rival would have to allow him that option, which would mean concessions to the losing bidder. Though Phelan acknowledged that the bid process forced commanders to do the best they could with their troops, the idea of an artificial limit on forces used to take a planet still shocked him.

He looked across the bridge at the large wall display that would show the bids and counter-bids. If Natasha chose, she could open with a bid to include all her forces. The computer would paint an icon for the *Dire Wolf*, three for aerospace fighters, three for Elementals, and nine for MechWarriors. Phelan knew Natasha was too shrewd to make such an opening bid, but he couldn't guess how much she would give away initially.

"Phelan, what is your assessment of the Third Drakøns?"

The young MechWarrior frowned. "They are a sharp unit, but the Precentor Martial's information places them on Skondia. All they have defending Memmingen are militia and a unit cobbled together from the Black Omen and the Outlaws mercenary units. They're tough, but there aren't many of them."

Natasha's eyes became like crescent moons. "But if they were there, they would tie up a Triple or two, *quiaff*?"

"Aff."

"Good." Tapping out a series of keys, Natasha put her bid up on the screen. Phelan was relieved to see no icon representing the *Dire Wolf* because that meant the ship's awesome firepower would not be used to raze the planet. Only one five-pointed blue star with white trim appeared to represent Natasha's aerospace element. Likewise, Natasha allowed herself only one four-pointed green daggerstar with silver trim to represent Elementals. She even sliced out three of her nine MechWarrior stars.

Phelan glanced down at the small box worn on his jumpsuit belt. Its little LED remained dark, as did the unit on Ranna's belt. He knew that meant Natasha had bid away the Stars of which they were members. Even if Natasha won the bidding, neither Phelan nor Ranna would see combat. He turned to complain to the Black Widow, but saw that the LED on her notification device was not lit.

He raised an eyebrow. *Natasha doesn't intend to win this bidding. What does she know? Are the Third Drakøns on the planet?*

Star Colonel Marcos countered with a bid pulling two MechWarrior stars from the display, but added back a Star's worth of Elementals and aerospace support. He smiled confidently across the holotank, where a vector-graphic hologram of the planet slowly rotated. Standing behind him, Conal Ward patted Vlad on the shoulder while Vlad busied himself at the bid computer.

Natasha closed her eyes briefly. "Two Stars of aircraft give him twenty fighters. The two Stars of Elementals counter the militia, leaving him four Stars of 'Mechs to take the Black Outlaws." She glanced over at Phelan. "Sound right to you?"

Phelan held up his left hand for a second, then finished punching

211

an information request into the computer. A file started to scroll up over the screen, and he froze it as the information he wanted appeared. "ComStar says the Black Outlaws have a combined air wing of fourteen aerospace fighters. The Third Drakøns also have twenty aerospace fighters, a reinforced air company. Most important," he said with a grin, "Memmingen is the home of the Vandal Air Force. They're a bunch of old fliers who have a full six-plane wing of MechBuster fighters. Neither the planes nor the pilots have been in combat since 3030, but they could still be deadly."

Natasha nodded appreciatively. "Good work, Star Commander Wolf. ComStar provided that information?"

"Nope. When the Hounds were trapped on Gunzburg, the Vandals came over and put on a demonstration, courtesy of Tor Miraborg." Rage almost made the man's name stick in Phelan's throat, but he swallowed past it. "I just kept it in mind and decided not to share it with Marcos. No reason we should make it easy for him."

"No, indeed. At this point, would you consider it an even fight?"

"What makes you think the Drakøns are there?" Phelan's green eyes narrowed. "If the Drakøns are on the planet, I give the edge to Free Rasalhague."

Natasha gave Phelan a hard, appraising glance before answering him. "I have word that the Kell Hounds and Wolf's Dragoons are heading into Rasalhague to shore up the defenses. That being true, it makes sense for the Drakøns to be released to Miraborg's command. Miraborg will want to surprise us, so he'll slip half the regiment in covertly while phantom exercises make ComStar think they're still on Skondia. He'll include the full air wing because the survivors can escape and be withdrawn to Gunzburg."

Phelan looked over at the ilKhan and the Precentor Martial waiting for Natasha's next bid. "With a little less air power, Marcos will be badly hurt."

"My thoughts exactly." Natasha punched her next bid into the computer. The screen updated itself, pulling only one of the blue and white aerospace stars.

Marcos chuckled aloud, having anticipated her bid. His counter instantly flashed onto the screen. That bid deleted one of the Elemental Stars, leaving Marcos with four 'Mech Stars, one Star of fighters, and one Star of Elementals. When Natasha raised her hands in surrender, Marcos shot a triumphant fist into the air.

The wide smile on Vlad's face made Phelan's stomach turn sour, but he forced the feeling away. "Promise me one thing, Natasha."

"You have a request, Star Commander?"

He nodded solemnly. "Whatever happens, we have to be the ones to take Gunzburg. I have an old score to settle."

Natasha folded her arms across the breast of her black jumpsuit. "A vendetta can be nasty stuff, Phelan. Having lived through a number of them, I know. They make you blind."

Phelan shook his head. "No, Natasha, it is not like that. Tor Miraborg humiliated me during the time he held the Hounds captive on Gunzburg." He glanced back at Ranna, who had heard the story before, and she gave him a supportive smile. "I knew his daughter Tyra, and Tor had me beat up so I'd stop seeing her. In fact, he wanted to imprison me on Gunzburg, even after the Hounds headed out. That's why I want to be there when he gives his surrender. To give him back what he gave me."

"That we might be able to arrange." Natasha turned from Phelan to greet the two men approaching her. "Precentor Martial, ilKhan, I apologize for so poor a performance in the bidding."

"Bargained well, but lost. There is no shame, Natasha."

The Precentor Martial nodded in concurrence with Ulric's assessment. "Marcos bid boldly, apparently ignoring the ten percent accuracy deviation I quoted him. You forced him to shave his force close to the line necessary for victory. As I understand your system, he will have to concede some things to you in order to win the world."

Natasha looked over at Marcos and flipped Conal Ward a little salute. "I hope you are correct, Precentor Martial. As it is, I want to take the time to prepare a bid for our next target." She gave Ulric an inquiring glance. "May I tell him?"

"By all means."

"We will hit Gunzburg next."

The Precentor Martial adjusted the black eye patch over his right eye. "Tor Miraborg will be commanding the Gunzburg Eagles. It will not be easy to take that world."

Ulric nodded slightly. "But then, no world should ever be easy to take, *quiaff*?"

"Well put, ilKhan." The Precentor Martial smiled knowingly. "The only worlds I have ever heard described as easy conquests were those that prove annoyingly difficult to take. I will relay the request for information on Gunzburg immediately."

Phelan touched the Precentor Martial's left arm. "If you could, please ask your sources to determine if Hanson Kuusik is still an aide of Tor Miraborg's, or find out to which unit he has been assigned."

Focht bowed his head. "I will include that request."

"Precentor Martial, perhaps you could request data on one more world in your transmission?" Ulric allowed himself the grim smile that Phelan recognized from previous times when Ulric had apparently been testing him. This time, to his relief, the look was directed at Focht.

"It would be my pleasure, ilKhan. Which world is it?"

"A target for the Smoke Jaguars and Nova Cats. It is in the Draconis Combine. According to what they say, it may be a world of some importance." Ulric frowned. "The name escapes me."

Focht's one good eye half-closed as he cycled through the names of the worlds in that theatre of operations. "Irece? Teniente?" The ComStar warrior hesitated as another name came to him. "Pesht? Do they mean to take Pesht? Pesht is a Military District capital."

"No, no, none of those, Precentor, but thank you. Ah, yes," Ulric said, "now I remember." As his smile returned, Phelan felt a sudden, horrible premonition. "The name is Luthien," the ilKhan said, pleased with himself at remembering quickly. "The world for which they want information is known as Luthien."

Myndo Waterly successfully hid her pleasure at the shocked expression on Huthrin Vandel's florid face. "Yes, Precentor Tharkad, I did say Luthien. Does that surprise you?" She looked at the other members of the First Circuit. "Did I not tell you that these Clansmen were bold?"

Gardner Riis, the platinum-haired Precentor from Rasalhague, looked over at Precentor Dieron, then back to the Primus. "Forgive me, Primus, but do we supply the requested information for the assault on the Draconis capital?"

Brushing her long hair back from her shoulders, Myndo strode down from her dais to stand directly on the gold star set into the floor of the circular chamber. "Is there a reason we should not, Precentor Rasalhague? The projected date is more than six weeks off. That is more than enough time to obtain the information, is it not?"

Riis nodded, flinching uncomfortably from her attention. "Yes, Primus, but that battle is likely to be hard-fought. Theodore Kurita will never permit Luthien to fall. This could be the place where the Combine makes its final stand."

"And you see that as a problem?"

Huthrin Vandel had recovered his composure enough to intervene. "Primus, I believe my colleague fears ComStar's association with what could be a grave loss for the Smoke Jaguars and Nova Cats.

215

If the Precentor Martial reads Clan politics correctly, we could be discredited along with the ilKhan. And should that occur, we would certainly lose our position as administrators on Clan-occupied worlds."

Myndo blithely ignored Vandel's protest and turned her attention to Sharilar Mori. "Precentor Dieron, what say you of the Combine's chances of successfully defending Luthien?"

"It is difficult to predict, Primus." Sharilar folded her arms and tucked her hands into the sleeves of her scarlet robe. "I believe Luthien is home to the First Sword of Light, the Otomo, the Second Legion of Vega, and both Genyosha Regiments. The Kanrei might also call in one or two of the Ghost regiments as reinforcements. It all depends, of course, on how much advance warning Theodore Kurita has and what are his current plans."

Ulthan Everson, Precentor from New Avalon, leaned forward on his crystalline podium. "That coincides with all reports I have seen concerning Luthien. I wonder, though, if Theodore mightn't also call in some of the Ryuken regiments. They are currently operating in the Pesht Military District."

Sharilar looked at the Primus. "If it would please you, Primus, we might use a projection map to clarify the situation." Myndo nodded and Sharilar commanded a map of the Combine from the computer. "As you can see, the line of conquest runs from Tamby on the Periphery on down toward Pesht. The Clans have not seen fit to enlighten us on why they do not sweep out in a push through the Draconis backwater. Nevertheless, I believe the Precentor Martial to be correct in pointing out that their current axis of attack makes for shorter lines of supply than if they tried to take everything at once."

She pointed at the world of Pesht. "The Ryuken are using Pesht as a base in preparation for a series of attacks against Clan-occupied worlds. This is a variation on the Davion strategy. Even if Theodore could recall these units to help defend Luthien, I do not think he would. Though an audacious warrior, he will continue with the attacks to the enemy's rear to distract them. Of course, he will bring in the Ryuken if the situation becomes grave."

Myndo flashed a smile at Riis and Vandel. "So you predict that the Clans could defeat Luthien?"

Precentor Dieron considered her reply just long enough to annoy Myndo slightly. "I believe, Primus, that the Clans can win against any forces they find on Luthien. I would not, however, wish to be present on that world during or after the fighting."

Myndo rewarded Sharilar's characteristic directness with a

smile. "I think your prediction of serious fighting is accurate, Precentor Dieron. I also share your opinion of the outcome for the Clans. I see no risk in providing the Clans with the information they request."

Huthrin Vandel hissed like a cat. "Primus, now is a time for caution. Recall that the Free Worlds League has agreed to create 'Mechs and parts for both the Combine and the Federated Commonwealth. These reinforcements could make a big difference in how battles go."

"How good of you to remind me of trivial matters." Myndo slowly returned to her dais, proudly refusing to acknowledge that she was in retreat from Vandel's attack. "You know as well as I that Precentor Atreus is on his way to the planet Atreus to speak with Thomas Marik about just this matter. Thomas was once one of us. We can persuade him not to assist the forces of the Inner Sphere."

"But the agreement has not yet been overturned, has it?" Vandel pressed his advantage. "Thomas has been quite independent since leaving ComStar and taking over as Captain-General of the League. I understand from Precentor New Avalon that Joshua is responding to treatment at the NAIS, though he is still quite ill. Do you think Thomas will renege on the deal while his son's life is at stake?"

Why have I tolerated you all these years? "I would remind you, Precentor Tharkad, that patience is a virtue at which ComStar excels. The 'Mechs Marik has agreed to turn over to Hanse Davion and Theodore Kurita would not come on line for a year or so anyway. That gives us ample time to formulate our own plans, including one that will lead to Thomas' replacement, if it comes to that."

Vandel shook his head. "Any such overt move would tip our hand and reveal that we are working with the Clans—which I do not think is a good idea."

"Your continual objections to our alliance have been scrupulously noted, though I acknowledge merit to your concern. That is why I ask you all to return to your stations for consultation with the leaders of the Inner Sphere." Myndo smiled cruelly. "Tell them that ComStar is deeply concerned about the invasion and will, therefore, cut our fees for military communications by ninety percent, with guarantees of instant transmission of data from intelligence agents behind the Clan lines."

"What?" Gardner Riis blinked at Myndo. "If the Clans learn of this, they will destroy us!"

Myndo laughed lightly. "Someday, Precentor Rasalhague, you will learn that there are wheels within wheels. You will make those pronouncements to the leaders of the Successor States. We will check

217

any information they pass through us for authenticity and then relay it to the Clans. You will also tell the Great House leaders that I, the Primus of ComStar, have gone out to meet with the Clans' ilKhan in hopes of working out a peaceful settlement of the conflict."

The only sound in the chamber came as Precentor New Avalon applauded the Primus. "This is masterful, Myndo. You should arrive at the Clans just in time to bring the ilKhan the news that Luthien has fallen."

"Precisely my intention." Myndo smiled coldly. "And when I return, I will bring with me the Clans' terms for the unconditional surrender of the rest of the Inner Sphere."

Unity Palace, Imperial City, Luthien
Pesht Military District, Draconis Combine
22 November 3051

The funereal silence of the briefing room shared by Hohiro
Kurita and his father shocked Shin Yodama. Finding himself neither
noticed nor welcomed as he crossed the threshold, the yakuza Mech-
Warrior knew how grave matters had become. Without speaking, he
went to his customary position at Hohiro's left hand and punched his
recognition code into the computer terminal.

Behind him, the leaders of the military units stationed on Luthien
filed into the room and took their places at the black table. Seeing
Narimasa Asano, leader of the Genyosha, seated across from him,
Shin drew strength from the man's calm demeanor. The other military
men showed more apprehension and irritation at having been summoned so abruptly. Some still rubbed sleep from their eyes, probably
having caught a few more moments of sleep as their aides drove them
to the palace in the middle of the night.

Though Theodore did nothing to acknowledge their presence, he
approached the head of the table when the last general was seated and
the doors had been shut. The Kanrei hit several buttons on the console
at his right hand, engaging the anti-listening capabilities of the room.
Though Shin had grown accustomed to it, Theodore's plodding,
methodical way of punching each button, like an executioner mechanically lopping head after head with an axe, struck him as a most
dire omen.

Theodore kept his voice quiet and low. He enunciated his words carefully, as though precision could somehow mitigate the disastrous message he had to deliver. "I have learned through an unimpeachable source that the Clans have chosen their next target in our space, and that it is Luthien."

Nausea twisted Shin's stomach like a python trying to crush a rabbit. *Luthien! They mean to decapitate the Combine, just as they have the Free Rasalhague Republic*. His hands clenched into fists as he looked around at the shocked expressions of the other military men around the table. Only Narimasa Asano was able to conceal his reaction to the news, though his composure was not perfect.

"Are you certain?" someone inquired from further down the table.

"*Hai*." Theodore took a deep breath and exhaled it slowly. "I learned of this intended strike only an hour ago and immediately sent for all of you. We have five regiments on Luthien, and can call up another three of militia and retired military, though our equipment is not so good."

Tai-sa Oda Hideyoshi, leader of the fanatical Otomo, pressed his palms flat against the table's surface. "We must defend Luthien. If we lose it, we lose everything."

Across from Hideyoshi, a wizened older man whose close-cropped black hair and big ears made him look to Shin like a monkey-spirit, nodded in agreement. "Kanrei, the First Sword of Light stands ready to repulse these invaders, but we are not able to do it alone. Acknowledging the spirit of the Otomo, the Genyosha, and your Second Legion of Vega, may I suggest that you recall the Ryuken regiments from Pesht to reinforce us here."

Theodore looked at the Genyosha leader. "Do you concur, *Tai-sa*?"

Asano leaned back in his chair, his dark eyes revealing nothing of his thoughts. "Forgive me, Kanrei, but we have not enough information to render that judgement. We have five regiments here, which translate roughly into a Clan force half our size. We have not seen a Clan assault with more than two of their regiments, except the rumored force they used to take Rasalhague. I also assume that the pattern of previous attacks means that we will be facing the Smoke Jaguars and Nova Cats, while the Ghost Bears and their new allies, the Steel Vipers, will strike further into our territory."

Theodore nodded. "I was not given any information on a Ghost Bear or Steel Viper attack, but I have no reason to assume you are wrong."

"Then I would have to agree that reinforcement is crucial, but let it be a general reinforcement of our whole line. Luthien may be the capital, but it is not the whole of the Combine."

The other officers stared at Asano as though he were mad, but Shin began to see at what the old man hinted. Shin knew the Ryuken were prepared to stage raids into Clan-held territory and that they had a sanctuary on Wolcott that the Clans would not hit. Pulling the Ryuken back would only keep the Combine on the defensive, while letting them loose would force the Clans to be more cautious.

Theodore leaned forward, pressing his fingertips to the tabletop. "Time and again, we have had to rediscover the key to modern warfare. We no longer have fronts, and ownership of planets means nothing. The only way to defeat an enemy is to destroy his capacity to wage war. This is done by destroying his troops and disrupting his supply lines. We all know this, but our pride often blinds us to this truth.

"Twenty years ago, we saw two sharp examples of this truth. The Liao strike at the Kathil ship yards was misguided and unsuccessful, yet could have crippled Hanse Davion's war had it come off as planned. There was also Katrina Steiner's strike at my JumpShips, preventing our invasion of the Isle of Skye, at no greater cost than a handful of agents."

The First Swords leader, Yoshida, raised a counterpoint. "What you say is true, but how can you discount how the loss of Luthien would affect our population? The dishonor..."

"Damn the dishonor! Yes, the loss of Luthien would be a blow, but a successful defense of other worlds would temper that, as would the reconquest of worlds the Clans have previously taken." Theodore's blue eyes blazed like a PPC beam. "So far all we have done is react to attacks by the Clans. But if they want to throw forces at Luthien, it means they do not have troops to hold other worlds. It means they're devoting too much of their munitions and spare parts to one world, making them vulnerable elsewhere. That vulnerability is exactly what I intend to exploit."

The Kanrei looked at Shin. "*Sho-sa* Yodama, please punch up Case *Tako*."

Octopus? Shin typed the request into the computer and saw a map of the Combine materialize and hover over the center of the table. Golden sparks of light glowed on each world where the Combine maintained troops. Slender golden threads representing supply circuits connected worlds in a wispy web.

Without his doing anything, the picture slowly changed. Ninety percent of the line units on the border with the Federated Common-

221

wealth—both along the Draconis March and the Isle of Skye—drifted up toward the Clan lines, and the supply web shifted to support them. More important, supply lines to frontline worlds increased, giving those units enough materiel to launch strikes at the enemy. Shin realized that even if the Combine's attacks were little more than raids, by the time the Clans could react to them, attack units shifted from the Davion border would be arriving to reinforce the planets they would attack.

"This is it, my Lords. We reallocate our forces to provide far more resistance than the Clans can imagine. The field modification kits are being shipped to the units I want to use for strikes, so the Clans will be facing 'Mechs that are close to their equal. We'll have the Ryuken strike at their rear and feint toward the Periphery, as though intending to backtrack the Clans and strike at their home."

Asano smiled ever so slightly. "Audacious, to say the least. Will you concentrate on reinforcing and supplying units with strong aerospace wings, the only combat arena where we seem to fight on even ground with the Clans?"

"Of course." Theodore straightened up. "We are also upgrading conventional air forces to aid in anti-'Mech activities. The cost will be high in terms of personnel, but it will give the Clan fighter pilots even more to think about, as well as keeping their 'Mech forces off guard."

The leader of the Otomo shook his head. "This plan certainly seems to offer the solution to dealing with the Clans, but I fear we are burning the roof to warm us against the cold night. Stripping forces from the Davion border is madness. Davion will be on us like a shark to a bleeding fish."

"Hanse Davion has given me his word that he will not strike."

"And you believe him?" Hideyoshi could barely disguise his incredulity. "That is a grave error, and one your father has never made."

Shin saw Theodore stiffen at the mention of Takashi Kurita. His father, still the Coordinator of the Draconis Combine, claimed the loyalty of many old-line military men who believed Theodore's reforms had emasculated the Combine and stripped it of honor. As a yakuza, Shin would never have been allowed to serve his nation or have risen to his present position except for Theodore's reforms. The thought made him flush slightly, whether in anger or embarrassment, he was not sure.

"*Tai-sa* Hideyoshi, I hasten to remind you that my father very nearly delivered us into Hanse Davion's hands twenty years ago. He also managed to alienate the most powerful mercenary units in the

Successor States through his Death to Mercenaries order. Had it been my father leading the defense of the Combine against Hanse Davion only ten years ago, he would have lost the Dieron district and half of the Galedon district as well."

Theodore's words came quietly, but the anger in them was enough to subdue his listeners immediately. "My father's hatred and distrust of Hanse Davion is born of prejudicial contempt. Takashi dismissed Davion as an inferior, which leads him to underestimate the Prince of the Federated Commonwealth. I do not make that mistake. I treat Hanse Davion as the deadly foe he is. That is why I understand that because it is not in his best interest to attack us, he will *not*."

Stubborn as a pit bull, Hideyoshi refused to let go the matter of the Davion threat. "Perhaps you do not find it odd to be considering Hanse Davion's best interests, but I have never approved of this alliance you made."

"Do you have more than your old traditions to back this distrust, or are you caught in a repetitive groove that will not let you free?"

"Let us assume it is as you say. Let us assume that Hanse Davion will not hit us right now. But the moment he learns that Luthien is vulnerable, he will have to strike us. This is his one chance to end our threat to him. And if Luthien falls, he must hit us. Not only will that be in his best interest, but he can claim merely to be bolstering your faltering realm. Then you marry your daughter off to his son, and Hanse Davion becomes the First Lord of the new Star League."

Watching Hideyoshi impassively through half-shut eyes, Theodore stroked the stubble on his chin. "I see that the court gossips have your ear, *Tai-sa*. Though we are here to discuss military matters, you seem determined to deflect the discussion into some dialogue on politics. I do not intend to honor that gambit because matters at hand are too grave for us to be sidetracked by fairy tales, rumors, gossip, or any other foolishness."

The Kanrei clasped his hands behind his back. "I likewise reject your distrust of Hanse Davion. I have been with him. I have looked him in the eye. He is a man of great power in our time, and we know he will never give it up easily and will always seek to increase the power he wields. We saw greed in his strike at the Capellan Confederation twenty years ago, and the same in his attack on us ten years ago. Hanse Davion, however, saw something else. He saw himself striking a blow for freedom and humanity.

"Misguided though he may be, that is his motivation. That is the force driving him. I would be the last to claim he is incapable of deceit or treachery, but I believe he descends to that level in the name of his

223

goal, something that he sees as a great vision. Besides, we must trust Hanse Davion. We have no choice."

Hideyoshi sighed heavily and Shin heard the resignation in it. "Then do not let Hanse Davion know that the Clans have attacked Luthien until you are able to inform him of our victory in throwing the invader back."

Theodore shook his head slowly. "Too late. A message informing Davion of the impending strike on Luthien is already on its way to him."

The Otomo leader raised his hands in despair. "We are lost."

"No, Hideyoshi, we are not." Theodore smiled carefully. "You are right that Hanse Davion must come after us if we lose Luthien. But there lies the solution to the problem. No matter what the Clans throw at us, we will never let Luthien fall."

Avalon City, New Avalon
Crucis March, Federated Commonwealth
27 November 3051

Hanse Davion watched as the muted light of the briefing room glinted off silvery scars on Justin Allard's black metal left hand. "I never expected to hear those words from you, Justin."

The Intelligence Secretary shrugged helplessly. "It grieves me to disappoint you, Highness, but our mutual discomfort does nothing to answer your question. The construction of the fax message—everything from the syntax to the brush strokes used—indicate it originated in the Draconis Combine. My experts trace it from Luthien and even suggest it may have come from the brush of Theodore Kurita himself. I have no way of authenticating beyond that."

The Prince looked to Alex Mallory. "Have you anything to add, Deputy Secretary?"

The slender blond man shook his head. "I can only echo what Justin tells you, Highness. The fax appears to have originated from within the Combine."

Hanse felt a flutter of fear. "Do you realize what you're saying? If the Combine has somehow gotten hold of one of our fax machines, they've been privy to our communications for the past twenty years!" He shook his head sadly. "No wonder we lost a war ten years ago. I'm more surprised Theodore Kurita has not shown up at our doorstep at the head of his army."

"You overestimate the threat, my Prince." Justin's expression

225

showed the reflective calm that Hanse had seen and learned to depend on over the years. "Every Black Box was accounted for at the end of the Liao war. We have proof that all were either destroyed or remained in our hands, though the possibility of deception cannot be dismissed. The evidence is less compelling in the 3039 war, and that may be when Theodore could have obtained one. It was just that danger that made us encode all military messages we have sent over the past two decades, and we have also improved the speed of the machines. In fact, one of our machines on Murchison picked up this message, then transmitted it to New Avalon. The original message won't reach us until the beginning of next month."

Melissa interlaced her fingers and placed her hands on the hardwood table. "So you believe that the threat to our security is minimal?"

"I would characterize no threat to the Federated Commonwealth as minimal, Archon, but the threat is within normal limits and has been handled in an appropriate manner. We treat faxes as subject to discovery and always include some disinformation to make things difficult for the ISF or ComStar if they are intercepting our messages."

Justin held up the sheet of paper from Theodore. "This merely confirms our suspicion that the Combine did capture one of our machines."

"Well, then," Hanse said, wearying of all the explanation, "what about the content of the message?" Hanse studied his copy again. "Can we believe Theodore that the Clans are on the way to attack Luthien?"

Alex punched a request for data into the keyboard at his place. "The reports we've gotten from our agents on the borders of the Draconis March and the Isle of Skye report massive recall of troops. The Combine has left a few worlds with 'Mech units in place, but it is usually one company from a crack regiment, with reinforcements cobbled together from yakuza elements and militia forces. They're stripping off all air and aerospace assets especially.

"I read that as a definite move to reinforce the front with the Clans."

"As Kurita moves the troops toward the fight, other troops move to Luthien." Melissa chewed on her lower lip. "A strike at Luthien could seriously damage the Combine's ability to fight. Their people are so tied to honor, they could start committing *seppuku* in droves out of shame for a fallen Luthien."

Hanse nodded. "Worse yet, you'd have a replay of the Ronin Invasions. Units would head out to avenge Luthien, without direction or supply. The front would be chaos, then it would collapse. This is very bad." *My buffer with the Clans is about to disintegrate.*

His head came up. "Assessment of the threat to Luthien, Justin?"

"Serious." Justin's hands curled down into fists, then opened again in a slow, rhythmic display of frustration. "At best, we show them with four line regiments, one political regiment, and another three weak regiments of reserves. The troops are some of their best, but we have no way of judging what the Clans will throw at them. The Wolves used three full regiments to pacify Rasalhague, but that was only a fraction of their available force. With the Clans' new strategy of hitting heavily defended worlds while skipping others, they will, undoubtedly, send whatever they need to take the world. With two Clans operating in that area, I have no doubt they will have the resources they need to do the job."

But Theodore is very crafty. "What if Theodore successfully outbids the Clans, as was done on Wolcott?"

The Intelligence Secretary nodded. "A good point, but I doubt the Smoke Jaguars will let themselves be humiliated again. Given their defeat on Wolcott, I'd wager they chose Luthien precisely to redeem themselves."

"Luthien." Hanse felt goosebumps rising on his arms. "For years, I dreamed of capturing Kurita's Black Pearl, but now the idea of its fall fills me with dread." *Or is it only that you hate the idea of someone else taking it instead?*

"The implications of Luthien's fall are not good." Alex's quick fingerwork on the keyboard brought a holographic map burning to life over the table. "Luthien's loss means Pesht would be isolated. If it goes, so does the whole Pesht Military District."

The top half of the Combine's red triangle went black. "If Theodore survived, he would have to pull all the way back to Benjamin to have a secure capital world. Benjamin, as a world, holds significance for the people of the Combine, so the loss of face would not be overwhelming. He could organize a defense from there, and with fewer planets to defend, he could hold out for a long while. However, he wouldn't have the industrial backing needed to defeat the Clans and reconquer the worlds he had lost. The Galedon District would go, leaving Theodore with the Benjamin and Dieron Districts, but no hope of ever again being a power."

The loss of the Galedon District reduced the map of the once proud Draconis Combine to a small rectangle of space roughly half again the size of the Capellan Confederation. The Clans' conquest of the Galedon District would put them directly on the border of the Draconis March, posing a direct threat to the Federated Suns portion of the Federated Commonwealth.

"Alex, I commend your projections, but do they take into account how long it would take for the troops that have been moved off the border to return to defensible lines?" Hanse studied the map closely. "Many of Theodore's troops could get caught without transport or supplies. That would accelerate the timetable of conquest, would it not?"

"I agree, Highness, it would."

"So, you're telling my husband and me that if Luthien falls, the Combine is destroyed?"

Justin nodded. "That is the long and short of it." He broke eye contact with Hanse and looked down. "Forgive me, my Prince, but I must now make a suggestion that I feel is my duty as your Secretary of Intelligence. We have fifteen regiments in position to consolidate the conquest of the Dieron District. If Theodore's time prediction for the strike on Luthien is correct, we could be at Benjamin and Galedon when the Clans hit."

Hanse felt an acid burn in his stomach. "Break my vow to Theodore? Hit the Combine?"

His face set in a mask of stone, Justin nodded solemnly. "They could not stop us. The Combine would be ours."

The Kurita curse lifted from my people forever! He pointed at the map. "Show me where we have units."

Little golden lights flared to life like muzzle-flashes all across the Draconis March and Isle of Skye borders. The line continued up the Rasalhague border, with two units deep in Rasalhague territory, and then traced a line that defined the Jade Falcons' incursion into the Lyran Commonwealth. Opposing his forces in the Dieron District, Hanse saw only a pitiful scattering of red pinpricks.

"The death of Luthien betokens the death of the Combine?"

Justin nodded with the finality of the Grim Reaper himself. "Without a head, how can the Dragon's body survive?"

The Fox shut his eyes as he came to a decision. "Orders will go out over my signature within the hour."

Melissa clutched his left arm. "Hanse, what are you going to do?"

"What I must do, beloved, just as with Thomas Marik. I have no choice." He stared at the gold sparks floating above the table. "I'm going to send them."

JumpShip Dire Wolf, *Assault Orbit*
Gunzburg, Free Rasalhague Republic
10 December 3051

Phelan Wolf could hear the thundering of his heart as it pulsed blood through his body. In the holotank, Natasha stood speaking with Marcos, against whom she would be bidding for the right to take Gunzburg. The young MechWarrior saw Marcos' fury at having been tricked in the Memmingen bidding, and he feared the worst. He and Natasha shook hands perfunctorily, then returned to their places.

"You didn't concede first bid to him, *quineg?*" From the flicker of anger in her eyes, Phelan realized he had spoken out of turn, too quickly and sharply.

"Is that a concern of yours for some reason, Star Commander?" Natasha skewered him with a harsh, sidelong glance as she turned the bidding console toward her. "Don't worry. We'll win the bidding. You'll get your revenge."

Phelan knew he should back off, but anxiety overrode common sense. "Dammit, Natasha, you know I'm concerned about more than bearding Tor Miraborg in his den. I've seen the casualty estimates from Memmingen, and I'm not referring to our people. Marcos had a temper tantrum down there and decided to level two villages as an example. I know he's going to force the bidding close to the edge, and I just don't want to see us backed to the wall the way he was. I don't want to see Wolves killed, and I especially don't want to see civilians killed."

Natasha kept her voice so low that none but Phelan could hear it. "I share your concern, Phelan," she told him in clipped tones, "but this world is not yours for the bidding. Were your estimates of Tor Miraborg and his resources correct?"

"They were accurate this morning and I've updated them four times since then with COMINT from radio intercepts."

"You still maintain that two Clusters are not sufficient to take it, *quineg?*"

Phelan punched the pedestal upon which his computer terminal stood. "No. Miraborg has half the Third Drakøns, most of their air wing, the Gunzburg Eagles, and one reserve regiment. He's put guns on anything that can fly and every citizen has a rifle. They handed out "fire and forget" inferno rockets that will have every city on that mudball burning down around our troops. The only way to beat the Iron Jarl is to deliver enough equipment that even he has no choice but to surrender for the sake of his people. That's the only way."

Natasha nodded grimly. "Then that's what we'll do."

Phelan felt a weight begin to lift from his chest. "Then you've got first bid?"

"No, he has first bid."

"Why?"

Natasha smiled cruelly. "Because, Phelan, I want to make him sweat."

And you want to give me a heart attack. His chest felt as though invisible chains enclosed it in a steel cocoon. He glanced at his force estimates, then looked up to see Marcos' first bid appear on the screen. *Dammit! He's a fool looking to regain the face he lost by having to ask Natasha for extra troops.*

The giant display showed the *Dire Wolf* icon on top. A large, eight-pointed red 'Mech star below it marked Marcos' desire for a full Cluster of BattleMechs. Phelan knew that would be enough to engage the Eagles and Drakøns on the ground. Six green Elemental stars and three stars worth of aerospace support rounded out the first bid. As Phelan watched the unit breakdown represented by the symbols, he saw Marcos had requested just under two full-strength Clusters worth of troops.

Phelan pointed to the aerospace units. "Natasha, that's not enough aerospace support. And the Elementals are no good. He's got too many of them and they will be less than useless in an urban assault. He's cut his bid too close to the edge."

"Has he?" Phelan watched in horror as Natasha slashed the Elementals in Marcos' bid by two-thirds and eliminated a whole

Triple worth of the aerospace fighters. As near as Phelan could tell, Natasha chose units at random, more intrigued by the pattern their elimination made on her console than out of any strategic concern. Before he could protest, she'd entered her bid on the computer, which appeared below her foe's on the overhead screen.

The only thing that kept Phelan's spirits from crashing to the deck was the stunned reactions of Marcos, Conal Ward, and Vlad as they studied Natasha's counterbid. Vlad hammered away at the keyboard of his information terminal, wiping away sweat from his head with the arm of his gray jumpsuit. His face brightened as he read some nugget of information, but Phelan's quick scan of new data from Gunzburg showed nothing to buoy his own feeling of doom.

He looked up at Natasha. "What are you doing? Vlad had things so close at the start that I don't see how we could win, and you keep cutting it down like a mad tailor armed with shears. I thought you shared my concerns for the people of Gunzburg."

Natasha turned on Phelan like a beast poked with a sharp stick. "I do share your concerns, but I do not have to make you privy to my every thought. There's more involved here than just the conquest of a planet, and whether or not a few innocents get splashed because they live in the wrong place. This is more than a fight between me and Marcos. It is a battle between the Wardens and the Crusaders. We hurt them with Memmingen, and they lost respect and materiel. Some of their bloodlines don't look so good now. If that happened at the cost of some civilian lives on Memmingen, too bad. Better they die that more can live."

The urgency in her voice convinced Phelan that she believed in the utmost importance of her task, but he still could not see her goal. "I do not understand, Natasha. I thought that both you and Ulric, as Wardens, would try to end the attacks. Instead, all I see are the two of you working to out-Crusade the Crusaders. How does that make sense?"

"You can't lead a group until you're out in front and know you will stay there." Her expression grew darker, as though a thin curtain had been drawn across her face. "It's a dangerous game, Phelan, but we must play it, and play it by *their* rules."

Marcos' return bid filled the line below Natasha's offer. The *Dire Wolf* remained available, but the 'Mech forces now appeared as fourteen smaller daggerstars. The bidding had trimmed the number of Elementals to a pair of Triples, but aerospace forces remained the same as the line immediately above.

Phelan shivered. The reduction of one company of 'Mechs did

231

not seem like much of a change, but he knew it doomed any chances for a clean, decisive 'Mech victory. With the aerospace and atmospheric craft Miraborg had assembled, the Eagles would dominate the skies after only a short series of battles, and that would make things harder on the ground.

Suddenly, unbidden, the memory of Tyra Miraborg filled his mind. She was the golden-haired woman as he'd seen her the morning he'd been freed from Miraborg's jail. Strong yet compassionate, she had ordered a prison guard to give Phelan a jacket and then presented him with the belt buckle she'd made, the same one Vlad wore as a token of conquest over Phelan. She had even gone so far as to oppose her father when he wanted to keep Phelan imprisoned on Gunzburg. It was Tyra who had won Phelan his freedom.

Tyra was a Kapten in the Eagles' aerospace force when he met her and she'd refused a commission with the Kell Hounds when the mercenaries left her world. *She was too much her father's daughter to ever leave Gunzburg. Now she'll be down there leading the fight against us.*

The sound of Natasha's voice dragged him back to reality. "Forgive me, Colonel Marcos, but I must ask you something. Is that your best bid?"

Marcos looked like someone forced to eat soggy bread soaked in vinegar. "What?"

"I asked if that was your best bid."

"I would suggest, comrade Colonel, that you make a counter-offer and find out."

Natasha rested her fists on her hips. "Listen up, Marcos, I'll beat whatever you bid. If you want me to make a counter-offer, I'll just close my eyes and shave something off."

Her hand hovered over the keyboard and Marcos blanched. He looked at Vlad, who seemed utterly perplexed. Conal folded his arms across his chest and said nothing, only watching it all with suspicion. Marcos pulled Vlad's terminal toward him and punched up his own request for data. He squinted at the information the computer reported back, his brow knotted in puzzlement.

He straightened up. "If you wish, I will revise the bid."

Natasha's finger poked one of the Elemental stars from the bid. "Just counter-bid this."

Feeling hollow inside, Phelan watching in fascination as Natasha tortured Marcos. If her opponent believed her boast that she would beat whatever he bid, he could wipe everything away and leave her with a single 'Mech star. Any bid even close to that range could be beaten, and would guarantee defeat for the leader beating it. Phelan knew that the main difficulty with so bold a bid was that Natasha could refuse it, leaving Marcos hoist by his own petard.

That meant Marcos would have to shave his bid as close to what he perceived as the edge, or even a bit below it, to successfully doom any effort of Natasha's. Phelan believed the bidding had already gone well below the margin he considered safe for the troops and citizens of Gunzburg, but Marcos, of course, did not have the same reservations about civilian casualties. Marcos' last bid had some slack built into it, probably in the form of a 'Mech star and an Elemental star. Natasha had removed the latter half of Marcos' safety net, so it was up to the Star Colonel to lop off the other half. When Marcos' bid appeared on the screen, Phelan saw he had done just that.

Natasha smiled cautiously. "Is that it? Is that your best?"

Marcos pulled himself up to his full height. "That is as low as I am prepared to go."

"So you mean that if I bid just one Elemental Star less, I will win the right to take the planet of Gunzburg? You do not think it could be done with less force than you have bid?"

Marcos faltered a bit. "No, Star Colonel, this is it. You will need everything I have bid to take this world."

"You're certain of that?"

Conal gently pushed Marcos to one side. "Warriors fight with 'Mechs, not words. Is there a point to this, Natasha, or are you stalling to work up the guts to make your bid?"

Natasha took two steps toward Conal. Phelan couldn't see the expression on her face, but her ramrod-straight back gave away her fury. "No, Conal, I've no need to stall for time on this bid. This is the one I've been intending to make since the start. I just wanted to know how far Marcos would go."

She pointed up at the screen. "I cannot use this thing for my bid because it will not register. I bid one."

Marcos hunched forward, waiting. "One what?"

"Just one." Natasha's hands curled into fists. "I bid just one warrior."

Marcos stared at her, stunned. "One warrior?"

"One warrior," Phelan whispered.

"One warrior," Natasha confirmed resolutely.

She turned from the Crusaders and graced Phelan with a hideous grin. "You want Gunzburg? It's yours, Phelan Wolf. Now all you have to do is go and take it."

Unity Palace, Imperial City, Luthien
Pesht Military District, Draconis Combine
25 December 3051

The irony of the situation almost gave Shin Yodama the desire to compose a haiku to describe it. Up above, on the surface, the Christian minority had decorated the streets of Imperial City with garlands of evergreen and ribbons of bright red. In small bands, they had gone throughout Luthien's largest city, doing what they could to beautify it, preparing for the advent of their savior. In Christian delirium, they rolled out a welcome mat for their beloved visitor.

Down in the bedrock beneath the city, Theodore Kurita's Defence Coordination Center was a stark contrast to the gaiety on the streets. Communication Techs remained hunched over scanners that monitored every cubic centimeter of the Luthien system. Other men, a select few that included Shin, attended the Kanrei—or, in Shin's case, his son—as the Kurita leaders studied various computer-generated battle simulations and actual spy reports.

Tai-sa Hideyoshi could barely contain his anger. "But, Kanrei, how can you ignore these reports from the Draconis March and the Isle of Skye? We have confirmations over and again that Hanse Davion has moved 90 percent of his troops from those borders."

Theodore's bright blue eyes were almost brighter than the muted lights of the command center. "I have not ignored his movements, *Tai-sa*. I merely chose to ignore the sinister motive you impart to them. Hanse Davion gave me his word he would not send his troops into the

234

Combine. We have no evidence that he has done so."

"Listen to reason, Kanrei!" Hideyoshi fought unsuccessfully to keep his voice from rising. "You know as well as I how many thousands of uninhabited stars he could use as stopping points to recharge his JumpShip drives. We would never detect them and his troops could arrive here without notice."

"Do you want me to fear ghosts, *Tai-sa?*" Theodore shrugged eloquently, though fatigue bled away some of the emphasis. "We have run the computer projections. Even if Davion has sent his troops, they would not get here before February. By then, we will either have defeated the Clans, or else we will all be dead."

Light glinted from the trio of gold bars on *Tai-sa* Yoshida's jacket collar. "Kanrei, our projections preclude the possibility of Davion having already put JumpShips in place to accelerate his troop movements."

Hohiro laughed aloud. "Because, *Tai-sa*, that is such an absurd idea that we rejected it in favor of taking more time to study projections of the battle for Luthien."

Theodore gave his son a nod. "I have Hanse Davion's promise. No F-C troops will invade our borders. End of discussion."

An inarticulate cry of terror erupted from one of the ComTechs. "I have multiple JumpShip contacts in-system. They've materialized within the orbit of our farthest moon!"

"Confirmed," another Tech cried out. "Fighters scrambling on the Orientalis moon base. Expect visual confirmation in two-zero minutes."

"I have deployment! Multiple DropShips with fighter screens!"

Even without the benefit of orders, Shin punched computer commands into his console. A three-dimensional model of Luthien and its system materialized above the briefing table where sat the strategists. The planet and its quartet of moons hung like blue-green marbles in the air. Around them whirled countless, sharp geometric forms matching the positions of orbital factories circling the world. Bright red as the holly berries on Christian wreaths, the JumpShips and DropShips clustered at a high point within the orbit of the most distant moon.

Shin knew that orbit formed the closest possible point of approach to the planet within the system. Most JumpShips appeared above or below the solar poles, but some intrepid pilots dared make their approach at "pirate points" that were much closer. The moon's orbit was swept clean of debris, its pockmarked face showing where most of it had gone, so the ships did not have to worry about emerging from their jump through hyperspace in the midst of an asteroid belt.

"The Clans are here already?"

Hohiro's question started a flutter in Shin's chest, but he shook his head. "Negative, Hohiro-*sama*. The equipment does not fit the Clan profile. This is Inner Sphere equipment."

The first ComTech's voice had returned to a workmanlike level, his concentration replacing panic. "DropShips burning hard. ETA one-one hours, repeat, eleven hours to landing. Vector plot puts them at Luthien."

Hideyoshi thrust a finger at Theodore. "Damn you and your trusting soul! Hanse Davion has launched an attack against us. I promise to see you dead before I see Luthien in Davion hands!"

Theodore's voice and face remained expressionless. "Save your threats for real danger."

The scanners on the surface of Luthien and on satellites spinning through space all turned on the invaders. Gradually, the red spheres resolved into shapes that coincided with the various known classes of DropShips. Small pinpoints of light represented the fighters arrayed to ward the DropShips as they burned in toward the planet.

Narimasa Asano's eyes narrowed as his gaze shifted from one ship to another. "*Union* and *Overlord* mostly. That's a lot of troops. I put it at seven or eight Regimental Combat Teams."

Hohiro offered a wan smile. "Not enough to take Luthien."

Theodore's expression hardened. "If they want it, we'll let them have it. Seven can't take it, and seven can't hold it against the Clans."

"IFF transponders negative," Shin reported, "but I have some unconfirmed correlations with ships we know. Shall I tag the incoming ships?"

Theodore nodded once, decisively, and Shin punched up the data onto the projection. As the DropShip formation split into three elements, little banners of *katakana* and *hiragana* symbols attached themselves to a ship here and there. Shin found himself suddenly surprised as more and more of the ships earned tags, with most of the data reports very recent in nature.

Hohiro's shock rode plainly on his face. "*Fitzlyon, Chieftan, Lugh, Manannan Mac Lir?*" He turned to his father. "These are the ships of Wolf's Dragoons and the Kell Hounds! Mercenaries have come to attack us."

Hideyoshi barked a harsh laugh of triumph. "There you have your ally's honor, Kanrei! He does not send his own troops, but instead dispatches *mercenaries!*" Hideyoshi managed to fill the word with utter contempt. "Hanse Davion does not even deign to dirty his own

236

hands with us. What a fool you have been."

Theodore said nothing, but watched the display intently. Shin saw the red dots of light reflected in Theodore's eyes, but could read none of the Kurita Warlord's emotions or thoughts. Hideyoshi and Yoshida clearly took Theodore's silence as weakness and hesitation, but Shin had the exact opposite reaction.

A light began to strobe on Shin's console. "*Sumimasen*, Kanrei. There is communication coming in from the DropShip *Chieftan*. Do you want me to run it through here?"

"Yes. Thank you, Shin."

Hitting the right keys, Shin supplanted the orbital scan with a holographic image of Jaime Wolf. "*Komban-wa*, Kurita Theodore-*sama*."

"*Komban-wa*, *Tai-sa* Wolf-*sama*." Theodore straightened up. "You realize that you have penetrated restricted space and appear to be on an attack vector for Imperial City?"

Wolf grinned cheerfully, and Shin felt the weight on his chest evaporating. "*Hai*, Theodore, I do realize that. Forgive any concern we may have caused you."

"Perhaps, Colonel." Theodore's expression eased. "Might I inquire what is your business here?"

"We request permission to land," Wolf said matter-of-factly. "Hanse Davion sent us a report that you would soon have a fight on your hands. How could we let you have all the fun by yourself?"

Kai Allard saw the surprise on Victor's face as he knocked at the open door of Victor's office. "Got a minute?"

Victor smiled quickly. "Sure." He stood and moved from behind his desk, eclipsing the diminutive Christmas tree set on a table in the corner of the room. "What are you still doing around here? I thought you were heading down to Mar Negro for some diving on your Christmas break?"

Kai nodded sheepishly. "I was planning to, but a storm front is threatening the peninsula down there. Leftenant Kimbal is from Alyina, so I let her have my leave to visit her family. Besides, I figure we'll see enough of Mar Negro when and if the Falcons decide to punt us off this rock."

Kai brought his left hand out from where he'd hidden it behind his back. "I also wanted to make sure you got this. Merry Christmas."

Victor accepted the gift-wrapped box and efficiently stripped it of the red ribbon and green paper. He opened the small box and set both the lid and the protective layer of cotton on his desk. Then he lifted out a carefully fashioned piece of dark jadework. Shaped like a monkey, cinnabar had been inlaid in the jade to give the creature eyes of red. In its right hand, it held a staff and its left hand clung to the leather thong to which the pendant hung.

Victor looked up. "A monkey?"

"Yes, but no ordinary monkey." Kai knew from Victor's voice that he was pleased with the gift, yet puzzled and curious about it. "That is Sun Hou-Tzu, King of the Monkeys in Chinese mythology. It wasn't because you remind me of a monkey that I got it for you, but because Stone Monkey and you are very much alike."

"Calling me a monkey, are you?" A smirk lit Victor's face. "You're digging yourself a deeper hole here, Kai."

Kai raised his hands. "I don't think so. Stone Monkey was royalty who hated anyone who gave him hollow titles and deferred to him because of his nobility. He was a mighty warrior who could not be defeated by even the fiercest of the gods. He was also cunning enough to win freedom from Yen-lo-wang for his people. Because of him, monkeys are not subject to death in the way we know it. Furthermore, Sun Hou-Tzu won for himself immortality."

He shrugged. "Being as how you stand to inherit all the worlds of two nations, it's not too easy finding a gift for you. This totem is meant to remind you to always be yourself, no matter what. And if there's any justice, the Stone Monkey will share with you some of his audacious good luck. He'll keep you safe."

Victor smiled and set the box on the desk. "I won't need his protection as long as you're around, or did Sun Hou-Tzu intervene on Twycross?"

Distant echoes of battle played through Kai's mind, but the gratitude in Victor's voice kept Kai's feelings of regret at bay. "I don't know, but I don't see any reason to take chances."

"Nor do I." Victor retreated to the corner of the room and pulled a box from beneath his meager tree. "I didn't think I'd have a chance to give this to you until you'd returned." He extended the package to Kai. "Merry Christmas, my friend."

Kai accepted the package wordlessly. Its white and red striped paper felt crisp and clean beneath his fingers, and the package felt weighty. Kai tipped it up and broke the tape on the narrow end. Carefully and slowly, he unfolded the wrappings.

Victor looked petulant. "That's not how to open a present. You're supposed to tear the paper apart."

Kai raised an eyebrow. "I must have missed that law."

"It's not a law yet," Victor laughed. "Just wait till I take the throne."

Kai chuckled as he slid the box from the tube of wrapping paper. He pulled off the top and secured it to the bottom of the box. "Victor," he exclaimed, "this is great."

Victor beamed as Kai pulled the stainless steel survival knife and

239

plastic sheath from the box. "They told me that it was treated not to rust even in what passes for oceans on this rock. The hilt is hollow and contains matches, some medical stuff, and a cord-saw. You can fix the sheath to your boot and keep it with you in your 'Mech."

"I'll bet that this baby could saw through some 'Mech armor," Kai allowed as he lightly passed his finger over the serrated edge of the blade, "but I don't think I'll want to get that close."

"I know that, but you're the one who had to find alternate transport home from Twycross, not me." Victor gave Kai a devilish grin. "I've got Sun Hou-Tzu to keep me safe, and you've got the knife."

For the first time since they'd landed on Alyina, the sense of impending doom that had weighed Kai down began to lift. "It's best to be safe, but we don't have to worry too much. I keep my bargains."

Victor's brows met, revealing his confusion. "Come again?"

"Don't you remember? When you said you'd get me a 'Mech so I could be in the fight on Twycross, I asked if I had to wait twenty years to thank you for that opportunity. You said yes, so that would mean we were certain to be alive in twenty years. Well, it worked on Twycross, and we've got nineteen more years to go."

The Prince nodded slowly. "Of course, Kai, now I remember. And thanks to you I'm able to hold up my end of the bargain."

"And I you." Kai closed the knife box. "Well, I'd best let you get on with whatever you had planned for today."

"Wait, Kai. How long until you've got duty?"

"About six hours." He hefted the box. "I'll go stash this in *Yen-lo-wang* and do some reading before watch. Or, if the rumors are true and they've got a holovid of Ken Tom's new discovery, Jake Lonestar, taking the title on Solaris, maybe I'll watch that."

"No way." Victor picked up the Stone Monkey carving and fastened the leather thong around his neck. "You're coming with me to Duke Kuchel's estate for Christmas dinner. I want at least one person there I enjoy talking with."

"But his estate's an hour from here by helicopter. For me to get back in time means we'll only be able…"

"…to spend four hours there." Victor's grin seemed to match the irreverent leer on the Stone Monkey's face. "You'll save me tracking Galen down and forcing him to call me with 'urgent business' later on. My original plan would have left me stuck there for six hours."

Kai shrugged hopelessly, but felt good. "All right. I'm happy to go with you. Four hours with the cream of Alyina's aristocrats?"

Victor frowned. "Yeah. If worse comes to worse, we'll manufacture a crisis and get back here faster."

Though they found the party was neither worse nor better than expected, the two comrades never did have to manufacture a crisis to save them. Within two hours of their arrival, Kai and Victor were in a helicopter headed back to headquarters. The reports were not good.

The Clans had appeared insystem and would make planetfall in eleven days. And with that news, Kai's premonition of doom returned full force.

Unity Palace, Imperial City, Luthien
Pesht Military District, Draconis Combine
26 December 3051

Theodore Kurita's decision to forego formal welcoming ceremonies for the mercenaries pleased Shin Yodama. Having been on Outreach, he disagreed with court protocol experts, who said that such a breach of honor would doom any hopes of a productive working relationship between Combine and mercenary forces. Theodore had reasoned, and Shin agreed, that a formal welcoming ceremony would only give many of the High Command who still felt contemptuous of mercenaries an opportunity to air their counterproductive attitudes.

Shin waited along with Theodore, Hohiro, and the leaders of the Combine defense forces in the cedar-walled reception chamber beneath the palace's helipad. He felt a mild tremor ripple through the floor as the helicopter landed and a shaft of sun streamed down the staircase from above. As the mercenaries began to descend, the whooping of the helicopter rotors drowned out the sound of their boot heels on the circular stone stairway.

Jaime Wolf was the first of the four men to appear. He bowed to Theodore, then approached to offer his hand. "Konnichi-wa, Kanrei-sama. I wish the circumstances were better for renewing our acquaintance."

Theodore, having returned the bow in both depth and duration, shook Wolf's hand heartily. "I agree this is not the most pleasant of occasions, but your presence makes it less oppressive. Still, I imagine a Christian hell or two has frozen over because of your arrival here on Luthien."

Morgan Kell smiled as he shook Theodore's hand. "We were speculating that Dante's Inferno would now have to be retitled Spark."

The Combine's Prince laughed politely at the joke and Shin smiled, though the reference went right by him. Theodore offered his hand to MacKenzie Wolf in greeting, then hesitated before the fourth man in the group.

Tall and broad-shouldered, the man wore the double-breasted shirt of the Kell Hounds' dress uniform, as did Colonel Kell. Shin noted that the man's eyes indicated an oriental bloodline, and his deferential attitude toward Theodore gave the impression that he must formerly have been from the Combine. His bronze hair and light-colored eyes led Shin to guess he was from the Rasalhague District. The ribbons sewn to the left ear of the wolf's-head on the man's jacket suggested he had been with the Hounds for a long time. Yet, even with those clues, Shin had no idea who the officer was.

The man bowed deeply to Theodore. "*Konnichi-wa*, Kurita Theodore-*sama*. It is the fulfillment of a life's desire to meet with you again and to stand with you as an ally."

"I am most honored to welcome you back to the Combine." Theodore bowed respectfully, then straightened up to his full height. "Akira Brahe, you have come a long way since your time in the Second Legion of Vega."

At the mention of the man's name, Shin began to recall the little he knew of the man. Akira was the son of one of the Combine's greatest MechWarriors, Yorinaga Kurita. In 3013, at the head of the Second Sword of Light, Yorinaga had killed Prince Ian Davion, Hanse's elder brother. Thirteen years later, he killed Patrick Kell, Morgan Kell's younger brother. Three years after that, Yorinaga and Morgan fought a duel on Nusakan that culminated in Yorinaga's committing *seppuku*. Akira repudiated his ties with the Combine after his father's suicide, left the Genyosha, and joined the Kell Hounds.

Shin shot a glance at Narimasa Asano. The gray-haired man smiled as Akira bowed, and then he returned the bow. "I recall that, twenty years ago, we did not look forward to meeting a next time because it could only mean contest in battle. How fortunate that life has proved us wrong."

"Most fortunate, Asano-*sama*."

Theodore completed introductions between the two groups. Hideyoshi and the First Sword's Yoshida looked less than pleased to see mercenaries on Luthien, but Shin knew their displeasure had even

243

deeper roots. Both men had favored formal ceremonies to greet the mercenaries, less to give honor than to keep Theodore's father away from such an event.

That would have been incredible, Shin thought as he visualized a meeting between Jaime Wolf and Takashi Kurita. The last such took place at Hanse Davion's wedding more than twenty years ago, and had become something of a legend. Jaime Wolf, whom the Coordinator had tried to have killed, took Takashi to task for his lack of honor. Later that year, after suffering a minor stroke, Takashi issued his infamous Death to Mercenaries order that had alienated so many officers, Akira Brahe included. As nearly as Shin knew, Takashi still awaited the day when someone would deliver Jaime Wolf's head to him in a box.

The Kanrei conducted his entourage to an elevator, which took them down to an auxiliary briefing room next to the command center. Shin and Hohiro both logged onto terminals in the room, starting data feeds pouring information onto their screens. With the flick of a finger, either man could summarize the data into charts holographically projected above the meeting table.

Theodore stood with his back to the double doors of the black room. Jaime Wolf and Morgan Kell stood facing him at the far end of the table. The other officers filled the space between the Kanrei and the mercenaries, with Akira Brahe and Narimasa Asano at Theodore's right. Near the center of the group, Shin and Hohiro formed a buffer between the Combine officers and the mercenary leaders.

Theodore wasted no time getting started. "Before your arrival, we were looking at five crack regiments of 'Mechs: the First Sword of Light, the Otomo, both Genyosha regiments, and the Second Legion of Vega. We also had three militia regiments. Two were to be assigned to field operations against the Elementals, using analogs of the armor suits we captured on Wolcott. The third is an Omega regiment that will make any enemy pay dearly if it comes to house-to-house in Imperial City."

With a nod from Theodore, Shin produced graphic representations of each unit's table of organization and equipment. Yoshida winced to see his unit's secrets revealed before men he had ever considered enemies, but Wolf's appreciative grunt and nodded salute clearly made him feel proud. Morgan Kell's dark gaze drank in all the information but, unlike Jaime, he did not reveal his thoughts.

MacKenzie glanced at Theodore. "With one regiment in Imperial City, you must be planning to fight nearby. What is your choice of position?"

The Kanrei signaled his son to provide a map. A green neon

topographical representation of Imperial City and the surrounding area floated above the table. Small red rectangles represented the units to be used in defense of the capital.

"Logistical necessities force us to battle within a fifty-klick radius of Imperial City. Luthien is so heavily industrialized that virtually any other venue would cause incalculable civilian injuries, not to mention damage to industry. We are fortunate that, aside from Turtle Bay, the Clans have fought a clean war. Even if they lost the battle but destroyed our industry, we would still be hamstrung. As it is, we intend to evacuate Imperial City the moment the Clans appear insystem."

Theodore pointed to a flat plain that stood beyond the hills that ringed Imperial City like fortifications. "This is the Tairakana Plain. We intend to defend here, then use the hills to fight a delaying battle as we come back toward the city. The hills will shorten ranges so that the Clans no longer have a gross equipment advantage. Our companies that have undergone field modification will act as a harassing force to keep the enemy concentrated on one front. If the Clan forces want to spread out and encircle the city, that's to our advantage, but we cannot allow them to flank our forces and cut them off from the city."

"Agreed." Morgan Kell stroked his snowy beard. "With us, you add seven regiments to your number, three of those—my first and two of Jamie's units—are equipped with Clan-type weaponry. With our strength added to yours, will you want to modify the plan?"

Theodore folded his arms over his chest. "Not substantially. What I really hope to do is use your regiments as reserves to bolster our line." He nodded to Hohiro, and symbols for the mercenary regiments appeared in several locations in the hills. "We will be holding the only quick route through the hills, so if the Clans pierce our line, they will lay open the way to the capital. If we fail, the fate of Luthien is in your hands."

"*lie!*"

The fear and fury breathed into that single word shocked Shin. As his head snapped around, he saw Takashi Kurita stalking through the doors. Silhouetted by the light from the open door, the Coordinator of the Draconis Combine gave off outrage like heat waves from a fusion engine. He stopped before Jaime Wolf, giving the mercenary a cobra-like stare. "So, the rumor is true. My son brings his treason home with him."

Takashi turned on his son. "It is not enough that you leave Luthien for nine months to consult with our enemy, but now you bring him here! Then I find you turning over to him responsibility for the

245

safety of Imperial City!" Takashi faltered. "Maximilian Liao was fortunate in his child. At least Romano had the mercy to assassinate him before destroying his nation."

"If that is truly your mind, shall I get a gun and shoot you?"

At Theodore's reply, Yoshida and Hideyoshi looked in horror at the Coordinator, who seemed refueled rather than crushed by his son's words. Takashi's head came up and his dark eyes flashed ominously. "Your acquiescence comes too late to bring me solace. I have acknowledged your right to command the military forces of the Combine, and I would not unman you by stripping you of your office now." He fought to keep pain from his face. "Do not emasculate your own nation by putting the fate of our Imperial City in the hands of *yohei* units."

Theodore pointed toward the map. "As you can see, father, our forces are arrayed to bear the brunt of the attack. We will do all we can to be sure we never need the mercenaries' help. It is the DCMS that defends the capital; the mercenaries are only here to offer support." The Kanrei fell silent, the muscles of his face working as he struggled for inner control. "Besides, father, what unit would we draw off to ward the capital? We have no others."

Takashi shook his head as though rebuking a foolish child. "You have one more unit, Kanrei." His tone dripped scorn. "It is the one composed of my own bodyguards and of MechWarriors who fought boldly long before you were born. These troops are known as the Dragon's Claws." The Coordinator raised his head and matched his son's stare without surrendering anything. "We will draw the line, and with me at their head, not a single Clansmen will cross it."

Stortalar City, Gunzburg
Radstadt Province, Free Rasalhague Republic
31 December 3051

To set foot once more into the Iron Jarl's antechamber sent a chill down Phelan Wolf's spine. With his ceremonial Wolf mask hiding his face, none who guided him toward Tor Miraborg's office guessed his identity or that he might have reason for unpleasant memories of the place. These guides had not been present two and a half years earlier when Jarlwards had conducted Phelan, severely beaten and half naked, to see their master.

And they wouldn't know that his office was the last place I ever saw Tyra. Phelan recalled the few minutes they'd had together, holding one another on the red leather bench in the room. *This is where she gave me the belt buckle she'd made.* He let his anger at Vlad rekindle his hatred for Tor Miraborg. If not for her father, Tyra would have come with him and the Kell Hounds, and he'd never have ended up on his odyssey with the Clans.

The hooded, charcoal gray cloak Phelan wore was just a shade darker than his leather garments and enamel mask. The cloak's wolf-fur trim broadened the shoulders of his silhouette and gave him a more imposing air. The mask, whose jutting muzzle and bared teeth resembled the head of his *Wolfhound*, made him look truly ferocious. None of his escorts got too close, nor did they speak to him unnecessarily.

As for Phelan, he spoke not at all.

He had disguised himself according to Natasha's suggestion because he relished the idea of fooling Tor Miraborg. Yet on the way down to the planet and after being met by lesser officials, his outlook on his mission changed. Were he there only to take revenge on Miraborg, he would have done anything to shatter the man.

I would have treated him as Vlad treated me.

That was the realization that struck Phelan just after stepping from the shuttle Carew had piloted down to the Gunzburg. While greeting Miraborg's envoys, he saw their unmistakable terror. All paid him great deference, continually apologizing for what they feared might be Tor Miraborg's hostile reaction to him. As one explained, "Well, the Varldherre is a military man, *ja?* You will understand him and his ways, *ja?*"

Suddenly Phelan's little game took on great importance. Not only must he win Gunzburg's surrender for the honor of the Wolves, he also had to win it for the people of Gunzburg. Should he fail and the mission fall to Marcos to complete, Phelan knew the Crusader would stop at nothing for a quick victory. Nor would Marcos shrink from acts of brutality if he thought they could redeem him.

First, I win the planet's freedom, then I make the Iron Jarl pay!

When a civilian official opened the door to the Iron Jarl's office, Phelan felt as though his last time here was only hours before, not years. Seated in his wheelchair behind a massive mahogany desk, Tor Miraborg still looked every bit the strong leader a world like Gunzburg needed. His silver hair was trimmed short and shaved at the temples as though he were planning to strap himself into a 'Mech when the invasion came. The stripes of dark hair in his white beard still tugged down at the corners of his mouth, reminding Phelan of a badger's striped fur.

Even more memories were aroused by the scar bisecting the left side of Miraborg's face from eyebrow to beard. Phelan remembered how the people of Rasalhague had hated mercenaries after Vinson's Vigilantes caused Miraborg's crippling and scarring. An identical scar marring the face of Miraborg's tall blond aide reminded Phelan of how fanatical had become the devotion of Gunzburg's citizens, many of whom disfigured themselves voluntarily. The scar also reminded him again of Vlad and the Clansman's hatred for him.

The official who opened the door and ushered Phelan in began the introductions, but Miraborg waved her off. "I think the ilKhan's envoy knows who I am. My aide is Hanson Kuusik, a Kapten with the Gunzburg Eagles AeroSpace Regiment."

Kuusik took a step forward and started to offer his hand, but

Phelan's silent disregard for the gesture stopped him. The other man's face flushed as he dropped his hand and resumed his position. Miraborg's restless eyes drank it all in, and a curious look of respect settled over his face.

The official retreated from the room, leaving the trio of warriors alone. Behind Miraborg, a glass wall gave Phelan a good view of Stortalar City. It looked far different in mid-summer than when he'd last seen it, and Phelan decided he preferred the flourishing green of trees and flowers to the white blanket of winter snow. From what he could see as dusk came on below, life continued normally in the city.

Miraborg interlaced his fingers as he rested his forearms on the leather blotter of his desk. "You surprise me by coming here. I thought all negotiations would be conducted via radio transmission. I had not heard that the Wolves negotiate in person."

"I am not here to negotiate." The mask's hollow muzzle let Phelan's voice echo back on itself, giving it a disembodied quality. "I have come to accept your surrender."

Kuusik's eyes narrowed and his urge to fight rode plainly on his face. Miraborg only stared at Phelan, as though his gaze could peel away the mask to reveal the man beneath it. "Our surrender?" He said the word not as though it were a ridiculous idea, but as though it were an option he had long ago dismissed. "Are your terms open to negotiation?"

"As I said before, I am not here to negotiate. Surrender, unconditionally, or your world dies."

The Varldherre sat back and stroked his chin. Kuusik, too tried to hide the expression on his face, but he failed. As he spoke, his nostrils flared and contempt edged his voice. "Perhaps we should be the ones offering terms for surrender. We have a formidable force on this world, and we know how to fight you. We almost beat you at Memmingen."

Phelan waited a moment to be certain Kuusik had finished speaking his threat, then he shook his head. "You are not dealing with the same commander who led the forces on Memmingen. As formidable as your force is, we have the equipment and personnel to destroy it. We know, for example, that half the fighters from the Third Drakøns may have made it to Gunzburg, but less than forty percent of them are operational. We also know that air strikes at Danzig, Felskinka, and Kosparris will destroy your ability to resupply and maintain your aircraft. Perhaps you will have air superiority for an hour or two, but destroying those three bases will cost us nothing because we can accomplish it through planetary bombardment."

"You are bluffing!"

Phelan ignored Kuusik and looked at Miraborg. "You are a warrior with a long and glorious history. You have fought against great odds in your time, but none have ever been so stacked against you. What I say about your forces should tell you how much more other information I have. If you choose to fight, many, many people will die."

The Iron Jarl frowned. "I can acknowledge the truth of your information, but that still does not answer the Kapten's charge that you are bluffing."

"Yes," Kuusik chimed in. "We hurt you at Memmingen. You do not have the resources necessary to fight us. We won't roll over and die for you."

"Remember, Kapten, war is not all glory and afterglow." Phelan's menacing tone took some of the sneer from Kuusik's face. "You may be prepared to die for your world, but is your family? Are your friends?"

He fixed Miraborg with a harsh stare. "You know I am not bluffing."

"Do I?"

The Clansman nodded slowly. "You do. What we ask is simple, and in return, we will leave you and your people in power. ComStar will act as liaison to keep us informed of what your government is doing. They will also advise us on your transportation needs for import and export trade with your usual trading partners. Your troops will be disarmed, of course, but they will not be Dispossessed."

"What good is it to have a neutered 'Mech?" Kuusik snarled bitterly.

"Is dying in the husk of an armed 'Mech somehow preferable?" Phelan brought his gloved hands out from beneath the cloak, forcing it behind his shoulders. "I offer you your lives and to spare your world the certain destruction that war would bring. It is your choice, Varldherre. The people will follow your lead. We do not ask that you embrace us as allies or friends, but only that you acknowledge us as master. Is not some loss of pride worth all the suffering it will buy?"

Kuusik dropped to his knees and took hold of Miraborg's right hand where it rested on the arm of his wheelchair. "Send this animal packing. You are the Iron Jarl. You are the champion of Rasalhague's freedom. If you give in to his demands, everything will have been wasted. Your daughter's death will have meant nothing!"

"What!" Phelan's surprise exploded through his mask. "Tyra is dead?"

He and Tyra had shared three months of passion, then been torn apart when the Kell Hounds left for the Periphery. Though they had said their goodbyes and made a formal end to their relationship, all that had happened to Phelan since his capture by the Clans had not left him the space to put his feelings to rest. No matter how much he loved Ranna, he had hoped to see Tyra again if only to learn how she had fared since their last meeting.

Tor Miraborg yanked his hand free of Kuusik's grip. "Do not tell me what to do, Kapten." A tear trickled down the scarred side of his face. He looked up at Phelan, his eyes lifeless. "Yes, my daughter is dead. It was she who drove her fighter into your flagship. Jaime Wolf said her action killed your warlord and bought us a year's respite from your attacks. Even if that were true, it was not worth my daughter's life."

Kuusik sank back on his haunches, his face utterly drained of color. "What are you saying?"

"I am saying that I have finally learned the lesson that might have saved my daughter. A leader must be more than simply a focus for his people's ambitions and desires. I am a military man, but my responsibilities extend far beyond soldiery on this world. Before, I could assure our people that their safety was inviolate because the Eagles could and would destroy all our foes. I cannot give them that assurance now.

"The time has come to truly act as a leader. Perhaps Tyra would not have left and joined the Rasalhague Drakøns had I done so before. I blame myself for her death."

The Kapten sprang to his feet. "You were not to blame for her defection! That mercenary seduced her. He wormed his way into her heart and confused her with stories of glory to be won on distant worlds." Kuusik drove his right fist into his left palm with a loud smack. "I only wish I had killed him when we fought."

"It was enough that you bested him in single combat…"

"Ha!" Phelan's hands clenched in anger. "Single combat? Perhaps you were the only one left standing, but that's because your confederates had been scattered."

Puzzlement knitted Miraborg's dark brows while fear flashed through Kuusik's eyes. Even as Kuusik started toward him, Phelan realized that the Kapten had never told the Varldherre he had jumped Phelan with a gang of men that night so long ago. *Of course, the Varldherre would have considered that an act of cowardice!* Kuusik had been able to hide the truth because everyone believed that Phelan's protests about the number of attackers was a lie intended to hide his

251

shame at defeat.

The Kapten's lunge came fast, but that mattered little. After Phelan's months of training with Evantha, Kuusik seemed clumsy and sluggish. Like a drunken brawler, the Kapten threw himself off balance as he punched, his fist looping through the air where Phelan's ducking head had been. The man stumbled forward.

Swinging with everything he had, Phelan hammered his right fist into Kuusik's chest. A hollow thump sounded as the blow landed directly below the Kapten's sternum, knocking the wind out of him. Hands clutched to his chest, Kuusik pitched forward and desperately tried to suck in air. Phelan's left hand clipped him behind the ear and accelerated his descent.

A sudden fire ignited in Miraborg's eyes. "Who the hell are you?"

Phelan wanted nothing so much as to tear off his mask so he could gloat over the Iron Jarl. His hands started up toward the mask, but a cold detachment replaced the urge and instead he readjusted the cloak that enshrouded him. *Revenge was something Phelan Kell would have demanded, but I am no longer Phelan Kell.*

It was Phelan Wolf who spoke. "You do not know me. We captured Phelan Kell in the Periphery. I know something of his last days on Gunzburg from his debriefing. He spoke fondly of your daughter, and I know he would have grieved her passing."

"He is dead?"

"He was on the flagship that Tyra rammed. Shortly thereafter, he was no more."

The Iron Jarl looked up slowly. "I see."

"Perhaps you do." Phelan looked beyond him, watching as the city's lights began to glow in the dusk. "You have a beautiful world and are responsible for safeguarding it. I must have your decision."

Miraborg sat so still and silent that Phelan wondered if the man had slipped into a state of catatonia. The office dimmed and Kuusik's moans ceased as he drifted into unconsciousness. Hardly daring to breathe, Phelan, too, remained motionless, waiting for the Varldherre's decision.

Finally, Miraborg's head came up. "I accept your terms for the surrender of Gunzburg. I will inform ComStar of my choice as successor, then I will retire from public life."

Phelan shook his head. "Do not retire."

"What?" Miraborg looked like a man at the breaking point. "All I have done is poison my life and the people around me. Kuusik there is only one of thousands more misguided men and women on this world, thousands whom I have led astray. I cannot continue in this position."

"Yes you can." The Clansman pointed toward the window. "Today, by agreeing to this surrender, you go from being a symbol for your people to a leader of your people. Your discipline, your love of Gunzburg, and your firm hand are still important and vital. And now you show the wisdom of knowing when to change."

Miraborg seemed to weigh Phelan's every word, assaying their truth. "Yes," he said at last, "I created the problem. It is for me to solve it."

Phelan nodded. "I shall return to my ship and inform the ilKhan of your decision." He turned to leave, but Miraborg's voice called him back. "Wait!"

The Clansman faced the crippled warrior. Miraborg slid open a drawer in his desk and took out a pair of mirrored sunglasses. Phelan recognized them instantly as his, and recalled his promise to Miraborg that he would recover them one day.

The Iron Jarl slid them in his direction. "I believe these belong to you." The man's lower lip trembled. "To the victor go the spoils."

Phelan made no move to take them. "If that is true, these belong to your people, for it is they who have triumphed today."

When Phelan and Carew stepped from the shuttle, they were immediately caught up in a frenzy of activity as bondsmen scurried around the shuttle bay. They waded through a sea of bodies securing the ship to the deck and found Natasha standing by the airlock bulkhead. She smiled broadly and offered Phelan her hand.

"Very well done, Star Commander. The ilKhan sends his warmest congratulations."

Phelan stripped off his right glove and shook her hand. Looking around at the furious activity in the bay, and the lack of people there to greet him, he felt confused. "What's going on?"

Natasha gave him one of those grins that said she'd managed yet another coup. "While you were down there enjoying real gravity, I've been working. I taught Marcos another lesson in bidding and won the right to take Satalice."

Phelan blinked. "Another assault?"

She nodded. "We've just been waiting for you before we jump. The New Black Widows will get their first battle inside a week." She chuckled slyly. "You didn't think we'd let you have all the fun, did you?"

253

Forward Observation Post, Tairakana Plains, Luthien
Pesht Military District, Draconis Combine
5 January 3052

The total lack of activity on the Skulker car's sensors made Shin Yodama uneasy. The Clans had grounded their forces fifty klicks east of Luthien, right where the Tairakana Plains began their gentle slope down to Basin Lake. The negotiation between the ground forces and the incoming Clans had not revealed much about the attacker's numbers, so recon vehicles like Shin's had gone out under cover of darkness to learn whatever possible about the enemy.

Shin glanced at the digital time display in the aft section of the boxy armored car. Dawn stood yet an hour away, and it was then that everyone expected the attack to come. Stooping down to duck into the driving compartment, he tapped the driver's shoulder. "Head out another klick. We have to find something."

The driver looked back at Shin with fear on his face. "Begging your pardon, sir, but I really don't think we need to see the whites of their eyes."

Shin gave the man a shrug. "I don't like this any more than you do, but if we can give our air support some fixes, it'll mean less for our 'Mechs to shoot." He turned back to the two Techs at the van's scanners. "We're pulling forward another kilometer. Stay sharp. I have a feeling we'll get our contact."

He slapped the dangling legs of the vehicle's turret gunner. "That goes double for you. If you see it, shoot it."

"Hai!"

The driver eased the vehicle forward and kept the pace at a leisurely 10 kph. At that speed, the triple-axle scout tank handled the relatively smooth terrain like a luxury car, and Shin knew that was important. No only did it make data interp easier, but it prevented shaking up the vehicle's electronics. Without them, the Skulker would be little more than a blind fish in a shark tank.

"Contact. I have a set of blips, intermittent, dead ahead."

Shin hunched over the Tech's shoulder. "Gunner, bring the turret to oh-ninety degrees at five hundred meters. Patch your periscope through to the monitor and magnify one hundred percent."

An image flickered onto the monitor near Shin's head, and he fiddled with the controls to sharpen the contrast. The starlight picture revealed a number of oversized humanoids stalking forward. Standing 2.3 meters high, they wore metallic suits with a laser muzzle where the right hand should have been. On the other arm, a laser was married to the hand. The back of the armored suit carried a boxy missile launcher that, from practical experience, Shin knew would detach after firing its complement of two SRMs.

Beyond these, he saw more similar shadowy forms moving through the night. "Six, seven, eight, nine. I mark nine Elementals."

The Tech at the radar scope cursed softly. "They have to be jamming us somehow because I only get five or six on the screen."

An explosion rocked the Skulker, bouncing it onto the passenger-side wheels. Shin flew back against the other Tech, cracking the man's head against his magscan monitor. As the Tech flopped limp to the deck, Shin leaped past his overturned chair and dashed to the driving compartment. "Move it! Get us out of here. Gunner, hit anything and everything!"

As the driver cranked the wheel around, the Skulker swung north, its headlights slicing the night. A ruby beam shot from the dome at the tank's center. In the distance, it illuminated the black form of a man and started a small brushfire. Another bolt coursed through the darkness and burned a scar into the landscape, but the tank's quick turn swept the target out of the windscreen's visual arc.

The driver stomped down on the accelerator, launching the Skulker in a sprint across the landscape. Shin glanced back at the conscious Tech, relieved the man had had the presence of mind to radio in their position and the readings for the Elementals. As the Skulker bounced up over one little hill, Shin braced for impact as the tank flew through the air. The landing shivered the whole vehicle like a hammer-struck anvil, driving Shin to his knees.

The driver cursed as the headlights pinpointed an Elemental standing in the middle of the unpaved track along which they raced. He started to shift his foot to the brake, but Shin jammed his own right foot down, crushing the driver's foot to the gas pedal.

"Full speed! Just keep it going! Don't stop for anything!"

The Elemental loosed a rocket from the launcher pod on his back. Shooting straight at the Skulker's nose, it exploded with a hellacious flash and the acrid scent of explosives, but failed to breach the vehicle's armor. The Scout's driver instinctively shied from the flash, but kept his hands locked onto the wheel, keeping it steady. The Skulker burst through the fire and smoke without slowing at all, then bucked and bounced as it rolled the Elemental beneath its entire length.

Through the rearview display, Shin saw the Elemental's body half-buried in the scrubby grasses and a number of his very alive comrades appearing. As those Elementals began to line up, he grabbed the wheel and jerked it to the right. As the tank swerved, heavy SRM fire shot through the air where the recon car should have been.

"Gunner, directly aft. Fire at will." Shin looked back at the radar Tech. "Raise HQ?"

"Help's on the way. We're to make for map coordinate A2536."

"Got it. Gunner, some fire! The Elementals are fast."

A scream and the rushing howl of the wind answered his request. Looking up, Shin saw the gunner's twitching legs disappear up into the turret. The wind gained in volume as the scream dopplered away to nothing. Replacing it was the shriek of metal being bent out of shape and the crackling of ceramic armor breaking.

Shin popped the driver's safety belts and steadied the wheel. "To the back! Blow the aft hatch and go! We've got one on top of us!"

The driver dragged himself out of his seat, and the Skulker slowed precipitously. Shin slipped into the man's seat, tugged the safety straps into place and snapped them together with the buckle over his chest. He heard a muffled whump as the explosive bolts on the aft hatch blew, then watched scraps of debris whirl up through the cab as they were sucked out the back.

The rearview monitor showed that all three men had gotten clear, with at least one up and moving. Alone except for the Elemental burrowing into the Skulker from above, Shin smiled with grim determination. In his first run-in with an Elemental, the damned Clansman had refused to die. "Let's just see if you're as hearty as your ally was!"

The speedometer reported a velocity of 112 kph when the

Skulker hit a meter-tall hump in the plains. Shin wrenched the wheel left while the machine was still airborne and clung to it like a drowning man. For a second or two, the only sounds he heard were the wind and the racing of the engine.

The Skulker's nose hit the ground first with a bone-crunching jolt that flicked Shin forward against the safety straps. Instantly, sparks and smoke streaked through the cab and the headlights shorted, blinding Shin to the world outside. The aft end of the car whipped forward from the right, then the rear wheels caught broadside and the Skulker slammed into the ground on its right side.

The equipment explosions from the back were drowned out by the din as the recon tank rolled up into its own roof. The great weight crushed the domed turret, shattering the ring assembly binding it to the Skulker. As the vehicle bounced up into the air, the turret sailed off like a wobbling saucer, then the Skulker pounded down into the ground and continued to tumble.

Shin couldn't count the number of times the Skulker somersaulted. His white-knuckled grip on the steering wheel snapped it off and warped it utterly out of shape. Tooth chips ground between his molars and blood was dripping from his nose. Even so, when the Skulker finally stopped on its right side, Shin knew he'd sustained no serious injuries, and he sent a silent prayer of thanks to his ancestors for keeping death at bay.

Popping the belts loose, he crawled back and got out through the escape hatch in the tank's bottom. Still dizzy and disoriented, he ran away from the Skulker, then sank to his knees on a hilltop twenty-five meters to the west. Behind him, the Skulker exploded as the ruptured gas tank poured fuel onto the sparking equipment in the back.

In the fire's backlight, he thought he saw the tank's other crewmen, but he could not be certain. Armed only with a heavy pistol, he couldn't afford to take the chance that it was an Elemental instead, though the body parts scattered around the turret's flattened disk told him it was not the Elemental.

Daubing at the blood from his nose with his sleeve, Shin estimated his position and figured out where rendezvous point A2536 had to be. Before he could begin to head toward it, however, a mounting roar echoed over the plains. Fearing the sound more by instinct and training than sense, he dropped to one knee and looked toward the sky.

Afterburners lit up with gold cylinders of fire, the First Sword of Light's aerospace wing shot toward the east barely fifty meters above the ground. Pulsed rain of scarlet laserfire strobed through the blackness. Brilliant clouds of yellow and red fire wreathed and defined wing-mounted rocket pods. The LRMs streaked off until they became pinpoints of light that erupted into boiling balls of angry red flame.

Even as the Combine's aerospace forces pounded the Clans, Shin felt the brief taste of victory sour in his mouth. The explosions lit by inferno rockets and cluster bombs silhouetted rank upon rank of enemy 'Mechs, then the night jealously hid them again. Even without trying to guess their number, Shin knew one thing for certain: The Clans meant to take Luthien, no matter what the cost, and they had brought with them more than enough 'Mechs to do the job.

I'm going to die if we don't get some support.

That realization came to Victor as his 'Mech's autocannon whined out a metal typhoon. The storm of projectiles sliced like a surgeon's scalpel through the knee of the enemy OmniMech. Armor shards sprayed back over the battlefield, ricocheting off the smoking hulk of Don Gilmore's *Archer*. The joint gave way and the falling 'Mech's stump impaled the dark earth, but still the machine did not go down.

Victor pulled his *Daishi* back to cover behind a granite outcropping. Because of its titanic size and dependence on lasers for primary weaponry, he'd named it *Prometheus* in honor of the mythic lightbringer. Glancing down at the auxiliary monitor's report on his armor status, he realized that the vulturelike Clan 'Mechs would like nothing better than to pick apart and eat his 'Mech. *Next time I name my 'Mech after something that had a peaceful life—like Bambi!*

Victor keyed his radio. "Zephyr One, bring the rest of your lance back toward me."

"Bill Davis is gone, Kommandant. Dave Jewell and I are it."

Victor knew the voice on the radio had to be Dennis Pesuti's. "Zephyr Two, work back to the north and east. You and Zephyr Three cover each other."

"Wilco, Tornado One"

259

Galen Cox's voice cut in on the frequency. "Victor, that'll leave your left flank open."

"No it won't. You and I are going to hit the Clanners from the flank as those two draw them up. Our field of combat narrows as we get near the bluffs. We can hold them, at least long enough to get some help. Relay those orders to the rest of our company."

Caution echoed through Galen's reply. "Victor, you know as well as I do that the Clans are herding us in that direction. We can't fall for whatever they're planning."

"Dammit, Galen, don't do this to me." Victor ground his teeth in anger. "It'll buy us some time. I'm going to see if Regimental has any support they can give us."

"Roger, Tornado One. I just want to be sure you understand the risks. As long as you do, I know you'll find a way out of it."

"Got it, Squall One. And thanks." Victor punched up the Regimental Support frequency, but all he got was dead air. Switching over to the secondary frequency, he got an earful of Babel. It sounded like hundreds of voices all pleading for the very things he wanted to request. Suddenly eerie static blasted through the speakers and one less voice demanded help.

"This is Tornado One in Sector 2660. I need fire support."

"Request logged, Tornado One." The operator sounded fatigued and hopeless.

"Regimental, what can you give me?"

"Be advised, Tornado One, that we have no resources for you at this time."

Victor worked his Omni back, then melted armor from a Clan *MadCat* with two well-placed laser bolts from his 'Mech's arm-mounted large lasers. "The situation here is a bit desperate, Regimental. I need support in 2660, now!"

"Things are desperate all over, Tornado One! The enemy has 2750 and 2650. If they push through to 2550, you're cut off—the whole peninsula is gone. We're holding the line, but we need everything we have."

"Good. We're coming in through 2560." Victor knew that the loss of sector 2550 would cut him off from the DropShips meant to evacuate his people should the tide of battle continue in its current disastrous direction. "Give me some cover and we can help out."

"Request logged, Tornado One."

Victor saw Dennis Pesuti's *Victor* reel backward, armor steaming off its left flank. "That's not a request, Regimental. That's an order!"

"Who in hell do you think you are?" The comtech's voice came back hot. "Clear the frequency, you idiot!"

Victor pounded his fist into the padded arm of the command couch. "I am Prince Victor Ian Davion, dammit! I own this goddamned army and my men are dying out here. Unless you want to explain to my father why I went the same way, you'll lay down a diamond pattern of artillery-deployed mines. Alternate with cluster rounds. Do it now! These coordinates. We'll be gone by the time they get here."

Fear rocketed through the comtech's voice. "Wilco immediately, Tornado One. Downloading coordinates now to Longbomb. Longbomb, mix ADMs with clusters. We've got to save the Prince's ass."

Victor reopened the link to his men. "Storm Company, hurry back on a heading of oh-four-five degrees, repeat oh-four-five degrees. Squall One, you can play rear guard. We're making for sector 2550."

He never heard the various acknowledgements of his order, and refused to look as the secondary monitor toted up the identities of the warriors calling in. At the start of the battle, his battalion had filled three full columns on the screen. Now he could see out the corner of his eye that the list had dropped to less than one column. He didn't know if those left behind were alive or dead, and he'd just called down an artillery strike to obliterate anything left in his sector.

The Clansmen seemed happy to let him and his men flee. Victor fought to present his enemies as poor a target as possible as he retreated, but none took the opportunity to make any potshots. He knew the Clans preferred one on one battling, which Victor admired, but he had no desire to play their game.

Pressed against his flesh, he felt Omi's gift where he'd sewn it inside his cooling vest. He thought of all the samurai tales he'd ever heard, most telling of the hero dying gallantly in defense of a pass or bridge while his lord escaped. *God help me, Omi, I don't want to play the Kurita game, either.*

He shook his head. That was exactly the way Prince Ian Davion, the uncle for whom he was named, had died more than a third of a century before. Victor hoped that sharing the man's name did not mean he would share his fate. *Great heroic traditions I've got all around.*

He fingered the jade amulet Kai had given him. *This marks a legend I'd much rather relive.*

Without warning, the first of the artillery barrages hit home. What had been a mottled green and gray landscape with spindly trees and majestic palms vanished in a sheet of flame. The cluster munitions sowed the area with countless little bomblets that battered and blasted the Clan warriors. As he shut his eyes against the intensity of the explosion, Victor saw one 'Mech reduced to a silhouetted skeleton that immediately collapsed in on itself.

The fire evaporated like an illusion, leaving the killing ground a blackened field pitted with smoking holes. Tattered 'Mechs began to move in the thick mist like zombies rising from their graves. One stumbled forward, and in a bright flash, lost a leg to a mine. The 'Mech toppled onto its side, but its companions kept coming.

Victor worked *Prometheus* east toward the coastline. Once there, he knew they would have a chance to link up with the rest of the Tenth Lyran Guards. The thought that the Jade Falcons were herding them toward that area niggled at the back of his mind. It meant the possibility of a trap or that the regiment had stopped the rest of the Falcons before they could trap the first battalion in a pocket.

As his ragged company reached the wooded plateau, Victor began to feel a bit safer. Directly east, only thirty meters from where he stood, the plateau broke off as though a big knife had sliced it away. Twenty meters below, the Mar Negro's dark waters pounded against the shore that marked the edge of the continental shelf.

The palm tree to his left burst into flames as a Jade Falcon's pulse laser laced it with kilojoules of energy. Victor whipped the crosshairs for both his large lasers onto the blocky outline of the Clan 'Mech. The dot in the center of each pulsed once and he stabbed his thumbs down on the firing button. The coruscating red beams converged on the *MadCat*'s right weapons pod, shearing it off at the wrist.

"Move them back, Galen. We're still being pressed." He used his trio of pulse lasers to lay down hazing fire. The lasers ignited the foliage they hit, creating a screen of fire between Victor and the advancing Clansmen, but that didn't slow the enemy at all. They kept coming and Victor sensed a change in the way they attacked.

Two of the vulture-like *Hagetaka* 'Mechs broke through the blazing barrier and thrust their arms at his Omni. Autocannons with pulse lasers riding sidecar made up their arm-mounted weaponry and it was all concentrated on Victor. The autocannons nibbled tiny chips of armor from the *Daishi*'s chest, then the pulse lasers cauterized the wounds by dripping molten armor over them.

Prometheus stumbled backward as Victor fought against the impact of the autocannon shots and the loss of balance caused by losing more than a ton of armor. That didn't keep him from realizing that the Falcons had worked together to hurt him. If they were willing to do that at this point in the battle, Victor reasoned, they were either desperate or the Clanners had been suckering them all along. *Given the panic at Regimental HQ, we must be dead!*

Galen's *Crusader* stepped forward to put itself between Victor and the Clanners. Its leg-mounted SRM launchers sent a dozen missiles corkscrewing in at one *Hagetaka*. They peppered the Clan 'Mech's jutting torso and right arm with a double handful of detonations that knocked the war machine back into the burning foliage. Its right arm hanging limp and useless, the 'Mech turned to engage them again.

Victor punched up the Regimental frequency again, but this time all he got was buzzing static. Ignoring precautions, he set his radio to broadcast across all the tactical frequencies. "This is Tornado One in sector 2560. We need any help we can get."

He thought he heard a reply, but the thundering detonations of a long-range missile against his *Daishi*'s head set his ears ringing and drowned out the voice. Spinning to his left, Victor cut loose with the autocannon. It caught a *MadCat* dead center and dumped it unceremoniously on its back.

Both he and Galen withdrew as quickly as they could. Already Victor saw on his scanner that the rest of his battalion had made it to the narrows, where they could hold off the Clanners. Heading away as quickly as possible, with Galen close on his heels, he reached a clearing where a granite fang separated a narrow trail from the plateau. The other 'Mechs had already strung themselves out along the path by the time he and Galen broke from the jungle.

Home free! Turning back to lay down cover for Galen, Victor allowed himself a smile. "We made it."

A panicked scream from one of the MechWarriors was Victor's only warning of the ambush. Shooting up to the level of the plateau, five OmniMechs with auxiliary jump jet packs strapped to their hulls leaped up from the Mar Negro. Water coursed off them and seaweed hung from the arms and legs of the 'Mechs, making them look like monsters from the bottom of the sea.

A Gauss rifle projectile smashed into *Prometheus*' right ankle. It crushed the joint, and when Victor tried to steady the toppling 'Mech, the clawlike foot sheared off. The shock of the ankle hitting the ground jolted Victor, but he successfully fought gravity and wrestled the 'Mech upright. He fired back with his lasers, sending melted armor bleeding down his tormentor's torso, but another 'Mech's autocannon burst to his left shoulder spun him to the ground.

Sparks shot from his control console and the light blinked out on one of the torso-mounted pulse lasers. More fire from the 'Mechs strafed his stricken Omni. They kept him enough off-balance that he could not aim well. When he tried to regain his feet, he went down instead like a punch-drunk fighter.

As much as Victor wanted to demand help from the other warriors, he saw they were in the same deep trouble. With all the holes in its armor, Galen's *Crusader* looked like a worm-gnawed corpse. Out on the bluff, the other members of Storm Company were sitting ducks for the newly arrived Clan 'Mechs. Though they fought back, their battered condition and lack of ammunition made their defense a piteous mockery of the power the enemy 'Mechs displayed.

Victor keyed his radio. "Storm Company, disengage. Just run for it. Galen, go." He pulled *Prometheus* into a low crouch. "Go on. I'll cover you."

"No! I won't do it, Victor."

"Go, Hauptmann Cox. That's an order."

"Then discipline me in hell, because I'm not leaving."

The *Crusader* got the granite fang between it and the ocean-going 'Mechs. Galen blasted away at the 'Mechs coming in from the mainland. Steam rose from fractured heat sinks as he launched volley after volley of missiles. The barrels of the *Crusader*'s arm-mounted machine guns glowed red as they relentlessly sprayed the enemy.

In his crouch, Victor presented a more difficult target for the Clanners. His large lasers punched through armor and started internal explosions on one of the five flying 'Mechs. It started to descend, but its loss did not help him at all. Instead of chasing the remnants of Storm Company, the other four 'Mechs turned their attention to Victor. As they jetted toward the ground, Victor thought of his uncle Ian who had also died trying to buy escape for his men.

"Thanks, Galen. I never wanted to die alone."

"Me neither, Highness. Me neither."

"Here they come."

Even as Victor dropped his sights on the lead Clanner and tightened down on all his triggers, he saw a flash of mottled green atop the fang. Coming faster than Victor had ever seen any 'Mech run, a battle-scarred *Centurion* burst into the fray. Without slowing at all, it thrust its right-arm Gauss rifle at a Clan 'Mech. In an electrical flash, a silver ball coursed from the muzzle, hitting dead-on target.

It nailed an enemy 'Mech in what would have been its right ear and crushed the cockpit. The 'Mech spun, its arms pummeling the 'Mech hovering next to it. Both war machines tipped in mid-air and started to somersault backward over the ocean. The dead 'Mech did a swan dive and rocketed down into the dark waters. Fighting to retain control, its companion completed the somersault, but had fallen too far to land on the plateau. Its jets carried it forward and smashed it into the bluffs.

Stunned, Victor breathed, "My God, that's *Yen-lo-wang*!"

The subsequent explosion of their comrade's 'Mech made landing difficult for the other two Clansmen. One flew through the fireball and touched down, but by that time the *Centurion* had leaped down from the fang and sprinted toward the landing site. Coming in low and fast, *Yen-lo-wang* held the fingers of its left hand hooked like claws. In a passing strike, it raked its fingers across the Clan 'Mech's belly, then filled the wound with laserfire from the forearm-mounted pulse lasers.

Its speed unabated, the *Centurion* continued its dash along the edge of the bluff. The last Clan 'Mech landed in a cloud of smoke left by its ill-fated companion. The Clan pilot had just started to turn toward the other Clan 'Mech, which was collapsing around its ruined middle, when *Yen-lo-wang* hit it at full speed. Victor saw armor buckle as the *Centurion*'s shoulder slammed square into the enemy 'Mech's chest.

Beneath the combined weight of the two war engines, the edge of the bluff crumbled. Victor reached out as though the arms of his *Prometheus* could somehow stop the disaster. The Clan 'Mech wrapped its arms around *Yen-lo-wang*, and both 'Mechs stood poised on the edge of the cliff. Victor screamed for Kai to push the Clanner away and save himself, but with a singlemindedness bordering on obsession, *Yen-lo-wang*'s legs kept pumping, pulverizing the bluff's lip into gravel, and carrying the last threat to Hanse Davion's heir away.

"Kai, no! Kai!"

Both 'Mechs vanished from sight. If not for the smoke in the air and the crippled 'Mech slumped on the bluff, there was nothing left to suggest the *Centurion* had ever existed.

Hot tears burning his cheeks, Victor pivoted his 'Mech on its maimed leg. Pulse lasers lashed out at the Clanners coming through the jungle and Victor kept his fingers on the triggers, heedless of the waves of heat roasting him in the cockpit. Beside him, Galen's *Crusader* added its power to the assault. Caution thrown to the winds, it was as though their sorrow and rage translated directly into their attacks and drove the Clanners back.

One by one, the computer shut down Victor's weapons as the heat they generated cooked circuits. He saw lights go out on his status board, but sent more missiles and laser beams to hold the Clansmen at bay. For a half-second, Victor imagined he had stepped into one of

265

those legends where a 'Mech fights of its own accord, regardless of what the machinery and instruments indicate. Then, as he heard voices buzzing in his ears, he realized others had joined them.

"Icestorm Deuce here, Tornado One. We've got your back door. Pull out."

Victor glanced at his holographic display and saw the crescent-shaped bite taken out of the bluff's edge. "Negative, Icestorm Two. We've got a man down in the water. Kai Allard went off the cliff. We have to get him."

"Tornado One, they've got reinforcements on the way." Down-loaded telemetry from a spy satellite filled Victor's auxiliary monitor. The computer showed a company's worth of Clan 'Mechs on a direct line for their sector. "They know you're here, Highness. They want you. You have to leave. Leftenant Allard ordered us to get you out of here, no matter what."

"No! We have to find Kai!"

"Victor, look at your monitor!" Galen's voice was full of dread, yet Victor could not ignore its urgency. "Look, Victor. There's no rescue beacon from Kai's 'Mech. There's no ID beacon. The shelf goes down a full kilometer here. He's gone. Don't let his sacrifice be a waste."

Victor hammered his fist into the radio panel, shorting it out. Teeth clenched to trap the scream growing in his chest, he began to limp the *Prometheus* back. As he worked his way along the bluff trail, he searched for any sign at all where Kai had gone under the water, but not even a ripple marked the grave of his friend.

Tairakana Plains, Luthien
Pesht Military District, Draconis Combine
5 January 3052

Sweat soaking his clothes, Shin Yodama continued to push himself as he ran toward the coordinates he'd been given before the Skulker exploded. By the time he was within sight of the small outpost that was his goal, the air strikes had met with stiff resistance and the burning wreckage of aerospace fighters littered the dark battlefield. He had approached two of the crash sites, but the intensity of the inferno had kept him back. He knew no one or nothing could have survived, but the debris gave him no clue as to which side the craft belonged.

He had wanted to stop when the ache in his side first began, and then again when it felt like a knife had been shoved deep and twisting into his guts. Whenever he did slow down to look back, the silhouettes of the pursuing 'Mechs grew even larger as they came on. Like demons from some childhood nightmare, the Clan 'Mechs lumbered forward despite the firepower hammering them. As hard as he ran to escape them, he could never lose sight of them.

The first sign Shin had of A2536 was a nervous young trooper half-hidden behind a fallen tree. "Halt or I'll shoot!" The excitement in the youth's voice made Shin certain he'd carry out his threat, but the wavering of his gun barrel told the yakuza he need not fear for his life.

He raised his hands. "I am *Sho-sa* Shin Yodama. Who is in charge here?"

The trooper jerked his head toward a low hill. "*Chu-i* Ashai. I'll take you to him."

Rounding the hill, Shin discovered that this forward observation post was nothing more than two soldiers, their leader, and a pair of scanning binoculars mounted on a tripod, radioing data back to headquarters. Ashai looked intelligent and eager. Probably a military academy recruit who'd graduated early, Shin concluded. His two young companions carried their automatic rifles awkwardly enough to convince Shin that they, too, must be very new to the warrior's life.

"*Chu-i* Ashai, we have to report back to headquarters."

The junior officer nodded curtly. "*Hai, Sho-sa*. There is a Skulker due here soon to take us back. It's been forward…"

Shin shook his head. "I was in that Skulker. It isn't coming." Shin held out his hand. "Give me your radio."

Color drained from Ashai's face. "I cannot. The microphone went out on our unit." He pointed up at the place on the hill where they had set up the visual scanner. "We were directed to leave this unit in place because they're still getting visual."

"Good." Shin ran up the hill as fast as his weary legs would take him. Reaching the summit, he positioned himself before the scanning binoculars. He waited until the device's motors whirred the lenses into focus on him, then quickly made a series of hand signals. He went through the sequence twice more, praying that at least one of the yakuza comtechs would be on duty.

As he stepped back out of the line-of-sight, the binoculars autofocused out at the advancing Smoke Jaguar 'Mechs. Their paint scheme showed circlets of black dots against a gray background, mimicking the coat of the animal that gave them their name. The dust and smoke they left behind in the bloody light of dawn blotted out everything to the rear of their lines. So heavily did the smoke hang in the still morning air that Shin imagined the Clan commander had arranged it less to obscure his troops than to warn them that they must go on, for no retreat was possible.

Shin saw aerospace fighters twist through martial acrobatics in the sky, then occasionally dive at their ground-bound enemies. More than one aircraft made it through the hail of ground fire to destroy a 'Mech, but Shin did not see that the attacks made the least difference.

To the west, facing the dawning sun, rank upon rank of Combine BattleMechs appeared to oppose the invaders. The crimson 'Mechs of the First Sword of Light occupied the center of the Combine line. The Otomo, their royal blue 'Mechs arrayed in staggered ranks, made up the northern flank. The two Genyosha regiments had been deployed as

268

the southern flank. The black and silver 'Mechs of their Second Regiment stood at a forty-five degree angle to the main body of Combine troops, giving the southern edge a hook to drive the Clan in toward the center.

Using their advantage of range, the Clan warriors engaged the Kurita units at long distance. Shin realized immediately that the Clans had abandoned their tactic of one warrior trying to engage another warrior in single combat. They concentrated their fire on individual targets, hitting hardest the 'Mechs equipped for LRM barrages. They kept coming as they fired, ever so slowly closing to a range at which the Combine's 'Mechs could effectively return fire.

The discipline of his comrades amazed Shin. No one moved or broke formation. It was maddening for Shin to watch them from afar as they stood there, taking barrage after barrage, but it had to be a thousand times worse for those in the BattleMechs. Even though the attacks mainly peeled off armor, Shin knew he would have been hard pressed to remain in his place. Even so, rigid adherence to Theodore's plan was the key to victory, and that knowledge would have kept him doing his utmost to hold and wait.

Ashai joined Shin atop the hill. "Look, *Sho-sa*, the Otomo are hurt."

A quick glance confirmed Ashai's observation. The long-range attacks had devastated the Otomo ranks. A dozen 'Mechs were down and many others looked fit for nothing but salvage. Even before the battle had been fully joined, the Combine's northern flank had started to crumble.

Shin noted that he and Ashai were not alone in observing the collapse of the Otomo. Smoke Jaguar 'Mechs surged forward. The Otomo stood furthest away from Imperial City, and the charge redirected the attack off its original line. The Smoke Jaguars broke into a gallop, increasing their speed as the Otomo's return fire came spottily and poorly aimed.

Ashai couldn't keep the fear from his voice. "They shoot like old women! It is a wonder they don't run!"

Shin smiled. "Watch, *Chu-i*. Watch and learn."

The swiftest of the Smoke Jaguar 'Mechs punched through the Otomo line. Their lead element had made it to the third and final rank of Otomo 'Mechs when the first Clanner hit a vibrabomb. In a flash of fire and steel that blew away the lower half of his right leg, it stumbled and went down, bowling over an *Archer*.

The *Archer* exploded. Shrapnel sprayed down in a forward arc that lifted the downed Clan 'Mech off its chest and blasted away its left

269

arm. Like a string of firecrackers, the other Otomo 'Mechs started to explode as well. From back to front, each of the blue war machines detonated. The thin armor over the chests of the 'Mechs burst outward, showering the enemy with a hail of death.

At the first explosion, Shin hit the ground and pulled Ashai down with him. "Theodore refitted industrial 'Mechs with armor to make them look like BattleMechs, then loaded them with explosives. A new variation on the old Trojan horse strategy. Instead of letting them take the horse into their castle, we had to lure them to our herd, but it worked nonetheless."

Into the chaos marking where the false Otomo regiment had stood, the real Otomo MechWarriors and the Second Legion of Vega charged. Their sudden appearance from the hills beyond the Kurita line clearly shocked the Smoke Jaguars. Their whole line had to stop to regain its drive toward the Kurita center. As they sought to regroup to do this, the Combine's line let loose with all the long-range weaponry it had.

What the attacks lacked in organization, they made up for in intensity. Individual Clan 'Mechs fell here and there, but the damage was far more widespread than that. Scant few of the mottled gray paint jobs escaped without revision. On the northern flank, where the Legion and Otomo blasted into the Jaguar's wing, the sheer force of their assault routed the Clansmen. As they began to push the Jaguar formation back in on itself, Shin could imagine the Genyosha doing the same on the other flank.

The thunderous flutter of a helicopter's rotor alerted Shin and made him roll over onto his back. A Combine copter touched down roughly a hundred meters back behind the line of hills, and he and the scout team ran gleefully to the streamlined craft. Once they had boarded it and were strapped in, the pilot got the chopper airborne again.

He kept the craft low, but when they bounced up over hills, Shin got another look at the battlefield. The Jaguar formation had been compressed into a wedge shape. The point of the wedge had engaged the First Sword, and the flanks were being hard-pressed by the other Combine units. Still, despite having given ground early and having suffered losses to the Otomo trap, the Clans had consolidated their position.

Just then, Shin thought he saw something in the smoke behind the Clan lines, but a hill cut off his view. It took him a precious ten seconds to convince the pilot to pull up his craft, and then the man did so only reluctantly. As the copter came up, the battlefield again came into view, but it no longer looked as it had only seconds before.

The movement Shin had caught in the smoke had been the charge of the Nova Cats. Their 'Mechs were black as death except for the brilliant blue star pattern in their center chests. Funnelling through the middle of the Jaguar wedge, their troops had sliced straight through the point of the wedge. Their charge carried them through the First Sword's line almost as though it were not there. The Jaguars split their wedge in half, forming up in parallel lines, then began to drive the Combine troops toward the east. At the same time, Clan aerospace fighters swooped in low to strafe observation posts.

Shin pulled the headset and mike away from the co-pilot and put it on. The screeching static of jammed radio frequencies drilled into his head. "Hanson," he said, noticing the pilot's name on his jumpsuit, "Take this chopper directly to headquarters in Imperial City, now!"

"I have orders."

"To hell with your orders. The Clans are breaking through. If we don't let the Kanrei know what's going on, Imperial City is lost. And the whole of Luthien with it."

Consulate of the St. Ives Compact, New Avalon
Crucis March, Federated Commonwealth
5 January 3052

"No, Candace, I don't think you're silly to be worried about Kai." Coming up behind her, he rested his hand on her right shoulder and gave her a reassuring squeeze. "After all, he is a warrior stationed in a war zone."

Candace glanced up at Justin's reflection in the mirror of her vanity table. "We have been together too long, my dear, for me to not hear the hesitation in your voice."

Justin smiled and bowed his head. "You know, had you not been inclined to seek a diplomatic solution to the differences between the Capellan Confederation and the Federated Suns so long ago, I do believe you could have turned me against Hanse Davion."

Candace reached up and pulled his hand into her own. "Are you not worried for our son?"

"Of course I am."

"See."

"But he's with the best forces we have. He's in a 'Mech equipped with the latest technology. And he's probably the finest MechWarrior who ever strapped himself into a cockpit." Justin disengaged his hand from hers and walked across the suite to his dresser. "To be quite frank," he went on, "I worry more about Victor Davion and his apparent disregard for his own safety. Yes, we all cheered the 'Fighting Prince' during the battle for Twycross, but poor Hanse's

272

heart was in his throat the whole time. I'm certain Hanse watches Victor go into battle and remembers his brother Ian's death."

Candace turned in her chair and pointed at him with a black eyeliner pencil. "You are correct that Victor is impulsive, but Galen Cox and Kai are there to calm him down. And to protect him, too. But who protects those who guard the Prince?"

Justin scooped up two cufflinks from the top of the dresser and returned to her side. Holding them out, he smiled sheepishly. "Could you?"

"Getting old, my love, or does your arm need new batteries?"

The diabolical glint in her eyes sparked a laugh from him. "Neither old nor in need of new batteries am I, Duchess. Cufflinks never were easy for me, even when both my hands matched." Justin stood rigid as she dutifully fastened the cufflinks. "And if my lady requires a show of my youthful vigor, might I boldly suggest she invent a way for us to leave this reception as early as possible."

In a melodramatic pose, Candace pressed the back of her right hand to her forehead and sighed, "Oh my, seduced by the Champion of Solaris…"

Justin shook his head. "I've not been Solaris' Champion for a long time."

"What is it they say—once a champion, always a champion?"

"And for that, you will always have my heart." He pulled her to her feet and kissed her, then held her tightly. "Trust me, my love. Kai will be back with us soon."

Releasing her, he glanced at his chronometer. "Damn, we're already running late." Justin turned to where he had tossed his black jacket on the bed. "I hate charity functions. Were it not for your company, I'd much prefer spending the evening in the war room reviewing reports."

Until the laser bolt hit Candace Liao on the left side of her chest and spun her to the floor, Justin had believed them alone in their suite. Mercifully, his wife fell on the other side of the bed, leaving only the sight of the hem of her evening gown and the black leather heels she'd chosen for the reception. The puff of white smoke curling up like a vaporous mushroom and the acrid scent of burned wool scoured away the scent of her perfume that he so loved.

Laser pistol in hand, the assassin stepped from the closet where he'd been hiding. He looked at Candace, then up at Justin and smiled. "Romano wanted her to die first, to be sure you knew you'd failed to save her."

As the black-clad murderer swung the pistol in line with Justin,

273

the Intelligence Secretary dodged to the right. His black metal left hand snapped back as far as it would go. Something tugged at the underside of the wrist, popping the cufflink free of the white shirt. With a fluidity born of years of practice, Justin thrust his left arm toward the assassin and willed its machinery to work.

The wrist-laser's green beam struck the assassin full in the chest. It cored a hole through him and flashed-burned a dark circle on the mirrored panel behind. The light reflected up to strike the crystal chandelier, but the forest of rainbows it unraveled were harmless. Yet fast as Justin's strike was, the assassin managed to tighten his finger on the trigger of his laser pistol before he fell.

Searing agony grabbed Justin by the throat as the ruby beam burned into his neck. He staggered forward a few steps, then dropped to his knees beside his wife. His right hand clutched at his neck and found it slippery with warm fluid. He glanced down and watched blood drench his white sleeve. Despite the pain radiating out from the wound, Justin forced his right hand harder against it, fighting to stop the precious fluid from leaking out between his slicked fingers.

With the clarity of mind that only imminent death could bring, Justin knew he had to sound an alarm. Yet the visiphone on the bedside table might as well have been two light years away from where he knelt. The consulate's soundproof walls made screaming futile.

A wave of nausea passed over him, then spots began to form before his eyes. Knowing he had no time to spare, Justin raised his left arm and pointed it upward. He triggered the wrist laser and slashed a black scar across the ceiling. He kept it moving for the three seconds until the beam died, then he slumped over, exhausted.

Until he felt the cool water spraying down onto his face from the fire sprinklers, Justin did not know whether his desperate attempt to summon help had succeeded. He never heard the alarm that had to be blaring, for it was not his own welfare that concerned him. He reached out to Candace to give her hand a reassuring squeeze, then the room, and the whole world with it, vanished from his sight.

42

Tairakana Plains, Luthien
Pesht Military District, Draconis Combine
5 January 3052

Shin's stomach lurched as the pilot jerked the helicopter up and over in a hard turn. Before Shin could demand the reason for that sudden, sharp maneuver, a pair of SRMs exploded on the ground.

The pilot yanked up on the pitch control and cranked the throttle wide open. "Clans fighter. He figures us as a spotter."

"Can you evade him?"

"If not, we'll die trying."

"What can I do?"

The pilot jerked his thumb back toward the crew compartment. "Man the twelve-five. I'll give you a shot if I can."

Shin tossed the headset back to the co-pilot and pulled on a gunnery harness. Snapping it into the restraining straps near the aircraft's left door, he slid the gun and mount from their stowed position. Locking it into place and laying the first part of the ammo chain through its chamber, he readied the gatling cannon for use. Ashai pulled the compartment door open, giving Shin a 170-degree arc of fire.

Shin pulled the gunner's helmet onto his head and adjusted the microphone. He flipped the eyeshades down and switched the gun's targeting laser to the On position. Immediately, a crosshair appeared on the eyeshade over his right eye. He knew that when he had the gun on target, a dot would pulse in the center of the cross, just as in a 'Mech.

Unlike piloting his *Phoenix Hawk*, however, he had to aim the gun manually.

"I'm in and ready, *Anjin-san.*"

"*Hai, Sho-sa.* Brace yourself."

The pilot stood the copter on its tail, then let it sidle over in a maneuver that pitched Shin forward. Despite the warning, if not for his firm hold on the twin grips of the 12.5 millimeter machine gun and the restraining straps of his harness, he would have followed Ashai's cap on the long drop to the battlefield below. As it was, he barely got his feet under him in time for the pilot to level off and give Shin a quick shot at an approaching Clan aerofighter.

Shin's thumb stabbed the firing button. The cannon's whine drowned out the flutter of the helicopter's prop. Bits and pieces of ammo chain rattled around the crew compartment as the six barrels spun their way through 100 rounds in two seconds. Shin fought the weapon's recoil, but having lost the target dot a half-second after acquiring it, he was fairly certain he'd not managed to keep the weapon on target.

Then the aerospace fighter exploded.

Black on red and red on black, Kell Hound and Wolf's Dragoon aerospace fighters swept through the air like fire-hearted thunderheads. A flight of LRMs from one of the approaching fighters blasted the Clan fighter from the sky. Trailing thick smoke, its wreckage spiraled toward the ground and the helicopter pilot brought the copter back on its express vector for Imperial City.

From his vantage point, Shin had a stunning view of the battlefield. The Smoke Jaguars still held off their opponents, but more by happenstance, Shin thought, than by strategy. Because the Combine forces on both sides of the line outnumbered their foes, the Kurita warriors had fewer targets and fewer opportunities to shoot. Anxious warriors in the back ranks crowded their comrades, driving them in closer than they wanted to get to the Clan lines. Already it looked as though the Kurita leadership was issuing orders to combat the problem, but the damage already done had won the Clans time to deploy the Nova Cats.

The Nova Cats had run head-on into the Dragoons and Kell Hounds. Airborne, Shin saw how the mercenaries had arranged their lines to stop the advancing Clans. One regiment of Dragoons held the roadway toward the capital, with the two Kell Hound regiments deployed in the hills on either side. Behind that trio of regiments, three Dragoon regiments repeated the formation. The Dragoons had held their last regiment in reserve, but it, too, now started to move forward to bolster the Kell Hounds' First Battalion.

Fighting down on the roadway looked particularly fierce. The smoke overlaying the battlefield still allowed the brilliant fire of missile detonations to burn up through it. The hot red light of lasers and the electric blue flare of PPC beams filled the gray haze with splashes of color, but they were nothing compared to the nova-white fireball of a fusion engine burning out of control.

Up on the northern flank, the battle between the Nova Cats and the Kell Hounds' first regiment looked particularly savage. 'Mechs equipped with long-range weapons laced the Clan lines with barrage after barrage of murderous fire. 'Mechs built for infighting closed with the enemy, but avoided direct physical contact. Concentrating their fire on Clan 'Mechs already weakened by their distant comrades, the Hounds took them down quickly and efficiently.

The Clan reprisals came swiftly, but did not have the same degree of organization that made the mercenaries so effective. Shin was at a loss to understand this confusion until he saw a Kell Hound 'Mech standing virtually alone on a knoll near the road. Even from such a distance, he recognized the blocky body of an *Archer*. It launched multiple flights of missiles at its enemies as they charged and directed more fire from its supporting fire lances, then picked the enemy apart with its lasers as they closed to shorter range. Alone yet very deadly, it made itself a perfect target.

The Clan warriors seemed to be doing their damnedest to make the pilot of that 'Mech pay for his arrogance, but their efforts were hardly successful. The Kell Hound missile fire fell with murderous effect, blasting Nova Cats back down the hill. As Clansmen rushed forward, the Hounds' close assault lances bored in, picking a target and savaging it until its smoking skeleton lay at the feet of the *Archer*. The *Archer* itself moved with a fluidity that told Shin a masterful warrior piloted the hulking 'Mech. As it dodged away from missile barrages, or squatted to make itself a more difficult target, Shin guessed that it could only be Morgan Kell, leader of the Kell Hounds, in the cockpit.

The chopper coursed through a narrow canyon, then popped up to give Shin another view of the battle. The Nova Cats and Dragoons had met in the roadway, and broken 'Mechs of both sides littered the ground. From the mixture of shattered hulks, it looked to Shin that the mercenaries had driven the Nova Cats back a hundred meters or so, blunting their momentum. The Dragoons had then begun an orderly withdrawal, forcing the Nova Cats to win back the ground they had taken initially.

As the slow snake of Nova Cat 'Mechs started forward, the Dragoons pounded them hard. From his vantage point, Shin saw the second Dragoon line moving forward. He assumed that just as the whole column of Nova Cats intended to continue pressing toward Imperial City, the Dragoons would charge and stop the advance. That would force the column to stop again. Not only would the stop-and-go progress be frustrating for the Clanners, but it provided more time for the mercenary airwings to hit the enemy.

The chopper pilot dropped the aircraft down behind a line of hills and shot it straight toward Imperial City. Shin directed him to land at a rear headquarters unit near a regiment of BattleMechs. The pilot radioed in for landing clearance, got it, and set the helicopter down on a spot midway between the BattleMechs and a nearby tent.

Shin unbuckled himself and dismounted. He gave the pilot a thumbs-up, then ran clear of the metal bird. When an orderly intercepted and handed him sealed orders, Shin recognized Theodore's chop on the rice-paper packet and tore it open. His jaw dropped open as he read the contents, then he refolded the sheet and sprinted toward the assembled 'Mechs.

Shin shivered as he mounted the ladder spilling down from the *Phoenix Hawk*'s breast. *I am not ready for this sort of responsibility, Theodore!* Once inside the cockpit, he hit the switch that retracted the ladder and sealed the 'Mech's faceplate in place. Stripping off his jumpsuit, Shin donned a cooling vest and helmet, then strapped himself in and went through his initiation procedure.

The second the computer made the *Phoenix Hawk* fully operational, Takashi Kurita's voice blasted through the helmet's speakers. "I warn you, I will not tolerate being ordered by one of my son's hoodlums. To him you may be special, but to me you are yakuza! I've dealt with your ilk before, and I can do it still. I demand you release my 'Mech!"

Shin swallowed hard. Theodore's orders, making him the liaison with the reserve unit Takashi had cobbled together, told him that the override code would allow the Coordinator and his comrades to bring their 'Mechs into full operational status. It also told him how crucial it was to keep them back until orders to commit them were issued. Being set 10 kilometers behind the initial lines put them midway between Imperial City and the front. This was not the optimum position for defense, but the valley they were assigned to defend gave them the latitude to move quickly to bolster any point that might break in the line. Theodore's message had communicated all that and more, and Shin felt like a grain of rice beneath a millstone.

"*Iie*, Kurita Takashi-*sama*. I have been given specific orders. I cannot release you yet."

"Damn you, Shin Yodama, and damn my son. He leaves the Combine in the hands of bandits and mercenaries. Free us!"

Takashi's imperious tone slapped at Shin's pride, but he fought back the rise of anger. "No! Your son has placed you here for a most specific reason."

"Ha! He has placed me here, defenseless, for only one reason: he hopes the Clans will kill me so he can be the Coordinator of the Combine."

"He has you here because he trusts you to accomplish what he needs done."

"You have been deceived by him, yakuza." Takashi spat out the last word like a piece of bitter root. "My son trusts me with nothing. For the third and final time, free us."

"No!" Shin turned his *Phoenix Hawk* and located the *Grand Dragon* with Takashi's crest on its right breast. "I have my orders and I will follow them."

"You will obey me now, yakuza! I am the Coordinator of the Draconis Combine!"

"Coordinator, I know who you are and have only the highest respect for your office." Shin gritted his teeth to keep his temper in check. "I understand your demands, but I cannot bow to them until I am given orders. If you wish to order me or your son to commit *seppuku* for this breach of honor, we will do so later. When the Kanrei tells me the time is right, I will release you."

"That time is now," gloated the Coordinator. "I have had my technicians review the software and I know what the release code is. Three times I have asked you to release us, and thrice have you refused. Honor has been satisfied. I am now free to act."

"If you do that," Shin intoned in a low voice, "you force me to use a second code I have been given. If I broadcast it, you will all die, and with you goes Imperial City."

"This is madness. My son is insane!"

"*Iie*, Coordinator. He is not mad, but only a man who knows his father so well." Shin's hand hovered over the keypad on the right side of the cockpit. "He knows you would be ingenious enough to find a way around his security measure. He also knew that if you knew nothing about the second code, you would have no time to find it in any analysis. He is serious about your remaining in position to deploy when needed. He could not risk your leaving this place."

"He was afraid I would steal his victory from him."

Shin shook his head. "No, Coordinator, not at all. He was afraid to trust anyone else with what must be done here."

Takashi's exasperation sliced through his words. "How can you continue to tell me my son trusts me when I know he does not?"

"I say this, Takashi Kurita, because it is the truth." Shin felt the packet of orders pressed against his flesh. "I say this because he told me your granddaughter refused to evacuate Imperial City. You and your men are all that stand between Omi and the Clans, and your son wants you here to stop them."

Satalice
Free Rasalhague Republic
5 January 3051

"I copy that, Firebird One. You have no visual on the *Ostsol*."
Phelan Wolf cursed under his breath. "Make another sweep. It has to
be around here somewhere."

"Roger, Dire Alpha." Carew did not sound too hopeful.

"Dire Alpha to Dire Star. Anything?" Phelan glanced at his
auxiliary monitor and its map of the local area. The computer updated
him with the locations of the rest of his command, with Dire Gamma
limping along in the rear. The terrain, as broken and uneven as one
might expect from a lava plain, was glossy with a treacherous layer of
ice. Live steam vents pulsed out mist like ethereal whales surfacing
from the rock to spout. The mist instantly crystallized in the cold air,
and Phelan had to keep his *Wolfhound* running hot just to keep the ice
from blinding his sensors.

All reports came back negative, but Phelan had the distinct
feeling that the others in his Star were deliberately holding back.
Though Natasha had harangued her Wolf Spiders into working coop-
eratively, the others in Dire Star were veterans who refrained from
interfering in what they saw as Phelan's rightful kill. The *Ostsol* had
attacked him first, which meant, under the old ways, that the target was
his. The others were willing to course it, but they'd not take it down
until Phelan had died trying.

Phelan shook his head in disgust. He knew why they deferred to

281

him, but he would have preferred a team effort. Because he was their Star Commander, was younger than any of them, and because he had singlehandedly taken Gunzburg, they offered him yet another chance at honor. *Well, change is bound to come slowly. The Star League wasn't built in a day!*

The secondary monitor gave Phelan an inventory of the damage he'd taken. Most of the armor had been blown off the *Wolfhound*'s right arm, but the extended-range large laser was undamaged. *Grinner* had lost a little armor from his chest and right leg, too, but other than that, the BattleMech was running at the top of form. The *Ostsol* might outmass his *Wolfhound* by twenty-five tons, but the two were closely matched in sheer firepower.

The humanoid *Ostsol* had toothpick-thin arms, one of which had been burned clean off by a snap shot with the large laser. That did little to hurt it because the 'Mech carried all its weapons in the torso. The pilot had recovered quickly and escaped, but not before Phelan savaged the armor on its chest. From what he could tell, though, both large lasers and the twin forward-pointing medium lasers were still operational. The *Ostsol* also boasted two rear-arc medium lasers in its barrel-shaped torso, but Phelan had not followed closely enough to give the pilot a chance to use them.

Phelan took another look at the map and switched his visual display over to infrared. The landscape instantly took on a cool blue tint. Steam jets shot tendrils of yellow fire into the air, and heat rose in red curls from the *Wolfhound*'s heat sinks. The jumble of colors, with streaks of red and gold marking ground warmth, was not so confusing that a 'Mech couldn't be spotted by the heat it generated, but the steam vents made sorting viable targets from spurious ones annoyingly difficult.

Still marching the *Wolfhound* forward, Phelan slowly worked toward a canyon that closely resembled a jagged scar ripped through the planet's crust by a dull knife. The legion of side canyons were large enough to hide a 'Mech or two. The cold wind twisting down through it could easily mix the hot air generated by a 'Mech with fresher air, hiding all traces of an ambush. As smart as the other 'Mech pilot had already proved himself, Phelan had no doubt that his enemy was, indeed, waiting therein.

"Firebird One to Dire Alpha."

"Go ahead, Firebird."

"Negative for heat. Magres is useless because of the ferrous content of the ground. Sorry."

"Roger, Firebird. Give me CAP if you can. Dire Star, I am going into the canyon. Beta and Delta, cut off the north end, if you please. Gamma, maintain your position. Epsilon, back me."

Phelan wiped a sweaty palm against the outside of his cooling vest. He started to work his way down into the canyon, but hesitated before he reached the floor. He hated the idea of offering the *Ostsol* the first shot, especially when all the enemy had to do was wait for a thermal signature to target and kill. *There has to be a way to decoy him, give him bait*.

A chunk of stone gave way beneath the *Wolfhound*'s left foot, but Phelan successfully kept the 'Mech on its feet by reaching out with its left hand to steady the 'Mech against the canyon wall. As he watched the stone rolling down to the canyon floor, it gave him an idea. Stooping the 'Mech, he picked up a hunk of volcanic stone. Holding it carefully by the thumb and forefinger of his 'Mech's left hand, he trained all three pulse lasers on it, dialed their power down for a three-second burst and triggered them.

The trio of beams filled the rock with fire. It glowed white hot on Phelan's holographic infrared display. He pulled the *Wolfhound*'s left arm back, then brought it forward in an easy underhand motion. Lofted forward, the rock bounded down through the canyon. It caromed around like a bowling ball in a surreal alley, then popped up and hung seven meters above the floor about halfway down the canyon.

Four laser beams flashed out at the rock. The two large lasers struck it full-on and smashed it back against the far canyon wall. The two medium lasers passed below it, but had it been the *Wolfhound*, they would have slashed through the armor on its belly. The rock, performing as would the *Wolfhound* had it caught that fire, dropped to the canyon floor.

The *Ostsol* stepped from the break where it had hidden, then halted only two steps clear of cover. Phelan, realizing the pilot had switched over to visual and discovered his mistake, brought the large laser up and punched the firing button on the right joystick. The hurried shot hit the *Ostsol*'s back leg, vaporizing armor from mid-thigh down to the ankle.

The *Ostsol*'s pilot pivoted his 'Mech to the left, bringing all its weaponry to bear on the *Wolfhound*. One large laser and one medium laser combined to make the armor on the *Wolfhound*'s right leg run like water. The air refroze much of it, and warning lights on Phelan's control console told him the knee and ankle had been fused. The other medium laser sliced armor from the right side of the *Wolfhound*'s chest. The remaining large laser did the most damage as it cored through the armor on the *Wolfhound*'s center chest. A wave of heat passed up through the cockpit, informing Phelan that part of the fusion engine's shielding had been damaged.

Phelan concentrated, despite feeling broiled alive in his cockpit. He dropped both crosshairs onto the *Ostsol*'s conical outline and triggered every weapon he had available. The large laser again blasted the *Ostsol*'s right leg. The spear of coherent light sheared away the last of the armor and boiled off the myomer muscles controlling the leg's movement. The 'Mech buckled instantly, and flailing impotently against the air, the *Ostsol* crashed to the ground. The trio of pulse lasers picked armor off other parts of the Rasalhagian 'Mech, but as the machine settled onto its chest, Phelan knew its fighting days were permanently over.

Phelan keyed his radio. "Dire Gamma, please relay to Black Widow Alpha that we have downed our bogey. Ask for a new assignment."

Switching the frequency control, he tightbeamed a message to the *Ostsol* across the frequencies he knew the Free Republic's troops used. "Whoever you are, you have my sincere respect. If not for a moment of inspiration, our positions would be reversed. You are now my prisoner."

The youth of the MechWarrior's voice surprised Phelan. "I may be your prisoner, but I will never surrender to you."

"Don't do anything foolish. Don't overload your engine. It won't serve anyone or anything for you to be that sort of hero."

"Oh, I don't worry. That would make it too easy on you." A fiery stubbornness entered the voice. "If I'm dead, I can't lead my people to freedom, can I?"

Before Phelan could think of a suitable reply, Dire Gamma's report buzzed into his ear. "The Colonel sends her congratulations. Satalice has been pacified. We are to regroup at the Den and prep for an inspection."

Phelan frowned. "Inspection?"

"Roger. She said the ilKhan will be reviewing us in two days, and he's bringing a very special visitor with him. The visitor is the one we're supposed to impress."

"This visitor have a name?" Phelan wanted to know.

"Not one of us, so who cares?"

"I care."

"No name, Star Commander, just a title." Dire Gamma hesitated, then sighed. "Does 'the Primus of ComStar' mean anything to you?"

Imperial City, Luthien
Pesht Military District, Draconis Combine
5 January 3052

Tempers flared as frustration eroded the last shreds of the
Coordinator's tolerance for either his son or Shin Yodama. For Shin's
part, he felt trapped in the battle between father and son, and had to
fight to maintain his composure. He knew Theodore had placed him
as a buffer against his father precisely because Shin could not be
blackmailed by the old samurai's demands.

It is precisely because I am not part of the centuries-old samurai
tradition that Takashi rails against me. Shin shrugged at the irony of
the situation, then sighed with resignation as a blinking light indicated
an incoming radio call on Takashi's frequency.

Shin punched the call through. "*Hai.*"

"Will my son let us fight *now*? We are almost to the gates of the
city we are to defend."

"My last orders were for us to remain here. I await the Kanrei's
orders to attack."

A quick button-lunch cut Takashi's strangled protest off in mid-
utterance. Even after Shin had issued the computer command allowing
Takashi's reserve unit to bring their weapons up, they had been
forbidden to engage in combat. Theodore, out with the Second Legion
of Vega, continued to coordinate the Combine's response to the Clan
assault. The Reserves had been shuttled from one point to another,
ready to intercept any breakthrough in the Combine lines.

So far, matters had not gone as well for the Clans as feared. Though the Nova Cats and Smoke Jaguars had pushed into the hills between their landing point and the city, the maneuver had allowed the Combine's forces into their rear. With the mercenaries harassing them through the hills, the Clans' progress had become slow, and the necessity of fighting a rearguard action slowed them down even more.

Shin realized that Takashi did not understand exactly how the Clans operated. The Coordinator believed that once the Clans had committed their forces, they would not call down reinforcements. Yet, prisoner interviews had suggested that their bidding system allowed them to call down more forces if and when needed. This put Theodore in the position of having to allow the Clans to progress until his troops were in a position to utterly destroy them. As reinforcements would take approximately two hours to land, the final battle would have to be very swift or Clan reinforcements might arrive just in time to do some good.

Of course, Shin reminded himself, *they could always raze the city with an orbital assault, as they did Edo on Turtle Bay.* The yakuza shivered and muttered a brief prayer to his ancestors to prevent that eventuality.

Shin immediately punched the radio call on Theodore's tactical frequency into his headphones. "*Hai*, Kanrei."

"Yodama-*san*, the Nova Cats are coming your way. The Kell Hounds have regrouped into a reinforced regiment and will be coming to support your southern flank. Colonel Kell says if you want to turn the Clanners toward him, he's ready to catch anything you pitch."

"*Hai*, Kanrei. We will stop them."

"Good luck, Shin. We'll be coming in from the north, and Wolf's bringing up the rear. It is now or never."

"Understood." Shin shut that frequency off and shifted to the Dragon's Claws frequency. "The Nova Cats are ours. The Kell Hounds will be coming in from the south and the rest of our forces will come from the north. We are to turn the Cats toward the Hounds."

Takashi's voice overrode Shin's. "Follow me, comrades. We will show these invaders how true samurai fight."

"No!" Shin let all his fury at Takashi's abuse of power flood the frequency. "Listen to me. We cannot and should not forget tradition, but suicidal assaults will not stop the Clans. We are a hammer, and the Kell Hounds are an anvil."

"I am samurai, Shin Yodama." The Coordinator's voice seethed with righteous fury. "My code demands I fulfill the dictates of honor."

"Your code also calls for the fulfillment of duty. Let your honor

286

be assuaged by attending to your *duty* to your son and the Combine. Otherwise, go down in history as the man who lost Luthien."

Shin's right hand hovered over the command console keypad he would use to type in the destruct code for Takashi's *Grand Dragon*. Though he tried to will his fingers to stop trembling, they would not. He had no fear of being unable to punch in and send the code if necessary, but he wanted to give Takashi every chance to avoid such a fate.

"This is not finished here, Shin Yodama."

"I understand, Coordinator. As I said before, you may command my death later." Shin saw movement on his holographic display and looked up to find Nova Cat 'Mechs beginning to enter the Kado-guchi Valley below Imperial City. "Now is the time to stop the invaders."

Takashi gave his men a sacred mission. "We are the Kamikaze that swept the Mongols from the shores of Japan nearly two millennia ago!"

With grim determination, Shin started the *Phoenix Hawk* in a lurching run that became smooth, swift, and powerful in a dozen steps. The BattleMech reached its top speed of 97.2 kph within 100 meters from its starting point, with each jarring step pounding meter-deep holes into the turf. Behind him, like a wolf leading its pack, came Takashi and the Dragon's Claws.

Centered at the top of Shin's display was the distance to the Clan 'Mechs. Numbers blurred as the distance spun down. The golden crosshairs that designated targets for his weapons bounced up and down wildly, making it virtually impossible to get an accurate shot at that distance and speed. Even so, Shin played with the joysticks on each arm of his command couch to try to keep them on target. Occasionally he got a gold dot, confirming a target lock, but at such extended range, he did not fire.

Because he was coming in at high speed, he knew the Clans would have almost as much trouble targeting him. In the four seconds it took his *Phoenix Hawk* to cross from extreme Clan range to the outer fringe of his own weaponry's effective range, only one Nova Cat successfully launched on him. An LRM rack sent a score of missiles burning across the battlefield, but less than half acquired and hit their target. Those that did blew almost all the armor from the *Phoenix Hawk*'s right arm. The detonations shook the 'Mech and threatened to unbalance it, but Shin compensated to keep it upright and running.

Another eight seconds brought him to a comfortable range for his weapons. He flicked fire control for all weapons to the crosshairs adjusted by his right-hand joystick. He centered it on the outline of the

Hagetaka whose missiles had hit him. His large laser missed high, but both the *Phoenix Hawk*'s medium lasers drilled through a rent in the *Hagetaka*'s armor. They filled its right shoulder with fire and subsidiary explosions pumped black smoke out the right arm's autocannon muzzle. The limb twisted, then hung limp like a flag on a still day.

Crossing the last 100 meters, the *Phoenix Hawk* suffered damage from two other Clan 'Mechs, but the attacks only chipped away at armor. In a last-minute adjustment, Shin altered his course just enough to drift toward the *Hagetaka*'s right side. He lowered the *Phoenix Hawk*'s left shoulder and barreled full force into the birdlike Battle-Mech.

The collision bounced Shin forward into the command couch's restraining straps. Metal screeched as the *Phoenix Hawk*'s left shoulder pounded into the *Hagetaka*'s right shoulder. The sheer mass of both war machines ground the ferro-ceramic armor on their hides to dust, while the impact of the attack itself snapped the *Hagetaka*'s arm off at the shoulder. The *Phoenix Hawk* slid on past the empty shoulder socket and hit the 'Mech's hip where it joined the forward-hunched torso.

The *Hagetaka* started to spin to the ground when the Coordinator's *Grand Dragon* hit it at top speed. Arms pumping like a sprinter, the *Grand Dragon* slammed into the *Hagetaka*, broadsiding it. The heavy 'Mech scythed through the Clan 'Mech's torso, popping the head and cockpit free to tumble across the ground.

Without the cockpit computers to monitor it, the *Hagetaka*'s fusion engine raged uncontrolled. A shimmering, silvery ball of boiling plasma shot like a comet from between the 'Mech's shoulders. Like a wraith leaving its body behind, its tendrils swiped at the *Grand Dragon*, but Takashi's charge had already carried him beyond its vengeful grasp. The energy-ghost imploded, leaving the *Hagetaka*'s lifeless husk smoldering on the ground.

Shin regained control of his 'Mech the instant it slipped beyond the Clan's initial line. He slowed his headlong rush because he had more than enough targets in the midst of the growing Clan formation. In addition, his task was to force the Nova Cats back into the Kell Hounds, and that would only happen if his force could form a line and drive the Clans before them.

A quick look at his holographic display told Shin that the shock attack had succeeded in penetrating the Clan line along a wide front. Clan 'Mechs were already falling back as Combine 'Mechs swept around him to consolidate the Reserve Regiment's position. The center battalion concentrated its fire in an arc that supported the northern flank.

"Yodama," Takashi radioed urgently, "I am bringing the center battalion around to stop them."

Shin glanced at his tactical map. "If you do that, we'll get their full attention. If they get through us, they have a direct shot at Imperial City."

"But if I let them flank us, they will strike at the city."

"The Kell Hounds' Crescent Hawk Company has our flank, Coordinator."

"Do they? I see no sign of them."

"They're there." Shin crossed his fingers. "They're there."

Venom filled Takashi's voice. "If they are not, I will slay you myself."

"If the Hounds aren't there, you'll have to fight the Clans for that honor, Takashi. I know my *duty!* I will do it!"

As the central battalion drifted to the south, the Clans increased their retreat, letting themselves get beyond the Combine warriors' effective range. The Reserves moved quickly and the Clans used their missiles sparingly, so the moving truce resulted in few casualties among the Kurita forces and fewer among the Clansmen. Even so, with the chase, the Clans managed to string out Shin's forces further than he would have liked. He slowed pursuit to consolidate his troops, and Takashi immediately rebuked him for letting the Clans slip around the southern edge of their line.

"You are a fool, yakuza, and a coward. As is my son for trusting you and your kind."

Shin saw a light flash on his command console. *Save the rhetoric for the historians, Takashi. It's time for warriors to earn their pay.* Shin keyed a command that downloaded tactical maps to all his 'Mechs. As a unit, they pressed forward as though initiating a second charge into the Clan lines.

As the Nova Cats readied themselves for the assault, the reformed Kell Hound Regiment came up and over the hills to the Cats' rear. They fell on the southernmost elements of the Clan force like a wave engulfing a sand castle. It seemed to Shin that the Clansmen were not so much surprised as overwhelmed. Unlike the way he had seen the Kell Hounds fight earlier, they did not hold back to fight at range. Instead they closed quickly, lasers and PPCs savaging targets at point-blank range.

The southern movement of the Nova Cats stopped abruptly as the Clansmen sought to regroup. From the north, Shin saw the arrival of the Second Legion of Vega and remnants of the Otomo and First

289

Sword of Light regiments. As they formed a wall to cut off the Clans from their line of retreat, the Reserve's northern battalion closed ranks with the center battalion to strengthen its position. Scouts from the Clans headed directly east, up the hills to the ridgeline lying between them and their landing zone, but those 'Mechs quickly retreated as elements of Wolf's Dragoons took the heights.

Shin knew what could come next and worked his way to the front of the Reserve position. The Clans determined that the Reserve unit was the weakest side of the box trapping them. With a desperation born of knowledge that defeat was certain, the Nova Cats turned and charged the Reserves even as the other three sides of the Combine formation fell upon them.

"Brace for it," Takashi shouted. "Now we're the anvil!"

A racing *Masakari* hit the *Phoenix Hawk* with a shoulder square into the middle of the *Hawk*'s chest. Sparks exploded through Shin's cockpit as his 'Mech folded up around the 'Mech's shoulder, then flew backward. Shin dangled from the restraining straps, then slammed down into the command chair when the *Phoenix Hawk* smashed into the ground. Realizing that remaining on the ground was to die, Shin arched his back and used the 'Mech's momentum to help it roll around so he could more easily get it up on its feet.

He knew completing such an acrobatic move was impossible, but he would have settled for a shift from supine to prone positions. What he got, however, was entirely different than what he wanted or could have imagined. As the *Phoenix Hawk* started to roll, its legs thrust between those of a running Clan *Daishi*. The Clan 'Mech's pumping legs shattered those of the *Phoenix Hawk* and sent it spinning off on its back like a turtle sliding across ice on its shell.

Feeling like a pilot in a centrifuge, Shin knew such violent motion threatened to snap his safety belts and leave him splattered against the interior of his cockpit. Shin reached out with the 'Mech's left arm, skidding the *Phoenix Hawk* to a stop. He brought the 'Mech up into a sitting position, but before he could make any sense of the surrounding chaos, a Nova Cat 'Mech stamped down with a cloven hoof, destroying the *Phoenix Hawk*'s right hand and large laser.

The loss of the support dropped the *Phoenix Hawk* flat on its back. Shin fumbled as he reached for the ejection switch, but stopped before he triggered it. The *Daishi*'s upraised foot eclipsed the sky and Shin saw the exact spot he would hit if he punched out.

It's done.

Electric blue light filled his cockpit and the crackling static that accompanied a blast from a particle projection cannon filled his headphones. The foot's dark shadow wavered then vanished as the *Daishi* pitched over onto its back. A momentary glance showed smoke trailing from the melted ruin of its head, and the shoulder-mounted LRM canister exploded when the 'Mech hit the ground.

Shin rolled the *Phoenix Hawk* over onto its right side and obtained a three-point stance on thigh stumps and a wrist stub. His 'Mech hunched over like a chimp, Shin lifted the 'Mech's left arm, ready to use the machine gun and medium laser mounted there. Scanning his holographic display for a target, Shin tasted blood dripping down from his nose.

Behind his 'Mech he saw a *Grand Dragon*. It showed battle wear and broken armor, but the crest over its right breast had survived. The gold dragon against a field of red, jaws agape and ready to devour enemies, told him who piloted that craft and who had saved him.

"Why, Takashi, why?"

"I may hate you and your kind, Shin Yodama, but you are a citizen of the Combine. No one or nothing will stop me from doing my duty to protect the people of my realm."

"So it is with the rest of us, Coordinator. Our tactics might be different, but our goals are the same." Shin licked the blood from his lips. "So if you'd be so kind as to lure some Nova Cats over here, we can both do our duty."

45

DropShip Barbarossa, *Outbound*
Alyina, Jade Falcon Occupation Zone (Trellshire, Federated
Commonwealth)
6 January 3052

Victor barely glanced up at Galen as the junior officer entered the lounge area. He saw the light reflect in rainbow spears from the surface of a holodisk, but attached no importance to it. Seeing Galen order the other officers out of the room, he realized the disk was more than data uploaded from headquarters on the planet they were abandoning. The grim look on Galen's face broke through Victor's distracted state enough that he guessed he would be called upon to do something.

Settled deep in a chair, with knees drawn up to his chest, Victor clutched the dark woolen blanket closer around himself. "It can wait, Galen."

Galen's eyes glittered like unforgiving chips of ice. "I am afraid it cannot, Kommandant." The scorn in his voice as he addressed Victor by rank stung the Prince, yet the pain felt very distant. "This holodisk was inscribed because of a Priority Alpha message transmitted by ComStar. It is for you, Eyes Only."

Galen held out the disk, but Victor shook his head. "That means it's from or about my father. I don't want to see it now."

Disgusted, Galen stuffed the disk into the viewer built into the DropShip's bulkhead and swiveled Victor's chair around to face it. "The message was urgent and your father entrusted it to ComStar. Given the current circumstances, you know that means it's very important. Let me know when you're done viewing and I'll come back and have it destroyed."

Galen started out through the hatch, but Victor called him back. "Wait, Galen. Stay for this."

The blond MechWarrior shook his head. "It's 'Eyes Only' and I don't have that sort of clearance. I must go."

"I want you to stay."

"I don't have that clearance level, Kommandant."

"You do now!" Victor knew from the sour look on Galen's face that his protest was a facade over the real reason he wanted to leave. "Stay. That's an order, Hauptmann."

"As you command, Kommandant!"

Victor reached out and punched the Play button on the viewer. The screen opened with a burst of gray-white static, then dissolved into a close-up shot of Hanse Davion looking very small against his throne. Seeing how old and tired his father looked shocked Victor halfway out of his lethargy.

Hanse Davion tried to put on a brave smile, but the effort seemed to die for lack of energy. "Greetings, Victor. I wish this message could be more pleasant, but it cannot. I regret having to make this request of you, but to do less would be a gross injustice."

Victor saw his father swallow hard, and he felt a sympathetic lump rising in his own throat.

His lower lip trembling, Hanse continued. "On the fifth of January, an assassin succeeded in slaying Duchess Candace Liao and Minister Justin Allard. He slipped into the St. Ives Consulate and awaited his chance there. First he shot and killed Candace, then mortally wounded Justin. Despite his injuries, Justin managed to kill the assassin and summon help, but it was too late."

Victor's jaw dropped open. "No, that's impossible! Not yesterday. No!" He glanced over at Galen, whose face wore the same look of blanched surprise that Victor felt. "God, no."

Hanse Davion balled his hands into fists. "We know the assassin was an agent in the employ of Romano Liao. He lived in the Sarna March on Shipka, but in 3042 moved to New Avalon. He became a full citizen in 3048. We had no way of knowing he was a sleeper agent.

"Tormana Liao has been appointed regent of the St. Ives Compact, though Kai's sister Kuan Yin attends to the actual running of the government. I have sent several reserve units to the Compact to discourage adventurism on Romano's part. Kai is, of course, the Duke of St. Ives and will be released from immediate duty so that he may assume the throne, or if he chooses, to head up the troops Candace lent to the war against the Clans."

Hanse's eyes narrowed. "We have undertaken an operation to avenge Justin and his wife, but it will not bear fruit for some months. If Kai wants to engage in a military solution to this situation, I would counsel him against it, but I would support any decision he makes. His parents will lie in state for two days here in the capital, then their bodies will be sent to Kestrel to be interred in the Allard family tomb. Cassandra and Quintus Daniel have been given the temporary duty of heading the honor guard taking the bodies to Kestrel.

"I know that it will not be easy, Victor, for you to break this news to Kai. Again, I apologize for asking you to do this, but I would not have him hear of his parents' death from anyone but a friend. Were it possible for me to be there, I would do it myself."

Victor tasted bitter tears on his lips. He wanted to shut the message off, but he also wanted to hear his father out.

"Victor, tell Kai that the loss of his parents hurts us all, as a nation and as a people. My relationship with his father and his grandfather was very special. If not for them, history would be very much different in the Inner Sphere. Your mother and I both take pride in your friendship with Kai because we know he can offer you the same support and wisdom his forebears have given us."

The screen darkened, and reading the end of message code, the machine shut off. Still staring at the black screen, Victor slammed his right fist down on his thigh again and again. "Damn, damn, damn, damn! Why did he have to die, Galen? Why was his life wasted?"

"How dare you!?"

The naked anger in Galen's voice snapped Victor's head around like a punch. "Wh-what?"

"How dare you say Kai's life was wasted!"

The furious spark in Galen's eyes and the rage in his voice kindled a reaction in Victor. "It was, dammit. Fifteen minutes after Kai died, we deserted Alyina, or have you forgotten? Kai died for nothing!"

Galen stood and looked down at the Prince. "Is that your judgement or a prophecy you want to fulfill? We may have lost Alyina, but Kai didn't die to save Alyina. You were there, you heard his men. He ordered them to get you out, and he knew he was buying time that only he, with those new myomers, could. The Clanners on the cliff, or the Clanners in the forest, it didn't matter. He never hesitated because he knew he was dead. He wanted to get you out of there and, damn you, he fulfilled his mission."

Galen grabbed the blanket and tore it away from Victor. "Look at you. You're still in your cooling vest and shorts. You've been curled up here like a child ever since we got on this ship. If Kai wasted his life, it's only because you're sitting here sulking."

"I'm mourning! I'm mourning a very close friend—my best friend." Victor's right hand caressed the jade monkey pendant at his throat. "Maybe you can't understand that."

"Victor, if you think I don't also mourn Kai and the others we lost on Alyina, then I hope your father never leaves the throne." Galen snarled, then closed his eyes and let tension bleed away. "Welcome to life, Highness. Welcome to the knowledge that war is more than toy soldiers and grand plans."

"You don't understand!" Victor smeared tears across his cheeks. "I keep remembering how Kai and I promised to meet again in twenty years. We had an agreement and I feel that somehow I failed him." Victor stabbed a thumb into his own chest. "Kai died because of me."

Galen squatted down on his haunches. "Kai died because he believed your life was more important to the Commonwealth than his. You didn't fail him. You'll only fail him if you make his sacrifice worthless. You won't be able to meet him face to face in twenty years, but if you make the best of your life, you can look in the mirror and know he'd be proud of you. He believed in you enough to die to give you that chance. You owe it to him to justify that sacrifice."

As Galen spoke, he heard the words echo through his mind in Kai's voice. So many memories of Kai, from their one-year overlap at the New Avalon Military Academy and time spent on Outreach to Christmas and that last glimpse of him going over the cliff, played through Victor's mind. His right hand closed again on the jade monkey and he recalled what Kai had said when presenting the gift to him. *I got you this totem to remind you to continue to be yourself, no matter what.*

Victor gritted his teeth to keep back the tears, then turned to Galen. "You're right. Kai was right." He stood up and began to unsnap his cooling vest. "I'm going to get cleaned up and changed. Meet me with some coffee in the briefing room and bring all the reports we've got. We're going to do a post mortem on this battle. We're going to learn how and why they beat us. We're going to know them better than they know themselves."

Galen stood and smiled. "Roger that, sir."

Victor looked beyond him and nodded to the phantom of Kai he saw in the porthole's view of the world they were leaving. "I'm going to do it. I'm going to be myself. I'm going to live up to my name. Next time, no matter what, I'm going to hand the Clanners their heads."

Sian
Sian Commonality, Capellan Confederation
6 January 3052

The draft slipping through the open door drove a wispy dust spectre across the floor of the office as Sun-Tzu Liao entered. He carefully pressed the door shut behind him, releasing the doorknob slowly so that the latch made no sound. With his back to the doors, his slender fingers turned the deadbolt, once again sealing the chamber. With a satisfied grin, he saw from the single set of footprints in the dust that no one had been in the room since his last visit.

Of course no one else dared trespass because my mother, the omnipotent Romano Liao, Madam Chancellor of the Capellan Confederation, ordered this room shut twenty years ago. He looked around at the cobweb-festooned furnishings lit by the small bit of sun that penetrated the ivy-covered french doors leading to the garden. The room had not changed since Justin Xiang Allard had betrayed Maximilian Liao and left Sian with Candace at his side.

It had taken years for Sun-Tzu's curiosity and courage to overcome his terror of angering his mother. At the same time that he learned he could control her, he'd decided she was utterly insane. To prove his independence to himself and to escape one of her rages, he had opened Justin's old office one day.

Even now I cannot believe he is dead. What have you done, mother? Sun-Tzu crossed to the desk and stood staring at Justin's chair. "You had a metal hand replacing the one taken in combat, yet

296

the layout of your desk does not reflect a right-handed bias. You worked with your handicap until it became an asset. This whole office is like that. It's no wonder you were able to bring the Confederation to its knees. It's only a wonder they ever found you out."

Sun-Tzu shook his head and cautioned himself against speaking to ghosts. *Leave it to Mother and Kali to speak to the unseen.* He shuddered. "How could you do this to me, Mother?"

Assassinating Candace and Justin was sheer lunacy. Yes, he knew it settled old scores for his mother. In her eyes, it avenged the death of her father and helped to restore the Confederation's honor. But it did nothing to weaken the Confederation's enemies, and Sun-Tzu dreaded the form Hanse Davion's retribution might take. There was a chance that the Prince of the Federated Commonwealth would find himself too busy with the Clans to strike back immediately, but Sun-Tzu had not the slightest doubt that Hanse Davion would make Romano pay for the killings.

But Sun-Tzu was not afraid of Hanse Davion. Not even the Fox suspected the game he had played on Outreach. It was true he'd failed in his plan to humiliate Kai in the final testing on Outreach, having grossly underestimated his cousin. But in the end it would all work in Sun's own favor, for everyone would underestimate him even more.

He'd played his role to the hilt on Outreach. He knew none of his enemies would dare trust him after his strange behavior, but they would not guess his true intentions, either. They believed him to be as mad as his mother, and would never suspect him capable of the bold moves he must soon make. *Yes, things are falling into place.*

Sun-Tzu's one wish was that he'd had more time to study his cousin and search out his weaknesses, as he had done with his uncle Tormana. For all his bluster, Tormana was more a holovid revolutionary than anything else. By his loud posturing, Tormana managed to keep donations flowing into his coffers from paranoid Feds from the Sarna and Capellan Marches. Some of that money did go to revolutionary cells within the Combine itself, but most of it went straight to Tormana's own Brazen Heart Cavaliers Regiment.

"Tormana is easy to control because the fighting of twenty years ago took the heart out of him. He has no real desire to rule the Capellan Confederation. Yet he is shrewd enough to know he must make some display of interest to earn the respect of his peers in the Federated Commonwealth. If conquest becomes difficult, if he feels himself vulnerable, he will do nothing to jeopardize himself. Come to think of it, Candace's death will be such a constant reminder of his own danger that it may yet serve a good purpose."

Sun-Tzu turned to look at Justin's chair once more. "But Kai is another matter. As long as he is fighting the Clans, he will not come after me. I am fortunate that he believes the Clans are a greater threat than the Capellan Confederation. Kai certainly is not a coward. I know now his bloodlines serve him well. When he is finally able to turn his attention this way, things will, indeed, get interesting. I must gather as much power as I can to oppose him. With Victor and Hanse behind him, Kai may well be invincible."

Sun-Tzu mentally played through a number of options and political scenarios as he decided what he must do to ensure his survival and that of the Capellan Confederation. Suddenly, a course of action presented itself to him in clear form. With a nod, he committed himself to a plan that would take at least five years to complete. The risk was great, but all he could lose was his life, and death seemed distinctly more desirable than life as he'd known it over the past two decades.

The sound of hollow laughter brought him out of his ruminations, but when he looked around, he saw only a shaft of sunlight impaling Justin's old chair. Sun-Tzu nodded in agreement with the room's phantoms. "It must be something in this room that nurtures thoughts of treason."

He smiled to himself and started for the door. "When the throne is mine, I will have this place destroyed."

Shin Yodama winced as the Kell Hound MechWarrior dabbed at the cut on his leg with a whiskey-soaked rag.

"Sorry about that." The silvery-haired warrior smiled. "It's better when ingested internally rather than applied topically. Still, we make what sacrifices we must in the name of medicine." He deftly cleaned away the dirt and dried blood, then smiled and adjusted his glasses. "Not very deep 'cept at the top. Couple of butterflies and you won't even have a scar."

Shin frowned and glanced at the name stenciled on the breast of the man's cooling vest. "*Sumimasen*, Murray Jack-*san*. Butterflies?"

The mercenary produced two small bandages from the pouch at his left hip. They looked like barbells to Shin. Jack pressed one square end above the cut and stretched the little center elastic piece, then fixed the other end below the wound. The elastic contracted, pulling the deepest part of the wound shut. The second butterfly went lower than the first and closed the wound even tighter.

"We call those bandages butterflies because they have two wings. For cuts like this, they're more useful than stitches." He looked around at all the bandage-swathed warriors milling around the ruins on the edge of Imperial City. "Besides, I'm out of thread."

Shin nodded in grim agreement. A couple of the Nova Cats had actually made it into the city and wrecked some outlying buildings, but a Dragoons airstrike had slapped them down. The Kado-guchi Valley had become a massive killing zone and the smoke still rising from burning 'Mechs streaked the sky with dozens of inky ribbons. The few Clanners who had survived the battle had been rounded up and held in a makeshift prison. Their DropShips had left before the battle ended, and Shin had heard a rumor that their commanders ordered them up out of disgust for his comrades' unsuccessful effort.

Shin helped Jack wrap gauze around his thigh. "For a MechWarrior, you are skilled in the ways of healing."

"Well, I was a doctor in a past life." Jack threw Shin a wink. "Morgan Kell encourages all of us to keep up on first aid techniques and the like. Given the occupational hazards of our work, it seems a wise thing to do."

"*Hai!* " Shin stood and tested his leg. "Thank you very much."

Jack shrugged. "My pleasure. I owed you anyway. If you'd not potshotted that *MadCat*, he would have roasted me in my *Rifleman*. Fighting from a legless 'Mech." He shook his head. "Damn glad you were on our side."

"As we were happy you were here to aid us." Hohiro Kurita patted Shin on the shoulder. "You are not badly injured, I hope?"

"Barely a scratch. I can walk, can't I?"

Jack nodded. "Just no running around. Keep it clean and you'll do fine."

"*Domo arigato*, Murray Jack-*san*." Shin shook the man's hand, then caught up with Hohiro. "Highness, I heard a rumor that you accounted for five kills."

Hohiro shrugged distractedly. "Really? I did not keep count. There were too many targets to worry about that."

Shin nodded. Reports had placed the size of the invading force at over eight hundred BattleMechs. The Combine had opposed them with just over thirteen hundred 'Mechs. If not for the added air support from the mercenaries, all the 'Mechs in the Combine would not have been enough to defeat the Clans. The battle for Luthien had been even closer than in Shin's worst nightmares.

With Shin in tow, Hohiro met up with his sister Omi, and the three headed toward the general headquarters. Throughout the journey, the Kanrei's children continually greeted and thanked the MechWarriors in the area. They made no distinction between citizen and mercenary, and as nearly as Shin could tell, neither did the warriors. Battling side by side had forged an alliance of spirit that made all their previous differences trivial.

Down in the valley, Shin saw where the MechWarrior units were stationed. Of the two Kell Hound Regiments that came to Luthien, just over two battalions remained operational. Wolf's Dragoons had started with five full regiments and been reduced to two and a half. The Combine's six regiments had suffered similar grievous damage, with the Genyosha and the Second Legion of Vega faring the best, with only fifty-percent casualties. The Reserve regiment had been hurt most, with only three 'Mechs remaining operational at battle's end.

As they neared the makeshift tent headquarters, Shin saw a tableau that gave him a shudder. Theodore Kurita stood with the two mercenary commanders, Morgan Kell and Jaime Wolf, while Takashi Kurita remained well in the background. Nearby he saw MacKenzie Wolf with his foot in an aircast and Dan Allard with his right arm in a sling. Captain Jason Youngblood of the Kell Hounds' Crescent Hawk Company was also there, among the other mercenary officers who looked as though they had survived the fighting without too much wear and tear.

Theodore glanced at the trio as they approached, but made no effort to keep his conversation confidential. "There is no way I can adequately repay you for what you have done."

Morgan Kell smiled broadly. "Payment is not a problem, Kanrei. You will recall that we're on Hanse Davion's payroll. Your offer to let us be first out to salvage is more than gracious."

"Hell, your not shooting us out of the sky when we arrived insystem was more than I expected," Jaime Wolf chimed in. "And a chance to fight the Nova Cats again was the fulfillment of an old dream. Battling them to keep Luthien free makes it that much better."

Theodore nodded his appreciation to both men. "I know the relationship between the Combine and your two units has not been pleasant. That you came here and did as you have is inconceivable to many."

Morgan Kell's dark eyes glittered in the early morning light. "Remaining angry for twenty years is difficult, yet some of us manage it with no trouble at all. What is important is that helping you has helped the whole effort against the Clans. This isn't a victory for the Combine. It's a defeat for the Clans at the hands of the Inner Sphere. If nothing else, they have to start respecting us."

"This really settles nothing in the old conflict, Kanrei, but that conflict does not involve you or the people of the Combine." Unresolved anger laced Jaime Wolf's words and Shin sensed they were meant for more than just the Kanrei's ears. "The problem between the Dragoons and the Combine is not for you to solve, and I have never held it against you. The Smoke Jaguars and Nova Cats had this coming

301

to them, so I'm happy to have been here to stamp 'paid' on their account."

Morgan offered Theodore his hand. "We'll have a chance to speak again, I'm sure. Right now, though, I've got some salvage parties to organize."

"Likewise." Jaime shook Theodore's hand after Morgan. "Your troops are damned good, Kanrei. In the old days, the Cats would have eaten you alive."

As the mercenary leaders left, Theodore turned to his children and Shin. "What are your impressions of our situation, Hohiro?"

"Morale is good. We've lost more than fifty percent of our machinery, but we had less than twenty percent pilot fatalities. In a month, we should be able to field 75 percent of the forces we started with and bring another five percent on line per month after that. Everyone is itching to have another go at the Clans now that we've seen they're not invincible."

"There was no doubt we would win this battle." Takashi Kurita entered their circle to stand between Theodore and Omi. "We had no choice."

Theodore turned on his father. "I agree with the latter half of your statement, but not the first. If not for the mercenaries, Luthien would now be in enemy hands."

Takashi's face closed. "We would never have surrendered."

"That's true, Coordinator, but we would have been fighting from another base of operation." Theodore frowned heavily. "Can you not bring yourself to end your conflict with the mercenaries? You owe them Luthien and you owe them your respect. Is it not time to admit you were wrong and come to peace with Wolf and Kell?"

"They have my gratitude and respect, and they know that. If I am to maintain their respect, however, I cannot say I was wrong, because I was not." Takashi's eyes sharpened. "Both Morgan Kell and Jaime Wolf believe it is unjust to expect noble warriors to commit suicide because they have not fulfilled their duty and their honor. They believe I could have prevented brave warriors they once knew from choosing such an end. This is the source of their enmity toward me, though other incidents have exacerbated it. Certainly their employer, Hanse Davion, has not tried to make them see the situation in any other light."

Theodore jammed his fists on his hips. "It was Hanse Davion who ordered their units here. Because he has agreed to send no Federated Commonwealth units into the Combine, he lent us his mercenaries instead. He has been able to change his thinking in the last twenty years. Why have you remained so...so..."

"Obstinate?" No flicker of amusement passed over Takashi's face. "I have remained resolute because I am correct. I no more doomed Yorinaga Kurita or Minobu Tetsuhara than I have any other man or woman who has committed *seppuku*. That act is one of personal atonement and redemption of honor. It is an individual choice that I respect. For me to do less, either then or now, would tarnish the honor of those who have the courage to cleanse themselves in such manner.

"However, my son, I will take issue with your assertion that I am not capable of change." Takashi looked beyond Hohiro at the remains of the battlefield. "Colonel Wolf was correct when he said that, given the old ways, the Clans would have destroyed us. You were correct in setting Shin Yodama as a brake on my anger and my need for glory. The defense of Luthien is not a victory for the mercenaries, it is a victory for your foresight and your generation."

Takashi's words, drained of the strident tones he used when speaking of the mercenaries, clearly shocked Theodore. "What are you saying, father?"

"I am saying that I see the wisdom of your vision for the Combine. I regret having opposed you because it made the changes you made more difficult to accomplish. Yet I rejoice in the strength you have discovered in facing my opposition. You will have to persevere now without my objections, though I hope you will welcome my counsel from time to time."

The Coordinator of the Draconis Combine draped his right arm over his son's shoulders. "This House, though divided against itself, has defeated the Clans twice. Imagine their distress when they learn we now devote all our energies to fighting them together."

Solsveda
Satalice, Wolf Clan Occupation Zone
7 January 3052

Phelan watched the young man he'd captured. The youth strode away from the detention camp with his spine straight and his head held high. The Clan MechWarrior recognized the pride in the young man's bearing, knowing it was the means he used to hold in his pain. *I must have looked just that way when I had to leave the Nagelring. Feeling like betrayed and betrayer at the same time.*

"You did well, Ragnar Magnusson. I thank you for helping quell the disturbance in the camp."

The tow-headed youth's eyes sparked anger. "I couldn't let them get themselves killed, could I?"

"No." Phelan shook his head. "You are part of the Wolf Clan now." He pointed at a piece of braided white cord encircling Ragnar's right wrist. "That means you are a bondsman to the Wolves. You must begin to learn our customs. Avoiding contractions is the first of these you can master."

Ragnar tugged uncomfortably at the rope bracelet. "Does this mean you own me, Phelan Kell?"

Phelan's head came up. *He's quick.* "You are a bondsman. Because I captured you, you are my responsibility, but I do not own you."

"Good. I could not stand being chattel to a traitor." Ragnar's face and voice sharpened. "I didn't know who you were, but some of the men in the camp remembered your visit to Gunzburg several years

304

ago. I would have thought a Kell Hound would die before joining forces with the enemy. I should have known better. You are, after all, just a mercenary."

Phelan could see that Ragnar wanted him to take offense, but he gave the youngster no chance to further vent his anger. "Understand this, Ragnar: I was captured, and like you, I was made a bondsman to the Wolf Clan. I earned my chance to become a warrior, and I embraced that opportunity. As a warrior, working from within the Clan structure, I have been able to help keep the native populations of the worlds from suffering as much as they might have otherwise. There is no way to stop this juggernaut, so I have resolved to make it tread more lightly.

"Right now, you speak from anger, and I understand that. I welcome your independence and will not try to extinguish it." He grabbed the white cord and twisted it so that it dug into Ragnar's flesh. "I look forward to the day when I can cut this cord and welcome you into the warrior caste. With you, Natasha, and some others, I believe we can persuade the Clans that their assessment of the Inner Sphere was wrong. Perhaps then we can stop this war."

Ragnar rubbed his wrist when Phelan released the cord. "If you are true to your intentions, I will join you. If not, I will become a warrior and kill you."

Phelan smiled. "Good. I would have it no other way."

Phelan started to guide Ragnar back to the bivouac established by the Thirteenth Wolf Guards, but before they completed the trek through the ruined streets of Solsveda's Drika section, they ran into the ilKhan and his entourage. Aside from the requisite phalanx of Elementals, the ilKhan was accompanied by Natasha Kerensky, the Precentor Martial, and a woman resplendent in long gold robes. Phelan recognized her instantly as the Primus of ComStar. Hearing the choked sounds coming from Ragnar, Phelan guessed that his bondsmen knew it, too.

Ulric gave Phelan a salute, which the MechWarrior returned. "Primus Myndo Waterly, this is Star Commander Phelan Wolf. You might know him better by the name he used before joining our people. In that time he was known as Phelan Kell."

The Primus smiled solicitously and held out her hand to Phelan. "IlKhan Ulric, I recognize the name Phelan Wolf from the Precentor Martial's reports of his exploits. My journey from Terra was hurried, but I kept fully abreast of your actions."

Phelan took Myndo's hand and brushed the knuckles lightly with his lips. "I am most honored that you take notice of me, Primus."

She continued to smile at him as she withdrew her hands into the sleeves of her robe. "Who could forget a warrior who negotiated the surrender of a whole world without a shot fired? Especially when that world was governed by a sworn enemy. I think you belong not in the Wolf Clan's warrior caste, but in a clan of sorcerers."

Myndo's gaze shifted from Phelan to Ragnar. "And this is the former Prince of Rasalhague. I see, from the bracelet, that you have made him your slave."

Phelan shook his head. "He is no more a slave than was I when captured by the Clans."

Ulric agreed. "His status relative to Phelan or any other warrior is roughly equivalent to the Precentor Martial's position in relation to your own, Primus."

"Ah," she said, clearly dubious of the explanation. "I hope, then, he will be as helpful to you, Phelan, as you were to Ulric." She smiled at the ilKhan. "And I trust Phelan will be yet even more more useful in the future."

Ulric lifted an eyebrow. "I have no doubt of that, Primus."

Obviously pursuing her own agenda, the Primus pressed on with that line of thought. "You can't let the defeat at Luthien cripple this strategy of yours. I can provide all the information you need, and with Phelan's help, your next target should fall easily."

"Next target?" To Phelan's eyes, Ulric, Natasha, and the Precentor Martial were as ignorant of her meaning as he was.

"Yes, the plan is so simple and daring that it cannot fail." Myndo smiled with the confidence of one divinely inspired. "I say, ilKhan, that we move now and strike at Tharkad!"

"Tharkad?" The panic in the Precentor Martial's voice doubled the dread gathering in Phelan's heart. "The capital of the Lyran Commonwealth. That Tharkad?"

Myndo fixed Focht with a look of surprise. "Of course, that Tharkad. What other?" She looked at Ulric. "You have the force to take it. With Phelan's knowledge of the world from his time at the Nagelring, and with the Precentor Martial's help, it should be far easier to take than the attempt on Luthien."

Ulric's face wore a look of amusement. "An interesting proposition, to be sure, but I am afraid it is not possible, Primus."

She smiled confidently. "Believe me, ilKhan, you have the troops and experience necessary to take Tharkad."

Ulric nodded. "Oh, I believe you, but taking Tharkad would deflect us from our goal and that I cannot allow to happen."

The Primus frowned and shot a quick, reproving glance at the

Precentor Martial. "Your goal?"

"You did not know?" Ulric feigned great surprise while the Precentor Martial's expression changed to pure puzzlement. "You truly do not know?"

The Primus shook her head. "I do not."

A predatory smile flashed across Ulric's face at Myndo's petulant tone. "Our goal is the conquest of Terra, my dear Primus. It was once the seat of the Star League, and it will belong to the Star League again. This is our will, our goal, and no one in the Inner Sphere can stop us from achieving it."

Epilogue

Nicholas Chung nearly jumped out of his skin when the gloved hand touched his shoulder. Dropping the small cargo crate to the spaceport's ferrocrete deck, he whirled and reached for the knife hidden at his back. His eyes focused as best they could on the face shrouded by the hooded cloak. He felt his heart flutter, then he leaned forward for a second, harder look.

"My God, I thought you were dead."

"As I recall, you thought the same thing on Spica."

Chung nodded slowly. "But you surprised us then, as you have done many times since. Why are you here?"

The cloaked figure pointed to the egg-shaped DropShip on the landing pad. "You have a ship and I must make a journey without anyone knowing who I am or where I am going."

Chung's welcome died as he guessed the intent of those words. "You can't mean to go *there!* That would be sheer madness. I have known you to be audacious before, even reckless at times, but never crazy."

"She called the tune, Chung, and now she must pay the piper." The figure reached its leather-sheathed left hand inside the cloak and withdrew it holding a sheaf of C-bills. "This is enough to buy you a jump to Daniels and from there into the Compact. This must be done and there is no one else to do it."

Chung accepted the money and bowed. "You saved me on Spica, so I owe you this. But you will find much has changed."

"Twenty years for some is a lifetime for others. I was born in the Confederation and part of me never left it." The cloaked figure's voice was low and even, a kind of deadly calm. "It's time for a homecoming, and I'll wager it's one Romano Liao will never forget."

EQUIVALENT RANKS IN INNER SPHERE MILITARIES, 3050

STANDARD MERCENARY	FEDERATED COMMONWEALTH	DRACONIS COMBINE	FREE RASALHAGUE REPUBLIC
OFFICER RANKS:			
	Marshal of the Armies	Tai-shu (Warlord)	Överbefälhavere
	Field Marshal	Tai-sho	General
	Marshal	Sho-sho	Generalmajor
Colonel	Hauptmann General	Tai-sa	Överste-Löjtnant
Lieutenant Colonel	Leftenant General	Chu-sa	Överste
Major	Kommandant	Sho-sa	Major
Captain	Hauptmann	Tai-i	Kapten
Lieutenant	Leftenant	Chu-i	Löjtnant
ENLISTED RANKS:			
Sergeant Major	Sergeant Major	Sho-ko	Fanjunkare
	Kashira		
	Shujin		
Sergeant	Sergeant	Gunso	Sergeant
Corporal	Corporal	Go-cho	Korpral
	Gunjin		
Private	Private	Heishi	Menig
	Hojuhei		

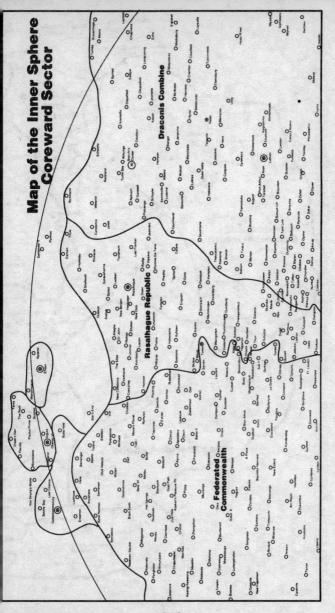

Map of the Inner Sphere
Coreward Sector

Draconis Combine

Rasalhague Republic

Federated
Commonwealth

313

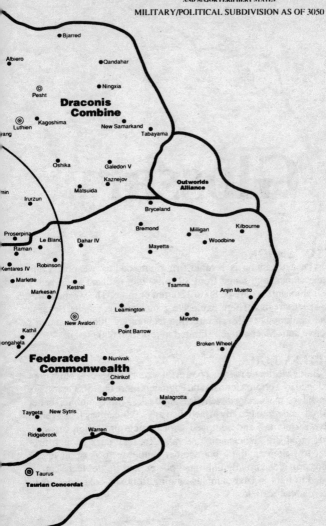

MAP OF THE INNER SPHERE

AND MAJOR PERIPHERY STATES

MILITARY/POLITICAL SUBDIVISION AS OF 3050

Bjarred

Albiero

Qandahar

Pesht

Ningxia

Draconis Combine

Luthien

Kagoshima

yang

New Samarkand

Tabayama

Oshika

Galedon V

Kaznejov

min

Irurzun

Matsuida

Outworlds Alliance

Bryceland

Proserpina

Le Blanc

Dahar IV

Bremond

Milligan

Kilbourne

Woodbine

Raman

Robinson

Mayetta

Kentares IV

Marlette

Markesan

Kestrel

Tsamma

Anjin Muerto

Leamington

Minette

New Avalon

Point Barrow

Kathil

Broken Wheel

ongahela

Federated Commonwealth

Nunivak

Chirikof

Islamabad

Malagrotta

Taygeta

New Sytris

Ridgebrook

Warren

Taurus

Taurian Concordat

Glossary

AUTOCANNON

The autocannon is a rapid-firing autoloading weapon. Light vehicle autocannon range from 30 to 90 mm caliber, while heavy 'Mech autocannon may be 80 to 120 mm or more. The weapon fires high-speed streams of high-explosive, armor-piercing shells. Because of the limitations of 'Mech targeting technology, the autocannon's effective anti-'Mech range is limited to less then 600 meters.

BATTLEMECH

BattleMechs are the most powerful war machines ever built. First developed by Terran scientists and engineers more than 500 years ago, these huge, man-shaped vehicles are faster, more mobile, better armored, and more heavily armed then any 20th-century tank. Ten to twelve meters tall and equipped with particle projection cannons, lasers, rapid-fire autocannon, and missiles, they pack enough firepower to flatten anything but another BattleMech. A small fusion reactor provides virtually unlimited power, and BattleMechs can be adapted to fight in environments ranging from sun-baked deserts to subzero arctic icefields.

COMSTAR

ComStar, the interstellar communications network, was the brainchild of Jerome Blake, formerly Minister of Communications during the latter years of the Star League. After the League's fall, Blake seized Terra and reorganized what was left of the League's communications network into a private organization that sold its services to the five Successor Houses for a profit. Since that time, ComStar has also developed into a powerful, secret society steeped in mysticism and ritual. Initiates to the ComStar Order commit themselves to lifelong service.

JUMPSHIPS AND DROPSHIPS

JumpShip

Interstellar travel is accomplished via JumpShips, first developed in the 22nd century. Named for their ability to "jump" instantaneously from one point to another, the vessels consist of a long, thin drive core and an enormous sail. The sail is constructed from a specially coated polymer that absorbs vast quantities of electromagnetic energy from the nearest star. Energy collected by the sail is slowly transfered to the drive core, which converts it into a space-twisting field. After making its jump, the ship cannot travel again until it has recharged its drive with solar energy at its new location. Safe recharge times range from six to eight days.

JumpShips travel instantaneously across vast interstellar distances by means of the Kearny-Fuchida hyperdrive. The K-F drive generates a field around the JumpShip, then opens a hole into hyperspace. In moments, the JumpShip is transported through to its new destination, across distances of up to 30 light years.

Jump points are the locations within a star system where the system's gravity is next to nothing, the prime prerequisite for operation of the K-F drive. The distance away from the system's star is dependant on that star's mass, and is usually many tens of millions of kilometers away. Every star has two principal jump points, one at the zenith point at the star's north pole, and one at the nadir point at the south pole. An infinite number of other jump points also exist, but they are used only rarely.

JumpShips never land on planets, and only rarely travel into the inner parts of a star system. Interplanetary travel is carried out by DropShips, vessels that attach themselves to the JumpShip until arrival at the jump point. Most of the JumpShips currently in service are already centuries old, because the Successor Lords are unable to construct many new ones each year. For this reason, there is an unspoken agreement among even these bitter enemies to leave one another's JumpShips alone.

DropShip

Because JumpShips generally remain at a considerable distance from a star system's inhabited worlds, DropShips were developed for interplanetary travel. A DropShip attaches to hard points on the JumpShip, and will later be dropped from the parent vessel after entry into a system. DropShips are highly maneuverable, well-armed, and sufficiently aerodynamic to take off from and land on a planetary surface.

LRM

LRM is an abbreviation for "Long-Range Missile," an indirect-fire missile with a high-explosive warhead.

NEW AVALON INSTITUTE OF SCIENCE (NAIS)

In 3015, Prince Hanse Davion decreed the construction of a new university on New Avalon, planetary capitol of the Federated Suns. Known as the New Avalon Institute of Science (NAIS), its purpose is to recover the lost technologies and knowledge of the past. Both House Kurita and House Marik have followed with their own universities, but neither is as well bankrolled or staffed as the NAIS.

PPC

PPC is the abbreviation for "Particle Projection Cannon," a magnetic accelerator firing high-energy proton or ion bolts, causing damage both through impact and high temperature. PPCs are among the most effective weapons available to BattleMechs.

SRM

SRM is the abbreviation for "Short-Range Missiles," direct trajectory missiles with high-explosive or armor-piercing explosive warheads.

STAR LEAGUE

In 2571, the Star League was formed in an attempt to peacefully ally the major star systems inhabited by the human race after it had taken to the stars. The League continued and prospered for almost 200 years, until the Succession Wars broke out in the late 28th century. The League was eventually destroyed when the ruling body known as the High Council disbanded in the midst of a struggle for power. Each of the Council Lords then declared himself First Lord of the Star League, and within months, war had engulfed the Inner Sphere. These centuries of continuous war are now known simply as the Succession Wars, and continue to the present day. As a result, much of the technology that had brought mankind to its highest level of advancement has been destroyed, lost, or forgotten.

SUCCESSOR LORDS

Each of the five Successor States is ruled by a family descended from one of the original Council Lords of the old Star League. All five royal House Lords claim the title of First Lord, and they have been at each other's throats since the beginning of the Succession Wars in the late 28th century. Their battleground is the vast Inner Sphere, which is composed of all the star systems once occupied by the Star League member-states.

DON'T MISS VOLUME 1 IN THE BLOOD OF KERENSKY TRILOGY!

MICHAEL A. STACKPOLE

LETHAL HERITAGE

BLOOD OF KERENSKY · VOLUME ONE

A BATTLETECH NOVEL

BATTLETECH ® is a Registered Trademark of FASA Corporation.
LETHAL HERITAGE is a Trademark of FASA Corporation.
Copyright © 1990 FASA Corporation.

FASA
CORPORATION

BATTLETECH®

A GAME OF ARMORED COMBAT

IN THE 30TH CENTURY LIFE IS CHEAP, BUT BATTLEMECHS AREN'T.

A Dark Age has befallen mankind. Where the United Star League once reigned, five successor states now battle for control. War has ravaged the once-flourishing worlds and left them in ruins. Technology has ceased to advance, the machines and equipment of the past cannot be produced by present-day worlds. War is waged over water, ancient machinery, and spare-parts factories. Control of these elements leads to victory and the domination of known space.

BATTLETECH ® is a Registered Trademark of FASA Corporation.
Copyright © 1990 FASA Corporation.

About the Author

ComStar ROM Division
Langley, North America, Terra
2 February 3052
Security Alert Advisory

Subject: Michael A. Stackpole

This is supplemental to the general alert the Primus sent out two weeks ago.

Recap:

The subject of our alert claims to be one Michael A. Stackpole, a 20th century game designer and writer who was raised in Vermont and graduated from the University of Vermont with a degree in History in 1979. The collapse of the Eastern Bloc in 1989, rending his education fairly useless, might account for his turning to fictioneering as a way of life. The historical Stackpole worked from his home in Arizona for companies like Flying Buffalo, Inc., FASA Corporation, Interplay Productions, TSR Inc., Hero Games, and West End Games. Despite persistent rumors that his volume of work indicated that more than one person worked under his name, we cannot confirm that nor can we confirm that the subject our search is indeed 1095 years old.

Recent Sighting:

We have reason to believe that the subject actually made it to the Clans along with Natasha Kerensky. The Primus, though she has no evidence to confirm it, is adamant on this point. If this is true, the Clans have access to one individual who has shown, through his previous work, to have a diabolically clear view of ComStar's inner workings. The possibility that he broke into our computers while a guest in one of our reeducation centers can no longer be dismissed.

Conclusion:

The Primus has issued a death warrant for the author as part of Operation Stiletto. There is no excuse for failure. He cannot live to complete his 3rd volume in the Blood of Kerensky Saga.